W9-DFH-748

Mea Culpa

Farhan Noorani

SxeolvkDphulfd
Edowlpruh

© 2010 by Farhan Noorani.
All rights reserved. No part of this book may be reproduced, stored in a retrieval system or transmitted in any form or by any means without the prior written permission of the publishers, except by a reviewer who may quote brief passages in a review to be printed in a newspaper, magazine or journal.

First printing

All characters in this book are fictitious, and any resemblance to real persons, living or dead, is coincidental.

PublishAmerica has allowed this work to remain exactly as the author intended, verbatim, without editorial input.

ISBN: 978-1-61582-787-9
PUBLISHED BY PUBLISHAMERICA, LLLP
www.publishamerica.com
Baltimore

Printed in the United States of America

Mea Culpa

Chapter One

February sixteenth. It is a bright, winter morning in New York City. The snow covers the city like a soft blanket and is as crisp and clean as the air. The birds are singing as if it were their last song. The cold would collect on the back of the neck while you slept so upon waking up you would have to shake it off just to avoid feeling stiff for the rest of the day. Robert Allen Heyward is a good and loyal man. Goodness and loyalty, two of the most fatal errors for a man in his position. Sadly, even he knows this, yet for some reason he refuses to turn away from his beliefs. It's hard to blame a man for his ways if it's gotten him to the position in which he is in today. Robert is the President of Orion Industries. Orion is one of the largest and most prominent energy source companies in the world, side by side with their rival, Highland Corporation. Even though they both are well known, neither of them has gone global yet, due to competition and readiness. Furthermore laws in the One World Organization, better known as the O.W.O., a group whose sole purpose is to regulate international business, are very strict; Orion plans to catch up sometime very soon though. Orion is Robert's most prized possession, which is second only to his family… sometimes.

Robert wakes up at the sound of the alarm, rolls over lazily hits the snooze button and then turns back to put his arm around his pregnant wife Sandra's stomach. *"She's just as beautiful as the day I met her."* He thinks to himself. He knows without her he's nothing, everything he has accomplished and all that he has done in his life is due to her support and belief in him. He holds her close, her arms are as soft as silk, and he rubs her arms softly and makes his way to her breasts.

"Now don't start anything you can't finish," She says with a smile as she wakes up, "you have to get up for work soon." Sandra says as she leans in closer to Robert as if to tease him.

"I'll go in late today." He says as he nibbles her ear.

He then kisses her softly on the back of her neck, and moves closer to her as he moves his hands under her night gown. Robert holds her tight and they remove their clothes. They make love as if they were new lovers. They haven't had morning sex in months so it was a good change of pace. When they finish Robert confesses his love for her in her ear softly as he kisses her. He then looks over at the clock to see the time.

"Oh my God, is it seven o'clock already?! I've got to hit the shower!" Robert jumps out of bed and runs into the bathroom that is connected to their bedroom. After an invigorating shower, he puts on his suit and ambles down into the spacious kitchen where his two sons and wife are already half way through their breakfast. Sandra is waiting for him with breakfast ready.

"Good morning kids." Robert says with a big smile.

"Morning Dad?" They reply in unison. It's odd to see their father so relaxed at the kitchen table; usually they see him only at the end of the day.

"Robby, you look so tired. Your meeting last night must have been exasperating." Sandra says with a concerned look on her face.

"Yeah it was. I'm still recovering from it right now."

"Well, don't worry about it, you just have a seat. Your coffee is almost ready."

"Thanks hon."

"Are you all set for school boys?"

"Yeah!" They chimed in agreement.

"Good."

"Kids, you'd better get a move on. I can see the school bus coming. Here, take your lunches. Oh, and Michael, don't forget to grab your permission slip." Sandra says as she peeks out the kitchen window.

"Right, thanks Mom."

Michael rushes up the stairs to get his permission slip while Ryan puts his coat on.

"Hey Dad, don't forget about my tournament next Saturday so remember to write it in on your calendar." Ryan says.

"I won't, and you have a game tonight right?" Robert answers.

"Oh yeah!"

"Oh yeah…" His parents mockingly reply.

"Hurry up, the bus is in front!" Sandra shouts out. The two boys kiss Sandra. "And one for the baby." They kiss her stomach.

"Bye!" The boys say as they leave. Michael holds Ryan's hand as they walk towards the bus.

"They're growing up so fast." Says Sandra as she drinks her orange juice.

"I know and with this third one on the way, we just might have to move."

"Yeah, well I think we're just fine where we are hon."

"Oh you never think big!" He says as he takes another bite of his pancakes, "Anyway, I think I'm going to change my schedule to work later on, I miss having breakfast with you and the kids."

"Yeah that would be nice and I sure can use some extra help around here as well."

"Oh I remember now why I started going in early." Robert jokingly replies. Sandra responds with an evil squint and a smirk. They both chuckle.

Charlotte, their white Labrador, runs excitedly into the kitchen.

"Charlotte, come here girl. Go get daddy's paper."

As their dog leaves, Robert turns to Sandra and asks, "Do you have everything set for tonight?"

"For the most part, yes. The caterers are coming in around six and all the guests should have arrived by six thirty."

"Good, then I'll bring Phil by at around seven or so. Oh and please make sure that Charlotte is chained in correctly in her house. Last time she almost ruined the whole dinner and…"

"I know, I know." She interrupts, "We'll make sure, and if you'll remember it was your job to chain her in last time."

Right then, as if on cue, Charlotte comes in with the paper in her mouth and stands expectantly in front of Robert.

"Ah, speak of the devil!" Robert attempts to take the newspaper from her mouth, "Charlotte! Let go. Come on, give it to me!" Robert says as he struggles. Finally, after battling over the paper for a few seconds,

Charlotte lets go of the paper and chases after a squirrel she sees in the window in the next room.

"Sandra, I think it's time to put Charlotte in obedience school. Look at how she mangled my morning paper!"

Sandra goes about cleaning the kitchen paying only half of her attention to her frustrated husband. Robert grumbles some more as he flips over to the business section.

"Damn it! We've lost another five and a half points! This is the largest drop in company history! I'm going to be getting together with the board members today and have a serious meeting on how we can improve Orion. This new technology we're working on better work. Meanwhile, Highland Corporations went up another three points; can you believe that? Goddamn company, with its stupid scorpion logo. Who the hell has a scorpion as a logo anyway? If anything, it should be a bull for bullsh…"

"You know I don't like you talking like that around the baby." Sandra interrupts. Robert nods his head irritated, but apologetic. "And honey, don't worry about it. Everything will work out just fine." Sandra assures him.

"Oh, I know. We are so close to a breakthrough in the Cold Fusion project. Once that comes about our sales will sky rocket. Production costs will lower by twenty percent and Highland Corporations will definitely start to depreciate." He says with a slight smirk on his face.

"That's good, but don't let your hopes get too far away from you. Like my father always used to say, a kite only flies as far as the wind takes it."

"Your father's sayings always got the best of me. I believe a man makes his own destiny. Anyway, I've got to go to work."

**

Later on at work, his secretary, Elizabeth buzzes in. She has been with the company almost as long as Robert. He trusts her with everything.

"Excuse me Mr. Heyward; Mr. Roderick is here to see you." She says with her usual monotonous voice.

"Oh, yes, please send him in Liz."

Soon after, a man in his thirties wearing a dark blue business suit enters.

"Good Afternoon Robert. Heard you're going to start coming in late now." He says with a smirk hinting he knew why Robert was late.

"Yeah spending more time with the wife and kids."

"Always with the wife and kids," He says mockingly, "anyway, guess what day it is today?" He asks expectantly.

"It's Friday. Do you have the paper work from Chicago? They're one of our biggest clients now, which makes them our top priority Phil." He says ignoring Phil's enthusiasm.

"Yeah, but you've been such a busy-body these days that you forgot your best friend's birthday. Even after working together for over ten years and all those years in college, you would think that you would at least remember that by now." He says sounding disappointed.

With a look of astonishment Robert replies, "Wait what? Oh, of course I didn't forget. Happy Birthday!" Phil gives Robert a stupid look. Robert knows he got caught. "Look, man I'm sorry, how about we go back to my house after work and celebrate with a steak dinner? It's been a while since you've seen the family as it is. They would be really happy to see you again." He says with a smile.

"Alright, sounds like a plan." Phil says returning the smile.

Phil is a single man and the head lawyer at Orion Industries. He handles all of the major business transactions and law cases for Robert. With such strong backgrounds in business, case, and trial law it's quite unusual to outwit someone at his stature, but somehow Robert always knows how to push his buttons. Phil doesn't care too much for family, in fact he doesn't even have one, the closest thing to family that Phil has is the company, and also Robert's family. He has a special soft spot for Robert's family, and would do anything for them. He has been very close with Robert since their freshman year of college; in fact they were roommates throughout college. Robert sees Phil as one of the most valuable assets to the company, of course his best friend as well. Every major decision that Robert has ever made, from which company to deal with, to which secretary to hire, and even to make sure that he married the right woman, Phil was always there to make sure that the legitimacy was never compromised. Being one of the best lawyers in the nation, Highland Corporation has tried to persuade Phil to work for them time and time again, but he never considered any of their offers on account of his loyalty to Robert.

Surprisingly, Phil's love for money didn't play much of a factor in this decision. Some nights he sits and counts the money in all his accounts, making sure everything is in place and accounted for. He developed this OCD, if you will, when his stepfather robbed him and his mother when he was sixteen. He was then robbed two months later of his dignity, when he caught his mother in bed with the same man who took everything from them. At least he had his pride…not anymore. To Phil, trust is just another word and money is power. Phil saves and saves, then on occasion he will overindulge in the finer things in life. The only one thing Phil always believes a good investment is, is a good finely wrapped cigar his favorite brand being Cohiba. ***Later that evening, after closing up the office, Robert and Phil hop into Robert's Jaguar and head over to his house. As they arrive, the house appears to be empty with no sign of anyone being home.

"Are you sure they're home?" Asks Phil.

"Oh, they're probably not back yet from Ryan's basketball game. We'll just have a couple drinks until they get home." Robert says as they make their way towards the front door.

Phil takes one more puff of his cigar, puts it out, and stuffs it in his front jacket pocket.

When they enter the dark corridor, lights suddenly come on and a room full of people shout, "Surprise!"

Phil shouts, "Wow! I can't believe this. I actually thought you forgot my birthday! Come here!" He hugs Robert and then notices Sandra. "Sandra, you get more and more beautiful every time I see you." He gives her a kiss on the cheek.

"Oh come on you know I look like a hot air balloon and don't even try to deny it." They all chuckle.

"What are you, at month seven now?"

"Very good Phil!" She says with a surprised look on her face.

"Uncle Phil!" The two brothers say as they run towards Phil.

"Boys! Oh my you just keep getting bigger and bigger. How was your game today Ryan?"

"It was okay…" He says sheepishly as he looks down at the ground, "I sat on the bench the whole time."

"Oh don't worry, the coach will put you in; you just have to show him you deserve to play." He says as he pats Ryan on the top of his head. "And if that doesn't work maybe Uncle Phil can give Coach Rocker a visit."

"Look what we got you Uncle Phil!" Michael excitedly says as he passes him a small box.

"Oh my, what's this?" He asks as he opens the small box. "A Movado watch, with matching cufflinks!" He says in shock, "Are you guys working for your dad now too?"

"No…" They reply.

"Well this deserves a tickle bug!"

"No!" They both shriek and laugh at the same time.

He tickles the two and picks up Ryan in his arms. "You guys really shouldn't have."

"Mommy helped us pick it out." Ryan points out.

"She did?! Well I guess I'm going to have to give her a tickle bug too!" He looks over at Sandra.

"Don't even think about it." She says moving behind Robert as she laughs.

Phil laughs as well, "Alright you get away this time, but seriously thank you Sandra, but this is truly too much."

"It was really nothing I just hope you like it."

"Like it? I love it!"

"Well it's settled then, you love it, so let's enjoy the rest of the evening shall we?" Robert puts his hand on Phil's shoulder and escorts him towards the rest of the guests. Phil puts down Ryan, "Thanks again boys." He gives them both a big hug. "You're welcome Uncle Phil!" They each say and run off to their mother. "Boy I tell ye Robert, you are one lucky son of a bitch."

"Yeah, I know, but tonight's about you so let's drink some wine, open some gifts, and have some fun!" Everyone cheers. They continue towards their many guests and they mingle with all of their friends and co-workers at the party.

"Mom can we stay up later tonight?" Michael asks.

"Yeah mom, can we?" Ryan follows.

"Okay just for tonight, but after cake you guys have to go brush up and get to bed."

"Fine…" They say sadly in unison.

With a bright look in his eyes Michael cries out, "Can I stay up later since I'm thirteen now?"

"Me too mom I'm eight and a half now!" Ryan follows.

"No, and if you keep asking me I'll send you both up right now."

"Okay mom." They both run off.

"You ruin everything!" He gives Ryan a small nudge.

"No I don't!" He pushes back.

The night had progressed as smoothly as Robert and Sandra had hoped and their guests had just finished their food. The caterers had brought steak, pasta, shrimp the works. Everyone was enjoying themselves and expressed it to both Sandra and Robert. Sandra loved throwing parties and watching her friends join in laughter enjoying each other's company. Sandra brought out the cake and everyone sang Happy Birthday in unison. Robert then got up and tapped his wine glass with his fork.

"Can I have everyone's attention please? I'd like to make a toast. This is to the person who helped me build this company when things looked dim, this is to a man who seems to be the only one who can do the least amount of work in the office and get away with it," Everyone chuckles, "and this is to my best friend Phil Roderick." Everyone cheers and drinks. "Now for the final part of tonight, my gift."

"Your gift? Come on you already gave me a gift Robby!" He says shaking his head with a smile.

"Now now, shut up Phil." Everyone laughs. "No, but seriously this gift is from all of us in the office."

"You guys are crazy!" He says looking around at everyone at the table.

"Ladies and gentlemen I honestly don't think this man likes getting gifts."

"No no, I'll be good." Phil says abruptly.

"Thank you. Now for your present Phil you will be enjoying a luxury *paid* two week vacation to the Florida Keys." Everyone oued and awed as they joined each other in quiet laughter and joy. "To get to your destination, you will *not* be flying in coach, you will *not* be flying in business class, and you most certainly will *not* be flying in first class. Instead my friend, you will be driving there in your brand new car!" Everyone cheers as Phil's jaw drops, "Where a private jet will pick you up from Florida to its beautiful islands!" Robert tosses Phil the keys to a brand new Porsche, and everyone cheers fanatically.

"Shut up!" Phil says, still in shock as he looks at the keys.

"I'm serious Phil, go look outside."

Phil leaps out of his chair and sprints towards the front door. There stood a brand new Porsche 911. "Oh my God, Oh my God, Oh my freaking God!" He runs and jumps on the car giving it a big hug, and smothering it with kisses.

"Well would you look at that, he hugs the car and not his best friend."

Everyone laughs and walks over to Phil to congratulate him.

"You all are amazing thank you so much."

"You know we were just kidding about the paid vacation right Phil?" Robert jokes.

"Yeah, yeah, come here man!" He hugs Robert as he attempts to hold back his tears.

"Come on now you'll make my wife jealous."

"You can keep him, just give me the car!" Sandra yells out as everyone laughs.

"Yeah, right!"

"Okay now all of you get out of here!" Robert yells jokingly.

Chapter 2

The next day, Robert wakes up to the hurrying voice of Michael.

"Dad, dad wake up we're going to be late!" Michael yells while shaking his father to wake up.

"For what?" He tiredly responds.

"Football practice." Sandra replies.

"Come on dad we have to leave now!" He starts tugging harder.

"Ugh, what time is it?" Robert rolls over and scratches his head.

"Seven thirty practice is at eight! Dad let's go!" Michael begins to whine.

"Okay, okay go down stairs Michael, I'll be there in a minute." He motions Michael to go away.

"Sandra, I don't care boy or girl, that child in your belly will not be playing any sports." He says as he gets dressed.

"Yes dear." She goes back to sleep.

Robert drives Michael to practice, during their drive Robert thinks of the special bond he has with Michael. His first-born. His first prince. His pride, his joy. Robert would do anything for Michael. Sandra knows Robert is spoiling him and discourages it, but in this scenario there is no compromise. Robert thinks back to just a few years ago at church Michael had gone to the bathroom and while he was gone the priest had asked everyone to move up so the other church members could find seats easier in the back. Robert's family had moved all the way to the front from the back pews. When Michael had come back he wandered the pews confused searching for his family and the face of his father. It wasn't long before his confused face turned frightened and the little boy in his little suit walked through the middle isle looking left and right for his family. Finally he had seen Robert's face, and tears started rushing down his eyes. Robert saw his boy, picked him up, and put him on his lap. "You okay?" He had asked. Michael nodded his head, and gave Robert a hug. Realizing what happened Robert vowed never to leave him again.

When Robert came back home he finds Charlotte waiting for him at the door with the newspaper. Sandra is just coming downstairs, still a little tired as she yawns going towards the refrigerator.

"Good girl Charlotte!" He pets her on the head.

"Did you guys make it on time?" She asks while pouring some coffee for Robert.

"Eight fifteen close enough."

"You know Coach Will hates it when Michael's late." She hands him the cup of coffee.

"Yeah I know I guess I forgot to set the alarm last night. Speaking of last night it was fun wasn't it?"

"Yeah it was I'm glad Phil liked his gift. Poor guy needs good people in his life."

"Poor guy? He just got a brand new Porsche!"

"Oh come on, you know money doesn't buy you love. He needs to settle down with a good woman."

"Well, he'll be getting some good women where he's going." He responds with a smirk on his face. Sandra stares at him with an evil look. "Alright I'm sorry, but a break will do him good." He starts reading his paper.

"Is Ryan up yet?" He asks with the newspaper covering his face.

"No he's still asleep." She responds as she brings Robert his breakfast.

"Who's babysitting tonight?" Robert asks putting his paper down to eat.

"Flora, from next door." Sandra replies, and then looks down with a sad look.

"You okay baby?"

"I was thinking maybe I shouldn't go tonight." She says while trying to avoid eye contact with Robert.

"Why not baby? You love the Orion Stars Gala."

"Yeah I know baby, but look at me, I'm huge! You're going to be there with this big disgusting blob and you'll have to drag me around everywhere." She says while staring at her stomach.

"Oh, come on love, I can assure you, you will be the most beautiful disgusting blob in the whole Gala." Robert says as he walks over and hugs her lovingly.

Charlotte interrupts them with a bark.

"See even Charlotte agrees." He says with a big smile.

"No you think I'm fat, and so does the dog!" She says yelling at the dog sarcastically.

"Oh come on, you know I'm just kidding. Look everyone already saw you yesterday and you looked beautiful. Besides, if I go without you by my side I'll feel all left alone over there." He says looking into her eyes.

"Oh you have all your friends and little suck ups to keep you company. 'Oh Mr. Heyward, Mr. Heyward'" She says mockingly.

"Ha ha, yeah but baby it's nothing without you, and I'm nothing without you. Please come?" He looks sadly into her eyes. There's a slight pause.

"Okay fine but just for you."

"Thank you sweetheart, and if you didn't come who would compliment me on my new tuxedo?"

They share a smile as Robert gives her a kiss.

***

"How was practice sweetheart?" Sandra asks as Michael comes through the front door.

"Dad was late *again* and coach made me run laps *again*." He replies in a frustrated tone.

"Yeah, but you got burgers and fries out of it, so don't look too down now mister." Robert interrupts, "Now, go upstairs and get in the shower, Flora should be over within a couple hours, and tell Ryan to clean up his room!" He yells as Michael runs up the stairs.

"I already did." A faint voice comes from up stairs. Ryan trots downstairs. "Can we have pizza tonight daddy?" He says with his hands clasped behind his back and looking up at his father.

"Only if I get the biggest kiss in the whole wide world!" He responds. Ryan runs up to Robert and kisses him on the cheek followed by an exaggerated hug.

16

"Oh it seems like someone wants only vegetables tonight!"

"No!" Ryan shrieks, and smothers him with kisses.

"Well then how about some raspberries!" Robert blows on Ryan's stomach, and Ryan giggles helplessly and so does Sandra.

"Charlotte wants some too!" They both turn towards Charlotte, and motion to tickle her, the dog looks at them strangely with her head tilted to the side and runs away.

"Okay you two," Sandra says as she tries to stop laughing, "Ryan go finish your homework so you can have fun tonight."

"But the magic eight ball said there's a snow day Monday!" He says trying to convince his mother.

"Ryan!" Sandra says with a slightly higher voice.

"Okay…but can we get extra cheese on the pizza tonight?"

"Only if you finish your homework."

"Aw man." He says as he runs back up the stairs in his red overall pajamas.

"And you mister need to go make sure Michael is cleaned up and Ryan finishes his homework while I go get ready." She says authoritatively with both her eyebrows raised.

"Yes dear." Robert jokingly hangs his head and slowly walks up the stairs as Sandra laughs at him.

Robert goes up the stairs to find Charlotte at the top of the staircase. He thinks back to when they first bought her. She was named Charlotte because, Charlotte's Web was Ryan's favorite book, needless to say no one in the family had much of a say in the decision.

"Here you are. Let's get out the way so mommy can come up. Honey you need help getting up the stairs?"

"No, I really want to do this on my own, I'm pregnant not disabled you know?"

"I know just trying to help baby."

Sandra slowly, but surely makes it up the stairs. She grew up as a simple woman in Chicago; she has one older sister who she holds near and dear to her heart. They talk almost every day on the phone. Her sister Sherry is also married with two children; a boy and a girl. Something Sandra always dreamt about. She and Robert met at a business convention in Dallas, Texas and have been together ever since. Sandra is a beautiful and straight forward person. She doesn't like to play games and despises

17

drama in her life. She believes the extra stress will only lead to an early grave, a lesson she learned from her grandfather when she was a child. Religion is very important to her; she believes that all of her good fortune is God's doing and not thanking Him for it is blasphemous. Because of her Robert has fallen closer in line with God. His relationship with God isn't golden, but it's better than nothing according to Sandra. She also believes her loyalty to God has lead her to Robert, even though she and Robert have struggled many a time throughout the building processes of their marriage and his company she has stuck by his side, and Robert knows how much she means to his livelihood. She even was the company's accountant up until she gave birth to Michael, which reminded her of her new coming child. She looks at her stomach from the mirror, and she smiles.

"With you the family will be complete." She whispers to her unborn child.

Robert walks out the shower as Sandra leaves the room to watch after the kids. "You ready honey?" He shouts out.

"Yeah. I'm glad I showered this morning."

"Yeah me too, I'll be out in a few."

"Okay hurry up it's already past seven thirty."

"Yeah, yeah don't worry."

About fifteen minutes later Robert comes out and Sandra and Robert see each other for the first time, and it's as if they're seeing each other for the first time ever. Falling hopelessly in love, he kisses her.

"Come on now you can't be late to the gala too you know." She says playfully moving back.

"Why not?" He says as he continues to kiss her neck.

"Because you're presenting tonight, besides you're messing up my makeup."

"Whatever, just tell me you're going to be there with the most handsome guy in town and I'll be fine."

"You didn't tell me Brad Pitt was coming!" Robert raises his eyebrow at her.

"Oh baby you know I'm just kidding."

"Yeah I know."

"I like George Clooney better." She laughs and gives him a kiss on the corner of his lips.

Whenever Sandra would get in trouble with Robert she kisses him there, and magically everything is fine.

"You're going to kiss me there and expect me *not* to miss the gala?"

Sandra gives him a mischievous smile as she walks away, Robert follows. The doorbell rings.

"Oh, that must be Flora." Sandra says. "Boys are you done with your homework?"

"Yes."

"Ryan."

"Yeah mom." They go to the door.

"Mr. and Mrs. Heyward you look amazing!" A girl standing outside the door says.

"Why thank you Flora," Sandra replies. "on the fridge are the emergency contacts, you can have anything in the fridge that you want, also the pizza should be here soon. Just make sure they don't have caffeine we have early mass tomorrow."

"Honey let them have what they want, we won't be home until later anyway, let's just skip tomorrow."

"I don't like skipping and you know that."

"I know baby, but come on you know it's going to be late."

"Okay just this once I don't want to make a habit of it. Flora if you need anything just call my cell phone."

"Yes Mrs. Heyward, and look your limo is here so I won't keep you any longer, enjoy your night!"

"Thanks Flora." They both say as they walk off.

"Honey, I left my speech in the office I have to stop by there for a few minutes."

Chapter 3

"You know what to do damn it so just do it!"

"I can't."

"Now either you do it, or we get rid of them ourselves, as well as completing the job and you can take the blame. You're getting your check so don't fuck around with us anymore. We're all busy people."

"Are you kidding me? Do you have any idea who you're taking to? You're all out of your God damn..."

"We know exactly who we're talking to." A sinister voice interrupts from the back of the round table. The darkness of the room couldn't fill his voice.

"Who the hell are you?" The man asks while squinting his eyes trying to make out the figure.

"I'm the man in charge now. You have been very fortunate lately. Don't let your fortune run out so swiftly. We know all your secrets, we know what you're capable of, and we intend to use your capabilities to their utmost potential. You don't have to worry, no one will know of this conversation or what will be carried out besides the people in this room...And we know what you want, you will get it, the spoils of war are always rewarded to those who are in the fight first."

"And nothing will happen to my family?" Everyone in the room laughs.

"Family?!" A man on the side yells out hysterically laughing. "That's classic!"

"They don't give a damn about you!" Another voice screams.

The man in the back slams his fists. A grave hush falls over the room. Everyone is startled and are as still as statues, all eyes turn slowly yet simultaneously to the back of the room. "Your...family will be taken care of."

Chapter 4

"What took you so long?"

"Nothing Liz accidentally shredded my speech and I had to dig through all my computer files to find it."

"Not a very good job for a secretary if you ask me. And now we're going to be late."

"Yeah well it was her son's bar mitzvah on Friday so she must have made a mistake; she normally never makes mistakes so let it go. And look this is our exit anyway, we're almost there."

Shortly thereafter they arrive at the Warldorf Astoria for the Orion's Stars Annual Gala. This is the one of the largest events in New York if not the country, and people are invited from all over the world to join in this gala. As Robert and Sandra approach the building they can already see camera crews and news reporters covering the gala events. The Limo slowly pulls up to the red carpet.

"Thank you for joining us. This is Amber K. with Highlight news, if you look behind me you can see most of the crowd has already made their way in. We met the man who we believe is closest to Mr. Heyward and has a great stake in this company, Mr. Phillip Roderick. We have seen such faces as the Vice President of the United States Ronald Jacobs, the Prime ministers from China, Japan, Engl...oh look it's Mr. and Mrs. Robert Heyward themselves! Mr. Heyward, Mrs. Heyward, can I get a quick interview? Mr. Heyward please?" She holds out the mic towards Robert hoping for an answer.

"Okay, but really short because I'm already late."

"Thank you Mr. Heyward, now is it true that Orion has a new product under its belt that will revolutionize the world, and bring cheaper energy sources around the world including third world countries?"

"Well that my dear, we'll have to find out tonight."

"Can you tell us anything about the recent drops in stock of your company?"

"Well we all hit road bumps once in a while, but after tonight I'm sure we'll be back on our feet."

"What are your plans for the company, once you get that energy source up and running, do you plan to sell?"

He chuckles then gets a little stern "Of course not my father built this company with his own two hands, and then I have made it what it is today, selling this company would be like selling my own child. So thank you, I have to go inside now."

"Mr. Heyward one last question!" Robert turns back.

"How many months pregnant is your wife?"

He looks over at Sandra and then back at the reporter "Seven months now. Thank you." He walks off as a wave of newscasters yell out to talk to him. He waves his arm to say good-bye and continues to walk.

"There you have it from the mouth of the shark himself Mr. Robert Allen Heyward. This is Amber K. Highlight news."

"And cut!" Yells the cameraman. "Wow, you're the only one who got the interview. Good job Amber!"

"Yeah whatever Harvey, there's more to this energy story and I want to get to the bottom of it, let's find a way to sneak inside!"

"You're gonna get us killed. Why are you always trying to look deeper than you have to?"

"Come on Harv you don't seriously buy his clean cut bullshit do you? A man with such a spotless record has to have something to hide, and I am going to find out exactly what that is."

***

Inside the Warldorf Astoria, a short husky man in a black tuxedo accompanied by a tall woman in a black dress with sparkling glitter begins to speak. He was a British man in his fifties and she was a young black woman in her late twenties.

"Good evening everyone and thank you for joining us at the fourteenth annual Orion's Stars Gala here at the Warldorf Astoria." Everyone applauds. "Thank you, I am Peter Lambard, and accompanying me tonight is the very beautiful, Miss New York herself, Starla Jackson!" Everyone applauds again. "I have been told that I am way too handsome and can not stand up here too long because then the ladies get out of control…and oddly enough some of you men. So without further ado let us eat before all of you lose your wives to me."

Everyone laughs, cheers, and continues in conversation. Meanwhile the orchestra begins to play in the background. Amber and Harvey sneak into the Ball Room disguised as waiters.

"Is the camera on?" Amber whispers to Harvey.

"Yes!" He responds irritably.

"Are you sure?"

"Yes Amber, Yes. I am the *camera*man I have only one job in life I think I know how to do it!"

"Okay, okay relax!" They walk past a few tables; they approach a table that seems to be talking about exactly what they're looking for.

"Frankly I think all this Cold Fusion talk is rubbish." A very young gentleman blurts out.

"Really, I think it's quite inventive." Says the lady across from him, "Countries like ours in Africa will really benefit if this actually goes through."

"That's exactly what I'm saying *if* it goes through, this juncture is costing millions upon millions of dollars and for what? A simple if! I say we use our money more wisely and just make bigger fatter animals and vegetables if you want to feed these poor people."

"Are you kidding me, is that what these people are to you just poor souls who need food?"

"Never mind the fact that we're all shareholders of an energy company and not a drug and food company." An older gentleman says in support of the woman.

"Well I'm sure they need other things to, all I'm trying to say is that this project is so dangerous, it can potentially kill as many people as it can help if not more. Is that a risk you'd really want to take?" The young man continues.

"And all I'm saying is that this can very well revolutionize the world as a whole, not only a company, or an industry." The woman responds.

"Did you get that? See I told you these people have some crazy agenda and we'll be the first to find out!" Amber whispers to Harvey.

"Yeah, yeah just shut up and go."

"Oh, oh let's go past Heyward's table."

"Hey you guys need to go get the salads first you have the wrong trays!" Says a waiter passing by.

"Okay sir," Responds Harvey, "sorry it's our first gala."

"Damn it, so close!" Says Amber. They turn and start walking towards the kitchen, as the waiter who coaxed them into changing trays watched carefully. As they walked closer to the kitchen they hear a yell.

"Hey, who the hell put this camera in here?!" Amber and Harvey both look at each other, then down at the tray. Harvey lifts the tray and discovers a big uncooked New York steak on the plate.

"Harvey!" Amber says running towards the kitchen.

"Man, I don't know the trays must have gotten switched!"

"I'm a cameraman you know, I have one job in life I know what I'm doing!" Amber says in a mocking and irritated voice, as they try to dodge pass the waiters and waitresses.

"I'm sorry I didn't know it got switched!" Harvey grabs the camera and they both dart out of the kitchen.

"Call the cops!" A waiter yells.

But it was too late they had already left the building and were about to take off into the night.

"What the fuck Harvey, the biggest story of my career down the fucking drain!"

"Look, relax you got the info you wanted and..."

"Yeah, with no proof. Shit all that work for nothing!" She says slamming her hands onto the steering wheel.

They then drive off into the dark. Back at the gala things are more subtle, the kitchen staff is confused and the cops were called, but no one dare ever would disturb the guests, not if you enjoyed living at least. The dinner moved in smoothly as scheduled. The steak was as succulent as ever with mash potatoes on the side topped with cheese and parsley, and for the vegetarians, juicy spinach and cheese lasagna also with the mashed potatoes, and spring rolls on the side. As the main course came out the traditional Chinese dancers took stage.

Everyone ate, drank, and laughed, as the night went on. After dessert it was time for the awards and achievements. Many of the speeches that were given by the board members were given during dinner. Most of them thanked the share holders and outside consultants for coming, others were talking about the company's future, and some talked about all the other events the company was involved in. It was Robert's turn to speak, and that meant the night was almost at a conclusion. The night's MCs had come on stage for the introduction.

"When you hear young thirty four year old millionaire what do you think of Starla?" Asks Peter.

"Well I'm thinking what's his name and is he single. Am I right ladies?" Everyone chuckles and applauds.

"Ah yes, well of course, but if the person is married with a beautiful wife, you would probably think of Robert Heyward, he is the chief executive officer of this beloved organization and he is here with us tonight. Please everyone join me in welcoming Mr. Robert Allen Heyward." Everyone applauds and whistles.

"Good luck honey!" Sandra says as Robert gets up.

"Yeah, good luck honey!" Phil follows as he blows out the smoke from his mouth and winks at Robert as he raises his wine glass towards him. His date chuckles as she holds Phil's arm. Robert kisses his wife on the cheek, winks back at Phil, and continues on to the stage.

"Thank you, and thank you all for joining us tonight." Robert reaches into his front pocket to pull out his notes, "My father had started this company twenty years ago; he just wanted people to see at night. He wanted to provide power to the people. He wanted less fortunate people to have the ability to do the same things that other people were able to do. Today, we are helping that dream become a reality." Everyone applauds. "When I was a child my father was just a mere electrician, and we would take walks at night in the park, and on a clear winter night we would look up in the sky and the most conspicuous stars were the ones of Orion's belt. He would tell me, 'Robby that's Orion, the hunter; you should always be in control of your destiny and make something of your self. If you want something go get, no one will ever get it for you, ever.' About nine short years ago both my parents passed away in a tragic car accident, it was the most heart breaking day of my life, and I miss them everyday. But I can promise you one thing I would not be standing here in front of you if it wasn't for the lessons my father had taught me and the support of my wife Sandra who I thank God for everyday."

Everyone applauds as Robert looks to Sandra and smiles, "Today we embark in a new era in energy. Ladies and gentlemen we are on course to a revolutionary energy source that will change the world as we know it. Cold Fusion." The crowd's attention becomes sharper. Robert feels as if he were talking to each person in the room individually. He looks over to his wife, and she nods her head yes. "Ahem, Cold Fusion is the name for effects supposed to be nuclear reactions occurring near room temperature and pressure using relatively simple and low-energy-input devices. When two light nuclei are forced to fuse, they form a heavier nucleus and release a large amount of energy…Simply put, we're making energy usage more vast from smaller amounts of energy."

The crowd uneasily grumbles a little bit talking to each other. Robert raises his voice to gain control. "I can assure you that we are going about this process in the safest, most in-destructive way possible. We have taken into account and would never risk the lives or the well being of our families, our friends, and our neighbors. Once we complete the project, whole third world countries will be lit up at the cost of merely a few thousand dollars. As we develop the project further it will become cheaper and cheaper. We will be the top competitors in the One World Origination group. Charity is good, but making the *world* self sufficient, is great. Let's bring this company to greatness, let us ourselves become great!"

The crowd goes into an uproar of applauds, cheers, and whistles. Robert looks around the room with a big smile nodding his head yes. His charisma always shined through in the most difficult times. His wife always accused him of getting out of trouble by using his charm whether it were with his college professors, clients, and especially her. After thirteen years of marriage she feels as she's coming on to his game, but lets him go sometimes because she still finds it cute.

It was now time for the ring ceremony. The ring ceremony is done very rarely. Only when a certain employee reaches a certain level in the company they are entitled to the ring. The look of the ring is of Orion shooting into the heavens and it has three spaces for his belt. Each time you reach a new level of trust and greatness within the company, more secrets are revealed to you, and you have a greater stake in the company. You become somewhat of a partner. Your level is determined first by the ring, and each time you reach a new level a diamond is added to the ring. Each diamond is worth over twenty five thousand dollars. The ring itself is worth somewhere near that amount. When your ring reaches a value of a hundred thousand dollars you know you're a somebody. Very few people have a full ring in the company. Of course Robert and Phil both have full rings.

"Thank you. Now it's time for the ring ceremony. This year we have an exceptional and promising young man. He has more than proven his stripes on many of occasion. He is one of the fastest growing members of our company, and one of our leading scientists in the Cold Fusion project; it would be an honor to watch him grow with this company during this exciting time. Please help me welcome on to the stage Mr. Dominique Walker." Everyone applauds; a young man nervously kisses his wife and approaches the stage to receive his prize.

"Congratulations." Robert says into the microphone.

"Thank you." Dominique says back.

As he makes his way to the middle of the stage the board members congratulate him with hugs and handshakes. Robert escorts him and they all take pictures together as the crowd continues to cheer them on. They all then make it off the stage and sit on a special table of ring bearers. The two MCs return to the stage.

"Well wasn't that just wonderful Starla?"

"Yes, congratulations once again Dominique. Come on everyone he deserves one more round of applause!" Everyone applauds.

"Well, this concludes our night as far as speeches and awards go, but please join us on our dance floor as our live band plays for you. Once again thank you all for joining us tonight. Goodnight!"

The music starts to play and the dance floor slowly fills as more and more people come to dance. The ring bearers sit at their own table as people come to congratulate the new member. Soon there after, the group goes into a separate room to have a meeting. Once they come out they join the party. When Robert gets back to Sandra she looks exhausted.

"Honey, are you okay?" Robert asks.

"Yeah, just really tired." She responds slowly and obviously out of breath.

"Okay baby let's go home."

She gets up slowly as Robert helps her up and they make their way towards the exit. He is bombarded by people, but tries to move along as quickly as possible.

"Leaving already Robert?" Phil asks as he puts his hand on Robert's shoulder.

"Yeah Phil, Sandra's not feeling too well."

"She okay?" He looks over at her.

"Just tired."

"Okay let me walk you guys out." He leads the way pushing people out of the way. He waits with Robert and Sandra until the limo arrives.

"Okay guys take it easy." He says as he closes the limo door.

"You're leaving Monday morning?" Robert asks through the open window of the limo.

"I'm not sure yet I might go tomorrow and spend a day in Florida before I take off."

"Alright well, enjoy and try not to be too bad."

"Yeah, I'll try." Phil says sarcastically. They smile and then shake hands.

"Good night Sandra." Phil says looking into the window.

"Night." She replies faintly.

Chapter 5

Early morning in some park a man in a black suit with a brown trench coat and a hat holds two briefcases and waits patiently on a bench reading the newspaper as people jog past him. *"Pretty lively for this time of day and especially in weather like this."* He thinks to himself. He lights up a cigarette and begins to smoke just as another man sits next to him. He's wearing a grey suit, also with a hat. He seems to be very nervous. To calm him down the man in the black suit offers him a cigarette and lights it for him.

"You're late."

"Had a late night."

"Are you prepared?"

"Unfortunately, yes almost." He takes a puff of his cigarette.

"Good, here's a small bonus." He hands over the brief case. The other man is reluctant.

"Don't be stupid, just take it. We're not always this nice. You'll also need this briefcase to 'aid' you in your venture." The man looks inside and sees what he feared it would be.

"I can't believe you guys are making me do this. Are you sure you want me to do this?"

"Are you sure you want to live?"

"Not so sure anymore."

"Don't worry, that to can be arranged."

The man in the grey suit closes the brief case, and begins to walk off with one in each hand.

"Where you going now?" Asks the man in the black suit as he still sat on the bench.

"Church."

"I thought you didn't believe in God."

He takes a puff of his cigarette, blows out. He drops his cigarette on the floor and crushes it with the toe of his foot. "I don't believe in a lot of things."

***

At a near-by church the man in the grey suit stands near the footsteps of the church. He catches another man's eye that is walking with a woman; he nods his head and touches the tip of his hat.

"Honey, go to the car. I'll be right there." Says the man coming out of church. "Man, what the hell are you doing here?" He says as he grabs the man by his coat.

"I don't think *God* appreciates such actions, now does he?"

"I don't think God appreciates you on his earth, but you're still here."

"Strong words for a man who got the opportunity of a life time just recently."

"Fuck you."

The man in the grey suit drags him over near the back of the church and punches him in the gut. Then he grabs him by the back of the neck and talks into his ear.

"Look I don't have time for low class scum like you right now. Here's the brief case you know what to do. You want to keep all that good stuff coming to you, then get the God damn job done. If you want to start coming to church to visit your family in the back graveyard, then I can make that happen too. Now put a smile on your dumb ass face, and take this briefcase and get the job done. You got it?" When he doesn't get an answer, he squeezes his victim's neck tighter. "I said, you got it?!"

"Yes!" His victim spits on the ground in front of the man's shoe.

Chapter 6

Sandra wakes up to the sound of the shower running. It turns off. She dozes off again. She then wakes up again to the movement of the bed. She looks up and sees Robert.

"Where were you this morning?" Sandra asks while rubbing her eyes.

"Went for a jog." Robert responds putting his arms around her.

"That long?"

"Charlotte was being frisky, so we stayed out longer."

"Have fun?"

"It was okay, not the same with out you though." She nods her head, "Are you feeling better?" She nods her head yes. He kisses her on the forehead.

"Robert?"

"Yeah love?"

"I have to pee." Sandra says, giving him an embarrassed look.

"Ha, ha okay." He helps her up and takes her to the bathroom.

They both are fully awake now and go down stairs. As they get to the last stair, the doorbell rings. Charlotte runs towards the door. "Back up Charlotte." Demands Robert.

"Who could that be this early?" Sandra asks.

"I don't know babe."

The doorbell rings again, they find Phil at the door. "Hey Phil, what's up?" Robert asks as he shakes his hand.

"Nothing, just about to leave, thought I'd stop by and say hello before I left." Phil replies as he tries to blow warm air into his hands.

"Well come in Phil, we just woke up. Have breakfast with us." Sandra says.

"No I don't want to bother anyone."

"Don't be silly come in."

"Yeah it's no problem at all. I wanted to see you before you left anyway." Robert adds.

"Well fine you twisted my arm." Phil says with a smile as he walks through the door.

"Alright that's what I'm talking about."

"What kind of eggs do you want Phil?" Robert asks.

"Scrambled."

"And for you baby?"

"I guess I'll take scrambled too." Sandra replied.

"Okay, I guess I'll have scrambled too then!"

"How are you feeling Sandra?" Phil asks.

"Much better thank you. You look a little flustered though." Sandra replies.

"Oh just had a little too much to drink last night, I suppose."

"Well are you sure you wanna drive that far like this? And the weather doesn't look to great out there either."

"Yeah I could use the fresh air."

"Do you guys want apple or orange juice?" Asks Robert.

"Apple for me hon."

"You have cranberry?"

"Um let me check," He looks in the refrigerator, "yep."

"Cranberry then."

"Okay and orange for me. So how do you like the Porsche?"

"I love it man. And thank you again."

"Oh don't mention it, you deserve it."

"Loved your speech yesterday by the way. Don't think anyone knew what the hell you were talking about, but it was cute." They all chuckle. "I especially loved 'the chemical reactions of low pressure molecules'..." Phil mockingly adds as they all laugh.

"Yeah, yeah well it's going to make me very rich soon and I'll be the one laughing then, now finish your eggs and get out of my house." Robert jokingly replied. "By the way what route are you taking anyway?"

"Taking the road straight there."

"No touristy stuff?"

"Nope just a straight shot. Don't want to keep the ladies waiting."

"Phil... no one says 'ladies' anymore." Sandra says shaking her head, as they all laugh.

Soon after they finish up breakfast and Phil prepares to leave.

"Alright guys I'm headed off. Don't miss me too much, and tell the kids Uncle Phil said bye."

"Will do champ." Robert replies.

The dog barks at Phil as if to call him. "Oh I'll miss you too Charlotte." He says in a childish voice as he bends down and rubs her ears.

"And please, drive safe Phil." Sandra adds.

"I'll try." He gives her a kiss on the cheek and hugs Robert. He jumps into his car and rapidly takes off. You can hear him scream for joy as he drives off. Robert and Sandra both laugh as they see the car disappear and they go back inside.

Chapter 7

A week and a half passes. Business is as usual and Robert is at the kitchen table with the kids. The weather is oddly warmer today, and Sandra feels extra tired. She comes down later when the kids are about to leave.

"Mommy, are you okay?" Ryan asks with a worried look on his face.

"Yeah sweetie, your bus should be here soon." Sandra replies in a slow and slightly pained voice. The kids give the usual kiss and take off.

"You okay love?" Robert asks worriedly.

Sandra looks pale; she walks towards Robert and faints.

"Baby?" Robert catches her as she falls; he lays her down on her back and immediately calls the ambulance.

***

"Hey sunshine." Robert asks with a smile on his face.

"Hey." Sandra replies softly. She looks around confused, realizing she's laying a hospital bed. "What happened?"

"Doctor says you fainted, some kind of stress problems."

"Is baby okay?"

"Yeah, just fine. They're going to keep you here for a couple days." He puts his hand on her forehead caressing her, and then he kisses her there.

"Are you going to stay with me?"

"Of course, baby."

"What about the kids?"

"I called Susan, Flora's mom, she'll take care of the kids and bring them here after school." Robert answers; Sandra nods her head, and closes her eyes. She sleeps until the kids come back from school.

"Mom!" Michael yells.

"Shh, she's still sleeping." Robert whispers stopping the boys at the door of the room. "You guys okay? I'll let you see her, but you have to be very quiet, mom needs her rest. Okay?" They both nod their heads yes. Robert walks outside into the hallway to talk to, Flora's mother, Susan as the boys enter the room.

"Is she okay?" Susan asks.

"Yeah, just stress pains I guess. She's a trooper."

"Look whatever you guys need, don't hesitate to ask John and I can take in the kids until she gets better."

"Are you sure?"

"Yeah, don't worry about it. You should get some rest, you look really tired."

"Yeah I know, I'll try. Come in you can see her."

They come in to find Ryan in tears, and Michael with his hand around him. Sandra is somewhat awake now, but still weak. They both have one hand clasping their mother's right hand. The IV is in the left arm. The whole room is pure white, kind of like heaven just sad. Susan sits near Sandra's head and she tells her that she'll be taking care of the kids until she gets back on her feet and not to worry. Sandra slowly closes and opens her eyes. The nurse walks in.

"How are you Sandra?" The nurse asks. Sandra nods her head towards the nurse trying to answer.

"Is my mom going to be okay?" Ryan asks.

"She'll be just fine. We're fortunate she came in when she did or there could have been trouble."

"Why does she look so weak?" Robert asks.

"She's just very tired, once she gets some more water and rest her color should return and her strength will come back soon too." The nurse changes the fluids in the IV.

"She hasn't eaten anything yet." Robert adds.

"That's fine for now the IV is giving her energy; once she comes closer to her normal state she'll get hungrier and start eating solids again." She finishes changing the IV then checks for any abnormalities.

"If you need anything just push the call nurse button, and a nurse will be here right away." She leaves with a reassuring smile.

"Thanks."

"Have you been eating Robert?" Asks Susan.

"Yeah a little bit."

"That's good, you'll need your strength for Sandra so make sure you get your rest and your energy."

"Yeah."

"Okay kids, let your mom rest now, you'll be staying with us tonight. Flora and Tommy are really excited that you're coming over."

"What about mom?" Asks Michael.

"Yeah I wanna stay with mommy!" Ryan follows. Susan looks at Robert, as if to ask what to do. Robert just shakes his head in the same confusion.

"How about you guys stay here and do your homework with mom, and I'll be back in a few hours to pick you up."

"Thank you Susan you don't know how much your help means to us."

"Stop it." She says firmly. "You've been our friends for so many years, and you've helped us enough when we needed it. It's about time we get to be useful." She says with a smile. "Now again Robert, do not hesitate to ask for anything okay?"

"Okay Susan."

She gives him a hug, and then turns towards the kids, "Make sure you guys finish up your homework, because we're going to need a couple extra players in monopoly tonight."

She leaves the room. All three of them sit quietly in the room. The boys start to do their homework, but keep looking back at their mother for some signs of life. Robert finally gets a chance to call the office; he explains the situation to Elizabeth and she relays the message to the Vice President of the company Scott Fisher. Scott is also part of the board members and a full ring owner. There's no better replacement than him.

The monitor in the background keeps beeping reassuring Robert every second. It's the only thing keeping him together. Every time Sandra awakens everything stops and all the attention moves onto her. She's in and out of consciousness. Every time she comes back though, it's for a longer amount of time, whether it be a second or a minute. The nurse comes back every hour to make sure everything is okay. Robert notices her color filtering back into her face which helps him relax a little bit more. Sandra wakes up and says hello to the boys. They all sit and talk for about half an hour and then Susan walks back in.

"Sandra, how are you?" Susan asks with a concerned look trying to smile.

"Susan, thank you so much for your help."

"Now am I going to have to scold you too? I have already told Robert not to worry about anything at all. You just make sure you're feeling better. I'm happy to see that you're up though."

"Thank you Susan," She looks over to the man standing next to her, "John how are you?"

"Just fine Sandra. Glad to see you're doing better." He looks over, "Robert." He walks over and shakes his hand followed by a hug. "How's it going?"

"Just fine John, thank you."

"Oh I almost forgot I brought food. Its roast beef sandwiches, chicken noodle soup, and some chips and some stuff to snack on." Susan says as she hands over a large bag to Robert.

"You shouldn't have." Sandra says.

"Oh Sandra, just worry about getting better, let me take care of the rest right now." Susan replies. "Okay kids, come with Aunt Susan now; we have a lot of game playing to do."

"Here are my house keys so you can get the boys' clothes and things, and also if you need anything else just feel free to take it." Robert unhooks his house keys from his key chain and hands them over to John, "Oh and if you don't mind can you please make sure to feed Charlotte? Her food is underneath the kitchen sink, the boys should know where it is if you don't see it."

"Yeah, no problem." He replies as he takes the keys then looks Robert in his eyes, "Everything will be just fine, okay Bob?"

"Yeah, thanks man."

"Okay Robert, make sure to call with any updates." Susan says.

"I promise."

"I love you mom." Michael says as he kisses her and then her stomach.

"I love you mommy." Ryan repeats the same actions. They both hug their father and then walk out with John and Susan.

Robert sits down next to Sandra; he begins to eat the sandwich, while she begins to eat the soup.

"This is good." He tells her. She gives an agreeing nod. Feeling so hungry she'd rather eat than talk.

Sandra and Robert were extremely thankful that John and Susan are there to help. When Robert and Sandra moved into the neighborhood, John and Susan were the first to greet them. They have been close friends ever since. One time Flora had broken her leg while playing soccer. John was just switching jobs and the insurance company from John's old job wouldn't help pay for the surgery. Robert immediately hired John, and put him on the company insurance plan. A few days later Flora was able to get her surgery, and was back in the game within the year. Not all good deeds go unnoticed.

***

A cell phone rings, rings again, and then again. The phone has been ringing for quite a while now, but the vibration wakes him up. He looks at the number…Private. It hangs up. 7 missed calls. It rings again.

"…Hello?"

"I've been reading the papers and watching the news, and yet I don't see you getting the job done."

"Do you know what time it is?"

"Why isn't it done yet?"

"It's all on schedule to get done tonight."

"See to it that it does."

***

The monitor beeps as normal. Beeps again. Then there's a change in the beep. Faster? Robert wakes up immediately, and looks at the monitor. The frequency has changed.

"Honey?" Sandra says moaning in pain.

"Baby?! Nurse! Nurse!" He yells as he runs out the room. "Nurse I need help!" A nurse rushes in and checks Sandra's pulse. She calls the doctor and a team of nurses follow the doctor.

"What happened?" He says with a concerned face.

"We don't know Mr. Heyward. Just let the doctor take a look at your wife." The nurse says trying to calm Robert down as she moves him out of the doctor and other nurses' way.

"The baby is choking!"

The doctor yells out to his team. They move Sandra from her side on to her back and the doctor twists the baby with his hands trying to be as careful as possible. Robert is asked to leave the room as he becomes more and more light-headed. This situation has Robert's mind going crazy. He uses the wall as a guide to lead him outside and down the hallway. The eerie sounds take him immediately back to the night of his parents' accident. And all he could think of now is what happened that night.

"We're losing him. I need a nurse with morphine, and let's get this guy to surgery." *The doctor tells his nurses.*

"The surgery room is full doctor!"

"Come on now, take him or lose him people!"

"She's flat-lining! We need a doctor here immediately!" Another nurse shouts out from the neighboring bed.

Robert stands there helplessly as his parents were dying in front of his own eyes. He looks over in Phil's direction. Phil was no longer standing next to him. "Where the hell did he go?" He thought to himself. He turned around and Phil was walking quickly out the door.

"Phil?!" Robert yells.

"I'm sorry man I can't take this! I need to breathe for a little bit, I'll be right back just give me a minute!" As he starts walking away he was cut off by doctors carrying a woman in a biker jacket with blood flowing down the side of her face. She looks at Phil and screams out for help. Phil just stares at her, he then turns around takes one last look at Robert and then he disappeared completely. Robert wouldn't see Phil for another couple months.

As he stood there about to crack, a hand clasped his hand he looks down at the hand then up at the face. It was Sandra. She was there to keep him strong. She was there to be his rock.

"Any vacancy at the O.R. yet?" The doctor yells.

"Yeah, hurry bring him in!"

"Let's go people. No time! No time!" They push his father's bed into the O.R. as fast as possible.

His father's dying body is rolled right past Robert's face. Holding back his tears he looks over to his mom.

"Allen?" His mother yells out, "Where's my husband?!"

"He's just fine ma'am, please hold still."

"Where's my son?!"

"I'm…I'm right here mom." Robert says with a broken voice. He runs over to her to hold her hand.

"Please help us keep her still; she's in an extreme state of shock." Robert nods and follows orders.

"There's way too much blood in the stomach area and lungs doctor."

"You'll be just fine, I love you mom. Just stay calm, please." Robert softly says in her ear as she shakes uncontrollably.

"Then pump it out nurse!" The doctor demanded in the background.

Through all the noise and chaos, Robert heard, felt, or saw nothing but his mother. She looked up at him and smiled as best as she could. She gripped his hand tight to help extinguish some of the pain.

"I love you Robby." She tells him. She lets out one more scream of pain, and then her body gives out. She leaves with the memory of her son holding her hand.

"Time of death ten thirty two P.M." The doctor announces. He looks over to Robert. "I'm sorry son."

Robert hangs his head. This moment is so surreal that it hasn't hit him yet. He looks over at the O.R. where they are operating on his father. He kisses his mother's hand and runs towards the O.R. as if his father makes it out alive then there is some solace to the night, some fighting chance that this craziness has an end, Sandra follows him. He looks up at the monitor near his father. The monitor starts beeping slowly again. "Is that good news?" He thinks to himself. He looks over to the surgeon to confirm his hopes. The surgeon takes off his masks with a smile and high fives for everyone. He walks over to Robert with a swagger in his step. He puts his arm on Roberts shoulder.

"Son, I think your father will be just fine."

With tears in his eyes Robert responds, "Thank you doctor."

Sandra puts her arms around Robert to comfort him. Neither of them forgetting what just had happened in the other room moments ago. Just as rapidly as the excitement built up, it came crashing right back down. A nurse in the O.R. yells out.

"*Doctor, his heart is failing!*"

"*What?*" *The surgeon sprints back into the room.*

"*Wha…what's going on?!*" *Robert asks confused.*

"*We don't know his heart's just giving up!*"

They started CPR, everything they did, just kept bouncing back. Time was running out fast. They kept injecting him with needles. Everything around Robert slowed down completely. His father turns his head and looks at Robert.

"*Robby.*" *He says faintly.*

"*Damn it, Damn it, Damn it!*"

The doctor yells out throwing things across the room as if in an angry trance. It was an eleven car pile up that night on the Brooklyn Bridge. A child had run on to the street chasing his own thrown ball. It was one of those big red balls; it bounced on to the first lane. He ran after it. A car swerved out of control, avoiding hitting the child, it barely misses the mother as she runs into the traffic to retrieve her boy. It bounced into the second lane. The mother ran after him and scooped him up with the look of fear in her eyes as she attempts to shield the child. She turned to run out of the street and an eighteen wheeler caught the back of her hand ripping the shoulder out of its socket. She twirled uncontrollably into oncoming traffic. The next car trying to avoid her cut in front of her but hit her knees and she was thrown back. The car swerved hitting the first car and they both fell over the bridge. The eighteen-wheeler went out of control and the whole truck fell on its side, as it took out people and other cars in its way. As the lady flew back, desperately trying to hold on to her child and her life, she is met by a minivan slamming its breaks, but it rammed her into the back of the fallen truck. The child falls out of her hands, as he cries attempting to run out of the way, a biker slides slamming and trapping the child between its wheels and the truck. The bottom of the bike cut him up and burned him, torturing the child until he died. Robert's father would have been the only other survivor that night. The lady in the bike hit her head pretty hard and had a ruptured spleen, even she would have died, but Robert let the doctors use his father's organs before it was too late. He wanted the donor and himself to be anonymous, for any living memory of his father or mother would crush him, since the lady also had the same name as his mother. Robert broke down into a downward spiral. Helpless tears ran from his eyes. All he heard was Sandra's voice, Robert! Robert! Robert! Just then Robert suddenly awoke from his dream at the sound of Sandra's voice yelling for him.

"Robert! Robert!" He ran back into the room. She was in excruciating pain. He runs in and holds her hand.

"What's going on? What's happening? Is she okay?"

"She's having a panic attack which is killing the baby. We need you to help us calm her down Mr. Heyward. Can you do that?" The doctor responds while looking straight into Robert's frightened eyes.

He nods his head, "Yes." He looks over at Sandra, "Okay baby I need you to calm down, please baby, it's for our baby. If you don't relax our baby will die, baby please slow down, just breathe okay?" He tilts her head slightly to look in his direction. "For me baby, just breathe. Just look me in the eye."

Sandra looks at him and they both begin to breathe at the same pace. A few moments pass and the doctor looks up at Robert. He takes off his mask and he walks slowly over to Robert.

"The baby and your wife look like they'll be just fine." Robert lets out a big sigh of relief followed by tears. He gives the doctor a passionate hug. Sandra had fallen asleep from the painstaking ordeal.

"Let Sandra sleep now, make sure she stays on her back. You should get some rest too Mr. Heyward."

"Thank you sir, thank you so much."

"Not a problem, you make sure you take care now. She will need you to have your energy as well."

"Yes, yes sir." He thanked every nurse as he or she walked out. Robert sat in the seat next to Sandra and fell asleep.

***

That night Robert was awakened abruptly by a beeping sound. Startled Robert woke up immediately. He looks over at the monitor it looks normal. He looks at his wife, she seems peaceful. He hears the beep again. "What the hell?" He looks down at his cell phone. He recognizes the number of his secretary. He looks at the time, it reads two seventeen A.M. Confused by what was going on he tries to shake off his sleep, takes a deep breath, and picks up.

"He…Hello?"

"Mr. Heyward?"

"Yeah, I told you not to call; I'm looking after my wife."

"I…I know sir, but we've got a problem."

"What problem do you have at two A.M.?"

"Sir it's Artemis. There's been an accident."

"What!?" He yells as he stands up, and then looks at his wife hoping he didn't wake her. He then steps outside. "What?"

"There's been some kind of explosion in the Cold Fusion plant."

"What the hell are you talking about?"

"Sir the police, the board members, Mr. Fisher, even *I* have been trying to contact you for the past hour. You need to come here now!"

"Let me call you back." He could hardly hear her through all the sounds of commotion in the background.

Robert looks down at the countless missed calls he's gotten.

***

"Hello?"

"Are you watching?"

"Yes. It took you long enough. Did you cover your tracks?"

"Yeah."

"Well you can thank God you get to keep your family and job."

The phone hangs up.

***

"We've been waiting for your call. Getting other people to do your job I see. I knew you'd weasel some way to get the job done. We'll see you at the next meeting."

"What about my family? You promised they'd be fine."

The phone hangs up.

Chapter 8

Robert looks over at his wife. *"She'll be okay won't she?"* He thinks to himself, *"This is something that needs to be done."* Robert makes tough decisions all the time, but this one has him torn apart. *"I'll be back by the morning won't I...Well I'll be back sometime tomorrow."* He runs towards the nurse. He runs back inside, changing his mind. *"Is it that bad out there? I can't show my face there yet. Not like this."* The television in the next room catches the corner of his eye. *"It's that reporter from the gala, and there's a fire behind her. Oh my God it's Artemis Labs!"* He turns on the television in his own room.

***

"Once again, CEO Robert Heyward is nowhere to be found! We have reports that there was some sort of bad chemical reaction, or some mechanical error, or even a bomb! Again this is all speculation, we are still awaiting answers. As you can see behind me the Binghamton Fire Department has been fighting these flames for quite some time now, and they have called the fire departments of neighboring cities for help."

An explosion goes off in the back.

"Oh my God, I think there's been another explosion! We're moving back now, let's just pray that the fire fighters are okay. We're being moved around due to the chaos, let's cut to commercial we'll be right back in a few. This is Amber K. Highlight news."

Robert hangs his head. He rubs his face with his hands, and runs them through his hair. He gets up, turns off the television, and walks towards the nurse. The nurse looks at him, he looks eerily calm.

"Mr. Heyward? Is everything all right?" She asks as she walks over to him.

"No. There's been some sort of explosion at the company plant, and I need to be there. If my wife wakes up will you please inform her of my whereabouts?"

"Oh my God, of course I will."

"I'll try to send someone to be near her side, is that okay?"

"Of course, be safe Mr. Heyward you haven't had much sleep."

"Thank you." He walks off.

He sits inside his car and puts his head in his hands. He collects him self as tears drop down the side of his face. He wipes them away, as his eyes turn a crimson bloody red with rage. His hands start to shake then from deep within, as if it has been put away for years a deadly scream comes rushing out of his lungs, travels through his throat and vocalizes through his mouth. He screams until his lungs give out as he clasps the steering wheel. He sits there and gasps for air while trying to collect himself. He looks at himself in the rearview mirror and takes a deep breath. He then turns his car on and a dinging sound goes off, he realizes he is nearly out of gas. *"Damn it, there's no gas station for miles and I don't have time."* He thinks to himself. He then figures that he should call a cab, and he can get some rest and prepare better on the way there. Luckily there were a few cabs sitting in front of the hospital. He runs towards the cabs, and stops at the closest one.

"Can you get me to Binghamton?"

"No man I'm on break." He runs to the second cab.

"I need to get to Binghamton right away please!"

"There's no way I'm going that far man." He runs to the last cab in line.

"Sir please I need to get to Binghamton."

"Yeah and I've needed a vacation for the past three years."

"Damn it!" Robert slams the top of the cab with his fists.

"Hey what the fuck, are you crazy?!" The cab driver speeds off. Just as he does another cab pulls in.

"Sir, please this is an emergency I need a ride." Robert says before the couple in the cab can even get out.

"Sorry man I'm going home now, my shifts over and I have a long drive ahead of me." The cab driver says in an African accent. He looks back, thanking the people as they step out of the cab.

"I need to get to Binghamton it's urgent, please I'll pay anything, can you take me?" He has the look of desperation in his eyes.

The cab driver studies the desperate looking man for a moment. "Aren't you Robert Heyward of Orion?"

"Yes!"

"So that's your factory that's burnin' down in Binghamton?"

"Yes, yes!"

"Get in! I actually live around there; I'll drop you on my way home."

The cab driver drives as fast as he can. He keeps looking back at Robert for his well being. He sees Robert's unshaven face, his red eyes, and the dark circles around them. How he recognized him was even beyond himself. Robert looks like he's in a daze of some sort, more like suspended animation. He's wearing a normal white t-shirt and blue jeans. Very few people have seen him outside of a suit. Even the people who know him very well think he looks out of place when not dressed up in the uniform of the business world.

Robert sits there staring at the cab drivers ID in the back seat. Though there are million things going through his mind he stares and reads the ID over and over again. The name was Mothusi Karim. 5'7". He got his license in 1992. Fast Track cabs, always fast never last.

"Sir? Are you okay?" Mothusi asks.

Robert shakes off the zombie like state he was in. "Huh, yeah." He looks down at his phone. It was off; *"I must have accidentally turned it off."* He thinks. He turns the phone back on and three new messages, all from Elizabeth. Now it shows another new message. It's from one of the board members.

"Robert where the hell are you? We need you here now!"

He dials the number to Elizabeth. "Mr. Heyward?!"

"Any progress?"

"No the fire, is setting off all the chemicals in the factory, they have brought in three more fire departments. Reporters…handling…fire…Mr. Roder" Beep, beep, beep.

"What the hell? What about Phil?!" He looks down at his phone. Signal faded. Battery also shows low life.

"Damn it!"

"Everything okay sir?"

"God damn signal faded!"

"Here use my phone, I get a signal all over this town."

"Thank you." He calls back his Elizabeth.

"Liz."

"Mr. Heyward?"

"Yeah, my cell phone isn't working, I'm using another number. What's going on now?"

"The fire is going crazy. All the reporters have filled the surrounding areas. We are trying to get some word out there to ease the media situation; right now Mr. Fisher is trying to handle the situation. Speculations are ranging from interior motives, to chemical failure, to terrorist attacks! We tried to call Mr. Roderick several times, but there's been no answer. We need you here to help bring some control to the situation! How far are you?"

"Mothusi, how far are we?"

"If I continue speeding two, two and a half hours maybe, depending on traffic."

"Around two and a half hours."

"Two and a half hours!? Sir what do we do in the mean time?"

"Get Fisher to tell the crowd we don't know what happened yet and as soon as we know they'll know. Take no further questions. Once that's done, get the police to get the camera's as far away as possible from the fire, we don't need any clear pictures from them on what's going on and we don't need any casualties on our hands. Make sure the whole board gets together and comes up with a contingency plan. Let's put this thing out!"

"Yes sir."

"Okay I'll see you when I get there!" They hang up the phone.

"Wow you're good Mr. Heyward! I can see why you're CEO."

"Thank you for your phone Mothusi."

"You're welcome sir."

"What does that mean by the way?"

"What sir?"

"Your name, what does it mean?"

"Helper, sir."

Robert chuckles, "No kidding." The driver smiles back.

"Sir, get some rest, I'll wake you when we are near."

Robert falls asleep. The driver looks back at him reassuringly.

***

A vibration startles Robert and he wakes up with a jolt.

"You okay sir?"

"Yeah, it's just my cell phone." He looks down, and it's Phil's number. "Phil where the hell have you been?"

"Sorry, Robert I was on the flight getting out of the keys into Florida, I wasn't getting good reception there so I thought I'd just call when I landed. Anyway what the hell happened? I heard terrorist attacks, and chemical malfunctions and so on."

"I don't know Phil; I'm on my way there as we speak."

"Why so late?"

"I was at the hospital"

"Hospital? Why?"

"It's Sandra, she had some stress pains and fainted."

"Oh my God is she okay?"

"Yeah, she's fine, she's getting rest now."

"Good, look they don't have any flights leaving right now, but the first flight I can get I'll be out there."

"Okay Phil."

"Okay you be safe now."

"Yeah." They hang up. "Mothusi, how far are we?"

"Less than an hour sir."

"Thank you." A beeping sound goes off, Robert looks down. His phone just died. "Great."

"Excuse me sir?"

"Nothing."

Robert lays his head against the glass of the cab. He looks up in the sky. The moon was only a quarter full and oddly close this night. You could even see the texture of it and it was quite easy to make out the shape of the moon, even on its dark side. It looked more so as a sphere tonight than a circle. The color was an odd yellow and flossy eggshell white. There were also hints of red accenting the giant quarter marble in the sky. Robert wondered if the red colors were of the flames from his burning factory. Through all the chaos though, it brought Robert comfort to see that the moon was as sad as he was tonight.

Chapter 9

"Nurse? Where's my husband?" Sandra asks in a faint voice as she turns her head towards the nurse.

"I'm not sure sweetheart. He hasn't left anything." She responds while grasping her hand.

"Where's the nurse that was here earlier?"

"Her shift ended a while ago so she's gone home now."

"I need my husband with me, can someone please call him?"

"Of course Mrs. Heyward, I'll be right back." The nurse leaves the room to call Robert. She comes back about ten minutes later.

"There was no answer Mrs. Heyward, it keeps going straight to voicemail."

"You don't understand I need my husband with me now!" She tries to gather all her strength.

"I know Mrs. Heyward, as soon as we can get a hold of him, we'll let him know." The nurse responds with a more firm tone.

The burley nurse tried to be as comforting as possible, but the uneasiness on Sandra's face was very apparent. The nurse tries to help Sandra get some rest. Sandra goes in and out of sleep, every time asking if any contact has been made with Robert. *"What an inconsiderate husband."* The nurse thought, *"Of course if you have money you don't need to be anywhere."* The nurse shakes it off and looks back at Sandra. Sandra is breaking into a sweat. The nurse checks her temperature, it has risen.

"Robert?"

"No dear it's still me. Are you feeling okay?"

"No, I want my husband, please!" The nurse goes out to call Robert again. After several attempts she comes back into the room to find Sandra in immense pain. The nurse yells for the doctor.

"What's the matter here?"

"I don't know doctor as soon as I saw her like this I called you."

The doctor checks Sandra.

"She's having early contractions." He says confusedly, "I think this baby is coming prematurely! Nurse let's get her into the delivery room, and let's have a team ready I'll get my things and meet you all there in two minutes!"

"Yes doctor."

Everyone rushes out of the room and prepares for the delivery.

"I need my husband please!" Sandra yells out to anyone who would listen.

"He's not here dear we need to get this baby delivered." Says the nurse as they start to move her out the room.

"No, not without Robert."

"We don't have a choice Mrs. Heyward."

Sandra screams out of pain. Everyone prepares in the delivery room. The doctor walks in and he shouts out orders to the nurses.

"Let's deliver a baby people!" The doctor yells as he walks into the room.

"No, no please no. Not now, not without Robert!"

"We need to get this baby out now!"

"Rob....!"

***

"...bert! Where the hell have you been man?!" A man the size of Robert yells as he walks up to the cab with his hand stretched out for a handshake.

Robert grasps his hand and looks behind Scott Fisher. The blazing fire is illuminating the skies like hell it self is rising up from the ground. In front of the fire are hundreds of people and news reporters, standing there like a plague just making his journey through this night even harder.

"I was at the hospital with my wife; sorry I'm late for the party." He says irritated, "Now, what the hell happened here Fisher?"

"We don't know yet, I got a call from the police telling me about the fire. I guess after you and Phil my number's next on the list."

"Has the media been informed of what I had told you?"

"Yes sir."

"Okay let's get to work."

He turns over to the cab driver, thanks him and then pays him, with extra tip.

"Do you need me to stay for anything?"

"No Mothusi, you've done enough, I've written down your cab number so if I need you, I'll give you a call."

"Very good sir…" He looks back towards the wreckage. "And good luck."

"Thanks."

He taps the top of the cab and starts his way towards the wreckage. He then walks towards the blaze. He has an odd confidence to him, a strange calmness, as if he's done this many times before in the past. His face is stern, and his walk is quick yet composed. When he has this particular look on his face the people in the office call it the "game face," If you were to stand in his way at this state, you were in trouble. As Robert approaches the fire, a swarm of reporters sprint towards his direction.

"Mr. Heyward, Mr. Heyward!" He breaks through the first flow of reporters. They are like blood thirsty wolves clawing away at him for any bit of information they can get a hold of. Scott does his best to ward off the reporters.

"Mr. Heyward! Can you tell us anything?" The second flow is behind him.

"Do you think this is a plot against your company, or some sort of chemical error?" Asks Amber. "Mr. Heyward please can you tell us anything?" He locks eyes with the reporter he saw earlier on the television, but keeps walking. "How about your wife, we have reports she's been in the hospital." Confused that anyone outside of the company knew about Sandra's condition distressed him. He turns around and walks toward Amber; he grabs her microphone and launches it over the sea of people and news crews. He gets in her face and points his finger straight into her face. Amber never gets taken aback or startled, but Robert put a new fear in her.

"Stay the hell out of my family's business!" He collects himself, as everyone looks at him as if he had just escaped an insane asylum. Then he says with a smile, "Now, as soon as I know something people, you will too!" He continues forward with determination. "Mr. Heyward, Mr. Heyward!" The reporters continue, as if nothing happened. Amber stood there shooken up.

"I'm going to get that son of a bitch!"

As he gets closer and closer to the fire, he can feel the warmth of the flames against his face. He approaches the yellow police tape. The officers greet him at the line as he ducks under the tape. The commissioner of the police department awaits him a few steps away. He's wearing a tan trench coat with a matching beret. He has a long mustache and an unyielding look on his face.

"Mr. Heyward, you finally made it." He says in a condescending tone, "Glad you finally found some time to join us."

"Yeah, I got a call that my most prized plant is burning down, so I thought I'd take a stroll on the beach and have a sandwich." He says, with a dark voice. The commissioner gave him a blank stare. "What the hell happened here?"

"We have to extinguish the fire first to figure that out. It's been burning for almost five hours now."

"How the hell does a building burn for five hours commissioner?! What the hell are these fire men doing? Taking pictures?"

Now the commissioner was beginning to get upset with Robert. "It's no easy task handling a chemical fire *Mr. Heyward*, as soon as the fire comes within controllable range something else blows up! But of course being the president of an energy company you already knew that."

Robert gets suspicious "Chemical fire? I thought you didn't know the cause?"

"I don't but the fire has to reach the chemicals at some point and that's when things get bad!" The commissioner gets stern.

A shattering sound rips across the sky. Everyone looks towards the inferno expecting more mayhem, but nothing. A few seconds later as if someone took a knife and cut open a bag of water, rain comes pouring down from the sky. The fire fighters cheer, as some back up finally comes down from the heavens. Sounds of cheers and thankfulness surround the area. A new wave of hope fills the firemen as they pull forward in attempts of extinguishing the fire. As the board members hang their heads, Robert pulls them together and begins to discuss how to correct this situation and how to make sure the company doesn't go under due to this setback. Everyone in the media, the police officers, and the fire fighters are astonished on how this group of people can sit and talk while everything they have invested in goes up in flames. No one knew that the fire burning within Robert was ten fold worse than what was going on behind them.

"Are you crazy Robert? What the hell do you mean calm down?!" Says one man.

"I told you all this shit wouldn't work from the beginning, and now look where we are, having a meeting while all our money is going up in that fucking volcano two hundred yards away from us!" Another man yells.

"Sit down the both of you! Don't you think I had stakes in this too? If anything I have more stake in this than all of you! Now instead of bitching about this problem let's figure out what the hell to do to calm the media and our investors."

"Oh, our investors are going to be very upset, if we have any investors left that is."

The meeting continues on. Within the next hour the fire finally dies down. The rain continues its strong-hold.

"Robert just look behind you, we're finished."

Robert turns around slowly, the fallen wreckage of his most valuable factory is nothing but ruins. Looking at it now, the horror finally sets in. Tears run helplessly down Robert's cheeks, he hides them well for a few moments thanks to the rain, but then he breaks down completely. He sits down and buries his head in his hands.

"I'm sorry Robert." Says Fisher as he walks towards him and puts his hand on his shoulder. He turns towards the board. "Look everyone, we're all tired, stressed, and pissed off. Let's all go home, get some rest, and tomorrow afternoon, we'll sit down and figure it out. I'll get Phil on the phone and we'll make this right."

Everyone gets up shakes hands and begin to leave for home.

"Robert go back to your wife, I'm sure she needs you right now. I'll handle the meeting tomorrow. I promise everything will be fine."

Robert looks up as the sun begins to rise. The damage looks worse in the light. "Thanks Scott."

"You okay Mr. Heyward?" Asks Elizabeth. She finally made it back from trying to tame the crowd.

"No, Liz, I'm not."

"We've been through a lot, we'll get through this."

"Yeah."

He starts walking back through the crowd aimlessly. The police help escort him to wherever he's going. Elizabeth and Scott are in front of him fighting off reporters. It's a mob scene and everyone is frustrated. When he reaches the end of the media circus, he sees a cab. He didn't think he'd see one, and hopefully this one will be empty. As he gets closer he sees a familiar face.

"Mothusi?"

"Yes, sir, I figured you didn't have a ride back to the hospital." He says with a smirk on his face.

"I thought you had to go home?"

"Yeah, but when do you ever get to see a show with a view like this?" He says with half a smile and a look of hope.

Robert puts his hand on Mothusi's shoulder with a thankful look on his face and sits inside the cab.

"Don't worry Robert we'll take care of everything here." Shouts out Scott as Robert's cab begins to leave. Robert gives a grieving nod, and puts his hand in the air for acknowledgement of the comment.

The drive back to the hospital was different. Behind him was one of the greatest losses in investment he has ever had, ahead was his wife. He looks down at his cell phone, it still wouldn't turn on. He asked Mothusi for his phone, but his phone had died too. He was on the phone most of the night with his wife, who is back visiting her mother in Africa. Normally during his breaks Mothusi stops by his friend's gas station to charge his phone, or he would charge it at home, therefore, buying a car charger seemed useless. This time was a different story. Mothusi could see the wreckage from his rear view mirror and shook his head. He looked back at Robert watching him as he would nod in and out of sleep. Such strains have punishing affects on the body. It's odd though, how the human body, the human mind still finds some reason to continue fighting. Mothusi always thought people who commit suicide was nature's natural selection to weed out the weak. Traffic on the way back to the hospital is a lot heavier now, due to the time. It's close to seven on a Monday morning, and everyone is headed to work. Five hours later, Robert finally wakes up.

"Oh my head is killing me."

"Good morning sir, or should I say good afternoon?" Mothusi asks looking at Robert through his rearview mirror.

"Afternoon? What time is it?" He asks as he rubs his eyes.

"Twelve fifteen sir, you've been sleeping the whole time. I had to stop for some gas and coffee to stay awake on the road sir."

"How far are we?" He asks while trying to clear his throat.

"Just about half an hour, Traffic has been pretty bad today sir."

Some time later they finally pull in to the hospital receiving lot. "Thanks again Mothusi, I'll never forget this."

"Don't mention it sir." He pays him and gives an extra tip then heads into the hospital. He stops by the flower shop to buy roses for the woman who he's been dying to hold this whole crazy night.

Chapter 10

"I need to fly to New York A.S.A.P.!" Phil yells at an attendee.

"I'm sorry sir, weather conditions are way too strong for any planes to go in or out." The attendee responds trying to be as calm as possible.

"But this is an emergency!"

"I understand that, and if I could let you on I would, but we are under strict orders to make sure there are no air activities."

"What the hell is so bad about the weather, you guys afraid of a little rain? I'm the head lawyer of Orion Industries and our plant just burned down, I need to get there right away. My God haven't you been watching the news?"

"Sir, the rain is starting to pick up; the air is way too strong. We're under an F-2 tornado watch. Haven't *you* been watching the news?" Phil then realizes that annoying beeping sound and scroll at the top of the television giving out a tornado watch warning while he was trying to get details on the fire.

"Look, is there anything I can do, or anyway I can get back?"

"Like I said I'm sorry sir, I wish I could help, but I can't. Either you can wait it out, or leave the city by car. Whatever you do, you should make your decision fast, 'cause then you're stuck with it."

"Damn it!"

He slams the desk, runs off and goes outside. He gets into his Porsche and speeds off. A strong forceful wind almost pushes him off the road, he regains control. Flustered by the situation he picks up the phone and calls Robert. "Damn it, voicemail." He continues calling, but gets the same result every time. The sky is a dark grey, and it's raining sporadically so he doesn't turn on the wipers. He then tries Scott, being the Vice President he would know what's going on. "Why is everyone's phone turned off?" He asks in frustration. Desperate for ideas, he calls Elizabeth.

"Orion Industries, this is Elizabeth."

"Elizabeth, thank God!"

"Mr. Roderick?"

The wind pushes him off the road again, and back as if he were a yo-yo. "Yeah, it's me."

"Where have you been sir, everyone's been looking for you, the board has stopped all investigations until your return, but if you're not back they'll go ahead with it without you. The…"

"Listen Liz, I know there's a lot going on I'm trying to make my way back. There's some sort of stupid tornado watch and they won't let anyone board. I'm sure it should all blow over soon! Please let everyone know. As soon as I get back we'll straighten everything out."

"Uh yeah, I'll let them know, just make sure you get back."

"I'll be there in no time sweetheart."

They hang up the phone. Just as Phil puts down the phone something catches the corner of his eye, some sort of dark massive cloud. He looks over and there it was the F-2 tornado. "Son of a bitch there it is!" He thinks to himself. He rolls down his side window and sticks his middle finger up at the colossal funnel. "Fuck you!" He yells out the window as the tornado crashes into one of the barns that helplessly stood in its way. He turns his head to look back at the road. When he turns back to measure where the tornado was, he sees an oversized wood panel darted in his direction. He tries to move out the way, but he was too late.

Chapter 11

As Robert makes his way up in the elevator he remembers how much he hated the hospital. He hated the look, he hated the feel, he hated the smell. He shakes it off, and remembers that he is going to go see his beautiful wife and that's all that matters right now. The elevator finally got to the tenth floor. With a sigh of relief, he steps out and starts his way down the hallway. All the nurses on the floor look up at Robert one at a time as he makes his way to his wife's room. The hallway didn't seem this long before. He soon approaches the end of the hallway, as he turns the corner he sees John and Susan outside the door.

"John, Susan! Oh I'm so glad you're here, I didn't get a chance to call you, but I'm glad you're here." He puts his arm on John's shoulder with a smile, John doesn't return the smile, he continues looking down trying to avoid eye contact. Robert then looks over to Susan and she has tears coming down her eyes.

"Wh…what's wrong?"

"Bob, have a seat…" John says.

"Why? What's wrong?"

John looks over to his wife, then back at Robert. He puts his arm around him.

"There's been some complication…"

"What the hell are you talking about John?!" He throws John's hand off of his shoulder.

"Look, the baby was born pre-maturely, Sandra had way too much stress which hurt the birth process, the baby lived for about an hour after the birth. Sandra, is very weak, the doctor said she as a fifteen percent chance of living."

"Fuck you John. What kind of sick ass joke is that?"

"Robert, I'm sorry." Robert runs inside the hospital room.

"Sandra!" The nurse and his kids look up at him. The monitor is beeping at a normal rate.

"Dad!" Ryan comes running to him and hugs his leg. Robert puts his arm around Ryan.

"She's resting now." Says the nurse.

"Will she be okay?"

"We don't know yet. She's suffered a lot."

"Oh baby." He starts to cry, "I brought these for you love." He puts the flowers at her bedside. "I should have never left. I'm so sorry baby." He kisses her.

They all sit there quietly. After a few hours, eventually John and Susan leave, they take Michael and Ryan with them. Both were reluctant, but everyone felt it was for the better. The two boys leave with John and Susan sobbing horribly and yelling for their mother. Robert sat there like a statue next to Sandra just watching her until the next day. The nurse walks into the room in the morning. Robert looks worse than Sandra. His hair was a mess and his beard was beginning to mask his face. His eyes are half open and it looks as if he is a sleep, but the nurse isn't sure. She goes around checking the monitors and the IV to see how Sandra is doing.

"I should have never left…" Confused the nurse looks in Robert's direction. He is staring at Sandra, with sadness that brought tears to even the nurse's eyes. His bloodshot eyes were unwavering.

"You had no way of knowing, and I saw on the television what had happened. If you didn't go, who knows what could have happened."

"I do…I would have had my child. I would have seen her alive." The nurse stands there silently. Robert touches Sandra's forehead.

"Mr. Heyward, there was no way for you to know…"

"Was it a boy or girl?" Robert cuts her off.

"Girl."

Robert lets out a tiny laugh. "She always wanted a girl."

"Would you like to name her?"

61

"Yes, Sandra, after her mother."

"Okay." The nurse replies with a supportive smile.

Sandra lets out a small noise. "Baby? You awake? Baby?"

"She can't talk right now, but she can hear you. When she makes noises like that it shows signs of improvement."

"Baby I love you, I'm sorry I had to leave. I love you so much." He begins to cry.

About an hour later, John and Susan visit Robert. They discuss funeral arrangements for the baby. Robert uncontrollably starts to sob and John just holds him as Susan cries with him.

***

"Emergency 911."

"He…Hello?"

"Yes?"

"Uh…yes hi, this…this is Charles Hymes, and…my wife and I just found a dead body in our barn."

Chapter 12

"What the hell are we doing here Amber?" Harvey asks as they try to step through burnt rubble.

"Just digging for the truth Harvey."

"If we get caught we're both going to jail! You do know that right? In fact, any reporting we do is illegal."

"What are you a cop now?"

"Just telling it like it is." He says as he puts his hands up.

"There's no way this was an accident. I know there's someone behind it, we just have to figure out who it is. Don't you find it a little odd that all the men in suits were extra calm during the whole fire?"

"What are you trying to say, that a bunch of rich old guys one day just woke up and thought to themselves 'hmm we have too much money, let's burn down our biggest factory'?"

"Exactly."

Harvey gives her an odd look. "…You know you're crazy right?"

"I know it sounds a little farfetched, but remember that one guy that was there…he kept walking around, as if he were supervising something?"

"The guy in the beret?"

"Yeah!"

"Yeah Amber that was the commissioner."

"No, not the commissioner."

"This guy was big, had some kind of army clothes on."

Harvey thinks for a moment, "Oh wait, I think I know exactly who you're talking about." He looks at his camera and plays it back and forward looking for the mysterious man. Amber continues looking through the ruble. After a few minutes of going back and forth he finally finds the man that he was looking for. He calls Amber over "Hey, is it this guy?" Amber comes back to look at the tape. They see the shadow of a tall muscular man standing like a statue with his arms folded watching the flames, the outline shows an army type uniform.

"Yes!"

"So?"

"So, what the hell was he doing there, and why was he exchanging glances with the board members the whole time? Don't you think for an army man he should have been more helpful?"

"No. What the hell is wrong with you? Just because he is trained to kill some people, doesn't mean he can fight a fire, and I'm sure he was just there like the rest of the people who live near by."

"But fully clothed in an army uniform?"

"You know how some of these army nuts are; I mean who the hell knows. We shouldn't waist our time on this shit."

"I guess you're right. Can you get a clearer picture?"

"No this is the best shot of him that I found." Amber stares at the image for a moment longer, and then shakes it off.

"Damn it, did you get any images of Heyward doing anything funny?"

"You mean like throwing your mic into the crowd?"

"Shut up!"

Harvey begins to laugh, "Oh come on it was hilarious!"

"I'm telling you he is up to something I just can't put my finger on it." She says as she looks away in embarrassment.

"Okay let's figure out what the hell is going on here."

They trek through the rubble in hopes of finding some clue.

"Harvey?" Amber yells.

"Yeah, what's up?"

"What the hell is this?"

"Let me see. Dude what the fuck? This looks like some C4."

"What the hell is C4?"

"It's a bomb."

"A bomb!" Amber drops the C4 into Harvey's hand and tries to run away. Harvey catches it with one hand and grabs Amber with the other.

"Relax, whoever wanted to detonate it would have done it already. This one must have been a dud. I guess whoever paid for it didn't get there money's worth. I know a guy who might be able to tell us some more about this."

"Let's get on it!"

***

"Oh my God, am I dead? Why is it so dark here? Ugh my head. What the hell is that?! Is…is that a ghost? Are you here to take me away?" As he thinks to himself, the ghost like figure walks away. He falls back to sleep.

Chapter 13

It was a bitter cold Saturday afternoon the wind felt like sandpaper rubbing against the face. Everyone was dressed in black. The cemetery field was filled with some of the board members, Elizabeth, close friends and family. Susan was at the hospital watching after Sandra.

The priest recited the normal versus from the Bible and the funeral proceeded. Robert sat there, quietly and completely still, with a single blue rose in his hands. If it weren't for the suit he would blend in with the tombstones. John was sitting next to him trying to be as supportive as possible, without saying a word. Robert could feel that. The guilt that Robert felt for his daughter's death was overwhelming, and now he was burying his child, without the one person who can help him through this. Robert was in a daze, it felt as if the afternoon was just flying by.

His child was buried, well wishers met with him and left. The dirt had been scattered on the grave. After some time John had finally left. Night fall had come, a cold brisk wind passed by Robert's face as if to slap him to wake him up. When he came to he could barely see at first in the unbelievable darkness, the only sources of light were the stars and the moon, which seemed to shine down directly on his daughters tombstone, an ambient lighting in the distance, and the blue rose in his hand. Everything was black and white, but the blueness of the rose was rich in color. He stood up walked over to his child's grave and apologized to her. Shortly after he threw up right there next to the tombstone, the hurling would refuse stop, it felt as if his stomach was attempting to jump out through his throat. The punishment had finally stopped. He broke down into tears, and sat on the other end of the rock. He sat there huddled up from the cold, telling her stories about himself, her mother, and her two brothers; he would look into the blue rose to search for his memories.

He told stories about how he and Sandra first met, about Michael's football team and Ryan's basketball team. He told her how him and Sandra would prank the boys and blame the other brother for the pranks that they did. Robert sat there and laughed with her and cried with her. Through the wind he could hear her laughter, and her voice. He told her everything, he talked about his parents and Sandra's parents, he told her about Orion and all of its secrets, he even told her about Phil. At that point he began to wonder where he was.

"Where the hell is Phil?" He asked her. He told her how Phil always runs away from situations like this one. He told her that he loved him though, and that he was his best friend. "But where is he?" He picked up the phone and called him. Voicemail…He should have been here by now. Robert shook it off, and just sat there with his daughter. It was his daughter's first funeral, and he was going to be there by her side tonight. Even though it was especially cold this night, he felt his daughter's warmth within him; he then slowly started to fall asleep. And as he began to nod off he whispered to her "I love you."

***

Later that night, the sound and vibration of his cell phone wakes him up. He tries to answer the phone, but his fingers are stiff from the cold. He fumbles the phone into the snow. He desperately digs for the phone. He finally picks it up, right before the phone hangs up.

"Hello? Hello?"

"Mr. Heyward?"

"Yes?!"

"This is nurse Roberts from the hospital."

"Yes?" He listens more attentively.

"Your wife Sandra has come to her normal status, and she's been asking for you."

"Really, Sandra's okay?!"

"Yes sir."

"Oh, okay I'll be right there!" He kisses his daughter's tombstone, "I'll see you later, make sure you look after me, I love you."

He leaves the rose at the grave and walks away from the cemetery. Once in the car he speeds off to see his wife. When Robert gets to the hospital he rushes down the hall to get to the elevator. "Finally, some good news." He thinks to himself. The news had given him some hope and a burst of energy. As he leaves the elevator he dashes down the hall. He looks inside the window of the door, and there she was crying her eyes out. Susan was there attempting to comfort her. He steps inside. Sandra looks up at him.

"Our baby Robby, our baby."

"I know baby."

He walks over to her and holds her as they both cry. Susan puts her hand on him. They glance at each other, and Robert could tell Susan had told Sandra everything. It was for the better; Robert knew there was no way he could tell her all that just happened.

That Sunday, Sandra came home. She had made a full recovery. It was either the child or Sandra, with no one to decide, the doctor chose for Sandra to live. Robert would have made the same decision, Sandra, of course, felt the other way. That Monday morning, the whole family went to see little Sandra. It was a sad heartfelt day; they had brought flowers and stood there for sometime.

Sandra broke down at the grave site, her family tried to comfort her, but Sandra needed her time with her daughter. Everyone knew they had to move on, they just weren't quite sure how. Michael felt in his heart that the death of his sister was his father's fault; he couldn't forgive him for that. Robert finally went back to work the next day, but took very few hours.

Chapter 14

"Well hello there."

"Ugh such a massive headache. Who are you? I can't move my mouth, my head, my arms, my legs. What the hell is going on here?"

"It's nice to see you finally awake during the day. All the nurses tell me that you only stay awake for a few moments at night, when your friend comes and visits and then you sleep the rest of the time. I was starting to get offended." The nurse jokes, "Now see I thought you had brown eyes all this time, but here you lay before me with those beautiful blue eyes." She giggles. "You, my friend, are actually very lucky the paramedics arrived when they did, anymore blood loss and you would've died. It was crazy, apparently a huge wooden board was flung at you and took your car off the road. I guess you spun off the road, and crashed right into a barn. Someone must really love you up there. After the third day in your 'coma' we were beginning to get worried about you." She stares at him for a moment, "You know you have a very familiar face, I just can't put my finger on it, but I feel like I've met you before. Anyway if you need anything I'll be here all day, okay sweetie?"

"Coma? What the hell happened to me? What friend? Robert? Is Robert here?" Phil murmurs drifting back to sleep.

***

"This next patient here is a remarkable study. He has suffered massive

69

blood loss, he has broken bones in both his arms and legs, and he also has a heavy concussion. Luckily none of the damage is unrecoverable...with proper care of course. You're one in a million Mr. Roderick. I hope you have thanked God for keeping you alive." The Doctor taps his bed side with a smile. "He should be ready for rehab in just over a month. Okay interns let's take a look at the next patient."

Phil looks over to the nurse with a confused look.

"Don't worry about him, he's not the warmest guy in the world, but he's very good at what he does. He's right though you'll be out of here pretty soon. I think you should be able to walk out of here and into rehab in about three to six weeks at best." She looks at his chart and double checks his IV. "It's Phil right? Hi, I'm Janis by the way... Is, is that a smile? Well, I sure as hell am flattered, that's the most movement you've had since you've gotten here!"

Phil lies in bed, everyday wishing he were able contact someone. Unfortunately, his injuries won't allow him to. He can't move at all. For some odd reason, the same man comes and visits him at the same time every night. He never got a good look at his face, but he can see anger and hate in that man's eyes. At first Phil felt as if the man was there to kill him, but then figured he would have already been dead if that were the case. Still it was pretty unnerving.

Chapter 15

It's early morning and Robert is driving towards the office. For some odd reason a board meeting was called at the last minute. Robert had gotten a phone call late last night. Carl McGuire had called him and told him about the meeting, he was peculiarly brief with him. All he said was, "Meeting tomorrow eight A.M. sharp." When Robert had asked for the reason, he had simply replied, "Company's future."

At home things have been strange to say the least, for the past week and a half. Sandra is always quiet, Ryan tries to act normal, but everyone gets annoyed of him and he is forced to quiet down. Michael is always angry, there's more hostility towards Robert from him than anyone else. Michael looks after his mother a lot more these days. Everywhere she goes he is looking in that direction making sure she is okay. His birthday had passed a few days ago, though no one had forgotten and a few gifts were given, there was no party, no hats, no confetti. Phil didn't even come. The family sat together and tried to make the most of it. The house feels unusually large these days. Everyone is so far apart. Everything seems to be bigger; the bed, the dining table, even the small kitchen table seems to separate everyone. Charlotte lives normally, but the new atmosphere in the house confuses her greatly.

Even though lately he dreaded going, work in fact was the only thing keeping Robert sane. He's been trying to call Phil everyday since the fire and yet no answer. He calls again during his car ride. "Where the fuck is he?" He feels as if Phil has left him hanging once again; as a friend he was great, but he could never trust Phil with things like this. Robert doesn't shave much lately; his appearance is sub par at best. He parks his car and walks into the elevator. He puts his ring into the top elevator slot and the elevator starts to make its way up. In the elevators there are four ring slots. The first is for new ring holders where some privileges were given at that floor. The more diamonds you earned the higher up you would go…literally. Every room revealed new secrets to the company, and the pampering you would get as you climbed the ladder was unmatched. As the elevator slows down as it reaches the top floor, Robert feels his body weight being pulled down and his heart sinks; The doors finally open to the top floor, this is where Orion's Board Member room was. Normally when Robert walks into this room everyone stands up and smiles, greeting him as he got to his seat. Today everyone just stares at him as if he were an insubordinate who was late. He looks at his watch to make sure he was on time; he was actually twelve minutes early. He looks at all ten of them as he makes his way towards his chair.

"Good morning everyone." No one replies, he looks at them strangely. "What the hell is wrong with everyone?" He unbuttons his jacket and sits down as he collects his thoughts. "Okay, I know you guys wanted to meet to discuss the company's future so I put together a few notes. I know what happened with Artemis was disastrous, but we'll pull through. We always have been able to pull through, and now should be no different."

As Robert spoke a new form of energy surged through him. He felt like his old self again. He talked about the falling stock, the company's new goals, and new projects he has had in mind. He stood up as he continued with his speech. "Guys, its time for a change!" He says with a smile as he looks around at his partners' undaunting faces.

"That's right Robert, and that's why we've decided to sell." Scott finally speaks for the board.

"What?"

"We've decided to go in a new direction, Apollo industries has been looking to expand, and this gives them the perfect opportunity to increase their market share. The company has a new plan and you're not a part of it. We're going public with the change in a few days."

"Why didn't anyone tell me?"

"Well, with new management coming by, and your stronghold personality, we didn't want a power struggle to form within the company. Of course, you'll get some money too, but we expect your resignation letter signed in forty five days." They pass over documents to him to sign. Robert looks up at all of them with a lethal look of rage on his face.

"You want me to do what?" He does his best to keep his emotions together. "I practically built this company, I made all of your careers, and this is how you repay me?! This isn't your company this is my father's company, and mine!"

"Robert in the past few weeks a lot has changed. We know. You're family needs you now, don't you think they need you more now than ever. You should be with them Robert." Adds Carl.

"Don't tell me what I should or should not do you fucking dog. And I'm not signing shit without Phil." Everyone sits there quietly.

"Robert, have you actually seen Phil lately? Where is he? No one knows. Robert, Phil hasn't been here at the company's most critical moment, he's fired. And just so you know, Phil knew we were selling the company before he left for Florida. Being your best friend he didn't tell you anything? Now don't you think that's a little odd?" Scott fires back, Robert sits there in confusion.

"You're unstable now. The company is going to be sold whether you like it or not. Either you can sign these papers and take the money, or you can be fired too." Says, Ronald.

Alex tries to console him from the side. "Look Robert, it's at times like these you have to decide, are you a family man or are you a business man?" Robert thinks of his wife, his kids, his daughter. He takes a brief moment as he stares down at the papers and then he did something he never dreamt he would.

"There you go Robert, we'll transfer the money to your account in cash and the rest of it will be paid to you with stock. You should move; a new scenery for you and your family would be a good change of pace."

"Yeah, well fuck you very much, but we're staying just where we are."

"Robert…that wasn't a suggestion, after everything that's happened we don't need the bad publicity. It's in the contract you just signed, if you want the money you have to move."

Chapter 16

"C4 that's all it is. Just your everyday run of the mill C4." A man with odd looking glasses says.

"So can't you tell me anything more about it? Aren't you supposed to be the great bomb guy that everyone talks about? We've obviously come to the wrong bomb guy." Amber says in frustration. Harvey holds her back.

He looks at her strangely for a moment. "I know everything about street exchange bombs and weaponry, everyone from kids who want to throw cherry bombs down the school drain, to gangbangers, all the way up to your corporate types who want bombs for insurance fraud, or to kill their wives lovers, and so on. All these guys, all of them either go through me or my guys. This bomb over here doesn't seem like street warfare to me, or anything we would sell. It doesn't have our stamp of approval on it." He says with a firm voice, he then thinks for a moment, "Well I've done some research and talked to some of the guys who do this business in the neighboring states, no one knows about any of this on their streets either." He studies the bomb a little further with his microscope glasses. "Well looky here." He says with a heightened voice.

"What, what?" Amber impatiently asks.

"You got something there bookkeeper?" Harvey asks in his deep voice.

"Some of these signs on this do suggest that this bomb may have come from the government." He seems confused.

"Now Heyward's connected with government bombs? This guy is nuts! I'm going to make sure this gets exposed." She says with determination.

"Whoa slow down there ace." Harvey says trying to calm Amber down, "We don't know whose bomb that was and how it got there." He looks over at the odd looking man, "So bookkeeper, you saying this is a government set up?"

"Yeah…I don't know. But I'll tell you this much if you're messing with the government or military for that matter I would keep my mouth shut about this, not only did you trespass onto private property, which was also a federal investigation site, if this is something bigger you could be in some big trouble."

"Yeah, well let me be the judge of that." Amber says as she takes back the bomb in her hands and walks off.

Chapter 17

"Phil, we have to blow up the plant."

"What? What the hell are you talking about?"

"Yeah, everyone's talking about how the company is failing, our stocks are falling, and so on. You're the only one who's closest to the company without being on the board."

"Fuck you; I wouldn't do that to Robert."

"You'd be doing him a favor. Look you know how cut-throat this business can be, and any sign of weakness and we can lose the fight. Apollo is already looking at buying us out. If this Cold Fusion thing doesn't work we're screwed, we'll all be out of jobs. Imagine for a second Orion got bought out due to incompetence and we all get fired. I'll lose my job and might get kicked out of other boards too, who knows? You my friend, you'll be fired from one of the top company's in the world. Who the hell will hire someone like that? If you can get fired from Orion, you're already overpriced for most of the market, and everyone else already has top lawyers, and they would think you did some shady stuff to get fired. This is also your career we're talking about. Do you think Robert was thinking about your career when we started the Cold Fusion project? We already started talking to Apollo Industries."

"Apollo, that shit hole company? What the hell for?"

"Well it's the United States Secretary of State's energy source, so they have a lot of financial backing."

"So?"

"So, they want to help us out."

"Yeah, you're fucking crazy. We're not selling out to a bunch of army freaks with too much God damn money."

"First of all, that's not your decision to make. Besides, they know things are bad, they're going to help us get back on our feet after the bombing, and want to help us since we're falling anyway. If we fail, you, me, Robert, we all lose and there's no coming back from that. They think of you as family Phil, and sometimes you have to let someone fall off their bike before they learn to ride. Listen, I'm not supposed to tell you this, but you can get someone else to do it, just get the job done. You'll also be rewarded handsomely. The insurance policy will kick in, and a large chunk of that will be given to you. Robert will be taken care of just the same. I promise you Phil, you and your family…I mean Robert's family, will be just fine, we will take care of you also, just get the job done. Let's keep this between us."

"If I say go to hell and tell Robert?"

"Well in that case we'll just have to take care of you and Robert, and anyone else that's involved."

"Look don't threaten me you scrawny little son of a bitch! If this doesn't work, I'll kill you myself."

"Phil, one more thing, we have a small meeting before the gala this weekend make sure you're there."

Just then Phil wakes up to a noise. He opens his eyes, it's that man again. His eyes burning into Phil's soul. He musters up everything within him.

"Who are you?" He says with his muffled voice.

The man steps into the light. Phil's eyes widen to their limit. He tries to scream, but his mouth is wired shut and is in extreme pain from the last sentence. It was the man who he forced to blow up Orion, Dominique Walker. He had promised Dominique that he would make him an Orion ring holder if he agreed to go through with the plan.

After the ring ceremony, Dominique needed further persuasion, so Phil had to rough him up a little bit after he had left church one day. Phil was certain that he had come to kill him. Phil continues to struggle in bed as his heart rate jumps complimenting the beeping of his monitor. He knew one day he would pay the price for what he did, though he didn't think it would be this soon.

"Relax you bastard, I'm not here to kill you." He says in a dark angry voice.

"The company sent me here to make sure you're still alive. I tried to convince them to go in the other direction, but I guess it's too bad I just became part of the club. Now hurry up and get your broke-ass well, I hate seeing your fucking face. I'm going back to my family; I'll be back once a week to check on you. Don't do anything stupid, just because I haven't killed you, doesn't mean I won't, it just means I haven't yet." The man begins to walk out and before he exits he turns around and looks at Phil. "And you can thank *God* for that."

***

Phil wakes up in the morning, he had fallen into a deep sleep after his encounter earlier that night. He tries to move, he needs to go back. He has to make sure his family is okay. He struggles and struggles, but can hardly move. The pain shoots from all angles and resides in his body. He starts to make noises, but it hurts. Pain is part of the healing process.

Chapter 18

"Welcome everyone to the new Apollo corporation board meeting. I am General Maximus Edward Johnson." A man in an army suit says, with his dark deep voice commanding everyone's attention, his dark eyes piercing into the hearts of the people at the table. "Recently there have been a few changes. I am here to make a few more. I will be stepping in as president of the company now. I will be keeping Carl, Ronald, and Jerry on board. I want to thank you all for your commitment to support our plans and work alongside with Apollo." A group of men and women walk in with perfect form and stand behind all the chairs, but three. "I will make sure all of you are rewarded as we had discussed in the beginning of this venture. These people will be taking your positions. You may all leave now." The old board members slowly get up and leave the room. He then addresses the people in the room. "These people here will be our new board of trustees, some of the closest people in my life. The people who have remained here from Orion, you are here for a purpose. Ronald, you have in check, all the company's accounts which we will need to look into as time progresses. Jerry, you have all the research from the Cold Fusion experiment. And Carl, I seldom meet a kiss-ass that I actually like."

"Yes, sir. Thank you sir!" He says nervously.

"Okay people let's talk business!" Just then a young man knocks on the door vigorously, it was Dominique. "What the hell do you want?"

"Look!" He turns on the television

"...site of Artemis labs. This bomb has been speculated to have been provided by the government. Why would anyone want to blow up the most innovative lab in the world? Why would the government be involved? Why is Robert Heyward suddenly out of the spotlight and nowhere to be found? And finally, does this new merger with Apollo, with the President of the company being General Max Johnson himself, have any indication of such a conspiracy? I'll leave that up to you America. This Amber K. just asking another question, with Highlight news." Dominique turns off the television and looks towards Max.

He hangs his head and then with death in his voice he says. "Get out."

"Yes sir."

"How the hell did they find the C4?" Max looks over at Ronald.

"I...I don't know sir."

"Fix it."

"Sir?"

"Fix it, get some research done and have a talk with this Miss Amber K. warn her, award her, do both. Whatever it takes to get her out of our hair, just do it!"

"Got it."

"We'll continue this meeting later on." Everyone leaves the room silently.

***

Later that night in Max's office off the shore of Florida, a man walks in unannounced with a gun in his hand. Max is facing the wall but knows someone has entered.

"Whoever you are, if you value your life, you should leave."

"You said *I* would be president."

"Mr. Scott Fisher."

"You said I would be the man in charge, you promised me." Max turns around slowly and his eyes meet Scott's.

"Are you here to kill me? Because I hate to break it to you Mr. Fisher, you're already too late. Now look, right now the company needs a better look for the public, and I'm going to do it, you wait for your stocks and your check and you'll be fine."

"It was never about the money, it was about being the man on top."

"Okay, how about this, let me run the company for now, in a few months when things settle down you can take over. How's that sound?"

"Fuck you!"

"You're making me angry now, Mr. Fisher. Now I have guns triggered all over this room, watching my back twenty four seven." He presses a button and guns come out of different corners of the room, from the ceilings, even from the pillars and they all face Scott. "Now this pin on my coat here," He shows Scott a pin attached to his coat glowing bright blue, "has a chip in it, and this chip tells these guns to kill any breathing thing in this room except for who has this chip. Mr. Fisher do you have a pin like this?"

The room is dead silent, Scott can hear his own heart beat out loud, and stands there quietly. "I did not think so. This room is my home. Now, no one has ever angered me and left this room and lived to see the next morning."

Scott begins to tremble.

"Don't worry Mr. Fisher, they won't shoot you, unless I give the order. Let's call this a trust exercise; now that you know I won't screw you over, will you please leave my office Mr. Fisher?"

"You promise I'll get the job?" He yells.

"I promise." The phone rings, "Will you excuse me? I have to take this. Outside you will see my private jet. You can take that back to New York, it'll get you back within the hour." They both lock eyes and then Scott leaves.

***

Earlier that night. A van pulls up next to Amber as she is walking down a dark street. The people in the van grab her, put a bag over her head, and pull her into the van.

"Somebody help me!"

"No one will hear you now Amber."

"Who the hell are you?" She says as she pauses for a moment.

"That doesn't matter. What matters is what you've recently stumbled upon, you nosey little bitch!"

"What the fuck are you talking about?"

"I'm talking about the C4 at Artemis."

"What? So you guys did bomb the place! I knew it! You guys are all going to jail starting with that son of a bitch Heyward as soon as I get out of here!" She yells as she begins to kick again.

"No one bombed anything," He says as he grabs her neck to shut her up, "but if you want to still see tomorrow, and make it out of this local *T.V. world*, you better keep everything to yourself, and forget about it. Do you understand?" He says as he gets closer to her ear. She keeps quiet. "Listen Ambreen Khowja, we know every little thing about you."

"You don't know shit!" She fires back.

"Really? Well let's see, your parents are from Pakistan."

"Fuck you, everyone knows that!"

"You were born in New Jersey then moved to New York." He continues as if ignoring her last statement, "Your parents moved back to Pakistan, because your father wanted to open up a steel factory there, after you graduated college. Your parents are Sadruddin and Rukhsana Khowja who both always disapproved of your career choice and thought going to school for journalism was a waist of time. Now, you work a go nowhere, *reporting* job sneaking around trying to make a name for yourself. Does that about sum up your pathetic little life?"

"How…how do you know all that?" She asks in shock.

"We know everything, now I'm going to ask one last time, are you going to keep your mouth shut, or will we have to shut it for you?"

"Fuck you, I'm going to tell the world!"

"Okay." The man says as he sighs. He picks up the phone and makes a call.

"Hello." The voice says.

"Yes, hello, sir?"

"What?"

"It seems like the reporter may need some convincing."

"Okay, well take care of it. Oh and Ronald?"

"Sir?"

"Mr. Fisher just left my office and is headed back to New York, he should be there shortly. Let's make sure he is taken care of as well."

"Yes sir."

Amber over hears the conversation. "Take care of what? What are you sons of bitches going to do?"

"Who's that cameraman that you report with?"

"Oh my God, Harvey?"

"Yes, Harvey, didn't you guys go to college together? He's one of your closest friends isn't he? Always there to protect you when you do something stupid? Well, it's too bad that all that has to change."

"Don't you fucking touch him, you mother fuckers!" She starts screaming and kicking violently. They hold on to her for a few more hours punching her and hitting her randomly, they made one stop and Amber tried to escape, but they held on to her. They brought in another man with a bag over his head also trying to scream for help. Soon after they throw Amber out of the van and they speed off. She runs for about a mile only to find her own news station. Luckily she worked at one of those local stations that never closed down for the night. Always open because news never stops, is what they would say. She rushes in and her boss comes walking towards her.

"Hey Amber, sorry about Harvey. If you need anything let us know okay? And oh my God what happened to you?" The man finally realizes the bruises on her.

"Harvey, what happened to Harvey?" She looks up at the television. There's a reporter on a bridge with ambulance, fire trucks, and police in the background.

"We believe Scott Fisher, in a suicide attempt took his own life by running his car off of this bridge. With him he took the life of Highlight news' very own Harvey Williams." The reporter begins to cry. "Back to you Leanne."

"Thank you Martha. In somewhat related news, Apollo Industries formally Orion Industries, has made a statement that the technology in their labs was so secretive, that attempts of robbery were guarded by a self defense mechanism. C4 was rigged through out the building; in the case of any sort of raid of the labs the entire building would self destruct. We will investigate that more as more information is available, and authorities are looking at previous plans of the buildings to verify the information.

We'll be right back after a short break, with Highlight News this Leanne Simmons."

Amber begins to cry and scream as she falls to her knees in the middle of the news floor. Her boss helps her up and takes her to his office as he tries to console her.

"I know this isn't any consolation, but we just got news from national and they gave me this letter for you." He hands her an envelope. She opens it. It was a letter of acceptance as a national anchor with United States News better known as USN. Behind it was another letter.

"Hope you believe we're serious now, keep your mouth shut and good things will come. Or else you can join your friend." She crumples it up and throws it out.

"Oh come on it's the best news of your career!"

"Fuck my career! I'm going to kill whoever did this to Harv." She storms out and goes home engulfed in the pain of her friend's death. *"If only I kept my mouth shut, Harv you'd still be alive. I'm sorry, but I promise you I'm going to get Heyward for this."* She thinks to herself.

Chapter 19

Robert and his family were almost done packing everything in the house. He figured the best way to put everything behind him and the best way to move on with his life was to leave as quickly as possible. Every day Robert called Phil and he would get no response. Every day he grew to hate Phil more and more for abandoning him again at the lowest point of his life. "Best friend my ass." He thinks to himself. Soon he stopped calling, and vows never to speak to Phil again. He begins to believe that Phil was involved with the board members on their decision.

Robert wants to end this chapter of his life and start over. He changes everything, he changed his look, where he lived, and he even changed his phone number. The 'for sale' sign has been up for a few days and already there was a buyer. Owners were set to change as soon as Robert's family was to leave. Robert and Sandra haven't had a real conversation since the death of their child. They grow more and more apart every day. Michael gets closer to his mom, Ryan gets closer to his dad. The split in the family is like a river flowing between the two sides. They can see each other, but that's about it.

"Hey." Robert says breaking the silence with Sandra.

"Hey."

"Did you hear about Scott?"

"Yeah I saw it on the news."

"Sad."

"Yeah."

"Boys did you finish packing!" Yells out Sandra.

"Almost!" Michael yells out.

"Ryan?" Robert asks.

"Yeah, almost dad!"

"Where's Charlotte?"

"With me dad!" Ryan yells.

Robert looks toward Sandra. "You talk to your sister San…"

"Yeah." She replies before he could finish her name.

That night the family sat together and had there last meal in that house. The next morning they will leave to go to Sandra's sister's house. It's just a pit stop until they find a home in Los Angeles; the real estate agent said that the schools were just better there. Sandra needs a break as well. She didn't want to move, but she knows it's something she needs. She wants to forget about everything that's happened and she wants to start a new life with her boys. She feels her and Robert are worlds apart and feels in her heart that he is the reason the baby died. She felt that he chose the company over her. She said she forgives him, but never really meant it. She's just numb. Her children mean everything to her. The only one above her children is God. She feels especially close to Michael, and she knows that Ryan is becoming close to Robert. She encourages it because otherwise Robert would have no support in the house. Charlotte seems to be the strongest link between the two sides.

Sandra still loves Robert, but the pain of her lost child just overpowers her life. She feels that some time with her sister will help, and maybe moving to Los Angeles will be for the better. She doesn't really know what to think anymore, so much has happened so recently that it seems like a dream that she can't wake herself up from. Whatever she does she's reminded of her child, and she feels the abandonment she felt in the delivery room when Robert wasn't there. All Sandra wanted was her husband, her knight in shining armor to be by her side, holding her hand. She wanted him to tell her everything will be alright. She wanted Robert to sometimes just walk up to her and hug her. She misses his touch. Every time she thinks of him she is immediately brought back to that day. "Why did he pick Orion over me?" She thinks, "Was I not important enough? Was I not his first priority? Wasn't the baby his top priority? He should have never left, I needed him, I needed my husband." She prays every night hoping to find some sort of sign on what to do, or what direction she should follow this night was no different. Unfortunately God usually wants people to figure out what path should be taken on their own. The next day they say goodbye to the lives they once knew forever. They tell no one.

Chapter 20

"Well good morning there bright eyes. I missed you yesterday. I know, I know you missed me too; it was just my day off. I spent the day with my five year old son. Boy I can tell you one thing though, they sure can be a hand full." Janis says, as cheerful as ever.

Phil looks towards her hands. "Yeah, I know no wedding ring." She noticed him looking at her hand. "He left us soon after Joshua was born. He's a good kid just needs special attention…but enough about me. So I heard you were a big time lawyer. For Orion Industries right? I heard they were just bought out, too bad huh…Wow, you look distressed, that must have sucked huh? Well at least you'll have more time to heal." She tries to be comforting. "As soon as we called the company, they made sure you had the best service. Well anyway I don't know much about business, and stocks, and all that noise. I'm just as simple as they come; I guess that's why I moved down here from New York, too many bad memories, and drama for me. I know I've said this before, but I have to tell you again you have the most familiar face; maybe you were on the news and I caught a glimpse of you, huh. Anyhow dear if you need anything just buzz."

Phil was horrified at the sound of Orion being sold so soon. "What the hell is going on there?" He thought to himself. Unable to pull together enough energy to talk still, he hasn't felt more frustrated in his life. He has had countless hours to think though. "Why the hell hasn't Robert or anyone called? How come no one from my family is here for me?"

After all he had done for Robert and tried to save him and his company, he didn't get one call to the hospital. "I'm never talking that son of bitch ever again." Sometimes these thoughts brought tears to Phil's eyes. The last time Phil cried was when he caught his mother in bed with the man who stole everything from him. As he thinks more of it, he begins to feel happiness in what happened to Orion, hoping that Robert probably got fired. If he can't come see his best friend in a near death accident, then why the hell should he care anything of him?

During his time at the hospital he becomes closer and closer to Janis, who is the only thing in his life right now that helps purge the anger. For the first time he feels like someone is watching over him, like someone is concerned about him and cares. Every time she walks into the room, he smiles inside. She always talks to him thus keeping him sane. As she checks the IV and makes sure everything is right he thinks to himself, "Wow she's beautiful and she's amazing. I wish I could just hold her and kiss her. Man she has a kid what the hell are you thinking? Who cares man you love her. Love her? This can't be love, can it? My God I just want her."

Janis begins to walk away. "Okay hon, I'm going to get going, I'll be back in an hour to check up on you." Phil's eyes widen as if he were troubled. "What's wrong Phil? Did you want me to stay?" She adds jokingly. Phil's eyes relax when she says that. "Well, are you sure?" He nods his head as much as possible. "Okay, but I don't know how fun I am." She sits with him and talks to him for as long as possible, they both wish it would last longer, but she would have to go soon.

After a week, Phil begins to talk, it is limited due to the pain, but it gets him by. He had more movement in his left hand where he had broken his wrist. Both his legs were slowly healing. He had a broken foot and ankle in his left leg and has broken his right leg. His right hand was crushed; soon he was able to move his fingers slowly. He tried calling Robert ever since he could talk even though he vowed never to talk to him again. Phil hoped that if he talked to Robert maybe something would make sense.

After a week of getting voicemails and no returned calls, Phil gets frustrated. His final call to Robert was the sound of the operator, "Sorry, but the number you have dialed has been disconnected." Phil knows at that point their friendship was over. He feels as betrayed from Robert as he felt from his mother. Phil swears in his heart that he will repay Robert for abandoning him, leaving him there to die. He thinks to himself that, being the president of the company Robert must have gotten wind of his situation and still did nothing. The only purpose Phil feels he has in his life right now is Janis.

Every day he fell more and more in love with her. Lucky for him, Janis feels the same way. Janis talks a lot about her son, who needs special help because he suffers from autism. It isn't severe, but it still holds him back from being completely normal. Phil and Janis share almost everything with each other from secrets, to embarrassing stories, to their greatest fears; they even shared their first kiss. Janis says it's a good way to build muscle in his mouth. Phil didn't mind the exercise. One night Janis decided to stay late after her shift to spend time with Phil. They watched Casa Blanca, and sat together, Phil was in a wheelchair, after being in the bed for so long it was nice to move a bit. Janis had a special love for old classics. After the movie Phil got back into his bed with Janis' help and they talked and kissed, as Janis stroked his hair.

"So what do you want to do now?"

"You can spend the night here." He says slowly, and painfully.

"Well I was thinking something more eventful." She says as she moves closer to him.

"Well, I guess there is one part of my body that didn't break." He says with a smile.

"Now that's what I'm talking about." She rubs the back of her hand softly across his face. She pulls it back as his beard pricks her. "You know a man's beard grows faster when he is anticipating sex."

"Is that right?"

"Mm hmm."

She kisses his lips then slowly gets on top of him trying to be careful because Phil's injuries are still tender. They kiss each other for a little bit. He looks her in the eyes and tries to stroke her hair as she kisses him on the neck. He thinks to himself how she looks beautiful in her tight scrubs. Her shirt fitted perfectly accenting her breasts and her pants complimenting her hips. She takes her top off and they make love in the hospital room.

Both being careful of each other, keeping Phil's injuries in mind and making sure no one hears them. They had both waited for this moment for quite a while. Janis lays forward so only Phil can hear her moans. When she comes close to finishing she grabs the pillow behind Phil and moans half into it and half into his ear. Phil with all his strength tries to caress her back. When he finishes, they both move their lips closer to each other as their cheeks rub against one another. Their lips finally find each other and kiss, falling deeper in love as every second passes. They didn't want time to move, but knowing with each passing moment, more love was being flooded into their hearts they couldn't wait for the next second to arrive. Janis sits up and they both smile at each other, she then lays next to him and puts her head on his shoulder.

"Don't you have to go home to Josh?"

"No, I called the babysitter tonight."

"All night?"

"Yeah my mother; told her I'm working all night."

"Oh…wait a minute, are you telling me you knew you were going to sleep with me tonight?"

"No, just hoped."

"Ugh, I feel so used." He jokes. They both sit there and laugh.

"Well aren't you the talkative one today, I'm glad my kissing exercises are working."

Just as she mentioned it Phil remembered his jaw and the pain. His mouth begins to swell a little bit.

"Mm…Hmm." He murmurs agreeably.

"Yeah that's right 'mm…hmm.'" They both slowly fall asleep.

***

Later that night around three A.M. The sound of a creaking door wakes Phil up. He was always a light sleeper. He looks up and it was him. Dominique.

"What do you want?"

"Ha, it's good to see you're talking now. Who's your little girlfriend? She's kind of cute."

"Don't worry about it, just leave us alone."

Janis wakes up. "Honey what happened?" She looks over. "Who are you?"

"Don't worry about it he's just a business associate sent from the company."

"Hello ma'am, I'm Dominique Walker, just here to make sure our friend Phil here is alive and kicking."

"He was just leaving though."

Dominique stares at Phil for a second, and then with a big smile he says, "That's right, I'll see you later Phil." He tips his hat walks out.

"Let's go back to sleep." Phil says as he motions her to put her head back on him.

Janis falls asleep on Phil's arm. Phil stays up all night trying to figure out what to do. If these people come checking up on him so consistently there must be a reason, there must be something he's missing. He needs to go back right away and figure out what exactly is going on. Phil lays there constantly calculating what he must do. Every day he wants to walk out of the hospital and straighten things out.

Another week passes; Phil improves greatly, but is nowhere near a hundred percent. Doctors estimate him being around sixty seven percent. Phil thinks to himself, "Who the hell estimates sixty seven percent on someone's health? It's either sixty or seventy; even sixty five makes sense, but sixty seven percent?"

He tries not to think too much about it, but odd things like that bother him. He and Janis become much closer, they sit and share stories of their past, they laugh, they eat, and watch movies together. It's almost like a high school relationship and neither of them is too ashamed to admit it. Janis tells him about how a while back she was in a terrible accident, but doesn't have much memory of what happened, that whole year of her life is a blank. As they get closer Phil wants to protect her and Josh more and more, but his past still haunts him and he feels as his spirit won't rest unless he finds out what happened.

"J."

"Yeah?"

"I have to go back to New York."

"What now?" She jokes.

"No, Monday morning."

"You can't, you're not healthy yet."

"I know, but there's some stuff I need to straighten out, but I promise as soon as I do, I'll be right back in this bed letting you take care of me."

"What kind of stuff do you have to do?"

"Just business stuff. I mean you heard about the merger, it's just some stuff I have to make sure is going the way it should."

"Well don't they have other lawyers for that?"

"Yeah, of course they do, but I have a lot of stake in this company too, I need to make sure things are right, ye know? I just hate being useless, and I like to be informed, and since I can talk a lot more know, I figured it would be a good opportunity to check in on things."

"So pick up the phone, why do you have travel a thousand miles to talk?"

"Come on sweetheart, you know how business is."

"Okay fine I'll come with you. I mean who else is going to roll you around in your wheelchair?" Janis replies.

"No, you have to stay. Look I promise you, as soon as I get things there straightened out I'll be right here. It shouldn't be that long at all, a few days at most. And then if you would like little miss I'll *come with you*, you and Joshua can come up, and we can see where things go, or we'll figure stuff out. I mean after all I bet I can pretend to be hurt for a couple months more." They both laugh.

"You promise you'll be back?"

"Only if you promise to be right here, waiting for me, and will take care of me when I come back." They both kiss. "It's funny how sometimes being hit by a tornado can be the best thing that ever happens to you." They continue kissing. "I love this exercise." He says as they both smile and kiss.

***

Early morning that Monday, Phil gets on the plane and flies back to New York. He has calculated as many scenarios as possible in his head and how to tackle them. He knows something is up, just not what. He continuously jumps back and forth from thinking about Orion to thinking about Janis. He hasn't told her much about the company, and his life in respect to it. He tries his best to suppress the whole incident with Artemis, hoping if he believes it enough it may be true that he didn't do it. As he inches closer and closer to New York, his heart gets heavier and heavier. He doesn't know why but an evil sense emerges in him, it grows like a disease. His sins are like a virus multiplying in his blood cells devouring his soul. As he revisits his past in his mind, his aura becomes darker. Once he lands he gets into a taxi which drives him to his condo in the city, once there he calls Janis with his new cell phone.

Phil doesn't believe in owning a house phone since all he ever used before was his cell phone, a house phone seemed useless. It's an odd feeling having to call someone to let them that you're okay, he thinks to himself. He didn't mind it too much though. He then debates whether he should go in today or not. The pain in his body was excruciating, partially due to not having taken his medicine on time, and without the luxury of the hospital it is inevitable for the pain to resurface. Phil takes his medicine and goes to sleep. The pain made the decision to go in, in the morning.

The next morning Phil makes it to Orion. The shooting hunter that stood twenty feet tall with waterfalls surrounding it in front of the building was gone. The fountain remained, but there stood erected a giant man with a bronze sun behind him. "What the hell is that?" He thinks to himself. He shakes it off and continues into the building. "Well at least the inside's still the same." As he continues everyone looks up and stares at him, but they try to be as discrete as possible. Phil believes it's because he's in a wheelchair now. He gets into the elevator and puts his ring in the ring slot. It doesn't work. Confused he tries it again. It doesn't work. He leaves the elevator and goes towards the receptionist, a new girl, he does not recognize her.

"Excuse me."

"Yes, how can I help you?"

"Yeah, I'm Phillip Roderick the company head lawyer, I was trying to get up stairs, but my ring isn't working for some reason."

She looks at him strangely. "Yes, Mr. Roderick, that's because they have been disassembled since Orion was bought out. For the new existing employees there was a change in rings."

"Change in rings?"

"Yeah." She answers back with attitude.

"Well can you call up Mr. Heyward and tell him I'm here." She looks at him oddly again.

"What?"

"Mr. Heyward has been gone for quite some time now, he no longer works here. Where have you been?"

"Look can you just call whoever is in charge up stairs and tell them I'm here." Phil begins to get very frustrated. She picks up the phone and makes a call.

"Yes, this is Hanna, a Mr. Phillip Roderick is down here. Yes sir." She hangs up the phone and looks at Phil. "Just go into the elevator, you'll get where you need to go."

"Um…Okay thank you." He gets into the elevator, it begins to move. *"What the hell is going on here?"* He thinks to himself. He gets to the top floor and a receptionist is waiting there for him.

"Mr. Roderick?" She asks him.

"Yes?"

"Mr. Johnson will see you now."

"Who's Mr. Johnson, and what happened to Liz?" Phil asks.

"I'm sorry I don't know who that is and Mr. Johnson is the president of the company."

"President?"

"Yes." She looks at him as if he were crazy. She escorts him to the office. Phil, goes in, there's a big muscular man sitting in there. The office looks like a long hallway. It seems dark, and very intimidating.

"Mr. Roderick, I've been waiting for you. It's nice to see you're back on your feet…well almost. You had quite the accident there. Anyway what can I do for you?"

Phil is taken aback by the extreme familiarity of the voice, "Who the hell are you?"

"Well, I surely am offended, you don't even recognize your old business associates." Just then Phil remembered the dark voice from the night of the gala. It was so dark in the room; Phil had a hard time making out faces. But it was him.

"You son of a bitch! What happened here? Where's Robert?"

"Easy Mr. Roderick, you've been through a lot lately, and I know much of this may be a shock to you, so I'll let a few things slide. But don't ever mistake my kindness for weakness."

"Don't tell me what to think you dirty, back stabbing…"

"Mr. Roderick, how is Janis?"

With a look of shock on his face, Phil yells, "Don't you touch them! You leave them alone! This is between you and me!"

"No Mr. Roderick, there is no you and me. Now, as I'm sure you've heard Apollo has bought out Orion. Unfortunately the explosion at the plant really hurt Orion Industries and was in danger of going under, thankfully we were there to repair the damage."

"What happened to Robert?"

"Ah yes, what did happen to Robert? Has he called you? Has he visited you? I'm sure he at least sent you flowers? And his beautiful wife? You always did have a thing for her, did she visit you?"

"Fuck you!"

"You're really beginning to try my patience Mr. Roderick. They haven't contacted you have they? If you get hurt, aren't they supposed to call the company and let the man in charge know what happened? I mean come on you're such an asset to this company surely somehow Robert would have gotten some notification, some clue as to where you were. He left here. Not even I know where he is. He left your sorry ass there to die. Well, we took care of you. We made sure someone looked after you as you lay there not able to talk, or feed yourself, or even wipe your own ass. So maybe you should reconsider who you express your profanities to as well. Now, since you weren't a good enough of an asset to Orion Industries, and I obviously can't trust you, you're fired. Get out of my office, and leave, don't ever come back here. If I ever see you again, I will promise you it will be the last sight you ever see." Max states slowly, his voice hard and icy.

Angrily Phil turns his wheelchair around, and begins to make his way out. As he gets to the door, he sees Dominique walking in.

"So I guess I won't have to visit you anymore." Phil stares at him and begins to continue out. Just as he does Max shouts out from the back.

"And Mr. Roderick." Phil stops and turns his head slightly to show that he is listening, "You might want to take a look at the New Montefiore Cemetery. There's something there that I think may interest you greatly." Phil leaves.

"Why didn't we just kill him?" Dominique asks.

"Because you fool, if he died, Heyward would have taken control of all of Mr. Roderick's stock in the company. I rather both these men keep their stock and hate each rather than one man have them all and hate me. Only few men in this world should have most of the power." Max states.

***

At New Montefiore Cemetery, Phil doesn't know why he came, but he did. The receptionist gave him a map of the cemetery on where to go. Apparently Max had faxed it down to her. As Phil made his way to the point in the map, he began to feel a great uneasiness inside of him. Something he never felt before. The map leads him to a tombstone. It was a brownish grey marble slab, the edges were straight and it was curved at the top. When he made his way around he saw the name on the tombstone. Sandra.

Just under the name a circle. Phil exploded into tears; he rolled his wheelchair close to the tombstone and hugged it falling out his wheelchair and onto his knees. He cried and sat there for almost four hours. He was interrupted by a phone call. It was Janis, he decided to ignore it. Explaining this would be impossible. He looked at the tombstone once more. "I swear I'll get whoever did this to you." He says out loud. He leaves the cemetery and heads back home.

The next day he flies back to Florida to finish off his treatments. He feels he needs to leave New York for good. He needs to start over.

Chapter 21

"Thank you Nancy, I guess you *can* put all your eggs in one basket after all, Jim."

"I guess you can Amber."

"With USN, I'm Amber K."

"And I'm Jim Rhines, goodnight America."

"And we're off the air!" A cameraman yells out.

"I'm glad that you're on board Amber."

"Thanks Jim, it's a good to be here."

"Amber walk with me, talk with me!" An older yet well kept man says to Amber as she gathers her notes.

"What's up Mr. Howard?"

"Mr. Howard? Please call me Greg, Amber."

"Okay…Greg."

"Anyway with you on board Amber, the numbers are going through the roof; you bring a new edge to the team. If you need anything you let me know."

"Will do."

He stops walking and stands in front of her. He looks her in the eyes as he puts his hands on her shoulders. "Hey, I know you've been through a lot lately. I can only imagine what it feels like to lose a close friend. With my line of work I've never had the privilege to have such company in my life. If you need anything, anything at all I'm not just your boss, consider me a friend, okay?"

Amber hangs her head, and then looks up with a smile. "Thank you sir, but I think I'll be just fine."

After Harvey's death Amber didn't know where to go, but away. Away was good. With Amber, out of sight out of mind, worked best. Moving to Atlanta was a therapeutic change more than anything. Maybe her parents would be proud of her now. After her whole life of being criticized by her parents for being a journalist, she finally made it onto national television.

Chapter 22

"You know I love you right?" Robert asks Sandra hoping for some light of affection.

"The broker called today, he said he found a house for us in LA." Sandra responds.

"Yeah?"

"Yeah, you should go take a look at it tomorrow."

"Why don't you come with me?"

"I want to stay with Sherry and the kids."

"Why do you act like this lately?"

"Like what?"

"Like this baby, quiet, distant, I don't know…so far away."

"I'm not."

"Sandra!"

She looks angrily at him. "I'm going to sleep with the kids tonight."

Robert leaves the next morning. Moving to Los Angeles seems like a good idea to him. He wants to move as soon as possible. He hates staying with Sherry, he has no privacy. He couldn't fight with his wife, he couldn't be himself.

On the plane ride to Los Angeles, he finally has a few moments to think. Not that he didn't have enough time to think already with Sandra being so distant. Even though he got a ten million dollar settlement and he got another fifteen million dollars in stocks, he felt there wasn't enough money in the world to bring him and Sandra closer together again.

Once again Sandra was right, money doesn't buy you love. Robert gets comfortable in his seat and reads the newspaper. He reads about Apollo Industries, it said Phil was nowhere to be found, but the company announced that he was fired due to unethical business conduct in the company, Ronald had resigned, and Jerry the head board member of R&D was on trial under suspicion of involvement in the Artemis Labs explosion.

Apparently they had found some video of him talking to another man in a grey suit, and handed over some briefcase. The story continued talking about all the allegations, Robert feels as long as his name wasn't brought up he was fine. He wants to distance himself as much as possible from his recent past. His plane finally lands, there is a limo driver waiting for him. He is then driven over to the house that his broker had called about.

"Robert!" A man standing in front of a giant house yells out.

"Alec!" He replies, with a hug.

"How's it going Bob?"

"Well, it's going. Let's take a look at the house."

"Of course."

Robert looks at the house and likes it immediately. There is nothing extraordinary about the house. There are no unique features, no bells, no whistles. The only thing that matters is that it is big enough and far away from everything. He is as far away from everything as possible. He was home.

Within a month the family moves in and gets settled. The kids try to get acquainted with the new neighborhood as the days and weeks pass. Early morning one of the days the two brothers had taken off in their bicycles with Charlotte that summer on one of their 'adventures of the city'.

"Hey the kids are gone, you want to go to the bedroom baby?"

"No." Sandra replies blandly.

"Well do you want to talk?"

"No."

"You want to do anything?"

"No."

"What the fuck Sandra!" He says out of frustration.

"Don't cuss at me!" She fires back.

"What the hell is your problem? Ever since…Ever since that day you haven't talked to me, you haven't touched me, nothing. Why the hell do you act like you hate me? I've done everything for you, for the family. For Christ's sake Sandra, I left the company for you!"

"Oh thank you for leaving your company for us Robert! Only if you did that the first time." She says under her breath.

"What? What the fuck did you say to me?!"

"Nothing just let it go Robert." She tries to stay as calm as possible.

"No, no, let's talk about it, if you have something to say, say it to my face instead hiding behind the kids or your sister. Nobody's here now, so say what you have to say Sandra."

"You left me and killed the baby, it's all your fault."

"What?! Are you crazy? I did what I had to. You and the baby were fine before I left. My whole life…our whole life was being burned down!"

"Our whole life is buried six feet under the ground in New York!"

"I know I buried her myself! I saw my baby go down there; don't you think I wanted to see her grow up? Don't you think I wanted her to grow up to be somebody? So don't tell me about her, I was there!" He screams as tears come rushing down his face.

"You left your family when they needed you. You picked them over us. You made that choice Robert. You made that choice!" She's also brought to tears now. "So if anything, fuck you!" They both stand there in silence, Sandra had never cussed at Robert before in her life, so it felt as if a thunder bolt came crashing through the roof and ripped the house in half, leaving each on their on side.

"I'm sorry." Robert says softly.

"No, it's too late."

"What do you mean too late?"

"You left us Robert, you left us. Why? You let our baby die."

"I'm sorry baby, I'm sorry" He goes near her to hug her. She moves away.

"Baby?"

"I want a divorce."

"…What?" Robert says taken completely off guard.

"I'm sorry Robert I can't do this anymore."

"Can't do what, what have I made you do? I do everything I can for you. Baby please…don't do this."

"I'm sorry."

"Baby, we can make it work." He tries to look her in the eye, but she looks away.

"It can't. I've tried to make it work. I'm tired of always having to make things work. I'm sorry I'm done with this."

"Yes we can! We can do anything we want! We can fix this!"

"I don't want to do this anymore Robert. We can't fix everything, you can't fix everything. All you ever want to do is fix things, our child is dead! You can't fix that! Sometimes when someone's hurt they just need you there, that's all, you haven't been there for me Robert you're too busy trying to fix things."

"What the hell are you…"

"I have prayed and prayed trying to find the right answer," She cuts him off in a much calmer voice, "I looked to God to help me through this, and it keeps bringing me back to the same place, and it's to be away from you."

"What? God told you that? Fuck God! This is about us!"

"Robert, please."

"No, I've gone through just as much as you have and I still tried to hold this family together. While you sat there, I was the one trying to make sure everyone was okay. And after all of that don't tell me your path is away from me!"

"Robert I'm sorry, you can keep the house and the money, just give me my kids and let me leave."

"Fuck you, there is no way you're going to get my kids. And what the hell, you think this is about the money? The money?! If it were, we'd still be in New York! And what about me, huh? What about me?! You don't care about what I want, what I've gone through? Every single day I stood there hand and foot, you would sneeze and I'd come running to you. Have you ever asked if I was okay? You ever once wonder what I was going through? And I didn't even ask you to do that. I stood there like a rock and served you like a dog. And your way of appreciating me was to go to your sister, or sleeping in another bed!"

"Is this all about sex to you?! And maybe you shouldn't be with a woman who doesn't care about what you want, or how you feel."

"Who the hell said anything about sex?!" He looks at her as if she were crazy, "See you just hear and say what you want? You don't even listen. You just want things your way, and when that doesn't happen it's time to pack up and leave! Is that what they teach you in your precious Bible?! To have kids and live with a man and then when you get bored or times get tough you should leave? What book is that in Matthew? I must have slept in during that sermon!"

Sandra gets up and begins to walk away. Infused by rage, Robert lets out a yell that has been hoarding inside him since that ratchet day. The scream is a release of all the emotions stirring inside him like a plague. He then picks up a glass full of water and with all his might, throws it across the room. It shatters into little pieces as glass flies everywhere and as it falls the two of them can somewhat see each other in the reflection of the falling shards of glass, and the water stains the pink wall.

Startled Sandra stands there for a moment. Then they hear another scream. They both look towards the door. The scream was from Ryan, he stands there frightened as tears ran down the sides of his face as he holds on to Michael. They had seen the whole fight. Sandra storms out and grabs the boys. Robert stands there in his house all alone. For the first time in his life, Robert felt alone. Something inside him told him that he should get used to the feeling.

Chapter 23

Two years later in an office, a man is standing behind his desk in his personal comfort room of his office building. The fire is burning on the side in the fireplace. There is red carpeting on the floor with the skin and head of a dead lion on top. There are deer heads and other animal heads on the wall. Another man walks in as they begin to converse.

"You want what from me?" A man says in a very thick southern accent.

"Look, I know what you've heard about me, but it's not like that."

"You must be crazy son. There is no way on God's green Earth that…"

"Look, just give me a chance, I'm telling you I am one of the best if not the best. I'll get the job done, no matter what it takes."

"If that were true, you wouldn't be at my doorstep right now begging for a job now would you? Funny how just a few short years ago we were the ones calling and asking *you* to come work for us, and now that we don't want you, here you are. We don't need extra help from scum like you."

"Okay, I know what you've heard, but let me just be an advisor of some sort, I'll do anything. I promise you I will gain your trust. Whatever it takes I will do it. It's not for the money right now, I just really need this."

"Fine, if you want to gain my trust then let's start off by playing a game of truth or dare, you start by giving me all of their secrets, and the dare, well we'll discuss the dare later on."

"Well of course, I just thought that was a given. But once I start, I have to fly back and forth from home until I get settled here."

"You do what you have to do."

Chapter 24

A year later.

"I guess this is good-bye Sandra." Robert says looking shameful.

"I guess so."

"Good-bye dad." Ryan gives Robert a hug.

"You be good now Ryan."

"Where's Michael?"

"He had to study for finals." Replies Sandra.

"Well, tell him I said I love him."

"Okay. You better get going your flight will leave soon."

Robert looks back at the airport then back at Sandra. "Of course." He starts to walk off. Ryan runs towards him and gives him another hug. "I don't care what happened, I still love you dad."

"Thanks son, I needed that." He begins to tear up. "Okay now, you take care of your mother."

He turns around and begins to walk away, Charlotte chases after him. Robert turns around and bends down to pet her. She has an expecting smile on her face.

"Oh girl, you know I'll miss you too!" He says as he rubs her ears, "But I have to go now okay?" She tilts her head to the side as if she were confused, then let's out a bark. Robert looks up at Sandra.

"Okay girl let's go." She grabs the leash and pulls Charlotte into the car; Charlotte keeps looking back and barking.

He then again turns around and begins to walk away. He gets to the outdoor baggage check-in area. Once all his bags were checked in, he turns around for some hope of light that would shine down upon him, some miracle. They were already gone.

After the divorce Robert has transformed into a new person. He feels dark inside. He split all his money down the middle with Sandra; he even gave her the two million dollar house. After his stock had dropped, Robert had about ten million dollars to keep for himself. For the past few years Robert didn't work, he slowly drove himself crazier and crazier. He would do things that he normally would never even think of, like splurging on unnecessary things, he would drink until he would pass out and so on.

He didn't care what happened. He would go out and do things just to spite Sandra, like going hunting and gambling, because he knew she hated it. He would even buy prostitutes, when it came time for sex he couldn't bring himself to sleep with them because he would always think of Sandra. He still had to pay though, he found himself paying a lot of money just to have their company. Even walking down the street sometimes he would pick up homeless people to walk with him and talk to him, and then he would take them to the most expensive restaurant in that neighborhood and eat with them.

At the end of the night he would hand them an envelope and instructed the homeless person not to open that envelope until he was out of their sight. Once they would open the envelope the person would find a thousand dollars in cash and a note thanking them for their time. Aside from helping the needy he did things out of character and out of nature so much so that it then became his nature and character. He soon became mad with sadness and loneliness. His whole life was taken away from him, his company, his kids, and most of all, his wife. What else was there to live for?

The only thing that kept him the bit most human was the book he was writing. It started off as a suicide note, and became much, much more. As he wrote and wrote the book became more and more of an extension of him. To say the least it became therapeutic for him. Even though it had much work needing to be done to it, he had already come up with a name. He named his book the Human Virus. Swiftly and surely as time went on ten million dollars became six million, and that soon after had become three million. Robert's cash flow was dwindling rapidly.

One day Robert was finally found by the media and was asked to appear on a live national television program. It was one of those 'Where are they now?' type shows, but more serious, named Fallen Stars. It was done by a very popular independent news broadcasting station. Robert showed up in rags and looked like any bum off of the street. The newscaster had bombarded Robert with questions on subjects like Orion, Apollo,

Artemis, and even his wife. Then when responses seemed monotonous he asked about Highland Corporations, and what they had done to contribute to the great fall of Orion.

He asked mockingly trying to at the very least provoke him, "Tell me Robert did the scorpion bite?" Robert continued to answer with very mundane average answers. The newscaster was getting annoyed with the uninteresting and almost famished story. Finally he asked "Looking back, what do you think of the life events that have happened to you in the past few years?"

Robert simply replies, "Look I don't think or care about anything anymore. I hate everyone. If I ever see that bastard who took my company, or that low life lawyer who said he was my friend, or even that son of a bitch Earl Hodges, I will kill them. I will kill every last one of them!" Everyone was in shock to hear what Robert had to say.

Recovering from the stun, the newscaster asked, "Do you realize on national television you made death threats, if I'm correct, against Maximus Edward Johnson president of Apollo industries and former military general, your former top lawyer and best friend Phillip Henry Roderick, and the president of Highland Corporations Earl Landon Hodges?"

"Yes and if you want to be added to the list you can be too."

"No...no sir. Not at all." They had ended the interview right then and there.

The newscaster began to fear for his life, and didn't want to move forward with the interview. Robert's family tried to stay by his side by being supportive of what he was going through. He would see Sandra and the kids twice a week at first, then it changed to once a week, and then once every two weeks. Both sides had trouble keeping up with time schedules. Sandra wanted to distance herself from Robert, and Robert would sit there idolizing his family so much that when he saw them they would only end up fighting.

The last straw came last year at Ryan's eighth grade graduation. All of Ryan's friends were there and everyone was enjoying their time. Robert had shown up drunk and was fumbling all over the place. Ryan only got a glimpse of his foolish looking father. Sandra had asked him to leave, but Robert stayed and fought with her. Michael finally came out and threw Robert on to the lawn and threatened to call the police if he didn't leave.

"Well at least just give him my gift!" He throws an envelope at Michael. When Ryan opened the envelope it was a card with a very old man buying a younger man balloons, inside the card it read, *'No matter what, you're always your fathers baby'* behind the card was a check for a million dollars to be paid progressively as Ryan graduates, elementary school, high school, and college. Robert slowly got up and straggled his way home.

Michael was a lot bigger now, and the captain of his football team. He was going to go to UCLA with a full scholarship after he graduated high school. A few days later, on his way home from a bar; Robert was arrested for drinking in public, harassing civilians, and getting into a fight with a young man. Sandra was on her way to bail him out, but then Michael had stopped her, wanting him to serve his sentence.

After the graduation and jail incident Robert felt it best to move away. Money didn't have meaning if you don't have someone meaningful to spend it on. With whatever money Robert did have left he had bought some land in Dallas, Texas to build a small flower shop and to buy a very small condo for himself. His mother had a special place in her heart for flowers, she would go out in the garden every spring and plant flowers and for the summer her garden was her family. Almost every year she would win prizes and awards for her beautiful garden. He felt as if opening a flower shop would bring him back to a simpler past, a past with no worries. Robert had traveled back and forth from California to Texas trying to settle in, trying to slowly push himself away further from his family. This was the last flight. This was the last time he would see them.

"Sir? Sir!" Robert awoke from his blank stare into space.

"Yes?" Robert looked up to see a flight attendant standing above him.

"Sir we're about to land please fasten your seatbelt."

"Oh, okay."

When they land, Robert gathers his things from the baggage claim area and takes a cab to his new condo. On his way to his new home Robert thinks to himself. *"Maybe God lives in Texas, maybe if I live closer to God, He will help me...Yeah right God's a joke, God is nothing but a manifestation of man's lonely imagination."* Loneliness has become Robert.

***

"Hello?"

"How's it feel to be a free man again?"

"Who is this?"

"We'll have time for reunions later. Don't you think it's time to get your cut, to get a little revenge?"

"Look I just got out, I haven't gotten comfortable enough to go back yet."

"You'll be in the clear; we just need some information from you."

"What kind of information?"

"Look outside your window." The man looks outside as the person on the phone instructs. "Get in that limo, and when you get here we'll discuss this a little more."

"I...I don't know about this."

"Well do you want pay back, or do you want to live the rest of your life shamefully. When was the last time you looked in the mirror and respected yourself?"

"How much does it pay?"

"Don't worry you'll be taken care of. It's funny, how the shoe is on the other foot now."

"What?"

The phone hangs up.

***

After moving into the new place in Dallas, Robert called Sandra and the boys a few times. He would get one word answers from Sandra, and never heard from Michael. Ryan talks to him the most, but even those conversations were limited due to awkwardness and Michael giving Ryan weird looks while he's on the phone. Robert didn't know why he continued to try to fight this uphill battle. It even astonished him that he was still alive. Why was he still alive? What purpose could he possibly have on this earth? Who would even notice if he died? Better yet, who would even care? Every suicide attempt he had would end the same way. He would go halfway through it, hurt himself immensely, then live another day to be ashamed of himself. He can't even kill himself correctly. After he would recover, he would go back to writing in his book. He would carry his book everywhere as if it were of some importance. It was just a bunch of ragged papers to the outside world. But to Robert, that book was his life line.

While sitting and writing, he hears the sound of a doorbell, as a door opens to his flower shop. Surprised, Robert looks up.

"Hello?" Robert asks from the back of the store.

"Hi." A woman responds, a man walks in behind her and holds her hand.

"Can I help you find anything?"

"Well, we're just looking right now." The man responds.

"Okay, if you need anything let me know."

"Okay, thank you." The couple looked around for a few seconds.

"Was there any particular flower that you were looking for today?" Robert tries again.

"No, just looking." The woman responds.

"A wedding?"

"More like a birthday." She finally answers; feeling if she didn't Robert wouldn't go away.

"Oh for who?"

"A baby girl."

"Really? What's her name?"

"Deanna."

"I had a baby girl once. She died. It was my fault. Make sure that baby doesn't die. The funerals are bad, but the days after are worse."

"Um…okay…we have to get going now, but we'll be back." The lady says; the man puts his arm around her as if to protect her as they begin to leave.

"No I'm sorry, don't go." He pleads.

They had already hurried out the door before he could finish his sentence. For the thirst of human interaction, Robert spent almost all of his time at the flower shop; a handful of people would come in and out every day. Robert would try to make as much conversation as possible to keep them there longer; unfortunately he would drive away many of his customers making odd comments. Frustrated with himself he would just break down and cry most nights.

Chapter 25

Sandra was in her art room painting her newest masterpiece. She loved painting, ever since she was a child. Once she and Robert were married, she had given it up due to the responsibilities of marriage and of course Orion. It had required so much of her time that she had forgotten about painting all together.

Once Michael was born she felt she would have more time to herself and her passion, but it was the exact opposite. Since their move to Los Angeles, things have changed so much and the only way Sandra felt she could express herself was through her art. She would leave hidden messages for herself in each of her paintings. Each art work told a short story about her. Her art brought her closer to God; she would speak to Him through her art. Even though she went to church every Sunday with the boys, for some reason praying doesn't always seem to be the best communicator.

Sometimes she would paint pictures of little Sandra, at least what she thought little Sandra would have looked like as the years went by. No one knew about little Sandra's paintings, except for Sandra herself. Those painting were her most intimate moments with God, and no one's eyes deserved to view them. The rest of her paintings though she began to sell. She believed wasting her time not having any income wasn't the smartest thing to do. The business didn't take off so well at first when Robert was still with them and her tensions were soaring. She still loved him, but the pain of her lost child would never be extinguished from her soul. Once he had left, she felt more free, but in her artwork she would passionately express how dearly she missed him.

One day during a church, adults only, group meeting somehow the subject of her paintings came up in conversation. Stanley Byron, one of the patrons of the church also owns an art gallery, and expressed great interest in her art work. Shy to the idea Sandra

reluctantly allowed him to, one day come see her work. As Sandra was painting one day
she was interrupted by Michael's voice.

"Ryan don't forget your shoes!"

"Oh right thanks Michael." He picks up his shoes half embarrassed. Charlotte barks at him.

"Yeah I know girl!" He responds with an irritated voice.

"Always forgetting things." Sandra says, as she watches Ryan fumble his luggage.

"I know mom, I'll get it together."

"Well as long as you don't forget who loves you the most I think we'll be okay." She says in a kid voice as she walks over to him and gives him a big kiss on his cheeks as she tries to tickle him.

"Mom!" He pushes her back now completely embarrassed.

"What, I'm still your mother you know."

"Yeah, but I'm too old for that."

"Yeah, but you're not too old to get your butt kicked by me." Michael tackles Ryan playfully. Charlotte tries to join in, as she barks.

"Mom!"

"Okay Michael, leave him alone." She says as she laughs.

"You're such a little baby Ryan. You always run to *mommy*." Michael says mockingly as he tries to get up.

"No, I just don't like being tackled by big monkeys like you!" Ryan replies as he pushes Michael off of him. Michael gets up as he laughs and puts his arms around Charlotte scratching her behind her ears.

"Anyway Ryan do you have everything for basketball camp?" Sandra asks with a concerned look upon her face.

"Yeah... I think so." He says with an unsure voice. Sandra and Michael look at each other.

"Okay let's take a look at your bag." Sandra demands. Sandra and Michael both look through Ryan's bag.

"Ryan, when did you start shaving?"

"Umm...last week?"

"Ryan! You have more things packed for pranks than basketball!" She yells.

"Ha, ha nice," Michael responds with a smirk, "I'm glad I taught you something right." Sandra looks at Michael with an angry stare and then smacks Michael on the back of his head. "Alright, alright I'm sorry."

She then looks over to Ryan. "Ryan you're going to *basketball camp* and you didn't even pack a basketball."

"Mom, they're going to have basketballs there!"

"And where is your inhaler?!"

"Oh…" He says while looking down.

"Look you are going to repack this bag," She then looks over to Michael, "and you are going to help him, and if I see any more stupidity, no camp for you and no Kayla for you!"

"You're going to take away my girlfriend?" Michael responds with a dumb smirk on his face.

"Yes, and lock her away 'til I feel like you can have her back."

"Yeah? Well if you take her away no painting for you for a month!" Michael responds jokingly.

"Oh yeah?" Sandra gets closer to Michael and picks him up by the ear.

"Ouch, ouch okay, okay sorry!"

They all laugh and Michael and Ryan go to his room to repack his bag. Charlotte follows as if she were supervising. As they pack, Sandra goes into the kitchen to collect some snacks to add to Ryan's pack. The two brothers reminisce about their past and how when they first moved to the new city they used to ride around in their bikes with Charlotte hoping to find abandoned buildings to start their own little secret club with their friends. They would call themselves the 'dog pack'. Eventually the 'dog pack' settled for the tree house in the backyard.

"Ryan!" Sandra calls out.

"Yeah mom!"

"Hurry up honey, we have to leave for your flight soon."

"Okay mom we're almost done." Michael helps Ryan pack some last minute ammunition for pranks at the camp. They finish up and head towards the door.

"You got everything you need this time?"

"Yes mom."

"Okay take this and put it in your bag, just incase you get hungry." She hands over a small bag of snacks.

"Oh, one more thing; I have to call dad and tell him I'm leaving!" He rushes over to the phone. Michael hangs his head in disappointment. The phone rings for about a minute and a half. He called a few times and each time the Ryan got the same result, no answer, no voicemail, nothing. Ryan tried to be as persistent as possible, but it continued to lead to failure. "He's not picking up."

Sandra now looks away with a familiar disappointment. "Don't worry about it sweetie I'm sure he got caught up with something." She replies.

"Yeah probably getting drunk." Michael says shaking his head.

"Leave him alone! He's not a drunk okay, he's trying to stop! Why can't you just leave him alone?" Ryan yells at Michael.

"Whatever! He was nothing but..."

"Okay never mind him it's time to go!" Sandra scolds interrupting Michael so the two brothers wouldn't get into another fight with each other over this. Ryan starts to walk towards the door. Sandra stares at Michael expectantly.

"Alright man I'm sorry, have a good trip." Michael says apologetically as he clasps Ryan's hand and follows it with a hug. Sandra and Ryan could both tell by the way he acted that he didn't mean it.

"Okay." Ryan rolls his eyes and puts his luggage away. He walks around to the front and sits in the car.

Sandra looks at Michael. "I've had just about enough of you and this." She says with a stern voice. Michael rolls his eyes and starts to walk away. Sandra grabs his arm.

"Hey I'm not your friend who you can walk away from like that. Now I know how you feel, and that's fine, but your brother doesn't feel the same so stop punishing him for that." She says as she holds his face. Michael looks back as if he's heard this speech over a hundred times. Sandra, sees the look and adds, "Hey come on, I know how you feel trust me I know, but there's no use adding fuel to a fire we're all trying to put out. It's only going to push us further away from God."

"Yeah mom." He replies.

"Okay, I love you."

"I love you too." She gives him a kiss on the cheek, then gets into the car and they leave towards the airport. *"It's so odd how we can go from laughing with one another to anger so quick."* She thinks.

115

Michael doesn't understand why his mother and his brother get so angry when he says anything against Robert. He was the one who left when things got bad. He was the one who chose the company over them. He was the one who showed up drunk to the party, and ended up in jail. Michael was there all the time to protect both his mother and his brother. So why did they act like he was a nobody? Why is it that he doesn't get the respect that he deserves? He blows it off and watches some television. A few minutes later he gets a call.

"Hello?"

"Hey!" He hears a girl's voice on the other end.

"Hey baby, what's up?"

"Nothing just missed you so I thought I'd call to see how you were doing. So what are you up to?"

"Aw. I'm just watching T.V. My mom just left a little bit ago to drop Ryan off at the airport for basketball camp."

"What city is he going to this year?"

"Sacramento."

"Nice, I hope he has fun. So you want to go to the mall?"

"Sure."

"Good I'm outside!"

"What?" Michael asks with confusion. He walks towards the window and there was Kayla in her car.

"What are you doing here?"

"Your mom told me she was dropping off Ryan, so she thought it'd be nice for us to spend some time together. We were so busy this last spring I hardly got to see you baby." She says as Michael goes to get dressed to leave.

"What? Really my mom called you?"

"Yeah, and honestly I don't think your mom trusts you being at home all alone. I think she thinks that you'll burn down the house, and really I can't blame her." She adds jokingly.

"Oh ha, ha, you know you're not funny right?"

"Whatever, I know you laugh on the inside. Now are you coming or what Michael?!"

"Yes, yes I'm coming just getting dressed."

He soon finishes getting dressed and heads out to the car. He gives her a kiss and they drive off.

Chapter 26

A limo pulls up to a gate. Behind it was a huge mansion. A man steps out the limo and looks at his cell phone, three missed calls. He can't be bothered with that right now. He has bigger things to worry about at the moment. He walks up to the gate and rings the doorbell. No answer. He rings it again. He hears a sound from the intercom. "We've been waiting for you." He hears the sound of a buzzer. He first looks up at the camera that was staring down at him and then towards the gate. He reaches out to push the gate, and right before he can even touch it, it eerily starts to open up.

The man moves out the way avoiding getting hit. He then walks into a garden like setting that sat in front of the massive building. As he walks closer the hairs on the back of his neck begin to rise one at a time. He brushes the back of his neck with his hand. In the other hand he had a large envelope. When he finally makes it up the footsteps of the mansion, the door opens up startling the man. As he walks closer he realized it was the butler who had opened this door. The butler is an old man possibly in his early sixties in a tuxedo. He has grey hair and was balding on the top. The man thought to himself how the butler actually looked like a typical butler, if there were such a thing.

"Mr. Hodges and company are waiting for you in the main room, I will a company you there." He says in a British accent as he extends his arm motioning the man where to go.

The man begins to think to himself as he makes his way down the long corridor.

"Mr. Hodges? Earl Hodges? Of Highland Corporations? No it can't be. Can it?"

They finally make it into a prodigious room. There were trophies from all over the world in this room. A massive fire roared in the back under the head of a great African lion, and behind an unparalleled desk. To the right, incased in two inch thick glass were two of the oldest copies of the Quran and the Bible. Behind it was a globe the size of a grown man. In the center sits Mr. Hodges staring down the man who had just entered, watching him as he was in awe of the glory of this room as he holds his glass of wine waiting patiently. On the floor is the most spectacular design of gold embroidery on a wine tinted red carpet.

"It's embroidered with real gold you know?" Mr. Hodges says in a very thick southern accent interrupting the man's daze as he takes another sip of his wine.

Startled the man looks up at Mr. Hodges. "Come, have a seat." There are six chairs around a cherry wood table that are taller than the average man; they look more expensive than most peoples cars. He sits down with a nervous stature.

"Here, have some wine." Mr. Hodges pours him a glass, "This is Chateau La Mondotte Saint-Emilion from the year Nineteen Ninety Six. I only ever drink wines like this when I know I will soon become richer. Boy I tell ye, it's a great feeling." He says as he holds out his glass towards the man and takes a sip of his wine.

"Here's all your information." He hands over the envelope to Mr. Hodges.

He swivels the wine in his mouth to take in the full taste then swallows. "Is this everything?" He asks.

"Uh ye…yes sir. All the research we have ever done, all the work that was ever done, and by whom is all in those files. Many of the information in there will tell you where to go if it's not in there already… Ca…can we talk about the money?"

"We'll get to the money." Hodges takes another sip, "Son, I don't like getting screwed, in fact I am the man who does all the screwing. Do you understand what I'm trying to tell ye boy?"

"Yes." The man replies as he nods his head.

"Good, so before I let you have a dime of my money, how do I know everything's in here?"

"Well…if you found me in the first place, what will stop you from finding me again?" The man replies with confidence.

Hodges lets out a whispers worth of a laugh, "Good point." He then studies the man for a moment, as the man sits there uncomfortably. Then just like that Mr. Hodges puts a big smile on his face. "Well okay then, I guess we have a deal then." He stands up and extends his arm to shake the man's hand. The small man stands up as well and he shakes his hand.

"Now about my payment."

"Yes it's always about the money right away for you northerners. I'll never understand that about you people. What ever happen to trust and good conversation, and just expect the check to come? Well I tell ye what, I have your payment here." Hodges says as he clasps the man's small hand even tighter. "Well it's not really a pay*ment*, it's much more like a pay*back*."

The man looks at Mr. Hodges with an awkward eye, and just as he realized what he had meant it was too late. He felt a piercing pain in his back that cut deeper and deeper. As soon as he let out some breath the knife was twisted inside of him. Then he hears a voice that speaks to him from behind, but right next to his ear.

"So tell me how does it feel to get stabbed in the back, Jerry?" The familiar voice brings Jerry back in time…

"Okay boys, just as we had spoken before, we need to get that poor excuse of a CEO out of this company. As the president of Apollo, I will finally provide for you guys a chance to win a losing battle with this imprudent product called Cold Fusion. We need to figure out how and when." Max says to the group.

The meeting went on for hours on how to create the perfect plan to overthrow Robert, and help Orion finally knock down Highland Corporation's scorpion.

"So now that we have the perfect plan how do we do it?" Max asks the group.

"Can't we hire someone?" One of the board members asks.

"I'm not sure if this will work." Another voice adds.

"This will work, and I'll tell you how. We'll get that dog of his to do it." Max says with an uncompromising voice.

"Phil?" Asks a woman from the side.

"Yes, Phil. If we convince him to do it then we can cover our tracks. This way we get them both out of the picture, and we can move business in our direction; the right direction."

"How do you plan on getting Phil to go along with this? I mean they're best friends for crying out loud." Says Jerry.

"Yes they are, aren't they Jerry? Now listen, you good for nothing scrawny pile of

puke. If you convince Phil that he would be doing Robert a favor by blowing up the plant then he'll do it. You just need a hook with a worm, and the hungry fish will always follow. And since we're on the matter I think the perfect man for the job is you Jerry."

"Me?"

"Yeah, Jerry you're the most inconspicuous one from us all. If you approach him he'll believe you!" A man from the side yelled out.

Everyone agreed and Jerry was forced into doing it. Being the R&D board member he actually believed in the Cold Fusion process, but he knew if he didn't follow through, this man who stood at the end of the round table could very well take his life.

Just then Jerry is pulled back into reality. Hodges grabs the wine glass from him so it wouldn't spill. Jerry turns around, to confirm who his ears had told him the voice came from. As he falls onto the table in front of him he saw the man, and looks into his eyes. His face was blank, with no emotion at all. With all the strength he had left in his body he points towards the man and says his last word. "Phil." He then closes his eyes.

The two men stand over the dead body. Phil still held onto the bloody knife. Mr. Hodges gives Phil a glass of wine. They both take a sip.

"So I got what I want, did you get what you wanted?" Mr. Hodges asks.

"Almost, there's still more business to take care of." He responds as he puts the knife down and pulled out his cigar to smoke. The butler comes into the room, and takes away the body and the knife.

"You're hunger for more can be dangerous Roderick." He looks at Phil with disgust.

"Well either I could die starving or I could die of gluttony, and I am a man who likes his food sir." He says putting out his cigar, remembering Hodges' distinct distaste for smoking.

"Well put…Oh, Hemmingway." Hodges calls out to his butler.

"Sir?"

"Please dispose of the body *creatively.*"

"Of course sir." The butler replies.

"You know you're lucky he had landed on the table, otherwise I would have been very upset. Anyway there's no use crying over spilled blood, let's get to work on this, Cold Fusion project, shall we?"

Both men look at each other, touch glasses, and take another sip.

"Son, we're going to be some rich son's of bitches I tell you what."

***

The next morning.

"Honey where were you all last night?" Asks Janis as she rolls over and puts her arms around Phil.

"I had some business to take care of baby." He says trying to deflect the question.

"Your business meetings sure go late sometimes."

"Just trying to take care of my wife and kid." He keeps a stern face.

"Yeah I know sweetheart, but I don't like sleeping without you and you know that." She says with sad eyes as she moves his head to look at her.

He looks into her eyes. "I know baby I'll try not to have too many more late meetings." He kisses her on the forehead. Then he looks at her for a moment.

"What's wrong hon?" Janis asks.

"Are you sure you're happy here?"

"In bed with you? It has its moments." She says jokingly.

"No, I mean here in Dallas, I know we've been living here for quite some time now, but still, are you sure this is what you want. How do you like your job? Is Joshua happy?" He asks with a concerned look on his face.

"Of course we are baby we're just fine. And you need to stop asking me all these questions all the time, and stop worrying. Work is just fine, I don't talk about it 'cause I know you're already stressed out from your job, so there's no need for more stress, the hospital has really taken me in and I really enjoy it. I mean don't get me wrong I miss home like hell, but we all make sacrifices. Josh loves the schools here; he's getting along just fine. Luckily we found a school that can accommodate his needs. He's made new friends and most of all, he loves you. And me, well, I have a handsome man who provides for us, loves me and my child, and makes me very, very happy. Phil I love you… and that is all that matters." She kisses him on the lips, "Now can you stop worrying about this please, because then you make me worry…Okay?"

"Okay babe no problem, but you know if you want to go home we can go back to Florida, you just say the word."

"I know babe."

"And don't worry about stressing me out, I want to hear all about your day and..." Janis interrupts him with a kiss.

"You know sometimes I wish they kept your mouth wired shut." She says jokingly with a smile.

He gives her a half smile. Janis then kisses him and lays her head on his chest as he strokes her hair. He lies there staring at his white ceiling as his memories of the night before replay over and over in his head. It was an odd feeling, though Phil has always had thoughts of killing people, he has never gone through with it. It also astonished him that he went through with it as if he had done it a hundred times before, and this was just another kill for him. It was almost as if all the rage from his past, with his mother, Robert, Orion, Sandra, and anything and everyone who had ever hurt Phil or did him wrong had come pushing through with that knife in his hand in that one moment. It was completely surreal to him.

He looked back at his wife. He knew he had to do this for her; he had to have a job that would look past his past. There was no one else in the world who would hire him. Mr. Hodges gave him a second chance in life and Phil was going to take it no matter what obstacles stood in his way. He had to support his wife and kid; he had to protect his family. Janis was right we all have to make sacrifices...some greater than others.

Chapter 27

The Dallas Grapevine

Former board member of Orion Industries, Jerry Weinberg, was hit by a freight train in the middle of the night; the body had been completely mangled, and was unrecognizable until DNA testing confirmed the identity of the man. Further testing has shown high volumes of alcohol in his system. No suspects have been identified at the moment, no witnesses were found. No one knows why he had come to Dallas, Texas shortly after his release from prison for conspiracy in the Artemis Labs explosion which was a technology laboratory for Orion Industries. No contacts near his New York estate have been confirmed him ever being there or having left there since his release, he also had made no further contacts to his ex-wife or children before he left from New York. Further inspection is yet to be deliberated; no trains will be crossing at the undisclosed crossing section until all the evidence is collected. Police speculate that Jerry Weinberg had gotten drunk and stumbled onto the tracks where he was ultimately killed. Police refuse to speak further about the case at this moment.

"Ha, there goes another one…" Robert thinks to himself as he reads the local newspaper, "I wonder if I'm next." Robert has been reading newspapers every day. His unstable state of mind has him going slowly insane. The book helps him somewhat, but even with that he needs to distance himself sometimes because then he becomes lost in his own book. He feels he will eventually lose himself to his book, become one of his own characters…space is sometimes good. The newspaper helps him stay involved with the

world in his secluded state. Every newspaper that Robert reads has its own writing style, it's own unique perception on current events, because of this Robert gets to relate to different people in that way.

Between the book, the countless newspapers, and the flower shop Robert feels like he has somewhat of a busy life again. He almost makes a routine out of it. He begins to notice odd things in the newspapers like how the same joke would be told in different comic strips of different papers, or the same clue in different crossword puzzles have different answers. Sometimes Robert would do odd things to break his vicious cycle of routine. Reminded by something in the news paper Robert decides to make a phone call.

"Hello?" Robert asks not hearing anything at first.

"Hey…" Sandra responds not sure what to say.

"Hey, is Ryan home?"

"No he left for camp a couple days ago."

"Oh I thought it was tomorrow."

"No, a couple days ago."

"Sandra where do you want this lamp?" A voice shouts out in the background."Who's that?"

"Just a friend helping me move some stuff."

"Why doesn't Michael help you?"

"He is, and so is Kayla."

"Is Kayla that guy's wife?"

"No, Kayla is Michael's girlfriend. Anyway Ryan tried calling you, you didn't pick up."

"He did?" Robert looks at his phone, "I didn't get any missed calls, the phone must be acting up. I left you guys a message the other day with my new cell phone number didn't you get it?"

"No Robert we didn't get your message."

"But I know for a fact I left it. Check it again please."

"Okay. I…"

"Sandra, come over here I need a little bit of help with this." The same voice in the background shouts out.

"I have to go Robert, I'll talk to you later."

"Why?"

"Because, I've got to get some stuff done, I'll talk to you later."

"Sandra…"

Sandra hangs up the phone and turns to look at her guest.

"Who was that?" A tall thin man in his early forties asks.

"Nobody, let's get to work shall we?"

"Yes ma'am!" He winks at her and continues on his way.

"Hey mom!" Michael says as he walks through the door.

"Where were you all day?" Sandra replies.

"I went out with all my football buddies. Remember I told you Morris is moving away? So we just had a get together, with just the guys. The real party is this weekend!" He looks over to the side. "Who's that?"

"Just a friend from church helping me move some stuff around, for my art business, I'm thinking of expanding, so I thought I could use some help and a second opinion before making any bold moves." Sandra explains.

Michael gives her an odd look. "So why didn't you just call me?"

"Well you were out, and I thought it would be nice to get to spend more time with some people from the church." He continues to look at her strange, "Don't worry nothing's going on." She assures him.

"Okay…"

"Stan." Sandra calls out.

"Yeah?" The man shouts back.

"Come here I want you to meet my son!" The man walks in.

"Hey buddy how's it going? Your mother is an amazing artist, with a little bit of good market placement, and some help getting things around she'll be famous soon!"

"Stan!" She hits him on the arm playfully, "I'm not looking for all that I just want to run my business and keep to myself. There's no fame and glamour in my future." She says with conviction.

Stan laughs it off and redirects his focus onto Michael, "I remember you from church don't you have a brother? You're Ryan right?"

Michael looks back at Sandra with a sarcastic look.

"No Stanley this is Michael." Sandra answers for him.

"Oh I'm sorry Michael, how are you?" He puts out his hand for Michael.

Michael stares at his hand for a moment, and then reluctantly shakes his hand. "Well, thanks for your help, but I'm here now so we'll see you later."

"Michael! Don't be so rude, he was just kidding Stan." She looks over at Michael, "Weren't you Michael?" He stands there quietly; Sandra nods her head demanding him to agree.

"Yeah, just kidding." The dog barks at the man, then growls at the unfamiliar face. "Let's go Charlotte, it's time for your walk anyway." They walk out the house.

"Hey, I'm really sorry, I didn't mean to cause any trouble here. If you want I can leave." Stan tells Sandra.

"No, don't worry about it, Michael's just a little over protective sometimes. He just needs some time to warm up to new people." She replies. "By the way I'm glad you're here, I could use a friend my own age."

"Well then I'm your man."

"Are you sure you're okay with this? I hope you're not putting anything on hold on my account."

"No not at all, it's a beautiful day, and I'm just here to help out a good friend. To tell you the truth I myself could use some good company myself lately." He smiles at her as he looks into her eyes, "Now how about we move one more batch of furniture and then we'll get something to eat."

"Good because I'm starving."

He smiles at her as they begin to move things around in the house, "Sandra, there is a closet in your art room that was locked is there any art work in there?"

"No!" She accidentally yells out, then covers her mouth, she then replies, "No, just some of my personal things, everything you see is all that we need to move." She tries to recover gracefully.

"Okay…"

***

"Is your *boyfriend* gone?" Michael asks with an over exaggerated sarcasm.

"First of all he is not my boyfriend Michael, and I know for a fact that I have taught you better than to be completely disrespectful to guests, especially your elders as you were earlier today." Sandra scolds him.

"Whatever."

"What is with your attitude?"

"Nothing."

"Hey did your father ever leave a message with his new number?" Sandra asks.

"Maybe."

"Michael, it was a simple yes or no question, and I expect you to answer it with *out* the attitude." She says with a sterner voice.

"Yeah he did so what?"

"So why didn't you give it to Ryan?"

"I did."

Sandra stares at him, knowing there was something more to the story, "Robert, are you lying to me?"

"Wait, what did you just say to me?!" He asks with anger and disbelief in his face.

"I asked are you lying to me?" She replies.

"You called me Robert."

"No, I didn't."

"Yes…you did. Why the hell would you do that?"

"Young man you better watch your mouth around me and that is my final warning." She says angrily, "Now, I don't think I called you Robert, but if I did it's only because you're growing into a man now. You look and act so much like your father it's scary." She says as she comes closer and puts her hand on his face. He aggressively pushes her hand away from his face.

"Don't you ever call me that again, and don't ever call him my father again. He is nothing to me, and we'll all be happier as soon as you realize he's nothing to you and Ryan also."

"Michael, don't talk like that!"

"Whatever…if you want to talk to him so badly, all I did was change the last two numbers of the phone number." He turns around before his mother can see his tears. "Now you can call him whenever you want."

"Why would you do that? Why would you do that to your own baby brother? This isn't even about me, it's about Ryan. Why would you take that away from him?" She asks with disgust in her voice.

"Because we don't need him." He walks away.
"Michael, where are you going?"
"It doesn't matter."

Chapter 28

Robert would do it for me wouldn't he? He would protect me from throwing my life away, right? Man I should just call the police and tell Robert the whole story and get rid of the whole board. If I do that then all our investors will know that there are trust problems within the company, and then we're really screwed. Robert would never forgive me for that, I wouldn't forgive myself for bringing the company down like that. I've made all his major decisions for him thus far, and I've been right. I mean look at Sandra...She's so beautiful, if he didn't take her I would have made her my queen. That lucky son of a bitch. He's done just as much for me though. He made me part of his family. Uncle Phil they call me. Yes I have to protect them; I have to make this decision for Robert. I have to protect Sandra, Michael, and Ryan, and the new baby. The board promised they would take care of them. I'll be the silent hero.

Just then Phil wakes up from his dream, rolls over in bed and sees his beautiful wife Janis sleeping facing in his direction. He has a new family now, one he can call his own. He moves closer to her pulls her hair back and kisses her on the lips. She responds with a smile. "Well good morning there." He doesn't say anything and kisses her neck. "Oh, I see how it is." She says. Just as Phil moves closer to her, Janis gives him the strangest look he's ever seen.

"Baby?" He asks. Janis jumps out of bed and straight into the bathroom. Confused, Phil sits there for a second, but then hears his wife gagging in the bathroom. He runs in and sees her throwing up.

"You okay baby?" Phil asks as he holds her hair back with his hand on her back.

When she finishes she wipes her mouth and responds, "Yeah, just a little sick. Must be something we ate last night. I told you I hate Chinese food." She continues to say as she washes her mouth.

"I'm sorry hon, we won't eat Chinese anymore, I promise. Are you feeling better or do you feel like you have to go again?" He asks as he flushes the toilet.

"I think I'll be fine." She begins to wash her face and brush her teeth.

"Okay..." He kisses her on the cheek and let's her be by her self for a few minutes.

A short while later the phone rings and Phil picks up. "Hello?"... "Right now?".... "Okay, I'll be right there." He hangs up and begins to get dressed.

"What is it honey? Where are you going?" Janis asks.

"Oh nothing, just have to prepare some paperwork for Monday."

"What's on Monday? And why do you have to go, today is your day off?"

"You'll see. It's a surprise. Just something I have to get done today."

"Surprise? What does your work and paperwork have as a surprise for me?" She asks with an odd look on her face.

He holds her hands. "You'll see Miss Anxious." He kisses her on her lips, "Now don't worry about it, just trust me everything will be just fine, okay?"

"No, I don't like you leaving like this all the time, coming home so late, we don't get to see you as often anymore, and when we do this happens."

"Baby, this is my job, you know I need this. After what happened with my last job, I really want to make sure things go well here. I want to make sure my family gets the best I could give them. You know I never really had a family before, so I want to make sure..."

"Hey, we're not going anywhere. You just make sure *you* don't go anywhere. And I know this means a lot to you, but we miss you sometimes. *I* miss you. I just don't want your job to take over your life."

Phil smiles, "Don't worry, I'll be right here with you, the company is just going through a lot of changes right now so they need me. As soon as things get back to normal I'll be right here with you and Josh."

"You'll always be here?"

"Always."

Janis moves closer to Phil's ear and whispers, "Tell me the surprise."

Phil looks up at her with a smirk, "No!" He tackles her onto the bed and gives her a kiss. "You'll find out on Monday." He then continues to get dressed and then starts to walk out the door, "Hey I should be back in time for a late lunch, I was thinking I'd bring back some Chinese." He says jokingly.

Janis raises her eyebrow at him with an unamused look on her face, "It's alright I'll cook something."

Phil laughs, "Okay, baby I'll call you when I'm on my way back then." He kisses her then leaves.

***

Later that afternoon Phil returns home to find Janis in the family room sitting and knitting something.

"Baby? You okay? Why'd you need me to come so quick?" Phil asks as he walks in.

"We need to talk." She responds.

Phil's heard those words before and hates them. "Baby, what's wrong? Look I know I've been gone for a while, I'm sorry I'm late, it's just this whole thing at the company…"

"I'm pregnant."

"What?!"

"I'm pregnant Phil we did it, we did it baby we did it!" She jumps up and hugs her confused husband frantically.

"Oh my God, are you serious?!" He holds her back. She nods her head with a big smile as she begins to tear up.

"Oh my God we're pregnant!" He yells as they begin to jump up and down. He begins to kiss her. "Wait a minute how do you know? Are you sure?"

"Yeah, after you left I bought some pregnancy tests and they all came out positive. I wanted to wait 'til you got home to tell you, before I told anyone else."

"You didn't even tell your parents?"

"Nope, not yet."

"Well we better call them then!"

Just then Josh walks into the room. "What happened?" He asks, Phil and Janis look at each other with a smile, Janis walks over to Josh and gets down on her knee to be at eye level.

"Josh, honey, you are going to soon have a baby brother or sister." She says with a smile. He stands there for a moment then responds, "Really! I hope it's a brother!" He looks over at Phil, and the expression on his face changes. The last time he had a family he was betrayed and his father had left him and his mom.

Phil saw the change of expression and had somewhat of an idea of what Joshua felt. He walks over to him and gets on his knee. The eleven year old child stood there with his head tilted away and his hands clasped behind his back.

"Hey Josh, I know how you feel, having an addition to the family like this can be a scary thought. A lot of things change and no one knows what exactly is going to happen. But look we're going to need your help with the baby, whether it be a boy or girl, and I promise I'm going to stay here with you, I'm not going anywhere. Trust me I know what it feels like to be abandoned and left alone. My dad left me when I was a kid, and then my mom left me too. I promise I won't let that happen to you." He tilts Josh's head up and looks him in the eyes. "Hey we have fun don't we?" Josh nods his head yes. "You like me don't you?" He nods again. "I like you too, and don't you worry about a thing, all you have to worry about is thinking about how you're going to boss around your little brother or sister." He says with a smile.

"Okay dad." Josh hugs him and kisses him on the cheek, and then he runs off on his toes.

Janis and Phil both look at each other with an astonished look on their face. "Did he just...?" Phil asks and stops mid sentence.

"I don't know...I think he just did," Janis responds with the same level off surprise on her face, "I love you." She says to Phil as tears begin to fall from her eyes.

"Wow...I...I love you too." He responds still stunned by the moment. They smile at each other for a minute as they let everything that is happening sink into their minds. Then they kiss.

"Okay I'm going to call mom, and then let's eat okay *dad*?!" The sudden rush of everything that just happened overwhelms Janis. She can't remember the last time she was this happy.

"Yes let's hurry I'm starving!" He kisses her then sits there for a moment as Janis calls her mom. He can hear Janis starting to talk to her mother.

Phil has to sit down as the blood rushes away from his head and into his heart. 'Dad' Phil has never known what that had meant. It was one of those words people would say that had no meaning. It finally meant something to him. "'Dad,' it has a nice ring to it," Phil thinks to himself as he smirks. Things were finally going to change now. He wouldn't have to worry about anything anymore. He has a son, a wonderful wife, and a child on its way. A child…his very own child. He was going to be a father. Never having one of his own, a sudden scare erupted inside of Phil; to think that he was going to embark in something he knows nothing at about.

He looked at Janis and noticed her excitement as she spoke with her mother. She would be there with him, they would do this together. He'll learn and do everything for his child to raise it the right way, not like himself, not at all. As he thinks more of Janis and the baby he realizes that nothing can stop him now, and with the news being announced on Monday, things will be perfect. For once, things will go Phil's way.

"Baby," Janis says as she kneels down and holds Phil's face. He looks back at her with a humble stare in his eyes, "You okay?"

He waits a short moment, "Yeah, for the first time, I am."

Janis smiles at him and kisses him, "Okay babe let's eat, I'm eating and doing everything for two now so I'm going to need you here with me."

"Yeah, anything you need, I'm here."

"Good." She grabs his hand and they stand up and walk towards the dinner table to eat. "Joshua! Let's eat!" She yells out.

"Okay mom!"

***

"Josh, Josh hurry dad's going to be on the news soon!" Josh comes running into Janis' arms.

"We interrupt this program this evening with breaking news. Hello everyone I'm Amber K."

"And I'm Jim Rhines with USN action news. We're just about to tune into the press conference area with Highland Corporations, one of the largest energy providers today. They have called this meeting just recently and have invited all the news groups from around the world, this must be big."

"Yes, and right now we have no idea what will be announced, all we know is that this will be huge. After the fall of Orion Industries, Highland Corporations suffered a bit due to the lack of trust within the industry, but business has been booming ever since. Market analysts believe that today's revelation will take Highland stocks through the roof. They hope to go global soon and personally I don't think there's anything out there that can stop them, Jim."

"You're right, Amber, speculations say that this announcement could be anything from selling the highly respected corporation, to expansion over sees."

"That's right and while we wait we have correspondent Anthony Straight with us to give us more insight on this great revelation on which we will soon embark. Thank you so much for joining us on such short notice this evening, Anthony."

"Thank you Amber, it's my pleasure."

"Anthony, Jim Rhines here, at what level or better yet, how are you involved with Highland Corporations?"

"Hello Jim, I have been following Highland for almost ten years now, I know Mr. Hodges pretty well, and he always makes sure that I am there before any mile stone is uncovered by this noble company. I am one of the few outsiders he actually trusts to be there to cover stories and make sure the public is aware of what is happening with Highland Corporations at all times."

"Well having such trusts with such a secretive yet world renowned company you must be able to tell us something about this press conference this evening."

"Unfortunately Jim, even though I have close ties with the company I do not know many of their secrets. As an outsider I get to look into the snow globe called Highland Corporations just like all of you, I just usually get the first glance."

"Anthony, Amber K. again, what can you tell us about what we should expect from Highland Corporations in the next few moments?"

"Lord knows what it will be Amber, all I can say is that whatever it is it will change the world forever."

"Wow! That's quite the statement there, Mr. Straight, what makes you so confident in what you have just said?"

"Nothing and everything Amber."

"Ex…excuse me?"

"What I mean is that obviously I have no concrete answer for you on why I have made that statement and knowing as little as I do about this announcement I could just be blowing smoke about this subject for all that anyone knows. On the contrary though like I said I have been following this company for almost ten years now and we have never seen Highland Corporations pull such a precarious stunt…ever. For any well known company to have such a last minute conference and to invite news groups from all over the nation and all over the world this has to be big. This is no joke my friends. So to reiterate what I had said earlier nothing and everything makes me state that this announcement…this revelation will change the world as we know it."

"Anthony, Jim Rhines here again, you had mentioned earlier in your last comment that you in fact do have some information about this announcement that we are waiting upon, can you please elaborate and provide more detail on that part of your statement in more depth please?"

"Jim I can only tell you what I have said before, that this announcement is big! This technology is unprecedented!"

"Technology?"

"Yes, technology, what we are about to hear is something that will bring other energy companies to their knees!"

"That's quite the hostile statement there Anthony."

"It's the truth and that's all I can say about that."

"So you're saying that there is no way Earl Hodges is going to announce a sale in this press conference?"

"Ha ha ha, you must be insane. Sale…that thought never even crossed the man's mind. He owns a top notch cream of the crop energy source company that will change…"

"I'm sorry to interrupt Mr. Anthony Straight, but we're being pulled into the press conference right now, we're going to put you on standby until after the conference if that's okay."

"Sure Amber, Thank you."

"Thank you, ladies and gentlemen we're going to pull you in live with Katelyn Alman our field reporter to take it from here until after the press conference. Katelyn can you hear us?"

"Yes, thank you Amber and Jim, we're here live in Dallas, Texas at the outer steps of Highland Corporations, the giant building you see behind me is the base of Highland Corporations, they have set up the podium in front of their trademark symbol and statue the scorpion, because the building is set in front of a lake, space to surround the podium is limited and much of the press was forced to move back. Mr. Earl Hodges and his team including his board of directors are set to come out now at any given moment, just bare with us as my camera man tries to focus in on the podium…can you see okay back at home guys?"

"Just fine thank you Katelyn, have you uncovered any news for us thus far Katelyn, or are you also in the dark with us?" Asks Amber.

"Well sources tell me that there is some revolutionary technology being uncovered, but no one knows exactly what it is."

"What is the atmosphere like out there?"

"It's pretty unnerving Jim, at moments the crowd becomes very quiet and at other times uneasy mumbles take over the people, but just as it gets too loud people begin to quiet down again. It is the most unusual sight to see." The conversation is broken up by a rumbling noise coming from the crowd, "Here come the board of directors now accompanied by a team of researchers and lawyers."

"That's quite the team Katelyn."

"Indeed it is Amber, Earl Hodges should be coming out soon."

As they watch the television Janis points out to her son. "Look Josh there's daddy."

"Where?"

"Right there sweetie." She gets closer to the television to point out Phil.

"Oh…" He finally recognizes Phil, "Daddy!" He then shrieks.

"Yes, daddy!" Janis responds with a smile. She gives him a big hug and kiss as they return to the couch. They watch carefully as they await the coming of the long awaited president of the company.

"Here he comes; you can see him as he is turning the corner to walk up the stage."

Everyone watches with an unmoving gaze as Earl Hodges walks up the steps onto the stage with a beige three piece suit, white shirt, and a bow tie. His goatee was white and long from the chin. The crowd had grown lifelessly quiet within the past minute; it was as even the wind had stopped in to listen in on the great news. Earl Hodges approaches the podium.

"Hello…for those who don't know me I am Earl Landon Hodges, President and CEO of Highland Corporations, and thank you all for joining us on this day, this day of unprecedented history. All my life I have spent to perfect myself, to be the best, to float on uncharted waters." He begins to say with an unusually humble voice, "Up until a month ago I truly believed I had done it all, I believed if I had died that day I would have left contently from this Earth. Then a few days after, as I sat on the front porch of my Texas ranch watching my son round up the cattle, waiting for him to take over my kingdom while I counted down the days with my wife to when we would finally meet our maker, I received a phone call. Second to my son's birth this phone call was the most fascinating news I have ever received. It was from the head scientist from my laboratory. After our conversation I knew my life would change forever. I had more to live for; new challenges have come my way…God himself had spoken to me. At first I wasn't sure what to make of it so I had rushed over to my laboratory to see the production process with my own two eyes, it was the most unbelievable site I had ever seen…Ladies and gentlemen, we," He looks at both sides of him towards his team, "have rediscovered and are close to perfecting the science and the technology of Cold Fusion!"

The crowd gasps and rumbles with uneasiness. The jaws of the world drop; Earl Hodges raises his voice to overpower the restlessness and re-quiets the crowd. "When our rival company first embarked on this revolutionary technology we were running for the waters. After their unfortunate downfall, we wanted to make sure that our company, our investors, and most of all our loyal customers would never go through such another scare again…ever. We have been working on this technology for years and countless hours, and have said nothing. We did this not to deceive the public in any way, but in fact for the safety of our laboratories, our workers, and of course our technologies. Today we know we are close enough to the point where we have unlocked almost all of the secrets of this awesome power; we feel comfortable enough to share this information with not only our share holders, but the world. Cold Fusion ladies and gentlemen…Cold Fusion. This will energize the world, soon we will go global, and the world will never go through another night in the dark again…I want to thank you all once again for being here with us on this auspicious moment as we walk upon a new stepping stone in our lives and as we push for new limits as we take part in changing human history. I am a man of few words so I will take my leave now, thank you and may God bless."

He turns and starts to make his way off the stage. The reporters bombard him with questions and attempt to block his pathway. Security ward off the press with little luck, back up is called for them to help keep their strong hold. Earl Hodges' team follows him as he continues to his company's front door. All anyone can hear is a field of journalists yelling at the top of their lungs, "Mr. Hodges, Mr. Hodges!" Without acknowledging anyone's presence he and his team make their way into the building leaving the media in shock.

"He's gone…" Katelyn finally addresses the public listening in on their television sets, "Cold Fusion, one of the greatest discoveries known to man to date. Well there you have it back to you…Amber, Jim."

Back at the news room Amber stares blankly into the camera in a stunned state as if she had just seen a ghost. The announcement of Cold Fusion had suddenly thrown her back into the past she spent most of her time trying to forget. Her dark thoughts acted like a black hole never letting her fear escape, only deepening it. Her mind was becoming a death trap for signs of light or blissful thoughts. The cameraman and side directors try to get Amber's attention, but are unsuccessful. Jim stares at her for a moment and gets into action.

"Uh…There you go folks, after over a five year hiatus Cold Fusion is here with us once again." He says as the camera focuses on him and off of Amber, "Let's take a short break and we will discuss this more with correspondent Anthony Straight. Anthony are you still with us?"

"Uh…Yes Jim."

"Great, we'll be right back America."

***

"Son of a bitch!" Max Johnson yells out as he throws his remote across the room shattering the television in front of him.

"Is…is everything okay sir?" Carl asks as he sheepishly comes through the door.

"I thought the Cold Fusion reports were secure." Max says.

"They were…I mean…they are. Why?"

"Then how does Highland Corporations now have the technology to produce it?"

"Sir?"

"You heard me." Max's voice becomes darker.

"Sir, he said himself they have been working on the project for years."

"They have, have they?" He begins to walk over to Carl.

"Ye…yes sir." Carl begins to tremble.

"And there is no way you let Jerry sell them the information?" Max asks darkly.

"No not at all sir."

"So you've kept your eye on him this whole time like I told you to?"

"Well see the thing is sir you've put me on six different projects and…" Before he could finish Max had snapped his neck and continued walking out the door.

"Cindy."

"Yes Mr. Johnson." The secretary in front of his office calls out.

"Cancel everything I have, I'm going on a business trip for the next few days." He continues to walk towards the elevator never breaking stride.

"Yes, Mr. Johnson."

He turns around and faces the secretary as he gets into the elevator, "Oh and Cindy?"

"Yes?"

"There's a mess in my office please make sure it's cleaned up."

The elevator closes.

Chapter 29

The Dallas Star

...And this Saturday night Highland Corporations will be announcing the details of the Cold Fusion project to its investors in Houston, Texas at their annual banquet held at the Westin Galleria in the Woodway Hall. Reports suggest that even the president of the United States may attend this event, accompanied by other politicians from around the world. Skeptics are concerned that this may be another flop on the Cold Fusion end, considering the 'accidental' explosion at Artemis Laboratories with the former Orion Industries over five years ago. Only time will tell if such an energy source will actual bring us to the future instead of setting us back once more in our struggle to achieve this priceless energy source to fuel the world's economy...

"No, no, no!" Robert yells throwing the newspaper across his flower shop. It smashes into a pot dropping it to the ground and breaking it, "This can't be, it just can't be!" He lifts up another newspaper. He reads the same thing, "This was my idea! Mine! They can't just take it." He begins to weep in the corner of the flower shop, the same corner where he always weeps. He covers his head with his dirty hands smearing the dirt onto his face. As he sits there he hears a voice.

"If it's yours then go ahead take it back." A dark high pitched voice says to him.

"Who...who's there? Store's closed for today." He says out loud as he cries.

"What's really holding you back Robert?" The voice continues.

He stands up. "Who's there?!" He looks around the shop. "How do you know my name? I'm going to call the police!"

"A man makes his own destiny, doesn't he Robert?"

He catches a glance in the mirror next to him and sees his own poor shape and soiled face. "Shut up! Shut up! Shut up!" He begins to pull the hair on his head realizing that the sounds are coming from inside his head. He begins to understand that he is going crazy and starts to laugh as he curls up on the floor.

"So Robby, are you going to go get what's yours?"

"They stole it from me…It was my glory…Mine!"

"Yes…yes they did…are you going to let them get away with that? Are you going to let your whole life's work just slip out of your hands?"

"No…" Robert whispers.

"You have to go get it back you have to crush whoever stands in your way."

"How?" He responds to the voice.

"The banquet."

"The banquet?"

"Yes, this Friday night the night before the banquet, you have to stop him take back what's yours."

"If I can't?"

"Then use force, do whatever it takes Robby even if it means taking his life."

"Murder?"

"No…revenge."

"Yes, revenge."

"Robby…" Another voice fires off in his head.

"Mom?"

"Robby what are you doing?" The woman's voice is oddly calm.

"Mom, they stole my idea, they stole my life."

"No Robby you did this to yourself, and now you have to pay for it. Stand up Robby, be the man you were meant to be. Be the man who you used to be."

"I can't mom, I don't know him anymore."

"You can be him by taking back what's yours." The dark voice reappears.

"Yes, I can do that. Then I will be Robert Allen Heyward." He tilts up his head with arrogance, "No one will be able to stop me again then. I have to kill Earl Hodges and take back what's mine!"

"No Robby you were raised better than that." The calm womanly voice comes back, "Is this what you want to teach Ryan, is this what you want to show Michael?"

"Isn't this what you want to show Sandra?" The dark voice fires back, "Don't you want to show her who's the man in charge? Don't you want her in your arms instead of fucking some guy in your bed?!"

"Shut up!" He covers his ears, but the images flash in his mind mixed with memories of him and her.

"Robby," The soft voice says, "you've lived too long like this…too long, it's time to make things right. Listen to reason, do it the right way, like your father, like you did before. You remember that don't you, how you used to be? How you became a big man without stealing one penny, without hurting one person?"

"And look where it got you *Robby*, look at you now laying on the floor with your hands over your ears rocking back and forth listening to voices in your head. Do you want to die like this or do you want to die respected? Who will come to your funeral Robby? Will you even have one? Die respected if nothing else Robert, die a man."

"You have to live like one first." The soft voice fires back, "You want to live respected, when your children look back at you, when your family looks at you, they should be able to look you in the eye. They should be able to have reverence in your existence."

"Family? She means the family that left you with nothing? Is that the family she is talking about? Or is she talking about your dead family? Because your dead family will never come back to see you. And that piece of shit family you had hates you. Your so called wife was too busy thinking about herself for you to ever be a part of her life. She took the first chance she got to run. Have you had any major problems or ridiculous fights with her before? No, because you couldn't, every time you would fight she would throw that conniving blood sucking God in your face. You started going to church, was God there? When Artemis burned down was God there? What about when little Sandra died was God there? Where is God?

God is just a stupid word made up so filthy humans like your wife don't feel that their insignificant lives have no meaning. God is an invisible false idle, nothing more. Even your own son turned on you. Your own flesh and blood. And the other one…Ryan…pities you…that's all. When you leave he laughs at you. You are nothing but charity to them, a stray dog. If you take what is yours they will see what they have lost, they will regret their actions. They will suffer from your success." The dark voice coaxes.

"Yes, yes!" Robert replies with great enthusiasm.

"Robby, don't you love Sandra?" The soft voice asks, reminding him of her eyes, "Look at her isn't she beautiful?" She asks about the memory he is seeing, "And Michael, he is just misunderstood that is all, just like you. Don't you know what it feels like, to be misunderstood? Don't you miss Ryan? Don't you miss how he looks up at you with those unrelenting trusting eyes? It's time to be noble again Robby." The voice stiffens, "Join forces with Hodges, work with him…perfect the technology. Wasn't that the point, to help the world? Or was the point greed Robby?"

"The world." Robert replies.

"Then go work with him, make this world strong, have them remember you for what you accomplished, not what you almost accomplished."

"Robert," The dark voice darts in, "don't be a fool, don't make the same mistake twice. Your father taught you that! Go to the convention the day before, meet Hodges and *have a word* with him. I'm sure throughout your life you've learned how people can be convincing. Do whatever it takes to *convince* the man just don't let the opportunity of your life slip through your fingers once again, there is no one standing in your way this time Robby…No one."

"You're right!" Robert stands up and walks out the flower shop.

Chapter 30

In a bar in Houston, Texas.

"For he's a jolly good fellow, for he's a jolly good fellow, for he's a jolly good fellow… That nobody can deny!" Everyone laughs and sings as they hit each other's beer mugs and drink.

"Ha, ha, ha! You guys are crazy you know that?" Says an older thin man as he drinks his beer.

"Man one more week then I won't have to see your ugly mug anymore Brown!" Says another shorter fatter man as he hugs him.

"Travis, if cheese ever had bad breath, I know for damn sure it would smell like yours." Everyone laughs.

"Well you're not off the team yet Brown so it's chief to you." Brown smiles at him and they both put up their glasses towards each other and drink. He turns to Brown's wife, "And how are you Melody?" He asks as he kisses her hand.

"Just fine Travis thank you." She responds with a smile.

"How are the kids?"

"Just great, I hope you and your wife will be coming over soon." Melody says.

"Well as soon as I can get that old bag off the couch we will definitely make that trip." He responds.

"Hey Brown do we get a speech tonight or what?!" Someone yells out from the back of the bar.

"Yeah Brown out with it!" A woman follows.

The whole room then goes in an uproar, "Speech, speech, speech, speech!" They yell as they pound their fists and beer bottles against the tables.

"Charlie?" He says to the bartender as if to ask permission.

"I guess they want a speech old friend." The bartender replies as he hands Brown another beer.

"Come on give the crowd what they want Franky, huh?" The chief says as he tries to convince Brown.

"Alright, alright!" He says as he slowly begins to stand up. He then takes another sip of his beer and points and smiles at one of his colleagues as he prepares to speak to his peers. "One more week boys!" Everyone cheers.

"And ladies!" A woman yells out from the background.

"And ladies, Martha," He responds, "one more week," he says softer. "I'm really gonna miss you guys you know?"

"We love you too Brown!" A man yells out.

"Ha, ha, but it's been fun you know? My whole career I've been trying to take this big good for nothing's job and I couldn't do it." He says while looking at the chief, "Well I guess it's up to you Greasy." He points to a man in the crowd.

"Don't worry Franky I got it!" He yells out as everyone laughs.

"Seriously though, Travis...chief...You've been like a father to me, you taught me everything I know. You've taken care of me and my family when in need and you never let me take it easy. I'll never forget that, so thank you." The chief raises his beer bottle towards Brown.

"To my beautiful wife, thank you. I know being on the force has taken its toll on our lives, but without your support I wouldn't have made it this far. All those nights working on cases not being able to come home was all for you. I love you baby, and thank you." He smiles at her

"I love you too." She says as she smiles back.

"And all of you..." He looks back at the crowd, and everyone cheers and hoots, "All of you are like family to me, but I want each and every one of you to know, especially you Tony...that I'm changing my phone number and address so none of you better try to find or contact me ever again!" He says jokingly as everyone laughs and claps.

"You know we're all trained to find you where ever you go right Franky?!" Tony yells out.

"Yeah, yeah unfortunately that's true, so I guess if you all ever need anything come on by whenever you'd like, and you can say hello every now and then too." The crowd replies with awes. Brown begins to turn red and tear up a little bit. He regains his posture. "Alright, alright now that's enough! Now, once again thank you all, seriously thank you. And let me end this speech by reminding all of you that tonight's tab is on Travis here so drink up everyone!"

"Yeah!" The crowd cheers, claps, and screams for Brown. The chief then stands up on a chair to get everyone's attention.

"Excuse me everyone. Excuse me!" He then whistles loudly and everyone immediately quiets down to listen to the chief. "Listen up…Thank you! Now let me start off by saying you poor losers are covering your own tabs tonight!" Everyone boos the chief, "Yeah, yeah put a cork in it! Anyway I'm standing here to make sure all of you know who this man really is." He looks over at Brown, "Franky you are one of the most modest sons of bitches that I know! People this man has never missed an assignment, never not completed a task, and almost never not solved a mystery…ever. Franky, we'd all be lucky to be half the detective you are. I want you to know even though at times we've butt heads you've always been like a son to me. We are going to be losing a great man from the force guys; it's up to all of us to try to fill these shoes as a team." He looks over to Brown, "They don't make us like they used to anymore do they son?"

"No they do not." Brown responds while raising his beer bottle.

"We're gonna miss you buddy, we love you Franky." He begins to tear up. The crowd also begins to tear up somewhat as well. The chief coughs then gathers himself. "Ah-hem…Alright, anyway, from the force we got you this old pal." He pulls out a small box, "It's an honorary chief medal of honor."

"What?!" Brown yells out. The chief opens the box and Brown's eyes widen. He then walks over to the chief as he has his arm extended to shake Brown's hand. Instead Brown moves his hand and gives the chief a huge bear hug. Everyone rejoices and laughs.

"You're the best kid." The chief whispers in his ear.

"Thank you so much." Brown responds.

The chief backs off and tries to gain control of the crowd again, "Alright, alright! Enough with the mushy stuff! I know all you good for nothings have work in the morning so don't get too piss drunk tonight!" He gets back down off the chair. The crowd responds by looking away trying to ignore the comment and continue conversation. Brown goes around and mingles with the rest of the crowd as they all drink and enjoy the night away.

Chapter 31

"Hey, you okay Amber?" Greg asks as he catches up to walk with Amber in the studio after work.

"Yeah Greg." Amber responds.

"You sure?"

"Yeah." She replies slightly irritated, "Why?" She stops and faces him.

"Well all this week you've been acting a little…strange." He says searching for the right words to say.

"Strange?" She asks with confusion.

"…Yeah…you've been off your game and everyone's noticed. I thought after a few days you would shrug it off, but it seems like something has you really bothered. So what's up?"

She shrugs her shoulders, "Nothing Greg just got a lot on my mind that's all."

"Like what? You know you can tell me anything you want." He says trying to be as comforting as possible.

"It's nothing, really."

"Here come with me." He motions her inside his office, "Okay no one else is here, what's going on with you Amber, was it the Highland story?" He asks already knowing the answer.

Amber puts her head down, "It's just when I heard the whole Cold Fusion story it just brought me back to a bad time in my life something I really didn't want to revisit. I finally had come to terms with it and thought it was behind me…but I guess not…"

Greg knew she was talking about Harvey and stood silently with her for a moment, "…Hey, you know I'm right here for you, I've always told you if you need anything you can come to me. You've become like a daughter to me over the years and I want you to know that if there is anything I can ever do I'll do it."

"I know…" She says with her head down.

He puts his hands on her shoulders, "Look, you haven't taken any breaks or days off for a very long time why don't you take a couple weeks off for vacation to take your mind off of things and then come back when you're refreshed. We'll have one of the interns take your spot for the time being as filler. This way we can all step back from the situation and come back strong."

"No!" She shouts out then catches herself in the act, feeling foolish she then lowers her tone, "I'm just fine Greg I'll blow it all off by the morning I promise, just give me one more chance."

"Amber I'm not firing you or anything I just think you need a break." He continues to be as comforting as possible.

"Well I don't, I know things have gotten a bit out of hand, but I'm telling you I'm fine and by tomorrow morning it will be the old Amber again." She puts on a fake smile as she says it.

"Are you sure about this?"

"Yes I'm sure."

"Amber in a couple days is the Highland Corporation annual banquet. They're going to be talking about Cold Fusion and I really need my lead anchor to be on her A game that day. Do you understand that?" She nods her head yes, "If that doesn't happen, we're going to have problems." She looks up at him, "Now that's not me talking that's the people who are on my ass to make sure that whoever is speaking is doing their job talking. Now I know it's only been a week, but look you really need to get it together. I've been busting my ass for you waiting for this to go away, but this business is tough. If you need to take a break please take it now, or else come back tomorrow with all of this behind you for good."

Amber shakes her head slightly disappointed and bites her bottom lip to not saying anything stupid. She then puts on a big smile, "Whatever you say Mr. Howard, I guess I'll see you tomorrow bright and early!" She says as she begins to walk away.

"Oh come on Amber don't do this, it's not my call!"

"Okay Mr. Howard!" She puts up her hand to say good-bye but only has her middle finger pointed up. She then slams through the doors in front of her.

"Amber...!"

Chapter 32

"Good evening Allison!" Phil says with excitement as he walks into Highland Corporation's office building. "Shouldn't you be home by now?" Phil coughs.

Confused to see Phil she replies "…Evening Mr. Roderick, I had to get much of my work done tonight and I have to make sure all the notes are together for tomorrow's gala, speaking of which, aren't you supposed to be in Houston right now?" She says back half playfully and sarcastically as she tilts her head down and stares at him from the top of her glasses.

"Yeah I am, but just like you I have to finish up some last minute details for tomorrow," Phil coughs again, "I'll probably be too worn out tonight to go so I think I might just leave in the morning with the family." He coughs and sniffles a little bit, "Are you leaving for Houston tomorrow as well?"

"No sir tomorrow I leave for Australia." She says excitedly, "Remember tonight is my last night with this company then I retire. You've been so busy lately that you didn't even stop by at my retirement party for cake." She chuckles.

Phil has a dumbfounded look on his face, "Oh my God Allison I'm so sorry. You know things have been insane…"

"Don't mention it Mr. Roderick," She cuts him off, "I know how it is around here, besides I'll be on a beach in Australia while you will be in a boring banquet." She says with a smile.

"Ha, ha you're right." Phil replies, still feeling somewhat speechless to the fact that he had forgotten her retirement. He searches his coat pocket for a moment then he finds what he was looking for, "Allison, I know I wasn't able to get you a good-bye present so why don't you take this as a token of my appreciation and as an apology?"

Allison looks at him strangely, "A cigar?" She asks.

"Not just any cigar, but one of my absolute favorites, a Cohiba cigar, one of the finest and most popular in the world. And it doesn't come that cheap by the way."

"Well thank you Mr. Roderick, but I don't smoke, but it was a nice try." She replies jokingly.

"Oh come on if you don't take it it'll break my heart, give it to your husband I'm sure he will appreciate a finely hand wrapped cigar while the both of you are lying on the beach enjoying the sun and drinking your wine coolers." He says trying to convince her with his smile and tone.

Allison thinks for a second then responds, "Okay fine…" She takes the cigar, "Thank you Mr. Roderick."

"Now how bout you leave me your address before you leave and I'll look you up sometime." He coughs harder now.

"Of course Mr. Roderick by the way are you getting sick, or is it all that smoking that is finally getting to you?"

"I think I'm getting sick Allison," He says as he clears his throat and raises his eyebrow at her, "with my wife being a nurse you'd think this would never be a problem huh?" He responds jokingly, as they both laugh.

"How is your wife by the way?"

"She's good and the baby seems to be healthy, so that's all I care about."

"Anyway have you seen Earl at all for the past week?"

Allison sits back and thinks for a moment, "You know, now that you've mentioned it I haven't seen him since the night of the announcement. A man in an army type suit walked in here they both walked out and I haven't seen him since. I mean I got emails from Mr. Hodges on things I needed to get done, but that's about it as far as communicating with him is concerned. Why, have you seen him at all?"

"No, not at all since that same day. Odd isn't it?"

Allison nods her head yes then abruptly stops. "Oh Mr. Roderick since you are headed to your office would you mind leaving this file in Mr. Hodges' office; I just haven't had the time to stand up and move from my desk all day." She says as she pulls out a large envelope.

"Sure." He extends his arm and takes the envelope and glances at the header.

"Apollo Industries? What's this for?"

"I don't really know Mr. Hodges said in his email to expect important mail from Apollo Industries and that it is of top importance."

"Did he tell you what it was about?"

"Nope, I don't ask questions Mr. Roderick I just follow orders."

"You said that the man that Mr. Hodges walked out with was wearing an army type suit?"

"Yes…"

"What did he look like?"

"Umm…He was a tall muscular man, didn't really get much of a look at him. Why? What's with all the questions?" She asks feeling as she was being interrogated for a crime scene.

"Max." Phil says softly.

"What?"

"Uh…nothing, just…just had a weird thought." He says as he coughs some more, "Anyway I will deliver this and then I'll see you on my way out then Allison?" He says trying to divert the conversation.

"Um…Yes Mr. Roderick.

"Please Allison, call me Phil." He says as he smiles then taps the counter with the envelope and walks away.

Phil makes his way through the long corridor to the elevators. As he makes his way up he wonders about the company and his future. He knows something weird is going on, but can't really grasp what. He stares at the envelope for a moment. As the elevator opens he decides to by pass Hodges' office and goes straight to his own. On his way there he notices that he has begun to walk faster and has become more anxious. As his pace picks up Phil checks his coat pockets again he notices that he has only one cigar left and pulls it out. He storms into his office turns on the light and gets to his desk. He then pulls out his lighter and lights the cigar. Once he takes his first nerve calming puff he looks down at the envelope. He then studies the Apollo logo on the seal of the envelope and tears it open to find official documents inside. The first document he pulled out was some sort of agreement document, which Phil begins to skim over.

This document states that Highland Corporation agrees to sell all of its assets to Apollo Industries…This turnover will take effect as a 'merger' to the extent of expanding the industry as we know it…in two months from the date this document is signed the merger will take effect. Earl Landon Hodges will forfeit all owned stock of Highland Corporation to Apollo Industries in care of General Maximus Edward Johnson CEO for the above stated price.

Phil ruffles through the other documents in the packet and finds out all the details about the merger. He screams as the rage engulfs his chest and flows into his arms down to his hands. He can feel the blood in his eyes. He takes the glass scorpion on his desk and launches it across the office. It smashes into the wall and explodes as the glass particles fall like hail onto the ground. Phil then barges into Hodges' office he remembered he had a spare key for emergencies.

***

Downstairs in the lobby of Highland Corporations, Robert runs through the doors and surprisingly finds a receptionist at the front desk.

"Ex…excuse me, can I help you?" Allison asks slightly startled.

"Hi…Uh yes…I'm Alex…Thompson and I was wondering if I could speak with Earl Hodges please." He asks looking flustered he gave her a fake name knowing Hodges wouldn't meet him knowing who he was.

"I'm sorry sir, but Mr. Hodges isn't in right now, and you'd have to make an appointment if you would wish to meet with him."

"He's not? Well do you know where he is?"

"Yes, in Houston for the Highland banquet tomorrow."

"Oh, he left early? Well I have urgent news for him and I need to see him immediately can you tell me what hotel he'll be staying in?"

"No, not at all sir. I don't even know who you are. And he didn't leave early, the banquet is tomorrow, when did you expect him to leave?"

"Please you don't understand the importance of this." He says desperately trying to convince her.

"Well if you tell me I'll make a note of it, and when he comes in Monday morning he will have it waiting for him on his desk."

"Well if that was the case it wouldn't be urgent now would it?!" Robert realizes his tone by the look on the receptionist's face. "I'm sorry, I really need to get to him right away. I need your help please."

"I'm sorry sir not even *I* know where he staying. If it was such an emergency why didn't you come in earlier like I don't know, yesterday?"

Robert thinks about his struggles he went through this whole week with himself. How he finally shaved and dressed up and how hard it was to look at himself in the mirror. "I just got the news now. Is there anything you can do, give me a phone number anything?"

"Sorry sir I can't."

Robert puts his head down on the counter out of frustration and disappointment he lays his head there for a short moment. Just then he feels a small wind, and then a muffled voice.

"Allison I've decided to go to Houston tonight after all, I have to see Earl on some important business. You enjoy Australia and take it easy okay?"

"Okay goodnight Mr. Ro…" He had left before she could finish her sentence.

Phil rushes back in, "To get to Comfort Inn Two Ninety what exit do I take?"

She stares at Robert, he seems to be asleep, then looks back at Phil, "Take forty five south to Two Ninety East I believe."

"Thanks Allison you're the best."

"Bye."

Phil rushes out the door again and as he gets to his car he hits a small pole that was only knee high to prevent cars crashing into the building. "Son of a bitch!" He yells out as he grabs his knee. The papers in his hands fall to the ground. He hurriedly gathers them all; He cuts his index finger on some sharp object on the ground, "Fuck!" He says angrily to himself. Frustrated he gets up rushes into his car and lights his cigar, the warmth of it helps soothe his finger. He puts the car in gear and speeds off.

Robert had heard the whole conversation and pretended to act asleep so the receptionist wouldn't think he heard her. The plan worked.

"Comfort Inn?" He had spent one night there because he wanted to originally open his flower shop in Houston, but decided on Dallas instead. He felt the torture of the memory of where he first met Sandra; the thoughts made him feel closer to her. He wonders if it's the same hotel though. He then feels a nudge on his shoulder.

"Sir? Sir? Sir! If there is nothing else I can do for you, you have to leave sir." She says trying to wake him up.

"Huh, yeah, well okay I guess I'll be back on Monday then." He says while pretending to wake up.

"Okay, you do that sir." She faces back to her computer working on some notes and checking email.

"Actually, can I leave my phone number here?" He says as he reaches for his pen, it slips out of his hand next to the receptionist's hands. When he reaches over to retrieve it she screams out of fear thinking he's attacking her and sprays him with her mace. He jerks back screaming and hits his head on the counter, giving him a deep cut on his cheekbone under his left eye. She picks up the phone and begins to call security. Robert begins to stumble away and out the doors. She watches as Robert hurriedly and painfully makes his way out of the building.

"God damn drunks always have to come and bother me! One last night and I'm finally out of here!" She says in an irritated voice as she gets back to her work.

Robert makes his way out and runs towards his car and as he does he is brought down to his knees. He felt as if a baseball bat was swung across into his right knee. He looks up as tears fill his eyes to find a small knee-high pillar. He slowly gets up and as he does something on the floor catches his eye. He bats his eyes trying to clear them, then he rubs them until he can see more clearly. He picks up the piece of paper and takes a better look at it. It was the check in itinerary for Earl Landon Hodges at Comfort Inn/Two Ninety Northwest, room five thirteen. Double Queen Non-Smoking.

"Yes!" Robert yells out in a sense of accomplishment, he then slowly gets up feeling the pain even more now in his knee and limps over to his car. When he gets in he looks over at the dagger he had brought and takes off. While sitting in the car the voices in his head start to go off again.

"Yes Robert, stare at that dagger…take it in your hands and bathe it in his blood. Take his life, and take back what's yours." The dark voice repeats the same lines over and over in his head.

"His life will be just the first step to your downfall Robert?" The womanly voice chimes in.

"Shut up, shut up, both of you just leave me alone!" Robert yells out trying to protect his mind from insanity.

"The first step to your downfall? Do you hear that Robert she's a fool? Listen to me that life has made you suffer through out your whole career…end it all, let this be a new beginning in your story. Make the pig pay for his mistakes let yourself rise once again Robert. This is your last chance!"

"He's right Robert this is your last chance to choose which path you will follow. Who are you Robert? Have you forgotten? Is this what your father taught you? Is this what your mother taught you? Do you think this is how you will get your family back? Make the right choice Robert, make the righteous choice."

"There is only one choice Robert and that is to take back your life…"

The evil voice is cut off by an odd sound coming from the car. The car slows down and then stops in the middle of the highway. A pickup truck nearly misses his car as it swerves out the way honking its horn profusely. Confused, Robert starts the engine again; the car starts for a moment and has enough energy to travel over to the shoulder. Traffic is light but the few cars that do pass him also honk at him urging him to get off the road.

"Yeah, yeah I'm moving!" He yells back at them. He looks down at his gages and notices that the gas tank is completely empty. "How did I not notice?" He thinks to himself. "Stupid voices see what you did!" He yells out but, he gets no response. He looks ahead to see any signs, and then sees a gas station it is less than a few minutes' walk ahead. He takes out the key from the ignition and locks the car leaving the emergency lights blinking. He begins his walk towards the gas station.

***

"Explain to me why we are in such a crappy motel again dad. I'm telling you we should have just stayed at the Westin just like everyone else."

"Because Bryan, before you embark on such a great venture that will change your life forever you must live life in a humble fashion." Hodges explains to his son. "You have to see that money and comfort isn't everything, your mother taught me that. You have to learn that if you let all of this get to your head, then you will lose your head. Besides I don't want any reporters, investors, or anyone else for that matter to know where we are to bother us the night before the grand gala. I don't feel like being a part of any weird scandals at this point in my career. I don't like people knowing where I am when they don't have to. Anyway instead of looking into why we are staying here, you should ask why I have finally asked you to come here the night before instead of the night of. And why you are here instead of your mother."

"Well...why am I here?"

"I wanted to talk to you son, just you and me so your mother will join us tomorrow at the gala. Anyhow, it's time for you to start venturing on your own, in just a few short months, you know, the company will no longer be ours, I want you to take whatever money you need and do something grand with your life. Be greater than your father, I was greater than mine, and he was greater than his. The moment you begin to digress is the moment you setback generations upon generations of building the Hodges' empire." Hodges walks over to him, "Look at me son, I never asked you for anything nor have I asked you to do anything this significant. Whatever you have ever wanted in your life I have provided for you. I don't want anything back from you, I want you to be happy, and I want you to be successful. The line of business I was in I had to do many things I'm not too proud of, but they had to be done. With what you have now, you will never have to go through that. I have given you something a Hodges man has never able to give his son, the freedom to be great without any barricades. Promise me you'll be great son."

"I promise, dad."

Earl smiles at his son, "That's my boy." He gives him a hug and pats him on the back. "Now that we got that out the way, I forgot some documents at the Galleria when we were there earlier today, and also I feel a late night hunger comin' my way so how bout you take the car out and get us some tacos or something and also see if you can get my papers?"

"You want me to take the Aston?"

"Hell, sure why not? You're a grown man, you can do it."

"Alright…I'll be right back, but the Galleria is like fifteen to twenty minutes away so it might take a short while." He says as he darts towards the keys.

"Well…I was hoping it would, I wanted you to get accustomed to your new car!"

"…What?" He abruptly stops.

"You heard me boy!" Hodges says with a big smile.

"Get out of here!" Bryan rushes over to his father and tackles him with a hug. They both laugh. "You're kidding right, please tell me you're kidding, dad don't mess with me. It's just not right."

"Son, you don't want me to change my mind now do you?"

"No, not at all…Thanks dad." He says with a sincere voice.

"Don't worry about it son, now get off of me I think you punctured my lung." He says jokingly. Bryan helps his father up as they both laugh.

"What do you want to eat dad?"

"It doesn't matter as long as it has cheese or steak…preferably both!" He says while laughing.

Bryan laughs back, "Okay, dad I'll see you in a bit." He rushes out the door and makes his way down in the elevator he is so excited that he can barely stand still.

The elevator finally gets to the first floor Bryan dashes out the elevator accidentally running into a couple. "Hey! What the hell are you doing?!" The man yells out.

"Sorry, sorry." Bryan apologizes and collects himself; he then helps up the young man and his wife. He apologizes again and runs out of the lobby and stares in awe in front of his new prize. He let's the joy sink in for a moment then gets into the car. He pulls out violently and speeds off almost crashing into a car as it is coming in.

"Son of a bitch!" Phil yells out, "Wait a minute was that Hodges' car that just pulled out? It didn't look like him in it…" Phil tries to redirect his focus and parks his car. "That son of a bitch is going to pay for this." He shuffles through his papers trying to find the itinerary for Hodges' room, but can't seem to find it. Frustrated he throws everything into the back seat of his car distorting all of the documents.

"Damn it what was the room number? Three fifteen? Three fourteen? Damn it, fuck, fuck, fuck!" He tries to think deeper going through the documents in his head. He reads the lines perfectly up until the line where it has the room number. He gets out the car and decides to try his luck. He opens the door to the backseat and gathers his papers once more, but more carefully this time and runs into the building. He takes the elevator to the third floor. He knocks on room three fifteen. "Open up Hodges!" No answer, "I said open up this God damn door!" A large black man opens up the door. It almost seemed as if he would do a better job in protecting the room than the door would. He steps out into the hallway almost pushing Phil backwards.

"What do you want man?" He says starring down at Phil.

Phil looks behind him and sees a naked woman then he looks back at the large man, "Sorry wrong room."

Without saying a word, the large man walks back into the room and slams the door closed. Phil then tries room three fourteen. This time he knocks more discretely, but still firm.

"Open up Hodges." No answer. He knocks again. "Open up damn it." No answer. He stands there knocking for about a minute and got the same result. "Maybe it was Hodges who left in the car," He thinks to himself. "Damn it!" He yells as he kicks the wall. Then a thought occurs to him. Maybe Allison would know what room he is in. He pulls out his cell phone and calls the office. It rings a few times no answer then voicemail. He calls again. This time there was an answer.

"Highland Corporation?"

"Allison!" Phil yells out in surprise.

"Yes?" She asks confused.

"It's Phil I have a question."

"Oh yes Mr. Roderick…I…I mean Phil."

"Do you know where Earl is staying tonight?"

"Yes at the Comfort Inn sir remember I gave you directions."

"Yes, yes I know, I meant what room."

"Oh let me check." She starts searching on her computer, "Ah, here I found it, room…five thirteen sir."

"*Five* thirteen?!"

"Yes sir."

"Oh thank you Allison! I love you!"

"Sir?"

"Just thank you Allison, you're the best."

"Well I do what I can." They hang up. Phil turns around, as the elevator opens behind him, and jumps in. He hits five and the elevator starts to make its way up. The anger within him grows with every passing moment. He clenches and unclenches his hands as they constantly become more and more moist. The elevator finally reaches the fifth floor, before the doors can completely open Phil is already walking out with a quick pace to room five thirteen. He stands in front of the door for a brief moment to collect himself and then knocks on the door with an odd calmness. There were three hard death ridden knocks. He hears a voice from the other end.

"Bryan? You back already?"

Knowing for sure that Hodges is on the other end this time Phil pulls out his partially smoked cigar and lights it again. The taste has an odd mixture blood, sweat, and smoke. The cigar seemed to have been dried out, but he didn't care. After he takes his first puff he knocks again in the exact same fashion as he did before.

"Who the hell is that?" Hodges says as he opens the door. He sees Phil standing outside, "Phil? What the hell are you doing here?"

"What the hell is this?" Phil asks shoving the documents into Hodges' chest. Phil forces himself into the room as Hodges is taken aback a little.

"Oh so you saw these huh?" Hodges asks as Phil walks past him into the room blowing smoke into the air, "Why don't you come in Phil?" He asks sarcastically as he eyes him, "You know if that bitch of a concierge wasn't retiring she definitely would be fired. Anyway what the hell do you want Phillip?"

Phil really didn't know how to answer that question. Flustered he takes another puff from his cigar and finally responds, "Why didn't you tell me about this? I mean I thought you trusted me. Why would you do this to me?" He says while desperately trying to keep his composure.

Hodges' walks over to Phil and looks him in the eye. He then removes the cigar from Phil's mouth, confusing and annoying Phil at the same time. "You know smoking *will* kill you, it's a disgusting habit, and I've told you never to bring it around me boy."

"There are a lot of things that can kill you." Replies Phil, knowing the only reason he lit the cigar was to annoy him, "So why the *hell* didn't you tell me what was going on Earl?" He asks in a deeper deadlier voice.

"First of all I don't owe you a damn thing to tell you what's going on with my business at anytime." Hodges responds as he makes his way to the suite's desk which is located in front of the open window where he was doing his work before Phil's arrival. "Secondly I only trust you from as far as I can shoot you." He rubs the end of the cigar in the ashtray and then looks at it to make sure it was out. He puts the cigar in his front jacket pocket. "And finally, this is my company. This is my legacy and I will do whatever the hell I please with it, including doing something like selling it. Now I would take it kindly if you would turn your good for nothing behind around and walk your sorry self out of my room."

"You know I changed my whole life for you. I moved here, I changed the life of my family; I even killed someone for you. I don't deserve this!"

"Son all those things are just part of getting a job. Three years ago you were in my office begging for a job. Not even the local law office would hire you because of your shadiness, and your ridiculously overpriced salary. I had the heart to help you provide that home for your family and that poor excuse for a ring for your wife. And by the way…" His voice gets deeper, "Killing that man was your idea not mine."

"I'll fucking kill you for this old man." Phil equivalently deepens his own voice. "You're going to pay for this."

"Killing a little weasel like you isn't as fun as you would think it would be. No I like to see pathetic people like you suffer. I knew you would try something stupid that's why I held onto the knife with your prints on it and with Weinberg's blood on it. Now you wouldn't want that getting to the police some how would you? I mean after all you are in Texas. With a possible death penalty or life sentence for a murder like that, how do think that would make the kid and the wife feel? Especially with my political pull, it wouldn't matter how good of a lawyer you were you would be sentenced before the bailiff could finish his own sentence. And what about that baby you have on the way? Who will take care of it, Phil?"

"You son of a bitch!" Phil runs in his direction about to swing a punch at Hodges' face, but is stopped with the sight of a gun pointed at his face.

"Son, you obviously are not from the south. Don't you know any respectable southerner always carries a gun in his pocket just in case he comes across some Yankee Doodle fool like yourself? Now you're really beginning to try my patience here." Hodges motions Phil to move back with his gun. Phil moves back and Hodges settles the gun down on his desk.

"I'm going to lose my job if you sell. I'm going to lose my home; I'm going to lose everything. No one will hire me at all this time. What do you expect me to do exactly? I have a family to take care of. I have a life to live. You make millions upon millions and live your happy life. I'll be stuck with nothing." Phil says as he backs down. "I've done everything for you, for this one chance to make my life straight, instead I've killed a man, I've taken upon immoral actions, and now once again I'm left with nothing. How do you want me to take care of my family?"

"Son...you're a lawyer, everything you do is immoral. Now having that said, have you heard the allegory of the Scorpion and the frog?" Hodges asks. Phil gives Hodges an odd look. "Well let me tell you then."

"Once, there was a scorpion and he looked around at the mountain where he lived and decided that he wanted a change, he wanted to be bigger and better than his father and his father's father. So he set out on a journey through the forests and hills. He climbed over rocks and traveled under vines and kept going until a river had halted him. The river was wide and swift, and the scorpion stopped to reconsider the situation. He couldn't see any way across. So he ran upriver and then checked downriver, all the while thinking and fearing that he might have to turn back. Even the thought of touching the water scared him half to death. Suddenly, he saw a frog sitting in the rushes by the bank of the stream on the other side of the river. He decided to ask the frog for help getting across the stream. 'Hello Mr. Frog!' Yelled out the scorpion across the water, 'Would you be so kind as to give me a ride on your back across the river?'

The frog gave the scorpion an odd look, 'Well now, Mr. Scorpion! How do I know that if I try to help you, you won't try to kill me?' Asked the frog hesitantly.

'Because,' The scorpion replied, 'If I try to kill you, then I would die too, for you see I cannot swim!'

Now this seemed to make sense to the frog. But then he asked. 'What about when I get close to the bank? You could still try to kill me and get back to the shore!'

'This is true,' Agreed the scorpion, 'But then I wouldn't be able to get to the other side of the river!'

'All right then…' The frog thought harder for a moment, 'How do I know you won't just wait until we get to the other side and *then* kill me?' Asked the frog.

'Ahh…,' Smiled the scorpion, 'Because you see, once you've taken me to the other side of this river, I will be so grateful for your help, that it would hardly be fair to reward you with death, now would it?!'

So the frog agreed to take the scorpion across the river. He swam over to the bank and settled himself near the mud to pick up his new friend. The scorpion crawled onto the frog's back, his sharp claws prickling into the frog's soft hide, and the frog slid into the river. The muddy water swirled around them, but the frog stayed near the surface so the scorpion would not drown. He kicked strongly through the first half of the stream, his flippers paddling wildly against the current. Halfway across the river, the frog suddenly felt a sharp sting in his back and, out of the corner of his eye, saw the scorpion remove his stinger from the frog's back. A deadening numbness began to creep into his limbs.

'You fool!' Croaked the frog, 'Now we shall both die! Why in God's name would you do that?'

The scorpion shrugged, and did a little dance on the drowning frog's back then replied, 'I'm sorry my friend, but I could not help myself. For it is in my nature.'

Then they both sank into the muddy waters of the swiftly flowing river…See Phil it was in the scorpion's true nature to kill the frog. It was born to take control and conquer all in its sight even if it meant its own death. There is no dance no fight, it sees what it wants injects its poison and finishes the job. That is why I love the scorpion. That is why this company has the scorpion's logo. We take no prisoners, we play no games, we shoot to kill. And just like that," His voice deepens, "*my friend* it is in my *nature* to kill you."

Hodges looks at the gun and immediately reaches for it. Phil sees the action and runs towards the desk. The gun slips off the desk and Phil punches Hodges in the jaw.

"Fuck you Hodges I won't let my life get ruined again!" He says as he knees him in the stomach.

"Boy I haven't been in a good old fashioned fist fight since my younger days, but I reckon I can handle you just fine." He swings at Phil hitting him in the side of the head.

They exchange punches for a few moments back and forth, then Phil punches Hodges in the face hard enough to make him lose his balance and walk backwards a bit, he then trips over a curve in the carpet and catches himself on the railing of the balcony. Hodges wipes the blood from his face as he collects himself and attempts to regain his balance using the rail. "Boy after I kill you I'll make sure that your wife will be taken care off…" He says as he laughs and winks at Phil, "And that retarded son of your wife will be calling *me* daddy!"

Phil let's out an angry scream yelling, "You son of a bitch!" and runs at Hodges punching him right in the middle of the mouth. The blow was strong enough to throw Hodges over the edge of the balcony making him fall down from the fifth floor. In shock Phil looks over the edge. Hodges appears to be dead. Blood starts to materialize from the back of his head. Worried, Phil runs for the door.

He looks out and there is a man that just walked out the elevator. He runs back and looks out the window trying to find some sort of fire escape or way down the window. He goes towards the door one more time and peeks out the door all the while thinking, "*What have I done, what have I done!*" He plays the scene over and over in his head. The man he saw seems to have gone the other way down the hallway. Phil runs into the stair well and makes his way down. He gets into his car and takes off. "*Shit, shit, shit!*" He yells out as he drives. "*I'm fucked!*" Sweating uncontrollably he continues to drive until he can figure out what to do.

***

"Son of a bitch where is this room?!" Robert thinks to himself. He finally sees an elderly couple leaving their room with all their bags. "Excuse me would you two happen to know which way is room five thirteen is?" He asks.

"Sir you walked down the wrong way it's on the other side of the hall." The woman responds in a soft voice.

"Okay thank you!" Robert darts off in the other direction as he touches his lower back to make sure the dagger is still there hidden under his shirt and tucked into his pants. Not knowing exactly what he was going to do, he continues down the hallway. He finally makes it to the room to oddly find the door open. He slowly walks into the room. "Hello?" He asks out loud, "Mr. Hodges, are you there?" He starts to see that the room was a mess; things were everywhere as if there was some sort of struggle in the room. He starts touching everything in the room and moving things around trying to figure out what had happened in the room. He picks up a pile of papers that stated the sale of Highland Corporation.

"Highland was going to sell? Ha, those poor fools didn't know what they had." Robert then walks out to the balcony and rubs his hands on the rail. He then looks over the edge to find a man lying in a pool of blood. *"What the hell?"* Robert thinks to himself. Just then he hears a voice.

"Who the hell are you?"

Robert turns around to find a young man holding a bag full of food. "I'm...I'm Robert Heyward, and I'm here to see Earl Hodges. Who are you?"

The young man gives Robert a strange look, "Earl Hodges is my father. He sees the condition of the room and then sees his father's gun lying on the floor. Bryan runs towards the gun and picks it up pointing at Robert. Robert immediately puts his hands up.

"Look kid I didn't do anything," Robert says to him, "but I think that's your father over the edge." He tilts his head motioning towards the balcony.

"What?" Bryan walks towards the balcony with the gun and his eyes pointed at Robert at all times, "Don't move, don't move I'll shoot, I swear to God I'll shoot!"

"I'm not moving." Robert responds fearing for his life.

Bryan looks cautiously over the edge of the balcony, "Oh my God, dad!" He yells as tears run down his eyes. With anger he turns towards Robert with his face and eyes bloodshot red. "You son of a bitch you killed my father!"

"I didn't kill anyone I just got here." Robert tries to defend himself.

Bryan runs towards Robert and gun whips him several times, beating him over the head as blood splashes all over the floor. Robert yells and screams for help. He tries to explain that he didn't do anything and has never hurt anyone. A maid sees what was happening in the room and immediately calls for help. The manager comes up and finally relieves Robert of the barrage of blows that came his way. The police came soon after.

***

"Damn it what the hell am I going to do now?! I'm going to lose everything...Everything! Janis, Josh, the baby..." Just then Phil gets a phone call. He looks down and it's a number he doesn't recognize. He chooses to ignore it. He fumbles around his front pocket. "Damn it, where the hell are my cigars?!" He thinks for a moment, "Fuck if I hadn't given that dumb bitch my cigar I'd still have one left!" The unknown number calls back again immediately, annoyed Phil decides to pick up this time. "Hello?!"

"Mr. Roderick?"

"Yes?" Phil answers.

"This is Bryan Hodges, Earl Hodges' son..."

"Shit!" Phil says under his breath, "...Uh yes..."

"I don't know how to say this sir, but my father's been murdered..."

"Wh...what?"

"Yes, the police have the murderer here and you were one of the only few men my dad actually trusted, are you in Houston or still in Dallas?" Bryan asks with an obvious hope that Phil was in Houston.

"I just got in the area a few minutes ago, son tell me where you guys are I'll be there as soon as possible." Phil responds trying to collect himself. He listens to Bryan as he gives him the address wondering what the hell could have happened after he had left.

"We're at the Comfort Inn off of Two Ninety East room five thirteen." There's no response on the phone, "Mr. Roderick, you there?"

"Uh yes, sorry I'll be there in about fifteen minutes, and don't you worry about a thing I'm here for you son."

"Thank you Mr. Roderick." They hang up.

"They caught the murderer? What the hell is going on here? They probably thought it was one of the cleaners or the maids. Right? As long as they know it's not me that's all that matters I guess." Phil thinks to himself as he sweats uncontrollably to the point where the steering wheel begins to slip. He finally gets to the hotel and sees countless police cars and yellow police tape surrounding all parts of the building. As he pulls closer a police officer stops him and motions him to roll down his window.

"Sorry sir the premises are closed due to a crime scene investigation. You're going to have to come back later." The officer says.

"Yes, I know officer I'm Phillip Roderick the man's lawyer, I was asked to come here." Phil responds.

"Okay go on in." The officer motions him to drive into the parking lot and then motions the other officers to let him through. Phil then parks his car and wipes his hands and face with napkins he had in the car. He walks over to the dead body, touches the face a few times as one of the officers accompanies him looking over his shoulder he then begins to walk into the building. He calmly makes his way to the elevator. As the elevator climbs so does his anxiety and confusion. He walks over towards the room and there are more police officers and more yellow tape. He sees Bryan and walks over to him.

"You okay son?" Phil asks. Bryan responds with a hug and cries on Phil's shoulder for a minute. Phil pats him on the back and tries to comfort the young twenty year old man. He then looks over to the detective and asks, "What happened here?"

"Well, it seems to be a homicide at the moment, but we just want to make sure everything makes sense before we take any actions." The detective studies Phil for a moment, "Detective Frank Brown by the way. I've been temporarily assigned to this case." The old thin man in a brown trench coat extends his hand for Phil.

"Phil Roderick, Earl Hodges' lawyer and personal friend." He responds.

"It basically looks like the man we have for questioning in the room right now got in some sort of fist fight with Hodges and threw him off of the balcony. He's been denying it, but it doesn't look too bright for him. We have also found a weapon on his person that we confiscated."

"A weapon?"

"Yeah, just a dagger tucked into the back pocket of his pants."

"Who is he?"

"Well, I think you should take a look." He says as he extends his arm motioning Phil to walk through the door.

Confused about what was going on Phil walks into the room. The man looks up at him with a ghastly shock on his face. Phil returns the same look at first, but then it turns into a smirk.

"Well, well, well, look what we've got here…Robert Allen Heyward."

Chapter 33

"Hello?"

"Hey."

"Hey you, miss me already?"

"Just got home so I thought I'd call to say goodnight."

"Well, aren't you just the sweetest man?"

"Any chance I get a second date?"

"Date?"

"Yeah, you know us two going out again, enjoying each other's company, laughing, holding hands, and so on."

"I thought we were just having fun."

"So it wasn't a date?"

"Well if it was you are pretty slick mister."

"Ha ha ha," The man laughs nervously, "well you've caught me. So…what do you say?"

"…Well I think it might be a possibility…"

"Alright…" He chuckles, "I can take that. You know I really did have a lot of fun tonight."

"I did too Stan, and thank you again."

"Hey, it was my pleasure, goodnight."

"Goodnight."

The phone hangs up.

"Who was that?"

Startled Sandra turns around, "Ou!" She puts her hand on her chest, and then lets out a sigh of relief after recognizing the face, "You scared me…What are you doing up at this hour of the night?"

"Who was that?" He asks again.

"Just a friend." She responds with an odd look on her face.

"Just a friend?"

"Yeah, why Michael?"

"It sounded like more than a friend. Who was it?" He asks in a calm yet bothered voice.

"I told you nobody."

"It was Stan wasn't it?"

"No…"

"I heard you say Stan, what happened to not lying in this house?" He says as he raises his eyebrows at his mother.

"Well I just didn't want to start anything over nothing." She responds as she begins to put away her purse to avoid eye contact.

"You're going on dates with this creep?"

"He's not a creep and it wasn't a date."

"I heard everything mom, what's going on?"

"Nothing I just had a good time with a friend okay nothing is going on, look ever since your father has been gone I've been all alone, okay? I need you to understand I need friends, and peers, and other people I can go out with. Stanley is just someone who I can relate to and that's all. So I went out with him and had a good time Michael. So what? I need to have a life too you know. Now, I know you get worried, but nothing is going on. Why are you up anyway?"

"Just got up to get something to drink." He finishes off his milk, sets down the glass, and begins to walk away. He makes sure his mother sees him roll his eyes as he turns around with a disgusted look on his face.

"Is Ryan asleep?"

"Yeah…" He says as he continues to walk away.

Sandra walks towards the couch and puts her face in her hands and let's out a big sigh. She is confused and has mixed emotions about everything. Stan is like a breath of fresh air to her, and she feels she might be starting to have feelings for him. She also knows she loves Robert. There's something missing though, something deeper than that. That feeling confuses her more and more. With every attempt she has made to move on something always pushes her right back. Stan was the first thing she had found where nothing has pulled her back…except for, of course, Michael. Michael…she thinks to herself. She named him after the archangel Michael. The one who is strong, the leader of God's great army, the protector of heaven, the angel of blessings.

He protects her everyday and she yells at him for it. He was a blessing to the family, the first addition, and yet she neglects him. She then thinks of Ryan. Robert had named him; it meant 'little king' as the years progressed it would become more and more true. What Ryan wanted, Ryan got. Never the less he is the sweetest child, any mother would be proud to have him. Sandra thinks about his innocent eyes, his caring nature, his strong faith. Every time she sees him she can't help, but smile. He is the baby of the family, yet he always tried like his father to hold everything together. Ever since everything had happened he had become so shy, so distant from the world. It is as if he has a shield held up against the world so no one can get in. You can see his thoughts and his heart through his eyes, but he will never speak of them, not to her at least.

She prays that his innocence and his pure heart never fade away. She thinks of Robert's face, then Michael…she can't tell the difference between the two. Michael reminds her so much of Robert. He talks and acts like him. The more she sees Michael the more she thinks about Robert. "Why couldn't things be different?" She thinks to herself, "Why couldn't he have been there, just that one time…why? Why did that factory have to burn down?" So many questions so few answers. This world has always had more questions than answers anyway. He was the unforgettable love who made the unforgivable mistake. She couldn't bear to see him; therefore she couldn't bear to see Michael. Angrily Sandra gets up and walks into her art room. She walks towards the locked closet and unlocks it with a key which was the Holy Cross itself that she wore around her neck. She pulls out all the forbidden paintings and then starts painting on a new canvas…her back wall. She paints with passion and zeal as the brush strokes surmount the white background. This was the largest canvas she had ever painted on and it excited her to know that the end of this painting would not come to an end soon. As the colors came together tears helplessly filled her eyes and flowed down her face like a river overpowering a damn, but it didn't hold her back or slow her down.

Sandra would wipe them away and continue painting as a new set of tears would follow like a never-ending cavalry. It was as if her heart was finally opening up and the window to her mind was becoming clearer. She was painting her prayers, she was painting her regrets, she was painting everything she ever wanted…

The next morning Michael walks across the art room on the way out the house as he was leaving for school and as he passes something catches the corner of his eye. He pauses for a moment and then slowly walks back towards the art room; surprised it was at all opened he decides to investigate further. When he looks inside the room he sees his mother on the floor hunched over with her arm on her painting stool and her head lying on her arm as she peacefully slept. Her dress from the night before was covered all over in paint. Her face was drooped somewhat and you can tell by the bags under her eyes that she had been crying the whole night. She has her other arm around Charlotte who is also asleep. As he walks in closer he notices drawings of a little girl. All the paintings were of the same little girl, there were some variances, but he could tell it was her. In one painting the girl was jump roping, in another the girl was walking into a school type building looking back holding onto the straps of her backpack for dear life, and then there was one of the girl running with her arms open looking for a hug it was almost as if she was going to jump out the picture and hug whoever was looking at it. She had the biggest smile and the most welcoming eyes, her pigtails came down the side of her head tied with a pink bow at the ends. He then looks up at the massive painting on the wall and is brought to his knees as tears come rolling down his eyes he had realized who the little girl was.

Soon thereafter he hears a sobbing sound and looks over at his mother, but she was still asleep, he then turns around to find Ryan behind him standing staring at the same picture also crying. Michael stands up and turns around to give Ryan a hug, as they hug the tears begin to come out stronger. Ryan can't get his eyes off of the painting. There are five people running in a field hand in hand. He continues studying the immaculate colors as they come together. All the way on the left hand side is Ryan as a child holding his father's hand, and all the way toward the right is Michael when he was younger holding his mother's hand. In the middle is a small little girl maybe about five or six linking the two sides together holding both Sandra and Robert's hands. They are all running in a field together with joined hands and with smiles on their faces as if nothing was ever wrong. As if they were in heaven. Ryan puts his head on Michael's shoulder, and then he feels a hand caress the back of his head. They both look back and it was there mother standing there with a tired look upon her face and half a smile. With mixed emotions about the painting and the joy she felt to see the two brothers comforting each other she couldn't help, but cry again. They all stood there in a hug in each other's arms.

Later that night Sandra gets a phone call...

"Hello?"

"Sandra..."

"Robert?..."

Chapter 34

"I'm going to Houston…" Amber says as she bursts through Greg's door and tosses a newspaper onto his desk.

"What? For what?" He asks confusedly as he picks up the paper. He studies the paper for a moment, "No! Absolutely not!"

"Why not?"

"Because Amber you are an anchor woman now and an anchor woman sits on her pretty little desk, with her pretty little notes, reading the news with her pretty little smile…And I thought I was 'Mr. Howard' now?" He says in a sarcastic voice.

"Come on Greg that was yesterday. You have to live life today and by the way how many times do we fight? Why should this one change anything?" She says in a sweeter voice looking at him innocently.

Greg always had a sweet spot for Amber; he knew when she first walked through his doors with her sad shy face that he would turn this rookie into a somebody one day. He always gave her what she wanted. He brushes it off and replies, "No, absolutely not, my bosses will have my head for dinner sending one of my lead anchors for a field workers job during the biggest national story since the Cold Fusion story five years ago. Besides it is way too dangerous. And I know how you are." He says as he looks at her condescendingly, "And you know better than anyone else that these people don't play games with anyone…" Amber looks down with a look of hurt, "Look I'm sorry sweetheart, but I just can't risk you getting hurt. I care about you way too much to let anything happen to you....And maybe you should take your own advice of living today and not in the past."

"Greg," She says as she walks over to him, "Robert Heyward has taken everything from me. My old life, my innocence, my best friend. I want to make sure that sack of shit goes to jail and gets the death penalty. This will be my final tribute to Harvey and to my past. This will bring peace to my heart and soul. I will be able to sleep at night without walking up in my own sweat and tears about that horrible night. Greg I need this..."

"Amber...you have to stop blaming yourself for Harvey's death. I know it was heart breaking to lose your best friend, but it wasn't your fault. It was these people who killed Harvey not you," He says as he slaps the newspaper, "and they can and will do it to you if they want. So it is best to stay away."

"Greg I know what the dangers are of my job, and I know exactly what can happen, but you have to trust me when I say I promise I will be careful. I just want to report a story and make sure the truth comes out. I want to make sure the world knows what this man did to other people. I just want justice to be served that's all. I won't get in anyone's way and I won't sneak around. I just want to report a story and that is all. Please Greg you have to let me go, I have been waiting for this moment for a very long time and it is finally here. Please don't take that away from me. It's my destiny Greg, I was meant to go there. I have to go there. Please don't take this away from me." She says as her eyes begin to water.

Greg sighs and pauses for a moment as Amber stares at him. He then says in a calm voice, "Amber I don't want you to get hurt..."

"I won't!" She interrupts.

"I don't want to lose you either..."

"You won't!" She says excitedly like a small child feeling he is beginning to sway her way.

Greg sighs again and reluctantly asks, "You promise?"

"I promise Greg." She says humbling her voice.

"I want you to take Ed...He's the best cameraman we've got, I don't want you to go anywhere or do anything without him." He stares at her; she stands there without responding, "...Okay?"

"You got me a bodyguard Greg?"

"Just someone to watch your step for you."

"Well I can handle myself just fine Greg."

"I know, but you're not going anywhere if he's not going, and that's final. I've agreed with you, the least you can do is meet me halfway."

They stare at each other for a moment then Amber says as she begins to walk out, "I'm taking the first flight out in the morning; make sure your bodyguard knows that!" The voice fades away.

"God, please be careful out there Amber…" Greg says to himself as he watches her leave.

"I'm going to crush that bastard Heyward." Amber says to her self as she leaves the building. She calls for a cab and takes off.

Chapter 35

"Tonight on headline action six news former CEO and president of Orion Industries, Robert Heyward, was taken in on first degree murder charges of the now former president of Highland Corporation Earl Hodges…"

"Hey turn it up!" A young man yells out.

"Mr. Heyward was caught by Earl Hodges' son Bryan Hodges and is now in police custody at an undisclosed location for further questioning. Bryan Hodges had allegedly walked into the room shortly after Robert Heyward had thrown Earl Hodges from the balcony of his fifth floor hotel room. Police believe it was an act of jealousy, and spite from his own life's shortcomings." The reporter touches her ear as she receives some news; "I have just gotten confirmed information that Mr. Heyward is being held in Harris county jail at the moment awaiting decision to go to trial. Many believe that Mr. Heyward could be facing the death penalty, on premeditated homicide. We will be right back after these messages with more details, with action six news this is Alicia Blacksmith."

"Hector! Did you hear that?" The young man says as he rushes through Hector's office door and into his office.

"Yeah looks like he's screwed. Oh well what can you do right?" He responds without much recognition of the young man's presence as he continues to study the documents on his desk.

"Hector, I'm taking the case!"

"What?" He asks as he takes of his reading glasses and looks up at the man, "No, Jack, this is a for sure lose case, you are not taking it and there is no way I'm letting you take down my firm either. We have a reputation here and there is no way we are representing a slob like that. You got it?!"

"Hector, I need this case man! Look business has sucked lately hasn't it?" Hector continues to stare at Jack, "Okay so being a newer lawyer there is no way in hell I'm getting anywhere without a big case like this. I know it's going to lose, but it will get my name out there. I just need the exposure. And you and I both know this firm needs the exposure."

"Jack, you know you're lucky to even have a job right? I mean come on, your resume is great, but like you said the market sucks right now and no one is getting hired. I actually had to create room for you and that ain't easy to do. You know your mother and I grew up together."

"Oh God not this story again!"

"Yes, and you better listen mi hijo, your mother and I grew up together. We were best friends since we were little kids. I was there for her and she was there for me through everything. And just like that we went through everything together. I was there at her wedding, your birth, and her funeral. I promised your mother I would take care of you and there is no way I'm letting you do such an ass backwards stunt like this. Now if you want to keep your job I suggest you get the hell out of my office." He says motioning to the door as he stands up.

"Hector, are you doing this tough love thing again? 'Cause I got to tell ye, you're horrible at this." He says as he smiles, Hector squints his eyes somewhat in anger, "I'm taking this case whether you like it or not. If you're going to fire me that's fine, I'll move on…But I want you to know I truly believe this will get this firm where it needs to be. Are you going to back me on this or what?"

"Have you even thought about this Jack? Like really thought about this. That man is broke, how is he even going to pay for this? Have you thought about that? And what are you an ambulance chaser now? You know you can't just solicit clients? Or has he called you?" Jack starts to have a torn look on his face, "So he hasn't, you just think you're going to go up to him and he'll say, 'Okay Mr. Jack Kennedy please take control of my future even though you have no experience or credibility.' You truly believe the judge is just going to hand over the case to you like that? Can I ask you a real question Jack? Is your name Jack or Jack ass?"

"Look I'll figure it out somehow okay. All I really need is the media coverage and…"

"You'll figure it out?!" Hector interrupts, "You've truly lost it haven't you Jack?"

"Hector, just hear me out," He tries regain control of the conversation, "all I need is the coverage of the news feed and I'll be set for life from there on. Heyward's probably going to get some no named states attorney anyway, why the hell should I just let this opportunity slip by when I can take it myself?" He replies with confidence.

Hector looks at Jack's overconfident face and studies him for a few seconds before he begins to speak, "How the hell are you going to help this guy? In fact with your lack of experience you're probably going to end up making things worse for yourself and him. Then what, huh? You're going to go on television being the stupidest inexperienced lawyer in the world, with my firm backing it! Have you even looked at all the evidence pinned against him?" He tries to look Jack in the eyes, but Jack is completely silent and looking in a different direction as he always does when upset or if he's being yelled at, "This guy is guilty Jack…there is nothing you can do for him. And say in this crazy world of yours you actually convince the jury to let him free, or even get to the point where they don't go through with the death penalty. Then what? You think you'll be a hero?" Jack looks down half angry and half sheepishly, "No, they will eat you alive! The only customers you will have are murders and ex-cons trying to get you to help them out of a murder or a rape that they committed. Is that what you really want? It's not always about the money Jack. You need to be able to go home and sleep at night with a clear conscious. I've seen it happen to a lot of kids I'm not going to let it happen to you…" They both stand there quietly for a moment, "I'm sorry kid I love you and all, but if you're going to go through with this then you're on your own with this one. If you leave then that's it."

Jack stands there for a moment completely torn apart. Then he finally speaks, "Thanks for all the help and experience Hector…" He begins to walk out, "You'll see me on the news!"

Hector plops back into his leather chair as he sighs out loud and shakes his head. He then puts his reading glasses back on and gets back to his document, "Oh God, please look after this dumb kid." He then looks up at the sky, "I'm sorry Clarice, I tried, but I guess they all have to learn one way or another."

Chapter 36

"Ready to pack up Franky?" Travis says as he walks into Brown's office.

"Yeah almost Travis…" He sits there studying papers with his right hand pinching the top of his nose almost ignoring the chief altogether.

"You okay there Franky?" He asks with a worried sound as he puts his hand on Brown's shoulder noticing Brown pinching the top of his nose. The chief knows when Brown does that, that it means he is in deep thought or frustrated, normally it's a little bit of both. "I didn't think leaving the force would be *this* depressing for you." He says with a small nudge and a smile.

"Huh? Yeah…I'm just fine…look at these evidence papers…something doesn't seem to add up here." He says as he spreads out the papers a bit.

"Oh leave it to the next poor sap who takes your spot. Don't worry about a thing; all you should be worrying about is what country you're going to visit. Paris, Greece, China, Alaska…"

Brown looks at him strangely then shakes it off, "Travis, I know its retirement time, I know and trust me I've been looking forward to it for a very long time. I just think that there is something fishy going on here okay."

"So what man? You don't have to worry about it anymore. The reason I gave you this case was because it's pretty straightforward. Now why the hell are you trying to tremble the waters? You know most guys would just say thank you, and be running out the doors by now."

"I'm not most guys Travis."

"Yeah unfortunately you're a pain in the ass Brown." He says firmly.

"I know chief I'm sorry it's something I've got to do."

"Seriously, you're driving into a dead end here, it's pointless and extra work on your end. Take my advice for once Franky, just let it go."

"Travis, how many cases have I ever just let go?"

"None, and I know what you're getting at so stop right now."

"How many cases have I not solved?"

"Oh God are we really doing this Brown, honestly I have a million other things to do besides play this stupid game of yours?"

"Just answer the questions for me Travis...Please."

"Ugh...seven." He says with disgust and annoyance at the fact of having to play along with Brown's game.

"Six, and six out of..." He edges on the chief.

"Six out of one thousand seven hundred and eighty four." He responds as he did earlier.

"And how many cases have I just passed onto someone else just because I was having a hard time."

"None, absolutely none you are a top notch detective and an asset to the force." He replies sarcastically, "There, is that what you wanted to hear Brown?"

"No, Travis I just want to finish this case and don't want any garnishes on my record that don't need to be there. Come on Travis let me retire with peace of mind man. What do you say? Just one more time for old time's sake and I'll be out of your hair forever in no time," He looks at the top of his head, "well at least what's left of it." He says with a smile.

"Brown, you're a moron, and if you want to work more than you have to then be my guest. But I'll tell you one thing," He says as he sticks his index finger out at him, "if you are going to take this case full on then I don't want you coming back to me crying about it later on how long this case is going and how you want out because you're supposed to be retired drinking pina coladas in Mexico. If you take this case then I expect it to be yours until the very end you understand me Brown?"

"Hey I never complained before and I never will chief." Brown replies with a smile and both of his eyebrows half raised in the air, "I Just want to make sure that I do my job and I do it right."

"Yeah you always did." The chief replies with half a smile. "Well at least I get to see your ugly mug for a few more days huh."

"I guess so." Brown replies. They shake hands followed by a hug, the chief then walks out. Brown returns to his desk and begins to study the papers once again.

Chapter 37

"You okay sweetheart?" Janis whispers to Phil as she leans over towards him.

"Yeah just fine." He replies.

Bryan approaches closer to the podium and begins to speak. "Ladies and gentleman thank you for joining me today as we say good-bye to a great man." He begins to tear up and looks down at his mother for strength; she nods his head at him. He takes a deep breath and continues. "To a man who taught us all to be greater than ourselves. A man who was never afraid to take on challenges and risks. A man who was my idol. Today we say good-bye to my friend, my hero, my father. Earl Landon Hodges…"

"I can't believe this." Phil begins to think to himself as the eulogy and other prayers continue to proceed, "I killed him! I killed him. Me. And here I sit at his funeral making sure that he is dead. I am a monster, but it had to be done." He looks over at Janis, Joshua, and the child, "For them…I had to kill him for them." He verifies. She smiles at him, he smiles back and looks back at Bryan. "I shouldn't have killed him I won't get away with this. I know it, shit like this always happens to me and now I'm really fucked. I'm going to lose everything! Even in death this son of a bitch is out to screw me. How the hell do you get rid of someone whom you can't kill?! I'll lose Janis, I'll lose Josh, the baby, my whole life!" He begins to get tears in his eyes as he holds Janis' hand tighter. She squeezes back knowing the pain of losing a friend. "She's so wonderful, probably thinking these tears are for that pig, for that poor excuse of a human being. No, these tears are for her, but I can never tell her that. How do you tell

someone that you have killed for them? That you have taken away someone's life for them when they never even asked. I can't even look at myself in the mirror anymore. They say that after you have killed someone for the first time, it gets easier the second and third time and after that you begin to lose your soul. I'm not sure how much easier this was. I guess I didn't think about it twice, but I never meant to kill him...I...I think. Oh God what the hell will I do now? I can't always weasel my way out of life. Yes I can. They will catch me. My prints are everywhere, but I touched everything when I walked into that room again, so my prints were everywhere again. They are going to get me for sure, it's only a matter of time."

He looks up at Bryan, "The boy! The boy trusts me. He will be my scapegoat. I will ride that horse out of town. I have to make sure that he stays on my side. He will, won't he? I mean after all, he did call me first. Who else would he have called? His face would turn into a mixture of expressions every time he would look back at Robert the night of the murder. It was a mix of anger, distress, and a sheepish look like some sort of fear. You could almost hear his thoughts almost asking Robert why he would do such a thing. Robert would return the same stupid look each time out of confusion. Ha, ha, ha, it was classic. It's amazing how things work out sometimes. I finally get my revenge. That bastard left me there to die. I had no one but him, and he walked away. He never walks away from anything, but he walked away from his best friend. He lost my job for me, when I was trying to protect him. And when I came back he had packed up and left hoping I was already dead. No note, no message, nothing. Janis was there for me. She kept me sane; she nursed me back to good health and kept me alive. Ha I still remember his face when I walked into the room. Surprised I was alive. In shock at his failed attempt. I wanted to yell 'you lose Robert! Ha, ha, ha you finally lose! And I'm still alive and kicking, you son of a bitch, I'm still alive!'...Thank God I had kept my composure."

"The evidence is all against him. All fingers and all the clues point to him; this is a win-win situation...So this is what it feels like to be in a win-win situation. Having so few of them and so far apart one tends to forget what such a good feeling feels like. It's kind of nice. Tomorrow I will begin to put together my notes for Bryan; the case shouldn't be too difficult seeing that Robert can't afford an attorney so the state has to provide one. Poor sap, they usually don't care much about their cases as it is and it looks like he's getting the death penalty anyway. Man it is literally like killing two birds with one stone! Got away with killing Hodges and now I get to make sure Robert pays for what he did to me, and I get to legally kill him in front of the whole nation, no...in front *of the whole world. That will be the single greatest moment of my life. And then I will convince the kid not to sell the company to that cold hearted, Max Johnson. Instead I will convince him to keep the company as a part of his father's legacy and I will help him become great. Since I helped kill the man who had killed his father he is bound to listen to me…and life…ha, ha life will be set. But how do I get involved with the prosecuting team…"*

"Ah hem," The priest clears his throat rudely interrupting Phil of his thoughts. Phil looks up at towards the front of the church, "If you all will join me we will now proceed to the burial services." The sea of black suits and dresses get up and exit the church as they make their way towards the burial site.

***

Up stairs in the balcony of the funeral home.

"These new unforeseen events are troublesome Dominique." Max Johnson says in a dark voice.

"You want me to take care of it sir?" Dominique replies as they both stare down at the people leaving.

"No, let us sit this round out, our time for action will come soon."

"Should I call in the chopper to go back to New York sir?"

"Yes. We need to remove ourselves from the situation and take a look at this from a different angle. Keep tabs on the boy, the lawyer, and find out about the selected jury. We must be cautious of our steps and weary of our surroundings."

"Roderick, sir?"

"Yes, he may know more than I'd like him to and considering events from the past he may pose an unneeded threat. Keep an eye on him for the time of the trial, and we can take care of Mr. Roderick afterwards. Just make sure he doesn't get in the way of our goals."

"Okay sir, I'll cancel our hotel reservations first." Dominique says as he begins to walk away and pulls out his cell phone.

"No, keep the reservations make it so as if we have never left." Max says as he continues to stare down.

Dominique turns around with an odd stare and replies in a confused tone, "Sir…In both hotels, New Orleans, *and* the house that was rented in Holly Beach?"

Max doesn't respond. Getting the message he then continues to walk away and begins to call in for the helicopter. Max then finally speaks halting him.

"Dominique."

"Yes sir?" He replies caught off guard from making the phone call.

"Get in touch with the district attorney. Let's see if we can convince them to get someone on our team assigned to the case." He says never moving his gaze from over the balcony.

"Yes sir, right away." He continues to walk away as he attempts to complete the call.

"There is no greater role to play in the theatre, than the puppet master."

Chapter 38

"Hello Mr. Heyward. How are you today?" The old lawyer says while looking at Robert as he walks into a cold feeling room. The only window is the small guarded one on the door. The room looks like a big metal box with a metal table and two metal chairs inside, it matched his metal bracelets. Robert sat in one chair, and the other one was empty across from him.

"I'm in jail for a crime I didn't do, how the hell do you think I am?" Robert responds as he looks up at his lawyer keeping his hands folded on the table, his voice matching the atmosphere.

"I know, just try not too think too much into it for now. Were you able to get in contact with your family?"

"No, were you?" He asks with a sarcastic tone.

"No…unfortunately I wasn't able to. Mr. Heyward didn't you say you talked to your wife, earlier this week?"

"Yeah, so?"

"So, what happened? Did you have any sort of discussion on what happened or was it a quick conversation?"

"Look I don't want to talk about it, let's just focus on the case and what needs to get done."

"Okay…" The lawyer stares blankly at Robert, "So I think we should get started on working on the case then. We don't have much time because there is a lot of evidence for me to look over, and we need to put our notes together as swiftly and as efficiently as possible."

"No not until my family is here. I won't do anything until I can see them." He says with determination.

"...But you just said let's focus on the case. I need you to get your head straight Mr. Heyward there's a lot at stake here and I don't think you fully understand that. You need to understand that..."

"Hey!" Robert cuts him off, "I know exactly what's at stake here okay! Don't you dare tell me what to do...I don't care if it is for free I don't work for you, you work for me!" He says slamming his fists onto the table. The outside guard looks in, but the lawyer waves him off.

"Look Mr. Heyward, I know there's a lot going on and I understand that you need the support of your loved ones in your time of desperation and need," The lawyer attempts to keep his calm composure, "but if we don't get started we won't have a case. I have been holding off for a whole week now waiting for you to get in touch with your family so you can do what you have to, but it doesn't look like it's going to happen so we need to move forward. It is the only way we can get anything done."

"Well, that's too bad. I want my family here and I want you to focus on this case. End of story."

"Mr. Heyward!" The lawyer tries to gain control of the conversation, "I *have* been focused on this case, in fact that's all I have been focused on. Now we need to discuss this so we can take further action is that clear?"

"What kind of further action?"

"Do you know what you're up against? You're up against the death penalty for first-degree murder. You can actually die for this. Do you understand what that means? I really need you to focus here."

"I am focused; I am focused on getting my family here. You wouldn't want a man to die alone now would you?"

"Oh my God you are impossible! I'm just going to spell it out for you. We need to do a plea bargain. That is; the only way you can possibly get anything out of this is with good behavior fifteen to twenty years of prison time."

"But I didn't do anything! I didn't kill anybody! Why the hell should I have to serve prison time for someone else's crime? You need to get me out of this, I'm not going to jail for anyone!"

"How the hell do you want me to do that? You won't even talk to me.

All you can talk about is 'I need my family, I need my family'." He says mockingly, "Well grow the hell up Heyward this is your life we're talking about not your family's." Robert faces his head down. "I'm sick and tired of representing you low lives in court going around killing people as if life was some sort of sick joke. Life and death isn't some fucking video game okay? You don't get points for every kill you get! You know I had to represent a twisted sick little sixteen-year-old boy who murdered his kid sister just a couple months ago. You want to know what he did? Well let me tell you, he killed her in the bathtub by cutting off her two middle fingers and shoving them through her eye sockets! And the reason? The reason was that she stuck her middle finger up at him in church and he wanted to teach her a lesson. Do you know how she really died though?…You're going to want to listen to this, because this is the best part…She drowned." Robert looks back up at the lawyer, "That's right, she drowned in the bathtub after what that sick fuck did to her, and since she drowned after the act and he didn't actually commit the murder all he got was eighteen months in jail and twelve with good behavior. You sick fucks are everywhere. But I'll still have to defend you, why? Because the death penalty and killing you for your crimes isn't my job, that's up to God." They both remain quiet and the lawyer looks over at Robert to break the awkward silence. "Now, are you going to work on this with me or what?"

"Yeah whatever…" He responds in broken down tone as he puts his hands through his hair.

"Good. I'm done for the day. I just need you to sign some papers before I get going." He opens up his folder and places it in front of Robert. Robert silently signs them with a disappointed look on his face and pushes back the folder towards his lawyer.

"Okay Mr. Heyward, I'll see you in a few days after I get all this sorted out and then we can really get to work."

Robert lets out a small sigh and nods his head as he looks away. The lawyer then turns around and knocks on the door. The guard looks inside and lets him out. As he walks out he thanks the guard and heads toward the exit. He takes out his cell phone to make a phone call.

"Hello?" A woman's voice answers on the other end.

"Hey hon I just got out right now I should be home in about an hour or so."

"Okay you hungry?"

"Um not really, I just had something to eat before I got here...I just want to get some rest."

"You okay?"

"Mr. Hailer?" A young man gets up from his chair as he approaches the lawyer on the way out of the building.

"Hang on honey." He says to his wife with his expression clearly annoyed, "Uh, yes do I know you?"

"Hi," He says with a big smile, "we've never met before my name is Jack Kennedy." He says as he extends his arm.

"Yeah what do you want?" He continues with the same annoyed sound as he shakes Jack's hand and continues to walk.

"I've actually have been looking at your case quite closely and I thought I could help." He begins to talk as they make their way outside.

"Wait, what?" Hailer says as he stops on the steps outside the building. He puts the cell phone back to his ear. "Uh honey I'm going to have to call you back." He hangs up. "Who did you say you are again?"

"Jack Kennedy," He says with a smile, "and I think that I would be a good addition to the team."

"Team? What team?" Hailer responds in confusion.

"Your legal team to support Mr. Heyward. Being such a hot case I figured there would be at least ten of you, but every time I ask about it I keep getting your name. So I figured you were the head guy."

"The head guy? Son first of all if you thought there was a legal team here then you obviously haven't been following the case close enough. Second how old are you like twenty-two, twenty three? Do you even have a law degree? And finally I work alone, so why don't you take your criminal law for dummies book and your cute hair cut and go bother someone else, I really don't have time for this okay?" Hailer says as he begins to walk away.

"What's the motive?" Jack yells out as Hailer continues to walk away.

Hailer turns around slightly annoyed and slightly confused. "What?"

Jack begins to walk down the stairs. "I was just wondering if you had any theories on the motive of the murder. Because I've looked at the case and I got to tell ye there's a few...trick is which one are they going to go with."

"What are you some kind of jack ass?" Hailer replies.

An angry look dawns upon Jack's face, then suddenly he pulls his fist back and throws a punch towards Hailer, but stops his hand mid flight. Startled Hailer ducks and holds up his brief case in front his face to avoid the punch. He then notices that there was no impact and slowly puts down his briefcase.

"What the hell was that you asshole!?" He then yells out. He looks back down searching for his glasses.

"See I could have kicked your ass there pretty badly huh?" He says as he stands their in an overconfident swagger while Hailer picks up his glasses, "But Earl Hodges being the respectable man he was would have probably covered himself from the first blow and somehow attempted to fight back. I mean just an assumption, but I think it's a fair assumption don't you?"

"So what the hell is your point?" Hailer responds, sweating profusely half expecting Jack to try something else.

"So my point is that even though I haven't really been in contact with Mr. Heyward I have seen recent pictures and mug shots of him and for some reason there...there doesn't really seem to be any significant marks from a fight on him, besides one scar. Now is it me or do you find that a little odd too?"

"Look all I know is that this mother fucker is going to get what he deserves, I just have to keep him alive okay." He says as he pokes at Jack.

"Oh is that what they taught you in law school...Just, just keep them alive?" He says acting sarcastically interested with his hand under his chin.

"Why don't you tell me since you probably just got out of there last week?" Hailer responds clearly fed up.

"Hey I'm just trying to help an innocent man get out of jail okay and if doing your job half assed so innocent men can die slowly in prison rather than dying by a needle helps you sleep at night then do what you got to do."

"Why do you really want this case huh? Is it the money? The fame? The experience? Which one is it? You really don't want this case so why are you on my ass trying to take this over? Look, why don't you do yourself a favor and save yourself the headache and buzz off okay kid."

"Look I'm doing this because something tells me this guy is innocent and I know that with me on the case he would have a real fighting chance." Jack responds in a more sincere tone.

"You know he has no money right? He's a bum Jack! Who the hell is going to pay you for this?"

"I'll do it pro-bono!" He blurts out.

"Pro-bono?!" Hailer yells out as he laughs at Jack. "You're out of your mind. This shit just keeps getting funnier and funnier. Where the hell do you people come from?"

"Hey at least I give a damn about my clients okay." Jack rebuttals.

"Oh yeah? You think you can do such a badass job son? You think you're some kind of savior helping out bastards like this? Look I don't know what you're really after or what your angle is, but you got it kid. Go ahead you take the case. But at least you'll go down on your own account. Thanks for the vacation kid," Hailer begins to walk away, "I'll have the transfer papers to you in the next couple days and you can explain to that poor soul how a young arrogant bad ass lawyer guaranteed him a one way express ticket to hell." He waves his hand in the air as he continues leave.

Jack stood there by himself in shock of what just happened. He knew he wanted the case, and oddly enough this is somewhat how he wanted the conversation to go. He always takes the risky route, but never goes all the way with it. Today was different. Today he got what he asked for and it scared the hell out of him. "Now what?" He thinks. Jack has never gotten this far with any of his off the wall ideas so this is all new territory for him. He was pretty confident in himself up until Hailer's last comment. "Heyward could die because of me..." Jack thinks to himself. All he really cared about was the publicity and never took into account another man's life. The sudden reality check froze Jack. He then is brought back to his senses and attempts to shrug it off as he walks away contemplating his next move.

A block down Hailer is approached by Amber.

"Mr. Hailer! Mr. Hailer!" Amber yells out trying to grab is attention while running and catching up to him.

"Oh my God now what?!" Hailer says as he turns around.

"Mr. Hailer just a few questions on Robert Heyward and the case. May we have a moment of your time?"

"This day just gets more and more annoying. Look you want answers why don't you ask Heyward's new smart ass lawyer back at the jail house."

"What?"

"Well since you're here, here's the scoop…I quit, and the new man in charge is that cocky S.O.B. Jack Kennedy." Hailer says into the camera. He then looks back at Amber.

"Well don't you feel privileged you have news that even Robert Heyward himself doesn't have yet. Now if you don't mind please leave me alone." He turns around and begins to walk away. Amber looks over to her cameraman.

"Did you get that?"

"Yep."

"Who the hell do you think this Jack Kennedy character is?"

"I don't know ma'am I'm just here to film."

Annoyed by the unsupportive demeanor of the cameraman she continues, "I wonder if it was that guy outside the building Hailer was talking to just earlier. We better start following him around now since Hailer's out the picture…Let's go." They try to make their way back as quickly as possible, but by the time they had gotten back the man they had seen Hailer talking to earlier had already left.

Chapter 39

It's a cool summer night, a zephyr flows through the white linen curtains and into the room as it settles in like a cold blanket. The room is all white; from the paint on the walls to the bed sheets to the blanket and even the carpet. The moon is like a spotlight aiming into the room tinting everything with a light blue color. The reflection of it off of the black water makes the moon seem even brighter. Another wind pushes in softly through the curtains opening the man's eyes lying in the bed. He turns over and sees a young woman who would be in her early twenties; Robert is near the same age. He thinks he recognizes her so he puts his arms around her. She responds slightly. He kisses her on the cheek and makes his way down to her neck. His hands move softly from her arms towards her breasts.

"Now don't start anything you can't finish, you have to get up for work soon." The woman says playfully. The sounds in the room are somewhat distorted and echoed. He feels numb and drunk and the objects in the room are shifting faintly and then returning back to normal. He turns her over and sees Sandra's face smiling at him. She bites her bottom lip as he stares at her falling in love with her all over again. He looks into her eyes as his pupils become larger and goes in for a kiss. They kiss passionately holding each other close, he suddenly feels a sharp pain and then tastes blood. He moves away for a moment and touches his own lips. He realizes she has bitten the corner of his lip and broke the skin as blood slowly trickles down the side of his face and colors the bed sheet. Robert's face changes to Phil's and Sandra's smile becomes bigger...Her expression is almost evil. She is lying on blue rose petals, a quick glimpse show blue rose petals everywhere. Everything is right, but something is wrong it was not him in that bed. He goes into bite her on the neck. He then sits up to go inside of her and the wind

blows away the soft white light weighted blanket and he could see her naked body in the moonlight. He leans forward a bit and another droplet of blood falls onto her hair changing its color to bright red and it glows like fire. He feels an urge that he hasn't felt in years.

Another familiar face takes over the man as he pulls inside of her. The pain continues in his head, but he can't stop. With his arms pinning her down, he looks at her face and sees the bliss in her smile and in her eyes. She gasps in pleasure. His face changes back to its original face and he feels some peace. She looks up and flips him over and gets on top of him. His face changes back to Phil's face. As anger rushes through his mind he grabs her breasts and holds them tight as she pushes harder on top of him. She breathes harder and all he hears is "Yes." The face changes again to an unknown person. In his uncomfortable state of mind he flips her over again and lies on top of her as he pushes deeper. She gasps again slightly biting her own bottom lip again. The wind rushes in cooling the sweat on their bodies. They move faster and faster to keep warm and the passion strong.

His face changes again and she gasps louder almost as a small yell. To stop her self she bites his shoulder. It hurts him greatly so he pushes harder. He cries in his mind not because of the pain, but because he doesn't own the face on that man's body. As the face changes once again he pushes even harder out of anger only to pleasure her even more. She digs her nails into his back and it helps to focus the anger inside his brain. There are lines of blood on his back that further color the bed sheets. She has a wicked twinkle in her eyes and he bites her hard back to cleanse his feelings for her. Her enjoyment of it hurts him more and causes a sharp pain in his chest. He squints his eyes and turns her around as he pushes from behind her. His face changes more rapidly now from unfamiliar faces to familiar faces back and forth each time a different face. He can't seem to find his own though. It sometimes passes, but he can't hold onto it.

The more attention he pays to the faces the more focus he loses on her. Her bright hair color changes at the same pace from red, to green, to blue, to pink, to yellow, to orange effervescently like a blaze caught in the wind. She continues to gasp and yell which brings his heedfulness back to her. He leans in to kiss the back of her neck as he touches her hardened nipples. He then makes his way to her cheek and then to her lips as he turns her head. He turns her around again as he kisses her and makes love to her at the same time. She tilts her head back as she begins to moan louder and louder with her eyes closed. He gets up and his face maintains to change rapidly. He pushes in at the same rhythm as her. And she violently opens her eyes and yells out. "Robert!"

Robert wakes up immediately and opens his eyes looking around as his lungs beg for air. He looks around the jail cell just to be aware of his surroundings; there is a small flicker outside from a dying light bulb. He studies himself for a few seconds and notices he is drenched in sweat. He felt as if someone had thrown him into a river and he had just made it out. He tries to wipe his face with his shirt, but it doesn't help due to how wet the shirt already was. He sits there trying to figure out what had just happened, but it pains him. This wasn't the first time he had this dream. It was the first time it had felt this real and hurt this much though. Realizing the extent of the dream a few teardrops fall from his eyes. Then sweat drops fall into his eyes burning them. He yells softly in his pain as he rubs his eyes furiously. He then searches under his bed. He notices blood on his bed sheets he searches his body to find where the blood came from. He feels the pain and touches the side of his lips as blood continues to drip. He tries to cover the wound by attempting to hold his lip inside his mouth then puts his hand under his bed again and finds what he was looking for. He creeps over to the edge of the jail cell to get enough light and begins to write in his book again. As he leans forward to get more light, another drop of blood stains the pages of his book.

Chapter 40

"Hey did you hear dad got a new lawyer?" Ryan excitedly asks as he makes his way into the family room with his laptop.

"Yeah I guess." Michael responds slightly irritated as he turns the page of his football magazine.

"Yeah well I was thinking about booking tickets to Houston today." He says as he focuses his attention towards the laptop, "How's next weekend? Did you tell your coach you might have to leave to go out of town sometime soon?" Michael sits there quiet acting as if Ryan didn't exist as he turns another page in his magazine. They both sit there slightly irritated now. "…You know we're going to have to go to Houston right?" Ryan finally breaks the silence as him and Michael sit in the living room.

"I don't have to do shit. But you, you can go do whatever the hell you want." Michael fires back.

"Michael you know he can die for this right? I mean the least we can do is be there for him." Ryan tries to be as convincing as possible.

"Just…like he's been there for us right?" Michael says with a high-pitched sarcastic voice.

"Why the hell do you hate him so much?"

"Why the hell do you love him so much?" He fires back.

"I just want things to be right Michael. I just want us to be a family again. I look at mom and I see that she's all alone. You can see it in her eyes…In her paintings. Come on man I know things suck, but…"

"We *are* a family," Michael cuts him off, "and mom, mom's just fine, she's got us to take care of her…Well me at least you keep running off talking to him or about him every chance you get."

"What the hell is that supposed to mean? First of all I haven't even talked to him in months and you know what Michael, I've been here for mom just as much as you have. No one has been there for dad, no one. The least we can do is support him here and now. Can you imagine what he's going through?"

"He killed somebody okay? Do you know what that means? He left our family and then he committed murder and you're still kissing his ass because he wrote you a big ass check for your graduation."

"Fuck you Michael, don't throw that in my face. Just because you hate him and treated him horribly and he decided not to give you anything doesn't mean you have to lash out on me okay. If your greedy ass thinks money is that important then just take the damn money you asshole. At least my father loves me!" He yells as he begins to stand and points his finger at his own chest, and gets somewhat in Michael's face while keeping some distance.

Angrily and as calm as possible Michael replies, "Back, off…" The look on his face is threatening.

"Yeah, that's what I thought, you've got nothing to say." Ryan looks him up and down as if Michael were nothing to him and turns around to reach for his laptop. With a fierce look Michael jumps up and tackles Ryan on to the ground throwing punches at him left and right.

"Get the fuck off me!" Ryan yells as he tries to push his bigger older brother off. He begins to claw at him and kick to make at any attempt to escape. Finally Ryan frees his right arm and punches Michael in the side of the head. It did enough damage to stop him for a second. Ryan then grabs the side of Michael's face and pulls it trying to ply Michael off of him. It works briefly until Michael regains his strength and begins to barrage Ryan with even more devastating punches. Blood begins to spray left and right and even splashes on to Michael's face. The taste of blood makes him hungrier for more.

Sandra and Stan walk in to the house and Charlotte darts towards the boys followed by Sandra.

"Oh my God Ryan!" She drops the bag of groceries in her arms and tries to pull Michael off of Ryan. Stan then jumps in and tries to muscle Michael off. They all struggle for a bit. Random punches hit both Stan and Sandra, but the adrenalin makes it unnoticeable. Stan and Sandra finally pull him off. Stan grabs Michael and pushes him back and stands between him and Ryan. Sandra holds Ryan's semi-conscious head on her lap as she attempts to wipe the blood to see where the bleeding is coming from.

"Michael what the hell are you doing?! I can't even leave you two alone anymore? What the hell were you thinking?" She yells as she holds Ryan in her arms as blood flows from his face mixed with tears. Ryan attempts to get up to fight back but is held down by his mother.

"What the fuck is he doing here?!" Michael's asks pacing back and forth while staring at Stan like a vicious tiger taunting its prey looking for any excuse to get back into the fight. Stan keeps his non-threatening composure.

"How can you do this to your own brother Michael?!" Sandra asks with a shocked look on her face as she tries to stop the bleeding from Ryan's head and nose. She pulls out her phone. "I'm calling the hospital."

"You don't need to call the hospital he's a man he can take it." He then looks at Ryan, "You can take it get up stop acting like such a little wuss." They all pause and look at Ryan.

"Mom…" He says softly as he looks over at Sandra.

"Stan, get the car we're taking him to the hospital." Sandra says as tears flow from her eyes while she tries to help Ryan up.

"You don't have to go anywhere he's just fine!" Michael starts to yell out of irritation, he starts breathing deeper and abnormally.

"Look at your brother Michael, does he look fine to you?!" Sandra yells back holding Ryan's face.

Michael looks at Ryan finally realizing what he has done and lets down his guard somewhat. His eyes become watery and he fights strong to hold back the tears. He feels greatly aghast by his actions and starts to feel weak in his knees. He begins to shake a little, but manages to act strong in front of everyone else.

Without another word, Stan turns around and carries Ryan to the car. "You okay buddy?" Stan asks trying to make Ryan talk to keep him conscious.

Ryan shakes his head yes and responds, "I just want to be with dad." In a faint voice as Stan helps him into the car. As soon as they settle in Ryan, Sandra sits in the back seat with him and they take off.

Michael expected to get yelled at by his mother before they left, but he got nothing not even an evil stare or a last minute word before they left. She didn't even care to acknowledge his presence. He just stared at the empty halfway open door as his knees finally gave out. He falls to the floor as a cataract of tears fall from his eyes. The emotions from the past few weeks are overwhelming and he can't take it anymore. He thought about suicide many times, but it never made sense to him no matter how appealing. Beating up his brother helped him extinguish some of his rage, but looking at his beaten bloody brother had only brought more anger upon himself. Life was like a never-ending uphill battle.

Chapter 41

"I want my lawyer!"

"Bryan, what the hell are you talking about, I *am* your lawyer." The man responds aggravated in his thick southern accent. "You're mother is going through a lot right now, and has advised both of us to work together, and I suggest we do so by starting to…hell I don't know…work together Bryan."

"Mr. Rogers, I want Mr. Roderick here now, and I'm not going to say another word until he is here."

"You're kidding right?"

The young man responds by raising his eyebrows as to challenge him. The lawyer lets out a sigh, "Unbelievable…okay. Lynn." He yells out.

"Yes Mr. Rogers." A woman's voice replies.

"Do you have all the files from the Hodges' case?"

"Yes, Mr. Rogers."

"Okay, there should be a number there under the name Phillip Roderick, can you please give him a call and ask him to stop by the office if he can?"

"Sure thing Mr. Rogers."

Mr. Rogers looks back at the young man, "There, are you happy Bryan? Now, let us get to work."

"There seem to be some papers missing from the pile Mr. Rogers." Lynn's voice interrupts.

"Ugh I must have taken them home and left them in my office there. I guess you'll have to wait 'til tomorrow for Mr. Roderick."

"Don't worry I'll call him." Bryan says as he pulls out his cell phone. "Of course."

"Mr. Roderick? Yes it's Bryan. Would you mind stopping by Mr. Rogers' office I really don't feel comfortable starting anything without you being here. All my mom and I really have left now is you...Okay thank you." He hangs up the phone and looks at Mr. Rogers. "He said he'll be here in about half an hour."

Mr. Rogers rolls his eyes as he sits back down to put together his notes. "Okay now can we get started?" He says more irritated by what's going on. Bryan just stares at him.

"You're seriously going to sit there quiet 'til he shows up?" Bryan answers with a sarcastic smile and starts fiddling with his phone. Rogers shakes his head and continues writing some notes onto his legal pad, trying to ignore the irritable sensation within him. About twenty minutes later a knock is heard at the door.

"Lynn would you get that please?"

"It's Mr. Roderick, sir."

Bryan turns around enthusiastically. Rogers looks at him and rolls his eyes, "Let him in Lynn." He says as he stands up.

Phil walks in with a tired weak look upon his face; with bags that were beginning to darken forming under his tired eyes and messy hair, and his face was drooping as if he hadn't slept in years. He locks eyes with Bryan; the young man gets up and gives Phil a hug. Phil returns the hug as he looks at Rogers and they both nod their heads at each other. "How are you?" Phil asks Bryan as he steps back and looks at him up and down to make sure he was okay.

"Better now." He replies.

"Mr. Rogers." Phil says while extending his arm.

"Anthony or Rogers is just fine no Mr. needed Mr. Roderick." He replies as he extends his arm right back. He then motions his hand towards the chair as to ask Phil to sit as he sits himself.

"Okay Anthony, and just the same, Phil is fine. So anyway, what's up how can I help?" Phil asks as he sits down.

"Well, you can start by telling Mr. Hodges here, since he won't listen to me that there is absolutely nothing you can do to help in this case. That you cannot sit in court and help prosecute this case, and you have not been hired to handle this case in any manner, and cannot do so legally. And the sooner he understands this fact, then the sooner we can start working on this case, and, therefore, the better it is for all of us."

"Why can't he help?" Bryan interjects. "I'll hire him, after all, my father has left me and my mother everything, and I believe I can afford Mr. Roderick."

"I'm sure you can Bryan, but unfortunately it is not up to you on the matter of who does or does not prosecute the defendant. The state appoints a prosecutor who they find fit to handle each case, and in this case they have chosen me. Mr. Roderick here can be there as a supporting audience behind the bar, but that is as close as he can and will, if he so chooses, get to you or this case."

"Do you have any idea what my father has done for this city, this state? For this country?! And now, I can't have the lawyer I want representing me in this case. What the hell is going on with this world?"

"Son, I know you are hurt and I sympathize completely, but please try to understand that even if Mr. Roderick did take the case, he would be representing the state and not you, therefore he would have to be a *states* attorney. And unfortunately, he is simply not that kind of lawyer."

"Well I'm not doing anything until we figure this out!"

"Mr. Roderick, would you please intervene?" Rogers looks at Phil as to plea with him for some support.

Phil turns to Bryan, "Anthony is right, Bryan there is nothing we can do. You are in good hands though; there is no reason to stress, and all the evidence is against Heyward. You were there you saw what happened. He will get what he deserves, and I promise you I'll be right there behind your chair every day. Don't worry, everything will be okay, I promise." He puts his hand on Bryan's back and gives him a supporting smile.

"I miss him so much." Bryan begins to sob uncontrollably as he leans toward Phil for support.

Phil takes him into his arms, "I know son, we all do. We'll get that bastard for what he's done to all of us. You have to start thinking about yourself now, and *your* company. Your company is a machine, and if it stops running for much longer many good lives, like your father's will be ruined."

"Will you help me run the company?" Bryan asks with hope in his voice.

Phil smiles, "I'll be with you every step of the way son." Phil glances at his watch, "Look son, I have to get going. My wife's pregnant and if I don't return with a chicken provolone Panini and cucumbers in one hand and a strawberry sundae in another soon I'll be in big trouble. You gonna be okay son?" Bryan nods his head. "Good, I'll call you soon. And if you need anything don't hesitate to call. Anthony, it was a pleasure." He says as he starts to get up and extends his arm.

"The pleasure was all mine Phil, and thank you…for everything." He says as he motions his head toward Bryan.

"Don't mention it." Phil smiles as he puts his hand on Bryan's shoulder then begins to walk out.

"Um, Phil." Anthony abruptly calls out.

"Yeah?" Phil asks as he turns around somewhat confused and caught off guard.

"I just had a thought, it's completely unorthodox, and if we do this it…it must be a complete secret," He looks at Bryan then back at Phil, "between the three of us. If anyone finds out it could cause a lot of trouble." Both Bryan and Phil look at each other for some clue of what's going on, but get none so they return the gaze back to Rogers. "I was just thinking." He continues as he walks towards Phil and closes the door behind him so his secretary wouldn't hear, and then motions Phil back closer towards his desk, "Since, you were also there at the murder scene, and considering your closeness to Bryan, the case, and of course Earl Hodges, it may actually be beneficial for you to help outside of the case, so we can, I don't know, prep the witnesses, put together notes, etcetera, etcetera. Besides if we do an outstanding job, I can probably move on to higher paying jobs, Bryan gets what he wants, you get to be a part of the case, and everyone comes out a winner. What do you think?"

Being caught off guard with such a proposal, Phil stood there for a minute, in thought evaluating all the different possibilities. *Is this a joke, or is this really happening?* He thinks to himself. *Do it you fool, this is your one chance to clear your name and come out on top, with you on the case there is no way to lose!*

"Phil?" Anthony interrupts his thought process. He looks over at Bryan still looking for an answer. His face was half confused and half brought to tears at the thought of his redemption and his sovereignty. Bryan's face was lit up and eagerly nodding yes.

"I...don't know if that's the best idea. Besides I showed up at the scene much later as it is, I'm sure I wouldn't be much help." He replies. *"No you fool!" The voice in his head rebuttals.*

"Please Mr. Roderick, I need you with me, this is my father's legacy, and our future legacy...Please Mr. Roderick." Bryan pleads.

Phil looks back at Rogers, "O...okay, but this must stay quiet."

"Of course Phil." They reach out to shake hands, but Bryan intercepts them with a hug for Phil. "Okay son I really have to get going." He looks at Rogers, "I'll hear from you soon."

"Definitely." He replies with a smile.

Later that night.

"Rogers."

"Mr. Walker, I have some interesting news for you."

"Are you on a secure line?"

"Always."

Chapter 42

"Hey."

"Hey."

"How are you feeling?"

"Fine."

"Doctor says you should be out of here by tomorrow."

"Good so I can go home, and you can beat me up again." Ryan replies then immediately bites his bottom lip.

"Look Ryan...I'm sorry." Ryan looks away not wanting to forgive Michael, and also not wanting to think back to a few days ago. "I know that there's no excuse for what happened. I...I just don't know what the hell is going on with me." There's dead silence for a few minutes.

"You really hurt me Michael..." Ryan finally breaks the awkward silence; Michael continues to look at the white and black-checkered floor in shame. "And you really hurt mom."

"I know man." Michael shakes his head as tears start falling down his face. He tries to fight them with his upper cheeks, but that only results in more tears. Ryan responds with a similar reaction. They both look away from each other. "Like I said man I'm sorry, you know I love you right, and I mean I would never, I mean you know that's not me Ryan...I..." He starts to cry and breathe oddly.

"Michael..." Ryan interrupts, "don't." They both look at each other and say everything without speaking a word. Ryan then looks down for a moment and then back at Michael and puts out his arm. Michael stands up, grabs Ryan's arm and reaches over to give him a hug. He then wipes his eyes and turns around to reach under his chair and pulls up a basketball. "So I got your whole team to sign this for you. I know it's not much, but I thought you might like this."

Ryan reaches for the ball, "So, what'd you tell them?"

"Oh just that you were being annoying and I beat the living snot out of you, they all laughed and thought that I was kidding and left it at that, and so I figured I would too." He chuckles a little nervously. Ryan looks up at him oddly with one eyebrow raised, and then shakes it off.

"So mom told me that you've been in here for the past couple nights checking up on me while I was a sleep."

"Yeah well, I didn't know exactly what to say to you, but I still wanted to make sure you were okay."

"Man you are *so* gay."

Michael somewhat embarrassed, smiles at Ryan's comment and starts fake punching him, and they both start laughing. Michael stops, and plops down back into his seat.

"Man I miss the good old days."

"Yeah, me too. You think things will ever go back to the way they used to be? It's funny you know, to think that the biggest fight we would have is whose turn it was to bathe Charlotte."

"Ha, ha yeah…I don't know, but I sure hope they do get back to normal. And even if things aren't like what they used to be, it doesn't mean we can't make the best of it right?"

"Yeah, I guess so."

"So are you guys still going to Houston?"

"Mom didn't tell you?"

"No, we haven't spoken much in the past few days, as you can tell I have a bad habit of not being on good terms with many people."

"Yeah no kidding…" Ryan lets out a little laugh, "Well, we're flying down there at the end of next week. Dad's new lawyer called and explained to us the situation, and we're going to try to make it there and discuss all the options we have and what path might be best. His old lawyer had called us to come down, he left messages and we were going to go then, but our schedules kept conflicting and we weren't sure what was going on."

"Wait, so when did he get a new lawyer?"

"I'm not sure, but just recently though, it's some guy named, um," He thinks for a moment, "Jack Kennedy, said he saw what was happening to dad and didn't want him to go down without a decent fight. He seems kind of cool, so we're going to go down there for about a week or two and then take it from there I guess. And the best part is he's doing the case for free."

"Pro bono?"

"What?"

"For free." Michael says as to define the word.

"Oh…yeah no one knows why, but who cares as long as things get done and dad gets the help he needs that's all that really matters, right?"

"Yeah I guess so, so who's all going?"

"Just me and mom, we figured you probably didn't want to come. I still think you should come, it might help more than you know."

"I don't know, I have some thinking to do, I just need to be alone for a bit, I think I should stay home, and come down the next time you guys go back. This trip might actually be good for all of us, and give us some much needed space."

"Michael I'm not trying to argue with you, but right now we don't need space, we need to be together." Michael just looks away quietly, "Look I know it's not what you want to hear, but at least promise me you'll think about it."

"Okay, I promise."

"And if you do decide to stay home at least you'll have Charlotte."

"Yeah, I guess so."

Chapter 43

"Um… Mr. Heyward?" Jack sheepishly asks, as he encounters the man he is defending for the first time.

"You must be the infamous Jack Kennedy everyone has been raving about. I was wondering what took the man who is supposed to be fighting for my life so long to visit. I'm glad you could finally make it. I would have baked cookies, but you showing up so scarce an un-announced hardly gave me any time to prepare. You must accept my apologies Mr. Jack Kennedy." Robert replies in a dark tone as he sits in the all too familiar cold box with the metal table and chairs with his hands cuffed and folded resting on the table.

Jack lets out a nervous laugh. "Ye…yes, well no need to apologize I, I already ate." He slowly approaches the other side of the table and cautiously stares, as if he were staring at a wild beast ready to pounce at his prey at any moment. He notices the cut on Robert's left side that he saw in the pictures. "That cut on your face, is from fighting with the other inmates or a bad day with the razor?" He asks with his nervous laugh trying to break the tension.

Ignoring his comments Robert continues. "So are you here to ensure my death sentence as everyone claims, or do you have some other agenda Jacky?"

"Believe it or not I'm here to save your life."

Robert lets out a short laugh. "You?"

"Yes me." Jack responds slowly getting aggravated.

"I'm going to tell you the same thing I told that other douche bag. I'm not saying a word, or starting anything until I see my family. If I'm going to die, for some other son of a bitch's crime then I should at least be able to see my family one last time. You got that kid?" He says in a degrading fashion. "Now unless you can do that Jacky, you can pack up your cute little unicorn folder, and take your smiley faced pen, and go back to your fancy little safe life."

"Mr. Heyward, I can assure you I am not taking this case as lightly as you may be assuming."

"Man I know how you punk fresh off the block young fucking gun lawyers are. Always trying to get in the spot light, looking for the next poor sap to screw, you don't even chase ambulances anymore, you pretty much drive the damn ambulance yourself, and ask the poor patients to sign before you even leave for the God damn hospital. I hate all you fucking lawyers; you're all nothing but a bunch of backstabbing liars trying to screw the last bum out of his last dime. Well I got news for ye kid; you're fresh out of luck because I don't have a dime to my name. So why don't you bring my other piece of shit lawyer back and you can go on your merry ass way."

"Look, I know all this must be hard for you, but we're going to get through this. Now, for the past week I've been running around working my ass off on this case and getting things organized."

"Hey, I don't need any favors okay kid, so spare me the fucking 'I've been working so hard story'." Jack closes his eyes while Robert continues to talk, "I hate people who spend more time talking about what they do than actually doing something. Like I said…"

Jack suddenly opens his eyes, "Look if you don't like me that's fine, you don't have to." Jack interrupts, "You really don't have to do anything, just sit there for all I fucking care, I might need you to sign a few things here or there, but since your being such a dick and aren't talking anyway I might as well just forge your signature on to whatever fucking piece of paper I want. And I'm sure in however amount of time, you'll be dead and I'll be on my way moving on to my next case in life, with the experience of defending someone who used to be one of the most respected people in the world even more so than the president, I'm sure I won't have too much of an issue getting a case. And if you do decide to actually partake in this case, it just might be too late, and if you claim that you didn't sign the papers that I forged for you, I just might be inclined to plead insanity for your lunatic ass and then we'd win the case anyway.

And as far as not having a dime, I know you have nearly a million dollars saved up and hidden somewhere just in case you need it someday. You, just for some reason, find the need to look and act like a bum. But don't worry about that either because like I'm sure you've heard I'm doing all this for free. Now look Mr. Heyward, like I said I know things are hard for you, but I'm here to help. I really, truly believe I can help you in this case and if we go down, I guaran-damn-tee we will go down fighting. I'm not asking for money, I'm not asking for assets, I'm not asking you for anything except your cooperation. Now having that said, I was able to get in touch with your family and they should be down here by the end of next week."

Robert looks up at Jack in disbelief, "And trust me I know your history," Jack continues, "I know all about you. I've been studying you long and hard. So, if you don't want your family to think your still some poor stupid bum then I suggest for the next week we both start working our asses off and put something together that's half way decent so when your family comes we have something competent to discuss. Now, if you're willing to work with me, here are the transfer approval documents stating that you agree and approve out of your own free will the transfer from your former states attorney to me in the case of the State of Texas versus Robert Allen Heyward." Jack opens up his folder turns it around and pushes it forward for Robert to study. He then pulls out his pen and sets it on top of the documents for him to sign.

Jack's heart is pumping so fast it feels as if he had just run a marathon. Robert stares down Jack as to mentally unlock a secret or mystery to some puzzle. Jack returns the stare trying to keep still and to keep his composure for any movement could be a sign of weakness. The silence fills the room like a deadly gas.

"You know you've got some balls Jacky, I don't know what your angle is, but I like you. You just better know what the hell you're doing." Robert takes the pen and signs his name on to the document. Jack smiles in disbelief of what just happened. As Robert finishes signing he pushes the folder back. Jack straightens his face to show little emotion as Robert looks up.

"Thank you Mr. Heyward I'm going to get started right away. Incidentally I have a meeting with the detective that's been working on your case. He was there the night of the murder; you might remember him, detective Frank Brown. Anyhow we'll be looking over evidence at one of the crime scene labs, and if there is anything in particular I should be looking for let me know."

"Nope."

Jack stares at him for a moment. "Very good, I'll keep in touch then." He begins to walk out.

"And Jacky." Robert says just as Jack reaches for the door. "Don't think I didn't catch you crack that little smile while I was signing the papers. Remember fear keeps you alive. You lose fear you'll lose yourself. Remember that." The statement made Robert feel like his old self again.

"Yes, sir." Jack replies then walks out the door.

***

Jack drives into a huge parking lot, there is nothing but a couple other cars besides his own. It was easy to see the exhaust in Jack's face, but the determination to the spotlight keeps him going. He parks his car then raises his eyebrows and looks down pulling his cheeks down as well as to stretch his face. He then rubs his eyes and picks up his folder. His folder was his life, it had all his notes all his documents in it, and it never left his side for one moment. He opens it to quickly go over points he might want to bring up with his meeting with detective Brown. The more he reads and learns about Robert the closer he feels to him.

"Come on Jack, focus." He tells himself hitting himself on the head. The closer he feels to someone the more vulnerable he gets. A man is an island, completely surrounded by the water of his own thoughts, his own fallacies, his own vices. His mother was the closest thing to him. She raised him made him who he was. His father would be back and forth from the air force, until one day he had died from an experiment gone wrong. He had few fond memories of his father. Cancer…cancer had killed his mother when he was seventeen. Hector had taken care of him since then. No matter what Hector

would do Jack would show no closeness. Jack would remain quiet soon after, but he then soon started to come out of his shell. Hector mentored him through college and law school. He had one day suffered a heart attack, while Jack was in law school. Jack vowed to pass the bar for him and his mother. Fortunately, Hector pulled through, but the experience deeply hurt Jack, he couldn't trust life, every time he got close to someone they would get taken away.

This strained his relationship with God, with Hector, and any intimate relationship he would get into. His smartass remarks and cruel attitude would shield him from any person who would attempt to make the mistake of getting close to him. So he stuck to what he knew best, the law. The law for Jack was his Bible, the courtroom his altar. There was no more perfect arena for battle. The greatest minds fighting, battling in the form of rhetoric. The greatest artist would take the win. This was always his passion everyone saw this in him since he was a child. Incidentally this great talent came with its own price, which made him socially awkward at times. Even though he would be a growing lion in his jungle, he was a sheep among men in the real world. For some reason he would always get bested in any argument conversation outside of the courtroom.

Many times during an argument Jack would close his eyes and imagine the courtroom around him, and immediately he would be in his home and would be able to fight back. He was almost like child outside of his comfort zone, which was narrow enough as it is. Jack shakes his head trying to get back into the working mind frame. He walks into an empty building to find a man in a white dress shirt and trousers held up by suspenders. He is standing like a statue with his hands in his pockets staring at what seems to be a clear lit up board. From his angle it was impossible to see anything on the board, but Jack was sure, that the man was studying something that could be beneficial to himself.

"Detective Brown?"

"Yes, you must be," He looks at the young man as he squints his eyes, "Mr. Jack Kennedy. How are you this," He takes a glimpse at his watch, it reads twelve twenty A.M., "morning, and your ten minutes early…good."

"Tired as hell and thank you. Punctuality is a big part of my life. How are you?"

"Confused." He returns his gaze to the board.

"Excuse me?"

"Just confused by this evidence. Nothing seems to add up."

"Well, I guess in the case of my client that actually sounds like a good thing." Jack tries to be humorous, but it goes unnoticed by Brown. "Um…So any reason we're meeting in the dead of night on a Wednesday…or Thursday now?"

"Yes, well my apologies for asking you to meet so late, but I feel that after the lab has closed we can actually do some research without the annoyance of other technicians, and no one will be getting in our way or, for that matter, me getting in the way of others as my brother-in-law likes to put it. He is the head technician here and he allows me to look through forensic files and what not this late so I can concentrate in peace. Honestly, I think he does it to make his and his lab assistants' lives better, but whatever gets the job done right?"

"So what happens if you have a question?"

"Well, then I just leave a note and he responds in the same way, and if it's something that has more than one question then I just wait or call him depending on the urgency of the matter. So, Mr. Kennedy I hear you have replaced Mr. Hailer, how the hell did that happen?"

"Jack would be just fine by the way. Is there anything in particular you'd like me to call you or…?"

"Detective Brown would be just fine, Jacqueline." Brown interrupts.

"Jeez what the hell is up with all the girl names today?" Jack thinks to himself, he shrugs it off and continues the conversation. "Okay…so I just felt that Heyward could use a better lawyer than some court appointed lawyer, and I'm sure with me on the case he would at least have a fighting chance."

"Wow, you really sound like you sold yourself that story pretty well. Anyone else buy it?"

"Wha…What do you mean?"

"You know the whole noble cause, fighting chance story. You sound like as long as you believe the story everyone else should too."

"Who the hell is this guy?" Jack thinks to himself.

"Seems to me you were looking for your golden ticket to the top and Robert Heyward was the goat that was going to take you there."

"What the hell are you talking about?"

"I read up on you princess, not a single major case under your belt yet, and…all of a sudden your defending the great Robert Allen Heyward. Just interesting why and how things happen, wouldn't you agree Mr. Kennedy?" Jack just stares at Brown, as Brown continues to stare at the board as if Jack's existence didn't seem to matter.

"I don't know what the hell you're talking about Mr. Brown, but this case is every bit my priority as any other case, and I would appreciate our focus to be on the case rather the believability of me taking this case for just causes or not. I'm sure we have a lot of work to do tonight." Jack answers.

"Of course, my apologies sometimes I feel like I can figure people out…" He finally turns and faces Jack, "but I guess sometimes I'm just wrong. No hard feelings I hope." He says with a somewhat condescending smile. He then puts out his hand as to lead the way. "Shall we, Mr. Kennedy?"

"Yes, let's get to work."

Before they start walking Jack finally takes a good glimpse of what was on the board. The angle he was standing in earlier wouldn't allow him to see the board too well…Damn technology! On the board were about ten or so diagrams, like a bolt it hit Jack that these were diagrams drawn by Brown on how he felt the murder may have happened, and only a couple pointed directly at Heyward. That still would give him a twenty percent chance in Brown's head. Jack stays on course continuing to move without stopping completely and staring at the diagrams, he tries to memorize as many pictures as possible, but it was no use. The two continue to move forward towards the table with Hodges' murder case and all the evidence left behind. It was just a mess of random "clues," that could have meant anything.

There were also pictures of the scene, which actually aided the confusion somewhat because anyone would be able to place the random objects in place of the scene of the crime. Both Jack and Brown stood quietly looking over the evidence and the pictures as if it would at any moment jump out and tell them the whole story of what had happened, but the evidence stood in the same fashion as the two men, in silence. Brown was holding up a pair of pants and examining it closely. Jack who was just trying to study the contents of the evidence finally went to reach over at Hodges' coat.

"What the hell are you doing princess?!" Brown yells out, startling Jack.

"What the fuck you freak!" Jack backs off immediately.

"Do *not* touch the evidence with your bare hands. We have enough to deal with here; we don't need extra particles, of your nasty hands contaminating the evidence. If you're that eager to look, grab a pair of surgical gloves."

"Wait I saw you touching stuff, in fact you have a pair of pants in your hands and I didn't see you..." Brown pulls out his right hand from under the pants only to show a white surgical glove on his hand. Feeling foolish Jack responds, "Yeah, well what's to say your left hand doesn't have a glove on it?"

"You're...kidding right?" Brown looks at him through the top of his glasses. He puts down the pants exposing his left hand, which was also covered. He then turned around and grabbed a box of gloves and tossed it over to Jack.

"Thanks. You know we could actually be nice to each other," He says as he puts on a pair of gloves, "I mean who knows we might actually end up working better together."

Brown responds in silence.

"Yeah, I was thinking the same." Jack then squeezes his lips together and raises his eyebrows and goes back to looking at the coat. "Man this must of sucked..."

Brown looks up at Jack, with a look that was almost intrigued by the fact that Jack could have spotted something that he did not. Jack spots the arousal of Brown's interest through the corner of his eye, and then continues, "Oh well that's too bad." Jack puts down the coat and continues to aimlessly look at other pieces of evidence.

"What?"

"What?"

"What must have sucked?"

Jack looks behind him both ways, and then points to himself. "Oh, we're...we're talking now? Because I could have sworn..."

"Okay come on sweetheart that's enough, what must have sucked?"

Figuring he had enough fun Jack decides to answer. "Well as big of a man as Hodges' was it seems this coat was actually pretty snug on him, considering his size and the size of the coat. Weird, I wonder if he had gained weight recently. I mean seeing what his size was after the autopsy this coat must have fit perfectly, meaning it must have been tight while he was alive. What about the pants, what size are they?"

Brown looks in the pants, "Forty two thirty four."

"Man, people really are much fatter than they are tall these days. Anyway the autopsy for his waistline was about forty-one.

"So what you're saying is that he decomposed to that size which means he must have been a little fatter before? What's your point?"

"I'm just saying it must have sucked to fight in such a tight suit. I mean look at the left armpit area, it's torn." Brown walks over to where Jack is standing to observe the coat. "Which is also weird because the way the holster is set on the left hand side in his inside coat pocket you'd have to guess that he was probably right handed, but now I'm not so sure anymore."

Acting as if he were impressed by Jack's keen eye, Brown takes the coat to confirm Jack's thoughts. "Wow, that's a pretty good eye you've got there Jacqueline, now you want to tell me the part where this actually has anything to do with the case, because, if you really want to continue stating obvious facts about stupid pointless things then I have a six year old nephew that might need some help in his *Naming Colors* book at home. My wife was babysitting tonight, but her meek intelligence couldn't possibly hold up to yours." He puts the coat down and moves on to the next piece of evidence.

Jack just stares at him, "You know you're a real son of a bitch. Why the hell did you want to meet me if you were just going to be a dick to me anyway?"

"Because, I want to talk to you about the case, and possibly get an interview with Heyward, I don't need you to look over the evidence, that's my job."

Jack closes his eyes for a short moment and the opens them. "Look I don't care what you think your job is; I'm here to look at evidence so I can try to piece together something to show in court, showing Heyward's innocence. Now whether you want to help me or not, I really don't give a rat's ass. I can even come here during the day. I'm sure they won't have a problem with me cause I'm not some asshole who puts everyone down trying to figure them out because you're on some bullshit power trip only to have someone to come up with some lame assed excuse that you're 'in the way' so they can push you off and have you stuck doing graveyard shifts by yourself. And the only way you even get to communicate with anyone is through little yellow sticky pads. So you know what? Fuck you okay?"

Brown stares at Jack for a moment, but Jack could tell by the look on his face, it had nothing to do with what he had just said. "Little yellow sticky pads...Jacqueline you're a freaking genius." He starts walking back towards the board. His walk was somewhat fast with a strange spring to it. Confused Jack decided to follow, he was sure he must have done some emotional damage with his comments, but he didn't think it'd make Brown go crazy.

"Hey man I was just pissed...you're not going to kill me or anything are you? Cause I've got to tell you I'm far too pretty to..."

"While you were giving you're cute little speech I was really thinking if my wife actually left me any food to eat tonight 'cause I'm kind of hungry. Then I figured it might be getting a little late and there's a taco cabana open down the block and I just might get some food from there real quick." Jack's face just drops in disbelief. "Then you said something that reminded me of something strange that I saw at the site, I kept it separate because it just might point to a motive. The strange part of the story is that if this gave Heyward the motive to kill Hodges, then why don't the rest of the pieces fit perfectly? See the thing is, to any idiot this piece of evidence would seal the deal, and that would be the end of the case. That's why I haven't really shared it so much with anyone, but since you're his lawyer you might actually find this interesting." Brown pulls out a small stack of papers.

"What is this?"

"Take a look, tell me if you see anything peculiar."

Jack studies the documents for a short while; on top are little yellow sticky notes. The notes read: ~~Set up meeting with Max. Consult final sales price with board. Set up final plans for Scorpion Banquet~~. Finish speech. Set up vacation plans with Julie-Anne. Keep 20% of stocks for Bryan. ~~Discuss new business plans/future with Bryan~~.

Behind the sticky pads were documents of talking about the sale of the company to Apollo…CEO General Maximus Edward Johnson…Behind that were other corporate legal documents of the company's recent activities.

"So, the company was being sold? Wow, that is weird. Is this the same Apollo that took over Orion Industries?" Jack asks.

"Exactly, now I feel that having this document as a big part of the prosecution, they would probably say something along the lines of…"

"Selling their company," Jack interrupts, "therefore selling the secrets of Cold Fusion, being Heyward's baby and legacy, to the same people who destroyed him and took over his company over five years ago! This would be perfect motive for the murder of the former CEO Earl Hodges."

"Uh…yes, thanks for interrupting douche bag."

"Sorry I got a little excited. So, what exactly is going on here?"

"That's what I've been trying to piece together. I think this murder is more than just a murder, I think there's more going on here than you and I know." Brown states.

"Who's this General Maximus Edward Johnson character?"

"I'm not quite sure, but I'm going to find out."

"So now what about Heyward, do you think he was framed?" Jack questions.

"I'm not sure, but I wouldn't be surprised. We both need to do a little more digging on our separate ends, but I don't think we have enough time to do it all."

"What the hell are you talking about, a murder trial could take up to years if we do it right, and especially if someone is up for the death penalty!" Jack exclaims.

"That's exactly what I'm saying. Sometimes more time gives us less time."

Jack raises one eyebrow at him as if Brown had gone mad. "Okay, now you've gone completely nuts."

"Listen the more time we take to solve this extra crap that is outside of the case the more time the prosecution has to build up evidence against us. We have a time crunch here to find all this information and simultaneously defend Heyward. I feel the best chance you would have is to ask for a no motions to delay the trial and work your butt off. If you really want to shine Jacqueline, this is your time."

"You're out of your Goddamn mind. If I ask for a no motion to delay not only am I going to be the first free lawyer to get fired in history, the judge is going to laugh at me, the media will tear me to shreds, and my career will go down the fucking drain. You must really think I'm some fool for you to seriously believe that I would actually even entertain such a suggestion."

"I'm telling you kid, this is what needs to happen. Just think about it okay?" Brown responds.

"No."

Brown shakes his head in frustration, "Look, do what you want, but I promise you the longer this trial ends up taking, the better the chances of Heyward actually getting that death penalty. I've been in the business long enough to know that as a fact. So if nothing else, at least think about that."

Jack looks at his watch. "Okay maybe you're right, but you have to understand I still have to do my job, and since I'm the lawyer I have to use my discretion in this case. Which means that I have to do my job, do what I feel is right, and if I think a no motion to delay will hurt my client you can bet your ass it won't happen, especially if I can help it. Now it's really getting too damn late. Let's meet up again in a few days, I still have to wrap my head around everything that I just saw."

"Fine I'll walk you out. Obviously I don't have to express the severity of the secrecy of the documents." Brown says as they start walking out towards the door.

"Of course." They start making their way down the long narrow hallway. "But the next time I come down here, I'd like to look over evidence that would actually help my case. I understand the whole conspiracy aspect that you're trying to tackle here, and trust me I would love to help a self-involved sociopath like yourself any day of the week, but I really would like your help deciphering some of these clues with the evidence. I think in about a week or so..." Jack feels a sudden thud to his chest. He looks down and it's Brown's arm extended stopping him from moving. "What the hell..."

"Shh…" Brown put's a finger to his lips motioning Jack to stay quiet. "Did you come with anyone?" He whispers.

"What? No. Why?" Jack responds in whisper.

"Did you leave that door open with a doorstopper in it?"

"No. Why are we whispering?"

"So no one hears us."

"So now that we think someone is here, we should whisper? Don't you think they would have heard us talking before we noticed the door?"

"What? Shut up."

Brown pulls out his gun, and walks outside as stealth-fully as possible. He sees a van and a small sedan that he did not recognize. He comes back in. "What kind of car do you have?" He looks back inside only to find Jack's not there. "Jack." Brown whispers, "Jack!" He whispers louder.

"What?" Jack whispers back as loudly as possible.

"Where are you?"

Jack steps out the door in the side of the hallway to show himself.

"What the hell are you doing in there?" Brown asks annoyed.

"You have a freaking gun in your hand! What the hell do you think I'm doing?"

"Oh my God, will you get over here?"

"And risk getting shot? You must be out of your damn mind!"

"Get over here!" Brown says angrily. Jack tries to be as stealth-full as possible in the empty hallway. Brown stares at him like he is watching a young stupid child.

"What? I'm just being cautious."

"Which car is yours?"

"The old Lexus."

"Okay, we need to go back. Someone is here."

"What? I'm not going back in there. Tell you what, since my car is like twenty feet away, I will quietly walk that way and take off. You on the other hand can be super cop and kill bad guys trying to steal lab coats in the middle of the night." Jack pats Brown on the shoulder and tries to take off. Brown grabs him.

"Stop, they probably have an accomplice in the van, and if they see you your life could be in danger."

"Damn it man!" Jack says as he kicks the ground. When he turns towards Brown again, he sees him looking through Jack's wallet. He then checks his pockets in disbelief.

"Hey what the hell are you doing with my wallet?!"

"Just making sure you are who you say you are."

"I guess your story checks out." He hands the wallet back to Jack.

"How did you do that?"

"When you've been in the business as long as I have, you tend to pick up a thing or two." He motions Jack back towards the hall and they start making their way back towards the labs. They try to check each door, but most of them are locked. They finally make it back into the room in which they were looking at evidence from Robert's case. Jack sees someone in the shadow move swiftly.

"Shit, right there!" He whispers to Brown.

"Freeze!" Brown yells out as Jack turns on the lights. They see a woman and she stops immediately.

"Don't shoot. I'm not here to hurt anyone." She pleads.

"Who the hell are you?" Brown says as he tries to get a better angle at the woman.

"Yeah, and what's your phone number?" Jack says with a smile, as he looks her up and down.

She looks at Jack in disgust, "Ugh, I'm just one of the lab workers from here. I forgot my key so I saw someone walk in here. I kept the door open with the doorstopper."

Brown looks at Jack and shakes his head.

"What?" Jack replies cluelessly.

"That was over an hour and a half ago. What were you doing here the whole time, because I definitely didn't hear or see you?" Brown asks the woman.

"I...I..." She stutters for a moment, "I was in the other room getting files and when I saw you two gentlemen leave, I decided to finish my work in here like I normally do." She says with a half smile and a nervous laugh.

"She's lying." Browns tells Jack.

"How can you tell?"

"Because she called you a gentleman." Brown says as he walks closer to her. Jack gives him a sarcastic look. Brown reaches for the young lady's purse.

"Hey what the hell are you doing? This is personal property." She tries to hold her purse away.

Brown manages to grab the purse anyway. He turns around for a moment then hands the gun to Jack. "Here, hold this and try not to kill anyone okay?"

"Yeah sure." He holds the gun and has it pointed at the young woman. "So how you doing?" He says with a smile. She replies by rolling her eyes.

"Oh lord." Brown says under his breath.

"Speechless? Yeah I have that affect on women." Jack continues.

"Can you hurry up, so I don't have to listen to this moron any longer?" The young woman cries out.

"Believe me I'm trying." Brown replies. "So how long have you been working here miss?"

"Lisa, Mona." She shakes her head, "Stupid." She says to herself under her breath.

"So, Mona huh? That's hot." Jack says.

"Please."

"So Miss Mona Lisa, it says here in *your* wallet that your *real* name is Ambrene Khowja from Atlanta, and you work for USN."

"Wait, are you Amber K?" Jack asks.

"Maybe."

"Oh my God you are! Can I tell you, I think you're so, freaking, hot." Jack says as he puts the gun down on the table next to him no longer feeling a threat.

"Wow, I'm always happy to see my fans." She says somewhat seductively as she moves closer to him.

"You…you are?"

"Stay back Miss Khowja." Brown tries to gain control.

"Amber, please." She says still walking towards Jack unmoving her gaze from his eyes, "You two know my name, but I don't know your names, how rude."

"I…I'm Jack. And he…he's." Jack stammers.

"Brown I'm detective Brown."

"Ou Jack I like that name." She says as she is face to face with Jack almost kissing him. Jack closes his eyes and puts out his lips expecting a hot wet kiss.

"Will you open your eyes? You jackass!" Brown yells out.

When Jack opens his eyes he sees a gun pointed at him. He looks down at the table next to him only to find the gun he set there to be gone. "Wait, so no kiss?"

"What are you, an idiot?" Amber replies.

"No."

"No, you really are an idiot." Brown confirms.

"Okay, now I'm going to take my stuff, and I'm getting the hell out of here. And if either of you try to stop me, I'll shoot."

"No you won't."

"Test me."

"I wouldn't doubt her Brown, she sounds serious." Jack says.

"Shut up."

"Just saying."

"Amber, put down the gun before I arrest you, for possession, trespassing, disobeying an officer, and so on."

"Wow, I'd put down the gun." Jack states.

"Shut up!" Amber and Brown both yell out.

"Okay…rude…"

"What makes you think I'm going to put down this gun, when I could have it pointed at you two and walk away completely free?"

"Well for one, you're a lead reporter for USN, which means many people know who you are, and for you to sneak around in the middle of the night in a lab, where there's much evidence lying around from many crime scenes means that you have a high interest in one of them. Having that said, with your high stakes, shooting someone would obviously mean jail time, and a murder would be far worse, especially for killing a cop, so you're probably not going to shoot."

"Don't act like you know me."

"He has a bad habit of doing that, and trust me it doesn't end there." Jack explains.

"Anyway," Brown continues.

Jack raises his eyebrows at Amber as to say 'I told you so.'

"…say you don't shoot and I find you to be an actually threat I have another gun in my waist right here." Brown motions with his eyes, Amber and Jack both follow. "Which I would have pulled out and have you shot before you even think about pulling the trigger." Amber stands there somewhat stunned in disbelief. "…and finally, now that you know the first two, that gun in your hand doesn't have any bullets in it."

"What?!" Jack and Amber both yell in shock.

"Did you actually think I would give a fool like Jack something like a gun, where he can actually have the possibility of hurting someone? That's like giving a monkey, open electricity in a pool."

"You're bluffing." Amber says.

"And you're still an ass." Jack adds.

"Am I?" Brown moves over and there is a clip sitting on the table behind him and a bullet next to it.

Amber looks under the gun only to find the magazine missing. "Shit." She says in a disappointing tone and hands back the gun to Brown. "So, I guess you're going to arrest me now?"

"Well it depends, if you can tell me what an anchor reporter all the way from Atlanta is really doing here, I might have a change of heart."

She takes a long sigh, "Alright, basically I wanted to be a field reporter for the Robert Heyward murder case, and I was here trying to find confirming evidence against him to make sure that son of a bitch gets the death penalty."

"You're here for the Heyward case?" Brown asks.

"Yeah, why?"

"I'm the assigned detective to that case."

"So who the hell are you, his assistant?" Amber asks Jack.

"Hardly, I'm Heyward's defense attorney."

"Are you kidding me? You're Jack Kennedy?"

"Yep, Excited? I don't blame you."

"No you idiot! I had to try and get an interview with you."

"Really…" He says with a big smile.

"Ugh I hate my life." She responds.

"So what do you have against Heyward?" Brown asked.

"Back in New York, when he was the CEO of Orion, I was trying to expose him for blowing up Artemis labs, when...let's just say some stuff happened and my best friend ended up getting murdered for it. Now this is my chance for me to make sure that bastard gets what he deserves."

"That's crazy! I remember watching all of that on the news." Jack says.

"Yeah same here." Brown adds.

"I'm sorry that you went through all that, but you have to understand that I have to defend him, even though what happened may or may not be true." Jack says.

"May or may not be true? It is true. So how does it feel to defend a world class villain?"

"Okay, relax, he hasn't been proven guilty for anything."

Amber cringes at the fact that she has been told to relax, "Don't tell me to relax. And he hasn't been proven to be guilty *yet*, but he will be soon enough. Now if you will excuse me I'll be on my way." She begins to walk out, when Brown notices something hanging out of her jacket.

"Um...Miss Amber...what's that in your coat pocket?"

"Nothing." She replies trying to keep stride.

"Stop Miss Khowja." Frustrated she stops. Brown searches her pocket and pulls out a rope like camera. "You like being difficult don't you?"

"Whatever. Can I go now?"

"Sure."

"Wait hold up." Jack intervenes, "Look whether we think Heyward is guilty, innocent, or there's some crazy conspiracy going on, we're all here to figure out the truth, and I think that's the most important part. How about we all exchange cards, so we can keep in touch and update each other with everything that is going on. Even though we all have different goals I think keeping in touch will help achieve those goals better and faster."

"I hate to admit it but I think the kid might be right." Brown responds.

"Ugh...Okay." Amber digs through her purse, "Here is my card." She hands it to both of them.

"Cool way to get your number huh?" Jack says with a big smile.

"Do you ever stop?" Brown asks as he gives them both his card.

"Just for that, you can only call me during the day." Jack responds as he hands Brown his card, "And you, you can still call me anytime you'd like." He hands his card to Amber.

"Yeah don't hold your breath." Amber says as she takes the card and then starts to head out again. Jack begins to follow, but Brown grabs his arm and keeps him put. He waits for Amber to leave.

"Look, I'm not sure what happened in New York, but this helps my theory that there might be a lot more to this than we know. Whether or not she might be involved, we should stay close to what she knows. The way she sneaks around could actually be more beneficial than anything. But this further supports my case for you to request a no motion for delay."

"Oh no, not this again."

"Listen! With people like her, and the power they hold over such things as the media, they can really help sway the case in any which way. Now again I'm not saying Heyward's innocent, I'm just not so sure he's guilty. Getting a no motion to delay will help people like her from collecting data and presenting it in any which way that they'd like. Now if you want to have any advantage this might be the best way to go about it."

"Okay you got me, I'll think about it."

Brown stares at him.

"I'm being serious. I'll look over the case tomorrow and see what I can do. I still have to talk it over with Heyward and explain this craziness to him."

"Okay do what you have to do, just remember what I said, we're pressed for time." Brown says with conviction.

***

"You might have taken my camera, Mr. Brown, but lucky for me the video feed went straight to the news van. I'll have to look over the tape tomorrow I can barely stay awake." Amber says to herself as she drives off in her news van.

***

"You should have killed him when you had the chance!" A dark high pitched voice screams from the distance, but seems like it's getting closer.

"No, no, no!" Robert covers his ears rocking back and forth. "I'm getting better; you were supposed to be gone. I was feeling better. Why are you back?! No, no, no…" He continues to rock with his eyes closed.

"Well I don't know what the hell you were thinking, but I'm here to stay. Don't worry I'll protect you, because you are the body in which I live. You are diseased, but you are my home and I am going nowhere, I am here to cleanse you with my fire. Now tell me, why didn't you kill that traitor? The one who took your life from you? He was feet, nay, inches away from your crushing hands, and you let him walk away with your head bowed down to him like some peasant. You were the king of kings at one time and look at you now… Answer me! Why didn't you tear is throat out and eat his heart?"

"He is not the reason for your downfall Robert." The womanly voice chimes in.

"Yes he is you wretched witch! Don't listen to her Robert; she only comes around when things can finally go our way. Only then she brings her ugly face around."

"Mom, make this ago away please…" Robert pleads.

"Mother? This witch is not your mother? She is a parasite that feeds on your body. She lives as you die. She becomes stronger as you become weak."

"Don't listen to him Robert, don't follow the darkness, there is no light at the end of that tunnel. He will eat away your flesh, and crush your bones. Every time he speaks to you, notice your stomach eating itself, notice your brain fighting to leave the body, notice the weakening of the knees."

"Yes Robert, notice the weakening of your knees, the same sensation you felt every time you laid your eyes on Sandra. Was that such a bad feeling?"

"No. Sandra…"

"No, it wasn't. You must get your life back; you mustn't let such opportunities slip away Robert. My son…"

"Dad?"

"He is not your father Robert! He is nothing. Stand up Robert and look at yourself…Why won't you go to the mirror Robert? If you are not willing to look at yourself than how can you expect your family to look at you when they come to visit."

"No one is coming Robert!" The dark high pitched voice yells. "No one cares about you, except for me! No one cares; now that everyone has gone, I am here."

"Robert, believe in yourself once again like you did earlier in that cold steel room. Control your life, and we shall disappear. Be who you were, no longer who you have become." The woman's voice tries to convince him.

"Robert wouldn't you rather rule in hell than serve in heaven! There is nothing more than this jail cell. There is nothing outside the walls. This is your sea now, and the sea awaits its shark, it awaits its king!"

"Robert a servant in heaven is a servant of God. Sandra is a servant of God. You must believe once again, you must believe in yourself. You must fight this case, you must win. Your family depends on it."

"What family Robert? Ask her what family! Ask her!"

"The family that will come visit you. Your family."

"Stop it!" Robert yells out and the voices echo away like a bad dream. The echoes stay in his head, but as long it isn't really them he can manage to deal with it. He quickly pulls out his book from under his bed and begins to write. The sounds of the pen scratching the paper soothe his ears.

Chapter 44

Phil is awakened by a slight sobbing sound. When he looks over in his bed to where Janis should be she is nowhere to be found. Confused, he gets up and looks around the room and he finds no sign of her anywhere. He then walks over to the bathroom in their room, still nothing. Phil quickly becomes more and more anxious from the thought of his missing, crying wife. He starts to recall many times he has been home only to find Janis with deep dark circles around her eyes, as if she were crying, but she would claim that she's just been extremely tired.

She looked like she had been possessed with her hollowed out eyes, and her slow uncaring walk. He tried to hire help for around the house for when he wasn't home, but Janis would refuse it every time, her defense would be that she is the mother and wife of the house and no one needs come in to take care of her home, but her. Phil didn't have much of an argument against it, except for when it came to her health, and even then he would be excluded in some parts. The doctors said it might be slight depression, and when they start talking to her about it, Phil would be asked to leave the room every time.

He figured it was a woman's sensitivity talk so he would never argue or ask about it. He tried his best to cheer her up as much as possible, but it would always seem that she would smile to entertain him. He thought about the baby, and how Janis would show more and more every day. She would look into Phil's eyes and sometimes be lost in happiness, giving Phil signs of hope. She would then turn her attention towards Joshua and begin to cry again.

Phil believed that Janis was afraid that the child would have issues, and maybe she thinks that Phil would not be able to handle the stress and leave. He tried to reassure Janis everyday of the baby's wellbeing and security, as well as his commitment to the family. Some days Janis would be receptive and other days she would cry more as a result of it. The doctors told Phil just to be encouraging and to stay by her side, because this was a highly hormonal time for her. Phil complied and did his best. He finally made it into Joshua's room where he found Janis sitting next to him as he slept. She was weeping yet trying to be as quiet as possible. How Phil heard her crying was even beyond him, but he was glad that he did.

He stood in the corridor for a second to make sure he wasn't interrupting anything, but Janis heard him, she got up and rushed to him hugging him tight and beginning to cry louder and louder. Phil tried to hush her, and walked her out of Joshua's room so they wouldn't wake him. He got a glass of water and sat Janis down on their bed and handed her the glass, as she sat and wept. He wiped her tears with his hand and sat next to her, but it was no use; her tears fell like water through a broken dam. They both wanted to speak, but the moment wouldn't allow either of them to say a word. So they continued to sit there, Phil held Janis close, her warm body comforting him, and his warmth comforting her.

They both sat there looking in different directions, they were close but tried to give the other space. It was an odd feeling, they both wanted to open up and tell the other what they felt in their hearts, they both wanted to reveal their secrets, but the words would get caught in their throats and the choking sensation would force them both to cry out even more. There were so many reasons for the tears; each tear was almost a different reason for crying. Neither of them truly knew why the other was crying, they had their assumptions and left it at that. With each passing moment they felt closer and closer to each other. Their love grew as they held each other. The crying was becoming softer as time was passing. It felt as if the whole world was moving faster and faster just spinning away as they sat in their home, the seasons were changing, they were getting older and the hair on their heads were becoming grey as their skin became wrinkled and soft. They felt as if they were dying, but it was okay, they were together, and as long as they were together they could fall asleep and die peacefully in each other's arms. The world was moving on, but they continued to stay stationary in each other's arms crying as if nothing else mattered, and as if the world outside their walls was nonexistent. Phil then turned towards Janis and tilted her head up to face him. The seasons move backwards even faster than they were moving forward, their hair returned to normal, and their skin became firm again. The everlasting journey had brought them back to where they had started.

It was easy to tell from the look on both their faces that they were building up courage for the other person, and as long as they had their strength and love then no secret could hold them back or tear them apart. They both smiled at one another in chorus to each other's song. With great passion Phil grabs Janis' face and kisses her as if he was off in great battle and he has come back home after years for the first time. And with all the courage within him he finally puts together the words he needed to say and he speaks.

"Janis, I love you, and…I need to tell you…"

"Phil we need to talk…" Janis interrupts; Phil is taken a back at her disruption towards his thoughts. Confused and stunned Phil replies.

"Okay…You okay love?"

"No," She looks down at her feet, "I'm afraid I haven't been completely honest with you Phil."

"Wh…What?"

Chapter 45

"Okay mom that's everything." Michael says looking into the back of the trunk of the car making sure there was nothing else.

"Okay thank you sweetheart." She says as she pulls her luggage to the side, "Now you make sure you pick up Charlotte from the vet by seven thirty and feed her…and make sure that she doesn't have too many treats. It will ruin her diet, I'm tired of that dog getting spoiled all the time."

"I know mom…"

"And I told Stan to call to make sure you don't need anything and…"

"Mom…"

"And I left his number on the fridge for you just in case you need anything. And finally I told Kayla all the things you need to do around the house so if you don't do it, I told her to stop coming over."

"Yeah right."

"Try me." She gives a smirk, Michael just rolls his eyes. "That's what I thought; now I'm going to call everyday so you better make sure you have your cell phone on you, no excuses."

"Mom…Your flight is going to be leaving…" He looks at his watch. "In an hour, now go…!" He says somewhat irritated and somewhat jokingly.

"Okay, but no parties, and be safe." Sandra sees that Michael is getting annoyed so she stops and sighs, "You sure you still you don't want to come sweetie? I mean we still can get standby, I'm sure there's still open…"

"Mom, I'm sure, trust me I'll be fine. I need this. Now just make sure you call me when you land okay?"

"Oh my boy," She touches his face, "grown up so fast."

"So yes, you'll call?"

"Yes, yes okay I love you sweetheart, I'll talk to you soon." She gives him a hug and a kiss.

"Hey mom, we okay?" He says softly in her ear.

"Yes." She looks him in the eyes as they still hold each other and then she gives him another kiss.

"Alright Michael, if your done kissing your mommy how about you say goodbye to your little bro." Ryan says as he finishes pulling their luggage to one side.

"Alright little bro, just make sure everything's okay when you go down there okay?" He says as he grabs his one arm and the hugs him.

"Yeah for sure, any message for dad?"

"Just make sure your okay, okay Ryan? And take care of mom." He gives him a smile.

Ryan squeezes his lips together looks down and nods his head, "Okay man, take it easy. We'll call you when we get there."

"Okay we really should get going now," Sandra says, "we'll see you hopefully in a week, if anything changes we'll let you know okay sweetie?"

"Okay mom." He looks at Ryan, "Later man."

"Later."

They finally entered LAX airport and a short time later, they board their airplane. Ryan still had a few bruises, but nothing major. His emotional scars from the fight were beginning to heal as well. Once airborne, Ryan puts on his headphones, as his mother falls asleep. He looks out the window as they quickly begin to pass the clouds. They were soon high in the blue sky above the clouds. "This is my home." Ryan thought to himself, as he looked down at the clouds trying to see shapes in them. He saw one that looked like a castle in which he lived alone waiting for the day the wind would push another castle nearby with a princess in it. He looked at all the cloud animals, who were all his royal subjects.

The patches in the sky were like lakes, and rivers to him, in which he can jump down in to the sky and bathe in its water. He saw dragons he would slay, and the people he would save. His, army didn't have real faces they were like toy soldiers, he could never ask a real person to fight and die for him. Off in the distance he saw his horse, silent night, to the world this horse was a white cloud, to him the horse was as black as coal, with hair as slick as silk. The two would ride through the heavens all through the night looking down at the Earth seeing all the great things in the world from the pyramids, to the Eiffel tower, and to the Great Wall of China. Soon enough these worldly objects bored Ryan so he took off into space with silent night and they would race around the rings of Saturn with other creatures.

He explored new worlds and brought together old enemies. He would have epic battles from twenty different worlds at one time, because they had captured his father. There were few worlds that would help him on his journey, and they were greatly outnumbered, no matter what difficulties, you must fight for, and protect, the ones you love. He truly was a prince of all worlds. Another airplane passes by breaking Ryan's concentration. He then closes the window curtain and lays his head back trying to lose himself in his music. His palms get sweaty in the anticipation of what was yet to come, he could save his father in the heavens, but how could he do it on Earth? Was he guilty? Did he really kill that man? Ryan could not wrap his head around his father being evil, his father was his superman. Ryan starts to feel hot and cold at the same time. The space he was in was becoming tighter and tighter. He starts breathing harder and harder; he reaches for his inhaler and puts it in his mouth, which immediately brings him back to normal.

Sandra is awoken by the sound of the inhaler. "You okay sweetie?" She asks, half asleep. Ryan just nods his heads yes, and continues to lose himself in his music. They both don't speak to one another, lost in their own thoughts, and from the uneasiness of the atmosphere. Sandra closes her eyes once again and tries to sleep, but it doesn't work. Her thoughts keep her up, so she decides to entertain them as the flight progresses. She already misses Michael. After the fight between him and Ryan, she couldn't bear to see him anymore. Her anger towards what he had done to Ryan was like a laceration to her heart. After she saw how much the fight also affected and hurt Michael she couldn't stay mad at him for much longer.

Every day he would cry for his brother and every night he would visit Ryan while he was a sleep. One night Michael left the hospital crying horribly when he came home Sandra saw the pain and tears in his eyes and came after him into his room. They both hugged as Michael incessantly apologized. Sandra could do nothing, but hold her child and forgive him. That night they talked more and became closer. Michael showed her the basketball he had gotten for Ryan and she loved the idea. Sandra opens her eyes and looks over at Ryan then closes them again. She's brought back to when her and Robert first meet, and the timeline moves forward as the images turn to water paintings. She sees their first dance, their first kiss, their wedding day. Time moves so fast, but yet it flows smoothly like the rivers. She sees the night of baby Sandra's death, and their fight back in Los Angeles.

She sees him becoming a drunk more and more everyday. As the images progress tears fall one by one from her eyes as if they were sneaking out. She wipes them away quickly so no one would see. She sees the silence that had become her life from the moment her child had passed. The silence only started to break when she started making friends like Stan. It was nice to be able to be part of groups again and laugh with people her age; her life was coming back on track up until she received the phone call of Robert's murder case. Murder…Robert. The two words just didn't fit in the same sentence and here she was discussing it, pondering it.

Sandra feels that she had led him to this, but his actions were his own. Day after day and night after night she struggled in trying to make the decision of whether or not to go to Houston. When the new lawyer, Jack Kennedy, had called, he somehow had convinced her to come. He said it was almost certain that Robert was facing the death penalty, and she and the boys were all he had. No one should die alone. Not even the devil was sent to hell by himself. So she decided to go be there for him.

For better or for worse, she had to do this; she had to see him once more. The kids deserve to see their father once more before he died. It befuddled her on how every thought she had was convinced that Robert was going to die. But she has rarely heard of defendants in death penalty cases like his, with all the evidence against his favor ever get away. She wasn't sure what she should be expecting when she got to Houston. She didn't know what she wanted, if she felt he deserved this fate, or if she wanted him to beat this. To escape any guilt she left it up to God. She didn't want to drown herself in hope, hope brings heartache. If you expect nothing then you get nothing, which is safe and safe is good. Safe was unlike Robert, Robert was a risk taker, a bull. Always running and crashing into the next project, but he had a keen eye for the right risks.

Unfortunately all of us lose sight of things sometimes, and if we take enough risks we all eventually fail. It is the nature of the beast, and the beast consumed Robert when he chose Artimis. He had chosen his true love over her, and he had to live by his decision and now he will die by his decision. Every time Sandra is brought back to such thoughts of Robert a new evil is brewed within her, like soup for the devil, and when he hungers again then more thoughts are brought into her mind. "Forgive us our debts, as we forgive

our debtors….For if you forgive men when they sin against you, your heavenly Father
will also forgive you. But if you do not forgive men their sins, your Father will not forgive
your sins." Forgiveness was the key to which Sandra could not find the door.

"Good afternoon ladies and gentlemen this is your captain speaking."
Both Sandra and Ryan are awakened from their thoughts. "We should be
landing flight number one nine two one in just about half an hour to
Houston Intercontinental Airport, the weather is approximately seventy
nine degrees and sunny, we will be landing on time, and at this time we will
be putting on the seatbelt sign so we are asking everyone to please take
your seats and fasten your seatbelts as we prepare for landing. We hope
you enjoyed your flight with us and hope to see you again."

As Ryan and Sandra join everyone as they stretch and prepare to get
off the airplane, they catch each other's eye and are immediately brought
back to the harsh reality for the reason of their flight. They could only
hope that their daydreams have prepared them enough for what they
were about to encounter. Ryan sees the trouble in his mother's eyes and
reaches out to grab her hand. They smile at each other. Ryan looks out the
window as he leaves his home in the sky, and Sandra begins to pray.

"You think he still looks the same?" Ryan interrupts her prayer.

"I don't know dear."

They finally make it off the airplane and gather their luggage. Once
outside they both notice that there is a man in a suit with a sign in his
hands that read, "Heyward" assuming it was for them they approached
the young man.

"Miss Heyward?"

"Hi, Sandra is fine."

"Ah, yes and you are Michael?"

"No, I'm Ryan."

"Oh okay, is Michael coming out?"

"No, Michael will not be joining us this visit. And you are?"

"Yes, sorry I'm Jack Kennedy we spoke over the phone. And I think
I spoke with you as well Ryan." He says as he shakes both their hands.

"Yes, we did." Ryan replied.

"Okay well I got us a cab, so let me help you with your luggage and we
can head over to the hotel. I'm sure you're tired so I'll give you a small

brief on the way there and we can get to more details, and get some work done tomorrow. How does that sound?" Jack opens his hands and gives them a look for an agreeable response.

"Sounds just fine Jack, and thank you for everything." Sandra replies with a hopeful smile.

Jack puts his arm on the side of her shoulder, "Of course. Now shall we." He begins to pick up their luggage and place them into the cabs trunk.

***

"Hello?"

"We just landed a bit ago."

"Okay mom, call me if anything important comes up."

"Okay hon take care of yourself."

"Okay, bye."

"Bye."

Michael was home alone for the first time. He had never been left alone for this long. There was always someone home, either his mom, Ryan, or even Charlotte for that matter. But the big house he lived in was a hallow shell now. He explored the house by himself expecting to find something he had never noticed before, but everything was just like it was supposed to be, it was a perfect house, but it was no home, not without his family at least.

Michael had stayed back, claiming his need to be alone for some time. Even he could not persuade himself to believing that. Everyone knew why he didn't go to Houston, and yet he stuck with his story. On the other hand this would give him time to collect himself, considering the events that had occurred in the recent past. He knows he should go to Houston and forgive his father like Sandra and Ryan forgave him, but he was too hard headed. Sometimes Michael's emotions consume him and he embodies them. The anger he felt towards his father was stanch and therefore his control over it was feeble. He was torn in what he should do, forgive and let there be more opportunity for disappointment and heartbreak, or stay angered and let the pain make him into the bitter person he was becoming. Neither seemed pleasing, but staying angry is what he knew, it was what came to him naturally and has worked for him thus far. He found dismay to be a good home for him. He wants to forgive and free his soul, but it is the fear of the unknown and the memories of the past, which keep him grounded. It always seems to be that when Michael gets lost within his thoughts, his thoughts will always repeat themselves, but in different words to sound new, but the results and the theme remain exactly the same. Michael is interrupted by a phone call. He looks over to see who is calling.

"Hey hon! What's up?"

"You okay baby?"

"Yeah, you here yet?"

"I should be there in about two minutes."

"Okay I'll be out."

Chapter 46

Janis,

That was the name of my mother. You don't know who I am, but I know very well who you are. One week ago was the day of your death, yet here you are, alive. Is this a miracle? No, this is a gift. From whom? You will never know. Why? It doesn't matter. You also have had a major concussion and you will most probably forget what has happened or who you were. Because of this amnesia let me remind you of who you were. You were a student here in New York, with fun friends, and a volunteer at the very hospital you are now residing in. Your school grades are less than even average, your friends are drug abusers and junkies who steal and prey on the lesser suspecting public terrorizing them for their own high. You were a volunteer at this hospital up until you were acquitted last month for stealing anti-depressants and other drugs for yourself, and to sell to your friends. Your death would be one more good thing for this city. Yet you are here, alive. You were in an accident on your motorcycle while on drugs. Don't worry you were not the cause. The details of the accident are unimportant except for the fact that you were the only survivor. Is this a miracle? No it is a gift. This is a gift from my father. He was a good man, and now the only last remaining piece of him lives within you. Do not go back to your old ways. It is impossible to do so by staying here. Enclosed is a plane ticket to anywhere in the world. Choose your destination wisely. Live your dreams and become better than who you are…who you were. In one man's death you regained life. If you do not do so, then remember, that the day

of your death was one week ago. This is no miracle, this is a gift. Take this
gift and the sun shall shine again.
    RAH.

"Who is RAH?" Phil asks completely confused staring at Janis as she
finishes reading the letter.

"RAH is the Egyptian god of the sun, who is represented by light,
warmth, and growth. So I'm guessing this person was someone who was
a person of God giving me a second chance to grow." Janis says.

Phil gives her a funny look.

"I don't know," She looks down at the box she is holding, "but I took
the plane ticket and went to Florida to be with my parents. I read about
the accident later on and what I did to that woman and especially that
child I could never forgot nor forgive myself; just thinking about it rips
my brain in half. I have never spoken of it since that day and even this here
is killing me inside. After I went to Florida, I finished nursing school and
met Nick." Phil turns his head and looks away, and the looks briefly back
at Janis before he brings attention to the bed underneath them. "I'm sorry
I'll stop."

He looks back at her, "No I'm listening, just please...go on." He takes
his hand behind his back and makes a fist as if it were to hold his tongue.
This story may never be told again and he didn't want to take the chance
and ruin it so he clenches his jaw for further insurance.

She takes a deep breath knowing how much this may be hurting him
and continues as if to plead her case, "Okay, we then fell for each other
and shortly after I had gotten pregnant with Joshua. During the
pregnancy there were some complications and the doctors thought that
Joshua would die. They said that there were irregularities near my womb
and because of it my child was suffering. These irregularities had
developed from the accident. I don't have many memories from that day
or remember much in detail about my life a few years before that and is
why I have never spoken so much about it. But I do remember a few
things and for some strange reason whenever I think of that day, I think
of you Phil. That day from the hospital...everything is hazy, but your
face...your face is clear like a crystal. I know I'm stupid, but every time I

have told you that you had a familiar face or that I remember you from some place that is what I'm talking about." She looks up at him somewhat expecting a ridiculous look back. Phil just looks at her with his eyebrows raised and squeezed together. "I know you must think I'm crazy so I'm just going to stop."

"No please love, continue. I want to know." Phil says as he takes her hand and holds it tight, trying to be as supportive as possible.

"Are you sure?"

"Of course."

Janis takes a deep breath and looks back down at the box she was holding for dear life with one hand now, "So every day was a new uphill battle in saving Joshua's life. Nick would be in and out, but it seemed with each passing day he would become more and more distant. I know I had my parents, but they could do only so much when you're pregnant and you need the father of your child. Eventually I went insane and my family had no choice, but to have me committed. I spent the rest of my pregnancy and six months more after Joshua's birth at an insane asylum. We named him Joshua because it means God rescues, and God had rescued my child. It was okay that I was in an institute as long as my child was safe." She takes another deep breath. "After about a year of me getting out of the asylum we discovered that Joshua had autism and then that's when Nick decided it was too much for him and he walked out the door and never turned back. From that day on I had to become stronger for myself, for my second chance at life, for Joshua. My parents helped me get on my feet, and soon after I became a nurse. A few years later I met the man of my dreams…and here you are. I have kept all my memories of the day of the accident in this box here." She looks up at Phil hoping for some sign of comfort.

"Come here." Phil gives her a kiss on the lips and holds her close. "Don't worry about anything I'm here now, and I always will be. If you get scared just say my name, and I will come to be by your side."

"Phil what if our child has problems too? What if our child doesn't make it? I'm so scared; I haven't stopped crying because of it. When the doctors close the door that is what we talk about, and I have been so scared to tell you, but every day I wanted you to be in that room with me.

I just…I just couldn't stand to lose you Phil, it would tear my whole life apart."

"Janis, you never have to be afraid to tell me anything, you are my life. Without you I'm nothing. I want you to be as open as possible, and I will always be there for you, you just have to let me." He kisses her on the cheek, "I am your man, and I am going nowhere…okay? And don't worry about the baby, if we live our lives in fear we'll never get anywhere. We have to keep faith, we have to be in this together and work together. If we don't keep a positive attitude then we won't make it through this pregnancy. I'll tell you this much, with you crying all the time the baby won't get any healthier, right?" She nods her head yes, "Like I said I'm not going anywhere, and we'll get through this together. And as long as we are together nothing will stop us."

"You promise?"

"I promise." They hug each other and hold each other for a moment. Relieved, Janis feels as if a hundred ton weight has been lifted from her shoulders.

"Mom?" The two turn their attention towards the door, and Joshua is standing there rubbing his eyes. Janis looks over at Phil gives him a kiss she folds up the letter, puts it into the box, and sets it on her dresser top. She then walks over to her child. He says something to her and she takes his hand and starts walking out. Phil just hangs his head in disbelief and overwhelmed by what had just happened. He feels closer to Janis and loves her more because of what she has just said. Then he thinks back to the whole conversation and tears of sadness and anger begin to form. Phil looks up at the ceiling as to act stronger even though no one was there to see. He realizes what just happened, shakes his head, and looks back down.

"So the one woman that can actually fall for me is a crazy woman…makes perfect sense now." He lets out a small laugh as he sniffs and tries to hold back his tears. He clenches his jaws tighter trying to break his own teeth. He is brought back to sanity and thinks to himself that Janis and Josh were all he had, no matter the past he had to look forward or be left out there all alone once more. After all, her past was before him and he can't help that. Whatever it took to suppress his anger for not knowing this information from the beginning he would do. *"And what about me, what about my confession?"* He thinks to himself. *"For now it must stay a secret, I must protect my family once again."* Some secrets are so for a reason and must stay that way. The days to come will be unbelievably challenging for him and his family, this was probably not the best time to burden them with his secrets, especially with how the trial may go, and anyone having the possibility to be a witness. The bliss of ignorance is a wonderful sedative for the belabor of knowledge.

Chapter 47

"Good afternoon Mr. Heyward." Jack says as he enters the room. Robert returns the welcome in silence. "I have some documents here for you to sign and I feel today we should really start working on what's going to happen during the trial. I have spoken with detective Brown and we have looked over…"

"I told you Jacky I'm not doing anything further until my family is here. Now you can take these papers and shove them up your…"

A knock interrupts Robert mid sentence and the security guard calls out. "Visitors for Kennedy Heyward meeting."

Robert turns around completely thrown off guard and sees Sandra enter the room behind her followed Ryan, both with their heads down and humble. With a big smile on hiss face, Jack lets out a small laugh and says, "Don't you just love the timing of some things Mr. Heyward?"

Sandra walks in and everything around Robert slows down immediately; from his breath, to his blood, to his thoughts. Her hair flowed slower as time becomes non-existent, she brushes her hair past her face and looks up, her steps were weightless as if she were walking on clouds, she was like a ghost brought back with a blink of an eye. Robert's heart was completely paralyzed and running a mile a minute, it was like he was having a seizure inside yet could not move one bit. It was as if he were looking at her for the first time in his life, once again. He shifts his gaze over to Ryan and his innocence melts Robert like ice thrown into a blaze. He looks behind them in desperation for Michael, and then looks right back at Sandra as she smiles because she finally got to see Robert's face. And just like that God had let his breath enter Robert and he was able to breathe out. From the relief of the suffocation Robert begins to weep unrestrained, as both Sandra and Ryan followed.

"Sandra?"

"We're here Robby." Sandra begins to cry as well. Robert then jumps up to give her and Ryan a hug. He looks at both of them as he holds them. "Where's Michael?" He asks as if he were greatly troubled by his missing son.

"Michael couldn't make it this time, but he'll come soon enough." Sandra replies. Robert hugs them both again as they all cry.

"Well I can see that our discussion may have to be delayed for a short while, so I'll let you all get reacquainted." Jack gathers his notes and begins to walk out.

"Jack." Robert holds Jacks shoulder. He turns around and looks at him. "Thank you." He says nodding his head.

Jack nods back with a half smile trying not to get caught up in the emotions, "I'll be back in a bit to get started." Robert nods his head in agreement. Outside Jack gets a phone call.

"Hello?"

"Mi hijo?"

"Hector?"

"How have you been son? I see you all over the news now, you weren't kidding about the exposure you were going to get. You better have brought you're A game Jack."

"Hector this is hard, and it's just getting harder, but the steps that I'm taking are too small for this playing field."

"Don't worry mi hijo, sometimes the smallest steps give us the biggest succor. You'll be fine mi hijo."

"I hope so, you think mom is watching?"

"You answer this; you ever think she is not?"

"No…"

Hector recognizes the distraught sound in Jack's voice. "Listen mi hijo, I know I said if you do this, you are on your own, but you know that I could never leave you by yourself huh?"

"I know, why do you think I went anyway?"

"Oh…Anyway, if you need anything you have all my resources, and my firm backing. Please Jack; call me if you need anything."

"I will Hector, thank you." They hang up. Jack takes a look at his watch and heads back inside to speak with Robert. As Jack enters the room all three of them look as if they have something to say, they look happy to be with each other yet restrained. It was a long rectangular shaped metal table. All three sat on the far end of the table, Ryan at the head and Sandra and Robert across from each other avoiding eye contact and acting like the opposite ends of a magnet.

Jack walks up to the other end of the table and it seemed as the table was getting longer and longer as Jack seemed to move further away. It was the oddest mix of emotions and it gave the atmosphere a sickening sensation. They would glance at each other and look away; just hoping the other would look back at them. There was so much raging to get out and be said; yet not a single word was being spoken. Jack makes a sound that disrupts the loud silence and all the eyes turn to him for a sign of hope or words to break the silence like a sledgehammer through ice.

Jack clears his throat, "So I hope you all have had enough time to catch up, I really think we should get started because unfortunately time is a factor." Everyone nods their heads as Jack takes his seat. "Um, okay first off I need you to sign these papers Robert so we can proceed with the rest of today." He opens his folder and passes it over to Robert with his pen. Robert notices that it is a smiley faced pen, he looks up at Jack with a raised eyebrow, Jack responds with a smile. After he signs the papers he passes it back to Jack. He makes sure everything is in order and attempts to start the discussion. He looks over at Sandra and Ryan, "Okay, first of all let me thank you both for being here. Having family by your side in such difficult times is more helpful then you know. At this time your support towards Robert is greatly appreciated and will help him through this trial greatly. If you have any questions at anytime please feel free to ask because any ideas we can put together are better than none." They both nod their heads. "Okay so we all know that it has been confirmed that Robert here is up against the death penalty for first degree murder, and has to stay in jail until the trial without bond or bail. Robert here feels that a plea bargain is senseless and would rather not to plea for something he is not guilty of, so we will fight this thing out until the bitter end, in court."

"What are the plea bargain options?" Sandra asks.

"Good question. There is seventy-five to life and there is forty-five to life with good behavior. And that is if the judge even decides to entertain the plea bargain considering the degree of how big this case is. Given that, I agree with Robert and feel like this case should be fought rather than throwing in the towel."

Ryan raises his hand as if he were in class.

"Um, yes? And you don't have to raise your hand by the way just ask away anytime you feel like it." Jack responds.

"Oh sorry," Ryan looks at his hand in shock that he even raised it, "but if you fight this in court my dad could die, right?" Robert looks over at him with hope because he hasn't heard the word "dad" in so long.

"Yes, and I understand your concern, but luckily for us, if a person is convicted of being guilty and given the death penalty they get two more appeals, which can take years upon years giving us a stronger defense when we get back into court. To actually die through the death penalty, though not uncommon, is very difficult, and I know that we're in the state of Texas, but the fact remains the same. Does that make sense?"

"Yeah." Ryan replies.

"Okay, so we had a meeting with the judge and I asked for a no motion for delay, and everyone had agreed."

"Wait what's a no motion for delay, and who is everybody?" Robert asks confused and caught off guard.

"A no motion for delay is saying that we have no reason to hold off the trial and we should get right to court. Sort of like a speedy trial. And everyone is the Judge, myself, and the prosecuting lawyer, Mr. Rogers."

"Are you out of your God damn mind!" Robert stands up and yells at Jack. Jack pulls back somewhat startled. A guard walks in and Jack waves him off. He then closes his eyes for a moment and opens them right back.

"Look Robert I understand your concern, and believe me when I say that I felt the same way when the idea first was brought to my attention, but let me put it like this; your case is one of the biggest in years and there is a media mob out their demanding for your head on a pike. Some of those reporters are determined to make sure you lose in court so they will do everything to help the prosecution's research. The longer we wait the more time we give the prosecution, the media, and the jury to think about what has happened and to look over the evidence. Whether or not you are innocent you have to understand *all* of the evidence is against you. Do you know what that means?....*All* of the evidence Robert. If we wait you will lose...we will lose. We just need to come up with what we need to talk about quick and hit them unexpectedly. The most surprising thing a prey can do while fleeing from the predator is stop and attack. You have to understand we are fighting a three-headed monster here. At least with the element of surprise we can catch them off guard and have a stronger chance of winning this by keeping everyone away from making things far worse for us than they already are."

"I'm not a big fan of magic tricks Jacky." Robert says calmly yet angrily.

"When the magician is doing his trick everyone's eyes are always on the sideshow until he is ready to show what's behind the curtain. This will be our sideshow I understand your concern by wanting to delay and fight it with more evidence on our side, but I'm telling you with certainty Robert, as your lawyer, that doing this will only pile evidence against us instead of for us, and I need you all to trust me when it comes to this case, because when I fight I fight to win." They all look at each other somewhat in worry looking for hope in each other's eyes.

"Well, I'm in." Everyone's attention shoots to the back of the table seeing Ryan there staring at Jack. There's a short pause as Jack looks around the table for more support.

"Okay me too." Robert adds.

Sandra lets out a big sigh and looks around the table until she meets eyes with Robert, "Okay let's put our faith in God and move forward. I'm in."

Jack smiles at them all. "Okay perfect the trial begins in two weeks."

Chapter 48

"With the State of Texas against Robert Allen Heyward trial only days away it has become a media circus out here at the Bob Casey Federal Court House which you can see here behind me." Amber says pointing at the large rectangular building behind her. "With talks of conspiracy resurfacing back from the burning of Artemis labs and the soon eventual downfall of Orion Industries, people are going wild with theories and supposed allegations of connections between the murder of Earl Hodges being linked to that day in history few of us will soon forget. Just to remind everyone out there of what had happened; after the collapse of Orion, thousands upon thousands of hard working people had lost their jobs. With great promises from Orion for uncovering the Cold Fusion mystery and joining the One World Organization or the O.W.O., stock holders had put complete blind faith into the energy giant and got nothing in return.

The financial market took an unforgiving downward spiral, with of course the stock market following, leaving Americans in great distress and many stock holders lost their life savings forcing many senior citizens and hard working laborers that were ready for retirement into soup kitchens instead of buying their dream houses. While industry tycoons like Robert Heyward and his money hungry board members were rewarded handsomely as they disappeared into thin air. Luckily for us Apollo Industries had swooped in and taken control of former Orion Industries.

With Highland Corporation holding strong while the American economics suffering, stock in southern energies skyrocketed. Not much later did Apollo Industries flex its muscle collaborating both their plants and being backed by the government strongly it showed promise for brighter futures. Before we knew it, the nose dive towards the second great depression had stopped on a dime and began its stronghold and triumphant return back to the top. As far as the American dollar is concerned I don't think we have seen such a scare or a rollercoaster ride for that matter in a hundred years. And this reporter hopes we won't see another one in this lifetime, and let's all hope we can learn from that crises and are better prepared in the future, no matter how sweet the sound of temptation is.

Having that said, we will all, with a bit of luck, take comfort in the fact that soon, as the trial begins to proceed, that murders, thieves, and people who lie to the American public like Robert Heyward will, before long, be put behind bars for good or at least they will get what they deserve. The prosecution has assured us that the evidence that has piled up against Heyward is impeccable and with such a weak defense this trial should be over in no time and Heyward will be filing for his first and second appeal which should both fail sending him straight to death row soon thereafter. Of course, it is more complicated than that, but hopefully justice will be brought simply to the lives this tyrant of the corporate world has greatly devastated.

When we asked the defense about their thoughts of how they feel about the trial and the previous statements about the Orion conspiracy, they responded by saying, 'Evidences are just things, and finding finger prints does not prove the guilt or innocence of any person. Robert Heyward is a stand up man and citizen who was caught in unfortunate circumstances and the world can be assured that there is no connection between the fire at Artemis labs, the downfall of Orion Industries, and the unfortunate event that caused the death of Earl Hodges.'

When asked why there was a no motion to delay the trial, there was no response given by the defense. Well, America help me answer this; if Robert Heyward is such a stand up guy, would a stand up guy run when the people, who were stockholders who supported him, were in trouble?

Would a stand up guy disappear for years and suddenly reappear at the murder scene with his prints everywhere of his greatest business rival? And would a stand up guy really want a no motion for delay so more evidence doesn't pile up against him, especially if he is innocent? No America, no he would not, but Robert Allen Heyward is no stand up guy, he is not even good enough to be a bum. Robert Heyward is scum, and soon enough it will be proven in the court of law that Robert Heyward is no stand up citizen, and he will finally be where he belongs, and we will all finally have justice. This Amber K. with USN."

"And...We're off air. Wow you really hate this guy huh?" Ed, her cameraman, says as he starts to pack up his camera items.

"Let's just say that there are some unresolved issues."

"Yeah, no kidding."

Ambers phone rings, "Ugh excuse me."

"Sure thing."

"Hello?"

"Did I ever tell you how sexy you are when you sound mad, all concentrating, in your hot little suit? You know I could just..."

"This call better have a point Jack or I'm hanging up."

"I just wanted to say how hot I think it is when you quote me. I should give you interviews more often."

"Good bye Jack."

"Okay, okay, okay wait. Just calm down."

"Don't tell me to calm down."

"Alright, sorry, I mean relax. Look I was going back to the lab to just make sure that I have all the evidence notes I need, and wanted to see if you wanted to check out the evidence as well. We could meet, I don't know tomorrow night around eight?"

"You wanted to make sure you had all the evidence notes you need?" Amber asks in disbelief.

"Yeah."

"I cannot believe an arrogant bastard like you is seriously going to ask me out on a date while the biggest case of my career is about to take place in less than a week from now. Honestly where do you get off..."

"You know what, you're right, a reporter like you probably couldn't use any more ammunition to shoot more holes into the defense to help the world see what a criminal I'm defending. Never mind I asked…I'll…uh…talk to you later then. Take care babe, call me if…"

"Alright, I'll come see the evidence."

"Well, see I don't know anymore. Come to think of it, it's actually a pretty stupid move on my part to invite the woman who single handedly is tearing apart my whole strategy before I even get into the courtroom. You know, I must admit that actually kind of hurts a little."

"Oh please like you have an ounce of blood in you that actually has feelings." Amber rolls her eyes.

"Well maybe, you just haven't been close enough to notice." Jack responds.

"You know what, you're sick."

"Yeah, you're probably right, I'm going to go now and probably see a doctor or something."

"Okay wait I…" Amber lowers her voice completely to a point where she can't even hear herself. "I'm sorry."

"You know I have to tell you, when I was kid I had this horrible firecracker accident and hurt both my ears, and ever since then I've just been really hard of hearing. So as much as I love when you whisper sweet nothings into my ear, could you do me a huge favor and repeat that, and act like you meant it?"

"I'll see you at eight tomorrow?" Amber replies, ignoring his request.

"So it's a date?"

Amber hangs up the phone. "Who was that, your boyfriend?" Ed asks as he closes the trunk of the van.

"Oh God no, just someone that might have information on this case that's all." She says dismissively as they both get into the news van.

"Okay, I'm just saying sure sounded like a boyfriend to me." Ed replies as they begin to drive off.

Chapter 49

"Hi, how's it going?" Brown says as he approaches a man working on his house.

"Just fine, I'm sorry, but you can't rent this here house, it's already been rented out. Try Barbara's down the block." A dark skinned man in overalls and a matching fisherman's hat says as he climbs a ladder to get onto the roof of his building to clean out the gutters. It was difficult to understand him, he mumbled a lot as he spoke and the straw in his mouth didn't help.

"Quite a storm we had last night huh?"

"Well yeah it's Louisiana. What can you say? It rains all the time, but when it rains it washes out the whole town, and we end up cleaning up after it. No matter, we do what can to survive. Wouldn't you so say so uh...what's your name there mister?"

"Brown, Frank Brown."

"Yes Brown, survive, survive, survive, then die eh Brown? Ha, ha, ha." The old man lets out a hysterical laugh, then looks back at Brown and doesn't get back the same enthusiasm, just a half nervous smile and a nod of the head. "Oh you city folk are all the same, just business, business, and business, never any time to laugh and look at nature. Your nature is hardwood and steel. No nature, just things made of nature. We have big black bears and you have bear skin rugs, we have alligators and you have alligator shoes. Ha, ha, ha, I love how you city folk think you're dangerous, but all smoke and mirrors, like the kids watch on the tele, smoke and mirrors." He then checks his pockets. "Uh speaking of smoke you got a burn there Brown?"

"Burn?"

"Yes, yes, a burn…" He looks at Brown like a child as he squeezes his index finger and thumb together and brings them to his lips.

"Oh cigarette, yes here you go." He hands it over to the man as he slowly gets off the ladder.

"I'm Ethan by the way," He puts the cigarette in his mouth, "my momma named me after her father, old family name, generations old." He checks his pocket again.

"Um…you got a light there Brown?"

"Yeah, of course." He pulls out his lighter and lights Ethan's cigarette and then his own. It was easy to tell by the look on Ethan's face after the first puff that this smoke was long awaited.

"So where you from Brown?"

"Not too far, over in Houston."

"Houston, big city, that's far real far, but south. I like the south. Friendly people, good homely folk. Traveled there once with my daddy had some trade work to do, helped to buy this house right here." He looks at the house behind him, "Hard worker traveled far, real far like Houston. Seen him maybe once twice a month. Good man, took care of us; got four brothers and three sisters. Youngest sister died when I was fourteen, alligator ripped her head off straight from the cradle while we were all a sleep, only left her bottom half." He looks back over at Brown, "Called it the midnight baby snatcher. Famous, real famous, but long time ago, probably dead by now who knows. Been living here a long time, know all the legends. Like the fire crackers."

"Fire crackers?"

"Fire crackers, what you city folk call them?" He looks at Brown expecting an answer. Brown shrugs his shoulders confused. "Fire ants or something like that."

"Yes, yes."

"Call them fire crackers 'cause when they bite it stings like a fire cracker burn. Like five six years ago they used to come out every day in heat just like this and try to eat everything alive. Targeted smaller things like rabbits and young children. Had to call the fire departments yelling the, 'the fire crackers got him, the fire crackers got him!' Ha, ha, ha!" Ethan slaps his knee and starts to laugh hysterically. "The kids would run from one block into the other and jump into a lake of leeches! Ha, ha, ha. The boys didn't know what hit 'em. Firemen came didn't know whether to feel sorry for the boys or laugh. Fire crackers moved on since then, was a long time ago." He puts his hand on Brown's shoulder, "Good old simple times huh Brown?" He asks as if Brown were there during the events.

"Yes, yes they were, old friend."

Ethan wipes his eyes from the tears he had gotten from laughing so hard. "Oh boy, don't get many folk like you 'round here much more Brown, get lonely sometimes. Anyway you want to come inside and have a drink, what you like beer or water?" He asks as he walks towards the front porch.

"Didn't you say someone was living here?"

"Yes, yes someone rented out the room, some really secretive fellow. Tall strong, with his son I think, don't look much alike, don't know business partner maybe. Wears some army type suit. Been cleaning up here for weeks, haven't seen them. Probably in Houston just like you, mentioned it a few times, also New Orleans. Sound like big travelers, but I don't ask too many questions, just listen, listen like the trees, don't bother nobody. They just send a check for the rent so I don't rent it out in case they come back. Can't have bad customer service as slow as it gets 'round here, ye hear? I go inside make sure everything is okay, no crazy stuff is going on, have a drink and then leave. Never had company over though, just stay here get away from people, problems, wife, just spend time alone." He says as he motions Brown to come inside the door.

"Yeah, I'll have a beer, so tell me about this army fella." Brown pulls out some photographs, "Oh and before that tell me something. Ethan, have you ever seen this symbol anywhere?"

Chapter 50

Amber pulled up to the Houston crime lab. She parked in a better lit area now that she wasn't sneaking around just to get in. Even though she was annoyed at the fact that she had to meet with an egotistical ass like Jack, she had to get her answers. She had to do what she came here to accomplish. She hated thinking about Jack; every time she thought about him it would bring annoyance to her character. Nonetheless she was here. She thought back to the day Harvey died, when she was taken into the van. She had finally moved on and was held back like a stone in a slingshot.

Then when she had heard about this murder case it was like someone had let go of the slingshot and she was thrown right back into the abyss of that chaotic night. It was like she became a child again and became vulnerable. She was seeking atonement the only way she knew how. This time she was going to get it, no matter what. This case will let her free her soul which is bound and sunk into that day, like a person thrown into the ocean with cement dried around their legs. There are few remedies to the death of a friend, we can all hope that at least redemption will give us one night to sleep without sorrow, and give us one dream without nightmare. Loneliness had become her jealous domineering lover that would never let her go. She had no choice but to befriend it, she knew nothing else, she had nothing else. Everything was languor after that night; she did nothing but focus to a point where all challenges were easily overcome.

But then there was this incompetent fool Jack. It was like his thick headedness was what was most attractive yet most uninviting about him, she couldn't figure him out. He would sound cute and intelligent, and then would talk further only to discount everything about him. It was frustratingly unbelievable. In the end, this was just another assignment and soon enough he would be out of her life, and that brought her some comfort. She looked into the mirror of her car to check her makeup, and made sure her camera purse was working. She hits it a couple times because the sound transmitter wasn't cooperating. She just hoped to piece it together when she got the video feedback. With a final check of everything she takes a deep breath, steps out the car and heads over to the door. She saw that there was a doorstop holding it open with a note attached onto the handle. "Hey sweetheart, I left the door open because I got tired of waiting. Do me a favor and pull the doorstop and make sure the door is closed...Can't wait to see your cute face again, Thanks babe."

"Ugh he's such a jerk." She thinks to herself as she crumples up the note and tosses it. She makes her way down the hallway and into the evidence room. There he is standing, studying the different pieces of evidence as if he were to actually care about them. She notices that he is more handsome when he's not acting a fool. As he takes a sip of his coffee, Jack looks up and takes a double take.

"Well, you could stand there staring all you want, but I promise you, the close up is so much better babe." He says trying to hide his smile so not to get in trouble as he puts his cup down.

"Yeah, whatever Jack let's get to work." She says as she confirms her thoughts from before, "Now why'd you want to meet me here? Because I don't have all night. I have a lot of work to do tomorrow."

"Really? What kind of work? Like bashing me and my client for more stuff you don't have any proof for?"

"Something like that, so are you going to answer my question or what?" She asks as she folds her arms.

"What was the question again?"

"Why did you want me here?" She says in a more aggravated tone.

"Oh yeah, well honestly I just needed some eye candy for the night, helps keep the mind sharp. Got me through all four years of law school," He takes a sip of his coffee, "and then some."

"Look I don't need this, I'm out of here."

"Okay, okay, stop." He says with a smile, somewhat laughing. He puts his coffee down on the table near the entrance of the room so it wouldn't spill as he chased Amber. He finally catches up to her midway into the hallway, "Look I was just being stupid, I wanted you here because I know how close you are to this case, and look I really think this guy is innocent, and I could really use your help."

"Help? Are you kidding, you want my help? Tell me Jack why the hell should I *help* you in this case? You know I'm here for only one reason, and one reason alone and that's to make sure that..."

"And that's to make sure that son of bitch goes straight to hell, God we all know the story, I'm just saying with the way you look at things, together we can probably uncover more in this case than just me alone."

She slants her eyes and stares at him for a moment, "Okay, let's see what the evidence says."

"Alright." Jack smiles as they walk back towards the lab. When they walk in Amber sets her purse down between a bunch of folders and Jack's coffee so it could see as much as the room as possible.

"What's all this?"

"Oh just a bunch of prep papers that were handed over to me by the old lawyer. He pretty much gave me a verbal prep so I never really looked too much into it. Just have it there as documents."

"Where's detective Brown?"

"He said he had to go out of town for some investigative work, said he might be back by next week. He told the head lab technician about me, and let me borrow his key card, so here we are." They walk over towards the lit up table with all the evidence on it. Amber leans over the table to take a better look at the objects that lay across the white ambient table.

"So this is all the stuff from the crime scene?"

"Yeah, pretty much." They both begin to piece together the story in their heads. Jack walks back and picks up his coffee again while Amber puts on surgical gloves noticing Jack already had his on.

"So, you look really nice tonight." Jack awkwardly breaks the silence. Amber raises her eyebrows and slowly turns her head towards Jack trying to figure out what had just happened.

"What?" Amber asks.

"I'm just saying that with the table glow shinning on you, and you have your makeup all done nice, it makes you look really pretty."

"Um, thanks." She looks back at the evidence, brushing off his comment.

"I'm sorry never mind, I'm just being stupid as usual." Amber just nods her head at the Jack's comment. Jack looks at her and does the same then goes back to studying the evidence as well. While looking at some notes, she searches for the knife that Robert had, blindly, only to find Jack's hand already on it. They both look down at their hands and then back at each other and pull their hands back.

"Cool…that kind of stuff never happens to me."

"Yeah I'm sure, being such a player as you probably are, I'm sure you dupe enough stupid girls to get what you want. So don't give me that."

"Okay I'm not sure where you got all that from, but I'm not saying you're a stupid girl, and I'm not trying any tricks, I'm just saying you really look nice, and I'd like to get to know you better…That's all."

"That's the best you can do?"

"Not good enough?"

"It's a start."

"I can go get us some food, we have the ambient table light, it could be a romantic first working dinner date."

"I'm sorry I'm just not that type of girl."

"Not a working dinner kind of girl?"

"Not a going on a date just when I meet a guy. I am an I-actually-have-work-to-do-kind of girl."

"I like how you already started to say you've met someone."

"You just don't give up do you Jack."

"It's not in my job description."

"Alright." She says as she smiles and looks away.

"Alright." He says with a big smile.

"So this gun," Amber tries to redirect the conversation as she randomly picks up an object to talk about. Jack stands up and tries to kiss Amber; she turns her head and pulls away. "I told you, I'm not that kind of girl."

"I…" Jack pulls back, "I know, I just thought I saw something in your hair."

"And you thought you could…I don't know kiss it away?"

"Oh that? No…I was going to blow it away." Jack's face turns somewhat red, "So…you were saying something about the gun?" He continues trying to forget what had just happened.

"Uh, yes so this gun wasn't fired once throughout the whole night?"

"Actually it wasn't, but before I talk more about the stuff here, I need to know everything said here stays between us."

"Well, if it's information I can use that's also open to the public I'm going to use it, the only difference is that I'm getting a closer look. Any information other than that, you have my word."

"Okay, fair enough. So yeah, it's weird it had Hodges', his son's, and Robert's prints on it and yet no firing of the weapon. Usually when so many hands have handled a gun with a result of death there is at least one shot fired. There was Robert's blood on the gun also, but that was from Hodges' son pistol-whipping Robert multiple times. And this is what was found inside," He retrieves a small plastic bag, "only one golden bullet. The man was so rich; he even killed in good taste."

"It was a family tradition more than anything."

"What?"

"Yeah, well I actually came across it in something I was reading about Hodges on the flight here. The Hodges' family was notorious in the olden days for taking on duals and challenging people to duals."

"Apparently these guys were very good." Jack states.

"Good? The best! These guys very rarely died in duals, and lucky for the ones that did they had successors." Amber replies.

"Like Bryan."

"Yeah, and they also have a long history of luck too. There's a story I read about a Hodges that was shot and lived to tell about it. It was when his opponent shot him in the side of the stomach completely missing every vital organ, so Hodges shot back shooting him straight in the heart. He later said that he shot him in the heart for not having enough heart to kill him."

Jack looked at Amber in awe, she looked back to confirm his feelings, "Anyway," Amber continues, "they would always use a golden bullet so when they killed their opponent or foe the family of the man they killed would have enough money for the funeral. The golden bullet went from being a family tradition to a symbol."

"Holy shit that's morbid as hell."

"Yeah, tell me about it. In fact from what I remember reading, this is the only time in over a hundred years that a Hodges actually died in a fight that didn't involve a bullet."

Jack lets out a small laugh, "Wow, you really know what you're talking about there Khowja, I'm impressed." Amber responds with a smile. Jack continues, "Well now that that mystery is solved, let's say we come up for an explanation for this knife. Now this knife only had Robert's fingerprints on it, and according to Brown doesn't seem like it even made and appearance at the crime scene."

"What do you mean?"

"I mean he didn't as much reach for it, let alone use it to kill someone." He says as he studies the weapon some more.

"How do you guys know that?"

"Well Brown says that the way he placed the knife in his back, under his underpants, it would have cut him pretty bad if he pulled it out in a hurry, and if he had a struggle with Hodges then he would have presumably had to pull it out at some point, and there were no marks on his back, nor was there any blood on the knife for that matter." Jack explains.

"So?"

"So, it's just weird, in this whole scenario, we have two men, both obviously have something to prove, both have weapons. And yet no weapons were used, and the defendant, Robert, denies the whole thing all together. I just find it weird, that if Robert was so vindictive, why he didn't actually just stab Hodges to death." He says holding the knife trying to place himself in Robert's shoes.

"Maybe the fight was going so well for him that he didn't need the knife, after all Hodges was thrown of the balcony."

"Yeah, maybe, it also seems like there wasn't much of a struggle at all since they didn't really find any extra skin tissue under his fingernails or anything. I don't know it just doesn't seem to add up. There has to be more to the story than what we see." Jack takes both his hands and rubs them on his face and then through his hair.

Amber is drawn closer to him out of his frustration. "Were there any cameras in the hotel?"

"Ha, I wish. It's such a low-grade hotel that camera's are probably considered a luxury there. And for some reason the place stays busy, must be a customer service thing. Even the night of the murder, there were so many people there going in and out, the concierge didn't remember seeing any unfamiliar faces, didn't even remember seeing Robert for that matter. Not a single witness could finger Robert; the only people that anyone knew are Hodges himself, and his son Bryan. For some reason to me, it all comes back to this knife. The unused knife is the reason for the untold story."

Amber thought for a minute, "Well, going back to the gun, I also remember that in the Hodges' lineage story that a Hodges would rarely make use of a gun if his opponent wasn't equally armed, unless they felt it has a complete need or had no other choice. So I was thinking maybe the gun wasn't used because Hodges knew he could kill Robert with a pull of his finger, and that would have broken the family code."

"Huh, and so are you saying that maybe therefore Robert was convinced to keep his knife put? That's brilliant! Maybe I can help tell the story in a certain way and claim an accidental death." Jack says.

"No, I didn't say anything like that." Amber says fairly uncomfortable with the fact that the conversation was starting to fall from her favor, "Knowing scum like Robert Heyward, Hodges probably pulled his gun out early on as a fair warning to Robert as to not try anything stupid. Feeling threatened he kept his knife in place. They probably had a small fight and Robert tried to reach for the gun. Hodges probably tried to pull him away and that's when the fight moved towards the balcony and then he was thrown off. For some reason slime balls like him always tend to win, but not this time."

"And see that's the other thing, if there was a major struggle, there should be some sign of it." Jack points out, ignoring her comments towards Robert.

"You mean besides the bruises and cuts on Heyward, and Hodges' death?"

"No like I said earlier skin under fingernails."

"Not everyone scratches during a fight you know Jack."

He looks up at her, "I know, but you know what I mean, there's always a tell tale sign somewhere. And also if there was a struggle, the knife in his back would have scratched him, and there would be some sign of that on Robert's back, which Brown didn't find, or some blood on the knife, which I didn't find. It's the oddest thing. I mean, imagine this knife being on your back, and when you lean back to dodge a punch it would cause discomfort and a high probability of puncturing the skin."

"Okay maybe, Heyward slowly took out the knife, and set it aside, to show some power on his end. Once the fight was over, he realized he didn't need the knife after all and put it back. Or Heyward threw something at Hodges blinding him momentarily and he backed up and fell over the edge." Jack looks at Amber as if she were insane, "What? It's possible."

"Look I know you have your biases in this case, but I feel like if you look at things at an angle where you put more meaning into it than there really is, then it is all a personal quest blinded by illusion. If we look at the facts and piece them together, this might actually make more sense."

"My theory makes perfect sense okay, if you read the report it says that Brown found the knife in his back pocket and *not* his back. Besides you're just worried about keeping your client from getting what he deserves. He had a motive to kill, he had intent, and he went through with it." Amber shoots back.

"Motive and intent do not equate to murder. People want to kill other people all the time and always at the last moment, hold back. Those people are not criminals."

"Yes, but Robert is."

"I'm just trying not to get my client killed, or serve more time for something he may have not done."

"He did do this!"

"You don't know that for sure." He puts both his hands on Amber's shoulders. "Look if this case is handled the right way, and we do it without much bias then this actually might help you put to rest what happened in your past."

"What the hell do you know about my past?" She pushes Jack's arms away and pulls back as if she felt an electric shock.

"Hey look I'm not trying to be a jerk or anything, I'm just saying that I know a lot happened a long time ago, and there is nothing you, me, or the outcome of this case can do to make that go away. I know you might feel that Robert getting the death penalty might redeem you for what you're feeling or what happened, but that's just not true. Trust me when I say I've learned the hard way. Holding on to stuff like that only ends up eating you alive from the inside. And I'm sure you know exactly what I'm talking about. Look I want justice to be done just as much as you do, but we have to do it the right way."

"Don't act like you know me." She says in an angry voice.

"What?" Jack says completely caught off guard.

"Shut up, don't patronize me. I lost my innocence back then." She begins to tear up, "My whole life came crashing down and I lost my best friend all in one night. The worst thing you ever went through was some stupid law exam. So don't you act like you know me or know who I am. Don't act like you know where I'm coming from because you don't. You don't know what happened there on that night, all you know is what you read. So don't you *dare* for a second act like you know what I'm going through!" She wipes her eyes and starts to storm out the room.

"Amber."

"No leave me alone, don't call me, don't try to contact me, don't even think about me Jack!" She goes to grab her purse, but hits her lower thigh against the table. Trying to play it off, she tries to show no pain, grabs her purse and storms out the room. Jack follows knowing he would have to let her out with his keycard. She stands at the door waiting and he finally lets her out. The whole time he just looked at her in distress, trying to comfort her, but not knowing how he could. He musters up the courage to speak.

"Look I'm sorry…"

"Don't Jack…just…don't."

He opens the door for her, and she continues her hasty pace out towards her news van. He watches her get to her car to make sure she reaches there safely, but he was watching more so for some answer to the confusion or some sign of hope. Maybe she would turn around, but she didn't. Amber kept pace and stayed on track towards her van, got in, and sped off.

Jack shakes his head as he makes his way back into the lab, "Ugh, what the hell was that?" He asks as if someone were listening. When he makes it back into the lab, he takes a look at everything, which was the mess he called his case. Once again he shakes his head in disbelief of how much work is yet to come. He rakes his hand through his hair and scratches the back of his head. Looking at all this he remembers what one of his law professors used to say to him, "Arbeit macht frei." It was a German term used by the Nazi's. There used to be big signs outside of their concentration camps with the phrase, which meant "Work will set you free." Jack lets out a small laugh out of frustration and then looks at his watch. It was already a bit past two thirty in the morning. Afraid he might fall asleep while working at the lab he decides to clean up after himself and take his notes home. This was a battle that would have to continue on tomorrow. "Arbeit macht frei, Jack, Arbeit macht frie."

Chapter 51

"Robby?" Sandra says as she walks into the dim lit cold metal box. Robert raises his head with a look of both distress and hope on his face. "Are you okay?" She asks, Robert responds by taking a deep breath and nodding his head yes. She pulls out the chair from the opposite end of the table, brings it next to him and sits down. The cold room was somehow different. It had a warm feeling to it, and his hands weren't bound by chains for the first time. His hands are folded and stretched across the table as usual though. Sandra mimics his hands and sets them on the table as well. Robert hangs his head trying to avoid being criticized. The room is completely silent; even each breath that came out had to whisper. The quiet was so piercing that the silence was envious of the deaf. Sandra closes her eyes and is suddenly taken to a dark place inside her mind as her thoughts pull her away from reality.

It's cold and it was easy to smell the dampness in the air. She starts to breathe deeply and her breath is easy to see even in the shadows. She hears scratching, screeching, and deep beastly breathing all around her, but sees nothing. She turns around trying to find her way out but finds nothing. Scared she reaches for her cross around her neck. When she touches it she notices that it has been replaced by something else, it had the shape of her cross but it was something new. When she looks down at it she sees a key in the shape of the cross it was different from what she was used to, it was more prominent. A bright light catches the side of her eye and she looks over. The golden light came from a small hole in the wall and she begins to walk towards it. The closer she would get the stronger the howls of the creatures around her would get. She stopped at first in fear, but the light drew her closer like a moth to a flame. As she got closer fear began to take over and she realized that the hole was a keyhole and the wall a door. She takes the necklace

269

that held her key off from around her neck and pulled closer to the door. She closed her eyes and put the key in and turned it.

***

Back in the metal box they sat there in suspended animation, like two sculptures in a wax museum. In the abyss of the silence Robert felt so much to reach over three inches and touch his soul mate. It was an array of feelings between rage and calmness. He wanted to grab his love and hold her tight, but was comforted by the fact of her closeness. Back and forth he would struggle on what to do. The struggle was so strong that he was literally at a standstill. Off in the distance the most grueling laughter tore through the silence like a knife slowly cutting through crisp paper. "No, not now!" He thought to himself. "No, God please not now…please…please…" He squeezes his hands together as to plead in prayer. The dark sound replied "God? There is no God here only me Robert. There will always be only me!" "No…" Robert's legs started to jitter slowly and began to speed up as a tear drop creeps out of Robert's eye like an ant coming up from the ground for sunlight. "Robert…" The voice tauntingly gets closer. The tear flows over his eyelid and begins its decent down his cheek scratching his face on its way down as he tries to fight more tears from coming. "Robert, listen to me!" He keeps strong. The tear finally reaches his cheekbone and jumps off his face making its way towards the ground gaining speed as it falls. "Robert…!" And right before it splashes on to the ground Robert feels a small nudge on his hand. Confused he looks up at his hands and there it was; the sign from God himself. There was Sandra's hand open asking for his. He slowly reaches for her hand to make sure that this too was no illusion. The warmth of her soft skin heated the blood in his body. He could feel her electricity energizing his body. He looks over at her and there she was with tears beginning to race down her face. "Oh Robby what happened to our family?…" And without another word he pulled her into his arms as the tears from their eyes fell so fast that they were threatening to flood the room and drown them. They held each other so tightly as if they were trying to become one person. They were brought to their knees onto the cold floor. As they held each other and had their heads on the other's shoulder with their eyes closed they found themselves on the highest peak of the tallest mountain. The cold wind brushed passed them trying to throw them off, but their bodies held strong and they kept each other warm as they listened to the song of their hearts playing the same song in harmony as if their hearts were long lost lovers finally finding their way back to one another. The smell of Sandra's hair warmed his lungs as it continued to induce more and more tears. Robert's body gave Sandra a long forgotten strength as she held onto him for dear life. Another wind passes through their bodies separating them as they fall from the mountaintop; they try reaching for each other's hand as they break through the clouds. The fear from being apart brings stronger tears into their eyes. All of a sudden there is a thumping sensation as their irregular breathing wakes them from their dream and they both look up only to see the other still in their arms. They touch each other as in disbelief to the reality of their lover being there. Above their bodies their souls danced in the joy of being reunited. They touched each other's face. "Robby." "Sandra." He wipes the tears from her eyes, and her brown eyes shined through the darkness like a guiding light. She pulls his face onto her mouth as if it were oxygen. Robert kissed her back returning to his dream of falling off the mountain he looks down and sees an ocean realizing that it was love he was falling into; he let go, and with a smile awaited the crash into the water. It would be the sweetest pain. Right before he hit the bottom he opened his eyes and ripped off his shirt as he picked her up and sat her on the table. He then pulled off her shirt. She looked up at him as he took deep breaths like a beast ready to take back what was his. She touched his stomach and moved her hands up to his chest. She felt as if she was home once again. She kissed his stomach and moved her way up to his chest. He ran his fingers though her hair and laid her onto the tabletop, as he unhooked her bra. They made love to each other as they fell deeper into love drowning in it almost forgetting to breathe in reality. "I love you." She whispers to him. The words he yearned to hear every day he finally heard for the first time in years. He kisses her on her lips as they look into each other's eyes while continuing to make love. He closes his eyes one more time as he crashes through the water, it splashes up into the air and Sandra screams out his name.

Just then Robert's eyes open only to find himself back in his seat while Sandra's hand still awaiting his. It was all a dream. "Robert." The scream was a whisper from her precious lips, and he joins his hand with hers. She lays her head on his shoulder, "I love you." She tells him as tears begin to fall down her eyes, she had found the door to forgiveness and when she turned the key her hand found his. "I love you too, we'll get through this, we'll be okay."

"You promise?"

"I promise." They held each other and for now, all was right with the world.

***

"So when are you all coming back?" Jack asks as he hands the last of the luggage over to the airport workers.

"We should be back hopefully by next week. How long do you think trials like these take?"

"Murder cases that have the death penalty as a punishment take anywhere from years to many more years. This is only the beginning Sandra, but anything can always happen. We just need to stay focused."

"Of course. I just wish I could stay longer, but I just have to make sure that Michael is okay and Ryan has school as well. I just need to be better prepared for when I come back."

"I know Sandra, don't worry about a thing just try to make it back as soon as you can. I'll stay in close contact with you, and I hope we'll be seeing you soon. With even this short visit I feel it has given Robert enough energy and the will power to want to move forward."

"Please take care of him Jack."

"I'll do my best."

"Oh and please give this to him." She hands Jack an envelope, "Tell him it's for strength."

Jack takes the envelope and looks at it, "I will. Now you guys have a safe flight, and let me know when you book your next flight back."

"I will, I wish we were closer. This is so difficult, having to miss the first part of the trial, and God knows what we may have to miss later on."

"Don't worry about a thing I'll update you as frequently as possible, I know this must be difficult for you we just have to keep working through it. We have to pay attention to what we all can do instead of what we can't."

"You're right, okay, well you'll be hearing from us soon." They shake hands.

"Sounds good," He looks over at Ryan, "okay Ryan I'll hopefully be seeing you soon too, and remember if you have any questions as well just feel free to call me, I'll try to answer them the best I can."

"Okay Mr. Kennedy." They shake hands. Sandra and Ryan then leave to go inside the airport.

Once they had boarded the airplane Sandra loses herself in the events that took place in the past week and a half.

"How long are you here for?"

"Just for a week and a half. When does the trial start?"

"I'm not sure yet, maybe a few months or so. Will you bring Michael next time you come?"

"I'll try my best."

"You guys don't want to be here do you?" Both Sandra and Ryan hang their heads in silence, "It's okay I wouldn't want to be here either."

"Did you do it?" Ryan sheep-fully and almost regrettably asks as he looks at the handcuffs surrounding Robert's wrists.

"No." Robert responds. Sandra looks up at Robert for confirmation, Robert then looks at her and assures her. "I'm not a murderer, I didn't do anything. I know what it says in the papers about me, but it's not all true. Yes I was there at the scene, but I got there after he was killed. I didn't see who did it or how it happened, I just showed up and he was dead. I promise you guys I would never kill anyone…ever. You guys believe me…Right?" Robert looks around for support.

"Ahem." Everyone looks over to Jack.

Sandra comes back from her daydream on the airplane and looks over at Ryan to make sure he's okay, he seemed to be lost in the clouds somewhere.

Chapter 52

"You nervous?" Jack nervously asks.

"No." Robert says as he kept looking back at the entrance of the courtroom while holding the envelope that Sandra had asked Jack to give him.

Jack notices him playing with the envelope then looks up at Robert. "Good. Being nervous is bad."

"Is that why your leg is shaking?"

"No..." Jack tries to stop his shaking then looks back at Robert, "Hey, I wish they were coming today too, but we need to focus on the case they'll be here next time, let's just get through the opening statements and the first couple witnesses okay?" Robert looks at him and submissively nods his head and then faces forward with his head down.

Jack looks forward into blank space trying to zero in on anything in front of him to keep his concentration. His hands feel so cold and sweaty that he was worried ice would start coming out his pores. His heart makes an attempt to escape and race away, but he takes deeper and deeper breaths to calm himself down. He looks over to Robert with half squinted eyes not sure what to expect. Robert had his head halfway down, looking at the wooden table. He had the most humble expression on his face, an expression of nothingness.

The courtroom seemed to get larger and larger and his confined space seemed to get smaller. Jack leans back and cracks his back and notices the prosecution lawyer, Rogers, walk in with another man and Bryan. Rogers looks over at Jack and nods his head as to confirm the beginning of the war. Jack nods back to complete the transaction.

"If you want, you can get forty years involuntary manslaughter thirty good behavior." Rogers says tauntingly.

"No, thanks."

"Okay…" The man that walked in with them sat behind Bryan and Rogers and briefly talks to them. Jack opens his folder to make sure he has everything memorized so no mistakes would be done. On top of his notebook was a quote his father had given him when he was young and he kept that saying as his motto. "No mistakes, not today." Jack gets lost in the quote and before he knew it the voice of the bailiff struck through both Robert and Jack's hearts like a lightning bolt.

"All rise…" The judge walks in to the courtroom. He was tall and carried a slight tired look on his face. You can tell there was much experience behind his eyes he didn't seem weak it was more of an unpretentious look. He took his seat and the bailiff continued. "The state of Texas versus Robert Allen Heyward case number nineteen, twenty one, seventy two, one is now in session. Judge Dayan Abidan Faisal is now presiding."

Phil just stared at Robert the whole time as he stood behind Rogers and Bryan with a solemn look. His retribution for what had happened was on its way. This time he shall win. Everyone sat down and the judge began to speak.

"Is the prosecution ready with its opening statement?"

"Yes your honor." Rogers says in his suave southern accent. He gets up and walks towards the jury, "Ladies and gentlemen of the jury we are here to investigate and prove that the accused here Robert Allen Heyward is a murderer, and a burden upon our society as a whole. He is one of the *reasons* our society cannot function in its utmost perfect manor, but due to our perfect system we have the opportunity to erase him from our system. But how can we do such a thing? Exile? No, we cannot risk the chance that he would soon infect another society, another habitat, another group of, of innocent people with the disease of who he is. Through our prosecution for the remainder of this case we will demonstrate motive from past instances going back up to five years ago up until that faithful day two months ago. We will ascertain intent and we will validate motive to kill.

Now, Mr. Jack Kennedy here and his defense will attempt to show that there was no single witness to the murder, that there was not one single weapon used though there where weapons available at the scene of the crime, and no one even saw Mr. Heyward walk into the building. Yet you will find that Mr. Heyward did end up in that room. You will find that his prints were everywhere, and you will find that Earl Landon Hodges is dead. Mr. Kennedy here will attempt to pull a rabbit out of what seems to be an empty hat, but we will all soon learn to see that the rabbit was in the hat all along. Ladies and gentlemen, I want you to think of it this way, we cannot see God, we cannot hear God, and we can most definitely not touch God, so how can we say that there is a God?...Huh?"

He looks around waiting for an answer to his rhetorical question, "It is in the *evidence* that God has left for us in the Holy Bible that proves his existence. And it is in the *evidence* that Robert Allen Heyward left behind that proves to us what he has done. The *fact* remains that Mr. Heyward acted in mens rea and we shall prove that to you without any question beyond a reasonable doubt that Robert Heyward is guilty as charged and deserves the ultimate punishment... the punishment of death. Thank you." Rogers bows his head and walks back to his chair.

"Mr. Kennedy." The Judge calls out.

Jack stands up and walks towards the jury. "There was a crime committed two months ago. There was a murder. And yes Earl Hodges is dead, and those ladies and gentlemen are the only facts of the case. That's it...Mr. Heyward here is just a victim of being in the wrong place at the wrong time. Why would anyone with the *intent* to kill not use a single weapon that was readily available to them? Why would anyone after murdering another human being just wait at the scene of the crime to be caught? Why no attempt to run? Why?...The truth is that Robert Allen Heyward walked into the room once the murder had already taken place and now he is on trial for his *life* for showing up early to a crime scene.

Ladies and gentlemen there was no intent there was no motive, there is only a dead body and no one to blame because there is no murderer to be found, so we point the finger of blame and allocate it to the first person we see, because we cannot sleep at night knowing that there might be a murderer out there somewhere and we did not catch him. But I want you to all know that we must look at this case without prejudice or bias and we must go to sleep knowing there is a murderer out there somewhere because Robert Allen Heyward did not commit this crime. There is no mitigating factor to Earl Hodges' death and sentencing an innocent man to death will not mitigate this tragedy, but only make it worse." He returns to his chair and takes a glimpse over to the prosecution and sees the man sitting behind Rogers looking over at him with the calmest yet deadliest stare.

"Is the prosecution ready with its first witness?" The judge asks.

"Uh yes your honor. If it'd please the court the prosecution calls one Sylvia Aluiza Gonzalez Perez to the stand. If it'd also please the court Miss Perez has difficulty in speaking the English language so we have asked a translator Miss Jocelyn Arnaz to help translate the witness' testimony."

"Okay." The judge replies.

An older lady approaches the witness stand accompanied by a middle aged woman in a business suit. The bailiff then meets her there before she takes her seat, "Please raise your right hand and place your left hand on the Bible." She does as he asks, "Do you solemnly swear that the testimony that you are about to give the court is the truth the whole truth and nothing but the truth under penalty of the law so help you God?"

"Si."

"I do." The translator follows.

"Please take the stand."

"Please state your name for the record." Rogers says to the witness.

"Sylvia Aluiza Gonzalez Perez."

"What is your occupation Miss Perez?"

"I clean the rooms after the guests leave. I work on the second and third floors."

"Miss Perez were you working at the Comfort Inn Hotel on the night of April the eleventh two months ago?"

"Yes."

"Can you tell me what you recall from that night?"

"Yes I was cleaning the rooms as usual and when I passed by room five thirteen I heard some arguing so I kept passing by. About twenty minutes later when I returned there was a boy beating up another older man with the back of his gun. That is when I ran and called the manager who then called the police."

"I see, can you please show the court who the man was that was being beaten?" The witness points to Robert. "Let the record show that the witness is pointing to one Robert Allen Heyward. And can you show the court who was doing the beating?" She points to Bryan, "And now let the record show that the witness is pointing to one Bryan Alger Hodges. Is Robert Heyward the person you heard arguing when you passed by room five thirteen two months ago."

"Objection your honor, speculation. Is the prosecution actually asking whose *voice* the witness actually heard on that night two months ago through closed doors?" Jack states.

"If it'd please the court there was no other witness to the fact and that there was no one else present in that room, living today, besides Robert Heyward and the witness' testimony would therefore be valid." Roger explains.

"There was also no witness for the fact that Robert Heyward had entered the room either." Jack argues.

"Except for the fact that the witness here discovered the defendant moments after the death."

"I'm going to allow this." The judge replies. "You will have your chance to rebuttal such questions during the cross examination, Mr. Kennedy."

"Miss Perez," Rogers continues, "was Mr. Heyward's voice, the voice you overheard in the argument when passing by room five thirteen on the night of April the eleventh?" He asks while pointing at Robert.

"Well there were two voices and one with a thick accent and one not so much. The one who didn't have the thick accent I think was Mr. Heyward's."

"And the other voice?"

"I'm sure it was Mr. Hodges, I heard him talking to the man at the counter before they checked in that night."

"Did you hear what they were arguing about?"

"I heard something about a job, but I didn't pay much attention I just kept going to the next room."

"If you heard arguing how come you didn't call the proper authorities then?"

"Well, I hear arguing from rooms all the time, husband and wife, mother and child, and even two men. I just thought it was just another fight I didn't think anyone's life was in danger."

"Thank you Miss Perez. Your witness."

"Miss Perez how long have you been working at the Comfort Inn hotel?" Jack begins.

"Almost three years."

"Really, what did you do before that?"

"I lived in Mexico."

"So one day you just decided to come here and start working as a maid?"

"Objection your honor this irrelevant to the case."

"If it would please the court the defense did not have enough time to interview the witness in pretrial."

"That was your own fault Mr. Kennedy, when you asked for the no motion to delay." The judge responds. "The objection is sustained. Please get to the proper questions Mr. Kennedy."

"Yes your honor. Miss Perez, what floors was it you said you worked on again?"

"The second and third floor."

"But Miss Perez what were you doing on the fifth floor cleaning if that is not where you're supposed to be?"

"We were short handed that month. One of the other cleaning ladies Almaz Iyella was having a baby and the boss had not yet hired a replacement for her. So my work load was increased to one extra floor which was the fifth."

"Why the fifth floor? Why not the first or fourth?"

"I don't know. I do whatever Mr. Joles instructs me to do."

"Who is Mr. Joles?"

"He is the hotel manager."

"Miss Perez, in the three years you have been working at this hotel have you ever overheard a fight or an argument escalate to such a point where you felt the need to call the proper authorities?"

"One time I heard a woman screaming and a lot of banging and ruckus. When I called the manager it turned out that the couple was having sex. After that I never called for help again until the day Mr. Hodges had died."

"Miss Perez after you had called for your manager what happened next?" Jack questions.

"Well the manger had called the police, and then I took him to the room. Mr. Joles then told me to go downstairs as he tried to break up the fight, and he told me to wait for the police."

"How long did it take for the police to arrive?"

"They were quick. It took them two maybe three minutes."

"I see. What happened once the police arrived?"

"When they came I took them to the room, Mr. Joles was trying to talk to both sides. There were some male workers there standing around both men so things don't get out of hand I think. Mr. Joles had taken the gun in his hand trying to keep it away."

"Did you then talk to Robert after that?"

"No then the police took me to the side and interviewed me. Once the interview was over, Mr. Joles let me go home for the night. The police said they would call me if they had any further questions."

"So in the whole time that everything had happened, you did not talk to Mr. Heyward one time?"

"No."

"Did you hear him say anything?"

"I only heard when he was screaming as he was being beaten."

"What did he say when he was screaming?"

"Nothing, it was just yelling out of pain."

"So if you never heard him say one word how do you know he was the man behind the door when you passed by?"

"I just guessed it was him since he was there after the murder."

"And how exactly do you know he was there exactly after the murder?"

"That's what the police told me."

"That's what the police told you."

"Yes."

"Miss Perez when did you find out there was a murder?"

"When the police came in one of the workers explained it to the officer and I overheard it, then the other police officer who interviewed me told me what happened…"

"I see…No further questions."

"The witness is excused." The judge directs the witness off by motioning his hands.

"The prosecution calls one Caren Joles to the stand." A middle-aged man bald on top with hair on the sides of his head takes the stand and follows the same ritual as the woman before him. "Please state your name and occupation for the record."

"Caren Montgomery Joles, hotel manager at the Comfort Inn."

"Mr. Joles do you recall the night of April the eleventh?" Rogers asks.

"Yes sir, I do."

"Can you explain to us what had happened?"

"Your honor," Jack stands up, "are we really going to hear repeated testimony from every employee at the Comfort Inn Hotel, with the unnecessary questioning and waste of my client's, the jurors', and the court's time."

"I believe the testimony of what happened in the room after Miss Perez had left it is quite important seeing that there were only two other people in the room at the time the defendant and the son of the murdered." Rogers answers back while facing the judge.

"The objection is overruled, but get to the point quickly Mr. Rogers."

"Yes your honor." He brings his attention back to the witness, "Now Mr. Joles, what exactly did Miss Perez say to you after she saw what was happening in room five thirteen?"

"Well she came running down the stairs and said Mr. Joles, there is a man in room five thirteen beating another man with a gun. I immediately called the police and the both of us ran up the stairs to see what was going on. Once I got to the room I instructed Miss Perez to wait downstairs for the police I didn't want anyone to get hurt."

"You mean anyone *else*, to get hurt."

"Well I didn't know Mr. Hodges' had been thrown off the balcony at that point. I found that out later."

"So Mr. Heyward was up in the room and then Mr. Bryan Hodges went up into the room then…"

"Objection your honor, the court can't possibly let Mr. Rogers here ask the witness a question he himself did not *witness*, move to strike." Jack argues.

"Sustained."

Rogers clears his throat. "Mr. Joles. Please tell the court in your own words what happened next."

"Well, after I told Miss Perez to go wait for the police, I immediately tried to run in and separate the two. I ran between the two, and faced Mr. Hodges' son, Bryan, held both his hands and told him to put the gun down, because someone could get killed. Mr. Heyward backed off and turned over in pain and held his head. Bryan then looked me square in the eye and yelled 'someone already did'. He then looked at the balcony. We all stopped for a minute and looked out the window. I took the gun out his hand for the safety of everyone, and walked onto the balcony and looked down. And there it was Mr. Earl Hodges' body in a pool of blood behind his head. All of a sudden a woman saw his body and started screaming. I instructed some of the men on our staff to secure that area and to make sure no guest went near it. Luckily the police had come soon enough and they handled the rest. I told them the same story, I just told you, and I handed over the gun."

Rogers looks over to Jack with a grin, "Your witness."

"Mr. Joles, how tall are you?" Jack asks as he walks towards the witness.

"About five five, five six."

"And how much do you weigh?"

"Objection." Rogers interrupts. "What is the point? I'm sure these questions aren't asked in pretrial, so how well does one need to know the witness."

"I'm getting to the point your honor."

"Please see to it that you do." The Judge responds.

"How much do you weigh Mr. Joles?"

"About a hundred and thirty five pounds give or take."

"I see, no offense Mr. Joles, but would you consider yourself a smaller man, wouldn't you?"

"I suppose."

"For a smaller man, what compelled you to jump between two larger men fighting in a room with a gun and a knife?" Jack asks.

"I…I don't know, I know that it was stupid of me, but I took it as a responsibility I guess."

"Is that right? So you just go all over Houston saving people, and stopping fights with guns and knives?"

"No, I just felt responsible because at that time I was the manager and the hotel was under my control. If someone died under my watch then I could get fired, and I couldn't live with myself."

"But someone did die under your watch Mr. Joles, isn't that right?" He gets no response, "Mr. Joles?"

"Yes…yes someone did die."

"When you jumped into that room and stopped the two men what exactly happened?"

"Your honor the witness already answered this." Rogers says.

"Mr. Kennedy?" The judge asks.

"Just refresh my memory please Mr. Joles."

"Like I said, I ran up to Mr. Bryan Hodges held both his hands and told him to put the gun down because someone could get hurt."

"Why didn't you run up to Mr. Heyward, the man with the knife, why Bryan?"

"Well I didn't know about the knife until the police had searched him."

"So you didn't even know there was a knife present?"

"No, the only threat I saw was the gun and that's where I went."

"Mr. Joles when you walked into the room, did Mr. Heyward look threatening, or give any threatening gestures that would make him seem harmful?"

"No, not really he just backed off and tried to cover his wounds on the top off his head. He seemed to have bled a lot."

"I see, at this point when you entered the room, Bryan not Robert, seemed to be more of a threatening presence, is that right Mr. Joles?"

"Yes, I…I suppose so."

"So, it is possible isn't it Mr. Joles, from what you *saw* from when you first walked into the room and what happened, that Bryan, not Robert had murdered Earl Hodges?"

"Objection your honor!" Rogers yells out.

"Is it possible Mr. Joles?"

"Objection! Your honor, the witness is by no means an expert on telling whether or not he can attest to the presence and mannerisms of someone concluding to them murdering someone. Motion to strike the question and the testimony on the side of the defense."

"Denied," The judge says sternfully, "the testimony will stand, take your seat Mr. Rogers. Mr. Joles please answer the question."

Mr. Joles thinks to himself for a moment and then begins to speak, "Well I don't think that would happen, but now that I think about it, it doesn't seem completely impossible."

"Mr. Joles were you working the front desk that night?"

"Yes."

"Did you ever see Bryan Hodges go upstairs in the room with Earl Hodges, or ever see Bryan Hodges before the murder?"

"No."

"One last question Mr. Joles. Did you see who was up in the room first, Bryan Hodges, or Robert Heyward?"

"No...no I didn't."

"No further questions."

"Redirect your honor." Rogers says to the judge. The judge nods his head in agreement.

"Mr. Joles, how long have you been the manager of the Comfort Inn?"

"About seven years, I move to different locations depending on need."

"And in your experience have you seen many fights?"

"Yes sir, plenty."

"And in all of those fights have you ever witnessed someone commit a crime and then accuse someone else of doing it?"

"No, no I have not."

"Mr. Joles, how long did you wait until the police had arrived inside room five thirteen?"

"Three, maybe four minutes at most. Some of the men on my staff came up in the room and helped keep things calm, I didn't think I could have handled it myself."

"And Mr. Joles what happened in those three to four minutes?"

"Well, Mr. Bryan Hodges sat there in tears, crying for his father, saying various things and asking various questions such as; 'I can't believe he killed my father. Why did you kill my father?' And so on."

"And Mr. Heyward."

"Well, he was sitting with his legs sort of stretched out on the ground as he held his head. One of my men put a towel on his head with ice over it to help the pain and stop the bleeding."

"How did he act Mr. Joles?"

"Well he was distraught, as if he didn't know where he was, sort of like an insane person. He didn't say much, and didn't try to leave. Even if he tried, I don't think he was in any condition to move much, he looked like he was in quite a bit of pain."

"He was like an insane person you say?"

"Yes."

"Thank you Mr. Joles."

"You may step off the stand Mr. Joles." The judge calls out to the witness, "The court is adjourned for today, due to unforeseen reasons we will meet in one week and one day from today, and continue from there. Any objection?" The judge looks at both the lawyers and the both shake their heads not objecting the decision. "Okay I will see you all in one week and one day." He slams the desk with his gavel.

"All rise!" The bailiff calls out. Everyone stands up and the judge walks out the courtroom.

Jack turns to Robert, "You okay there?"

"Yeah, you think Sandra and the boys will be back by then?"

"I'm working on it. Sandra said something about all of the boys' school stuff ending within a week or so I believe, so I'm hoping everything will work out." He looks Robert in the eye, "Hey, let's focus on the case for now, and let me worry about the other stuff. I need you to be less stressed okay." Robert just nods his head as the police officer comes up to them to take Robert back to his jail cell. Jack looks back at the man who accompanied Rogers as he walks out the room. He gives Jack a quick glimpse back and leaves the courtroom with Rogers and Bryan.

***

Back in Robert's jail cell he begins to hear a small snicker. He ignores it. "Robert…" The voice calls out tauntingly. "Who's there?" He calls out. The voice starts to giggle. "Who's there?" Robert raises his voice. The voice starts to giggle even louder, and then bursts out into an evil laugh. "Who's there?! Who's there?!" He yells out. The voice responds in a ceaseless laughter.

Robert collapses onto the ground and sits there rocking back and forth holding his ears. He then falls onto his side and sees the envelope that was given to him by Jack. He reaches under his bed and pulls the envelope towards him. When he opens it slowly not knowing what to expect, he sees a picture of him and his family. It was him pushing Michael and Ryan on a tire swing while Sandra is laughing as she leaned against the poll and held her pregnant stomach with her left hand.

He could hear Sandra's voice in his head. *They say you should hold your stomach with your left hand so the baby could recognize your heart beat through your pulse.* Robert could hear all the voices of the past. He could hear his family laughing and enjoying each other's company. He heard Michael scream, "Push harder daddy, spin it faster!" And then Ryan, "Yeah, faster daddy, faster!" And they would both scream and laugh.

Robert pulled the picture close to kiss it, and as he did a note fell out from inside the envelope. He could tell right away what it was. Just like Sandra would always do for him in times of trouble, she put a prayer in an envelope and gave it to Robert to help him through his difficulties. *The Lord is my shepherd, I shall not want. He makes me lie down in green pastures; he leads me beside still waters; he restores my soul. He leads me in right paths for his name's sake. Even though I walk through the valley of the shadow of death, I fear no evil; for you are with me; your rod and your staff, they comfort me. You prepare a table before me in the presence of my enemies; you anoint my head with oil; my cup overflows. Surely goodness and mercy shall follow me all the days of my life, and I shall dwell in the house of the Lord forever.*

After the prayer she wrote on the bottom, *Keep hope alive Robby, we are with you. Sandra.* Her name was signed in the most elegant fashion. He takes his hand and touches the words and then brushes his fingers across her name. Each letter was perfectly in sync with the next as the bumps of the ink send vibes up his fingers and send energy towards his brain. He then kissed the letter and held it to his heart. When he looked back at the letter he saw some markings under her name. It was hard to make out, it seemed as if she tried to erase it or scratch it off, and didn't notice it was still there. He brings the letter closer to the light in the hallway. He could barely make it out, it read, *Mea Culpa*. Robert begins to cry as he held the letter back to his heart. "Mea Culpa, my love this was not your fault, none of this was, Mea Culpa."

As Robert sits there on his knees under the glow of the single light in the hallway he drops his head. His hands come together as if they were controlled by a strong magnetic force clamping the letter in between his hands. And for the first time in years, for the first time since before he could even remember, for the first time from his heart he begins to pray. He took the name of the Lord and could not stop. Prayer, man's final gleam of hope.

Chapter 53

"You okay?"

"Yeah."

"Is there anything I can do?"

"No."

"Look, if you want I can help out around the house more often, or drop off food or…"

"Stan, thanks, but right now I just need to be with my family."

"What are you saying?"

"I'm just saying with Robert's case on hand, right now I need to figure stuff out for myself."

"So you're going back to him, the guy who's on trial for the death penalty, the guy who walked away…from you?"

"I didn't say that, I just have a lot going on right now."

"So that's what I'm saying, I can be there for you, I can be there with you. We'll get through this…together."

"Please Stan, don't make this harder than it already is. I really need this, you have been an amazing person and friend to me, and I don't want to lose that, I just…really need to figure things out right now. I hope you can understand that." Sandra doesn't get a response. "Stan?"

"Yeah…" He says in a whisper, as if it hurt to talk.

"We okay?"

"Yeah."

"I still need you as friend Stan I hope you know that."

"Yeah."

"Look I'm sorry, I didn't mean to..."

"Hey uh listen, I'm umm getting another phone call here...I'll...I'll just talk to you later."

"Stan, don't do this."

"I'm not doing anything just taking a call."

"...Okay."

"Bye."

"Bye."

***

"With the first day of the Heyward trial over we are now waiting less than a week for the next day to proceed. There have been no comments given by the defense, nor any sign of Robert Heyward's family. Mr. Rogers, of the prosecution on the other hand has this to say when asked about how they felt the first day in court went, 'We clearly see as expected that Mr. Kennedy would have plenty of tricks up his sleeve, nonetheless there are no aces in the deck he is playing with and therefore no bullets in the guns he is holding only 'bang signs' we shall soon show the court all the holes in his theories and expose him and Mr. Heyward both for what has happened. Don't worry Miss Amber K. I can assure you that this trial will hopefully be over soon enough.' When asked if the defense has presented any arguable or strong evidence in their favor Mr. Rogers responded by saying, 'Mr. Kennedy's arguments are all smoke and mirrors and when the dust settles at the end, we shall all see what is true and what is hoax.' The prosecution seems to have a stronghold on this case, and with further investigation we will truly see whether Mr. Kennedy's defense is truly a hoax masked in smoke and mirrors, because it looks like even Houdini himself could not get himself out of this one. This is Amber K. with USN."

Ryan turns off the television and looks over at Michael, "You think she's right? You think dad won't win this? I mean how possible do you think it is?" Ryan looks at Michael searching for some sign of hope.

"I don't know. We'll all have to see at the end."

"School's over tomorrow and your football stuff doesn't start for a month. Jack, dad's lawyer, has been talking to mom about the case every now and then, and we're going back before the trial starts again."

"So?"

"So? What do you mean?"

"I mean so what?"

"So, aren't you coming? We're leaving in two days."

"No."

"Come on Michael, you can't have that much hate. You've got to give him some sort of a break, he's getting bashed left and right here."

"He did it to himself."

"So what if he did or didn't, he told me and mom he was innocent. He looked me dead in the eye and said he didn't do it. Now whether or not he brought it on himself I believe him, and if we all held each other accountable to the fullest extent for all our actions, either everyone would be dead, or no one would talk to each other...And you know that Michael."

"What do you want from me Ryan?"

"I just want you to give him another chance, like everyone has given you."

"I can't..."

Chapter 54

"Daddy!"

"Hey, how's it going champ!" Phil says as he picks up Joshua to give him a hug.

"You're finally home, how was work?" Janis asks as she takes off her cooking glove greeting Phil at the door with a kiss.

"Work was busy, but it looks like I made it home just in time for dinner. What are we having today?" He asks as he puts Joshua down.

"Pot roast and mash potatoes."

"Mm smells good."

"Yeah, well go wash up I'll set the table."

"Okay, dear…Hey Janis?"

"Yeah?"

"I love you."

She smiles at him, "I love you too…Now hurry up I don't want the food to get cold!" She gestures him towards the bathroom.

"Alright, alright." He says as he laughs. He walks into to the bathroom and begins to wash his hands. Phil then looks up into the mirror and doesn't like what he sees. His face is a constant reminder of what happened and what is happening. He remembers from his younger days from law school how he learned that one of the better ways to see if a person is lying, especially if they don't do it often is to show them the mirror. Since humans for some reason can never remember what their faces look like, that once shown their own image, it was hard to lie to themselves to their own face, as they look into their own eyes. How remarkable the mind is, capable of so many things and it can barely

remember what the vessel it is carried in looks like. Commit enough crimes and you begin to detach your actions from the person in the mirror and become criminally insane.

Phil hears Janis call out for him, indicating that the table was set and the food was ready. He sat there and ate with his family, for when he was home he was a different person. He was a family man. He was a husband and a father, but a murderer he was not. He ate the food that Janis had prepared, and he laughed and joked with his wife and child. He talked about the parts of work that he could. He listened to stories that Janis had and how she spent time with her friends shopping today. He listened to Joshua explain how the monsters in the movie he just saw would knock down the buildings. He had built a city out of building blocks in the living room just like the movie, but his were all color coated. He was going to knock them down during dinner, but Janis had stopped him. They sat there and enjoyed each other. It's good to have a family to fall back on, Phil thought to himself. It is good to have a piece of heaven on earth. Being so caught up in the case he had forgotten much of the dismay from Janis' confession. He was happy, his family was happy and that's all that mattered. No one backstabs each other here; no one lies to each other.

"Peace, my home is my temple I am the king and in front of me is my queen, bearing my awaited prince or princess and with us sits our oldest prince. In no time at all the final annoyance will be put to rest out of my life. What better ending to my life than this?" He thinks to himself. After dinner they all sat and watched a movie in the living room as they ate ice cream in bowls. Joshua soon falls asleep so Phil carries him to his bed, Janis follows after putting away the dishes. After they put him to bed they walk into their own bedroom and kiss, they finally find their way to their bed and make love. Afterwards Janis lies on Phil's shoulder lost in deep thought, as she plays with the hair on his chest.

"Remember that night in the hospital?"

"I don't know what you're talking about." Phil responds with a smile as he looks up at the ceiling.

"Yeah, you do!" She says as she laughs and hits Phil on his chest softly.

"Ou, you're so violent." He says as he laughs and holds her hand, "Really J, I don't know what you're talking about must have been some other guy." Phil continues jokingly.

"Yeah?" Janis asks. Phil just shrugs his shoulders, "Stop." She says with a smile trying to warn him.

"Alright fine." He says letting out a small laugh and kisses her on her head.

"I think I fell in love with you that night."

"Yeah?"

"Yeah."

"I think I fell in love with you that night too."

Janis then holds Phil closer to hear his heart beat as they both fall asleep. His heartbeat was her favorite lullaby.

Chapter 55

"You know no matter how long you stare at the evidence it will stay the same."

"Jesus! You scared the shit out of me Brown!"

"Sorry, just came back in town and I wanted to look over some stuff from my investigation. Didn't think I'd find you here." Brown takes a sip of his coffee.

"Yeah, well here I am." Jack says, as he looks back down at some of the evidence remembering his own cup of coffee and takes a sip.

"So if nothing changes, why are you here?"

"I'm here to put the pieces to the puzzle together. See finding evidence is like opening a brand new puzzle box. You pop it open and there are pieces everywhere. And the stories of the people are the glue that helps these pieces fit together. It's unfortunate when we have a crime that there is no picture on the box to help put these pieces together, but I guess that's where people like me come in."

"Well, if that's so what information did you get, or how much *glue* do you have to help make sense of this."

"Nothing that would help you."

"Damn."

"Don't worry kid you'll find your way. How did your first day in court go?" Brown asks, as he gets closer.

"It was okay just opening statements and the first round of witnesses." Jack tries to keep his focus on the evidence.

"Any witness account helping your case?"

"I don't know I guess we'll find out."

"How's Heyward holding up?"

"Well he's on trial for his life what do you think?"

"Fair enough."

"And his family?"

"They're coming in tomorrow."

"Weren't they here already?"

"Yeah, but they had to go back, and now they'll be here tomorrow."

"Are they going on the stand?" Brown asks.

"I don't know they're on the list just in case."

"So do you work stuff out or do you just go by the fly?"

"I just say what comes to me and go from there?"

"And that works for you."

"The courtroom is my home, I just take in the situation and go with it. None of my law professors ever agreed, very few of my clients ever agree, and any other colleague that hears of it pretty much shuns me and looks down upon my 'professionalism' as you can imagine, but it is what it is. There was one professor though, he said 'a true artist, even though there is planning and preparation involved, in the moment in the *true* moment of painting or artistry the painter does not anticipate where his next stroke will go, a true writer does not stay up all night pondering what his next words will be, a true lawyer does not fear and over study his own argument. All of these things come to the true artist of his field when he is in the moment while in action, while in war. A true artist will let his hand push the brush and it will paint for him. A true artist is a master of his realm. And in school we are here to understand the mechanics, but in our hearts lies the true lust of mastery.'" Jack says.

"Sounds like the man knew what he was talking about."

"Yeah, he does. The man was my hero in college. He was like a father to me through law school he got me through some tough times."

"Yeah what happened to him?" Brown asks.

"Of course like everyone I ever cared for, he almost got taken away from me. Thought he would die of a heart attack, but he survived, one of the few breaks I got in my life. I don't know what I would do without him backing me up." Jack laughs a bit thinking of recent events, "The man then became my boss, but anyway, yeah that's how I am in court I go with my gut, it's definitely not always the best way to go, but my mind can't recognize any other way."

"Well, as long as it works. So why are you here so late?"

"Just like you, trying to glue the pieces together so I can tell a better story when it comes time to go to court. Winning is about the side who tells the best story. The one who champions rhetoric wins the hearts of the men and women who listen, but with such a talent of the raw power of words, we must take into account the lives we affect and the ears that listen to us."

"Your professor?"

"Yes sir." Jack keeps his focus on the evidence.

"Impressive, so you going to put Heyward on the stand?"

"I'm sure that's what eventually is going to happen, I mean I don't think there is any way around it. Not that I'm trying to avoid it, I'm just sure that it needs to be done." He sips his coffee.

"Boy you lawyers really have your way of talking."

"Like I said rhetoric, you wouldn't know anything about it."

"Is that right?" Brown stares him down.

"No offense it's just that…"

"Rhetoric is the art of ruling the minds of men." Brown interrupts.

Jack smiles and looks at Brown from the corner of his eye. "Ah Plato, very good Brown." Says Jack comically as if he were in a kung fu movie. "I must say, now I am the one who is impressed."

"Good I'm glad all that studying finally paid off. Now that you're impressed I can finally die."

Jack just stares at Brown nodding his head slightly trying to figure out what just happened. "Okay smartass, Did not the heavenly rhetoric of thine eye, 'gainst whom the world cannot hold argument, persuade my heart to this false perjury? Vows for thee broke deserve not punishment."

"Shakespeare, very good Jack, but everyone quotes him. Do you know why I am the detective and you are the lawyer?"

"Ugh, why Brown?" Jack rolls his eyes deciding reluctantly to play along with Brown's game.

"Well let me put it this way." Brown tilts his head and looks up at the ceiling as if he were a professor and someone was beaming information down into his head. He begins to pontificate, "It is the mark of an educated man to look for precision in each class of things just so far as the nature of the subject admits; it is evidently equally foolish to accept probable reasoning from a mathematician and to demand from rhetorician scientific proofs." He looks back at Jack and smiles.

Jack's jaw drops as he stares at Brown speechlessly, as if the wind were knocked out of him. His eyes slowly close and then open and Brown remains there with his overconfident smile. "You." The words finally utter through Jack's lips.

"Yeah." Brown nods his head continuing to smile.

"You, you read the Nicomachean Ethics? You?"

"Yeah..."

"But you're a cop, I've studied law for years before I could understand Aristotle and here you are quoting him as if it were Doctor Seuss."

"Hmm I guess I am. So either I'm really smart or you're really dumb. Which one is it Jack?"

"So why are you a cop?"

"My father was a cop, my grandfather, and so on. It's just what we do, we all try to make the world right or wrong in our own little ways no matter how big or small the job, we all have to do our parts."

"You know you're alright Brown." Jack says as he toasts his coffee cup to Brown.

"You too Jacqueline. You too." Brown returns the gesture.

***

"Hello?"

"Hey."

"Michael? Are you guys there already?"

"No, I didn't go."

"What, why not?" Kayla responds having a hard time hearing Michael.

"I don't know, you want to come over, I'm having a hard time sitting standing straight right now."

"Oh my God Michael, are you drunk?!"

"No...Yes..." Michael slurs as he begins to cry.

"I'll be right there." She hangs up the phone. About half an hour later Michael hears a knock at the door.

"Kayla! You're here...What, what are you doing here? I'm supposed to be in Houston. Are, are you cheating on me in my house, because I, I want you to know that I would never cheat on you in my house...or anywhere. Come on, come on in. I have beer, wine, beer, scotch, oh yeah and beer. What, what's that?"

"This is Thai food, and this is a thermos full of coffee you need to sober up and we need to talk." Kayla starts walking into the kitchen.

"You, you know nine out of ten times when a woman tells you we need to talk it's a bad thing." Michael says stumbling as he follows Kayla.

"Well it is ten out of ten times with me."

"Ouu you're feisty, I love you..."

"Give me the beer."

"No!..." He bring the can close to himself, and then he looks at the beer, "I, I love beer too, it's a love triangle." He makes a triangle in the air with his fingers. "Well I love football too, it's a love square...yes."

"Michael, what are you doing?"

"What? Just having some fun, lighten up babe."

"Seriously, what are you doing Michael?"

"What do you mean?"

"You know exactly what I mean." She gets closer to him and takes the can of beer out his hands.

"Just getting my mind off of things, you wouldn't understand be...because you're perfect, you're not like me. I hate my dad...and now...now he's going to die..." Michael belches then begins to cry as he moves back until he hits the wall and slides down.

Kayla pours a cup of coffee and brings it over to him as she joins him on the floor. "Look sweetie I know things are tough but avoiding the problem won't make things better. You have to go see your father."

"He's not my father, he's just some man who slept with my mom."

"No Michael, he's your father."

"I know enough to know that he's been calling, asking for you. And when they went down there the first thing he asked about was where you were."

"How do you know that?"

"Ryan told me. And you need to understand that if he wasn't your father he wouldn't have ever asked."

"It's so hard to let go of what happened."

"What happened Michael?"

"I don't want to talk about it."

"Come on baby you never want to talk about it, but I think it's important that you do. I need to know, and I need you to talk about it. Please Michael."

Michael looks back at her to see if he could trust her with his most sacred thoughts. She seemed to be trustworthy enough after all she stuck by his side so far even after tonight's despicable show that he put on. Here she is by his side, willing for him to give an excuse a reason, she is willing to hear his story even through everything. He thinks of how much he loves her. He thinks back as far as he can to his childhood, and as the first tear falls down his cheek he begins to tell his story.

He hates opening up, he hates telling his story because it is his story and no one else's and he couldn't share it with them. He hated when he would be telling his story to anyone and that person would break his concentration and interrupt. Everything he expected from the world Kayla was not. As he opened up he felt stronger for it because she was there, she listened and didn't say a word. She shared his tears; she poured more coffee as he finished it. The more he told the closer she would get. Always facing him, but he kept his head down as he told his story. He would turn his back on the world only to turn around and see her face. Only to see her smiling at him showing him the way to back to the world, and bringing him back to reality. When Michael finished telling his story he looked up at Kayla with half shameful eyes not knowing exactly what to expect hoping for some look of understanding. As soon as their eyes met, Kayla wrapped her arms around Michael and held him tight. She kissed him and told him not to worry about anything because she was right there with him, and Michael believed her. Then for a while they just sat there in each other's arms.

"You know after what you told me, you have to go down to Houston." Kayla breaks the silence.

"What do you mean?"

"I mean I see all you have gone through and then I think of your father and what he must have gone through, and what he is going through. You lost your sister and your father. And no matter what happened you really didn't give him a chance to talk to you about it, and I think that is where all your strong feelings are coming from."

"Look I don't want to do this."

"Just listen for a second, and if you still think it doesn't make sense and you don't want to take it any further I'll drop it."

"Okay…"

"Even though you had your losses and things you went through were rough, your father lost his daughter, he lost his two sons, he lost his wife, and now he may even lose his life. I mean God forbid that would happen after losing everything, do you want him to believe he didn't have his family by his side? Do you want him to believe he didn't have you by his side?"

"Please, let's drop this."

***

"We're being followed sir."

"By whom?"

"The detective assigned to the case."

"Hmm…"

"Do you have a profile on him?"

"Yes, here sir." Dominique hands over a folder to Max. "Shall I take care of him?"

"Patience Dominique…" Max begins to study the files in the folders, "Hmm detective Frank Brown…let the hound sniff out the trail. I'm sure he will find a dead end. It will keep him out of the way."

"Sir?"

"To be on our trail he can only be searching for clues on the Cold Fusion project. Goddamn Hodges got too careless and now we have this mutt on our case. None-the-less the detective is researching therefore no specific leaks are getting out to the press. Says here he is on the verge of retirement. We can make sure to give him a good send off in return for his silence. Until then let him dig. Hopefully if our lawyer does well we can get Heyward out the way soon as well."

"Why is Heyward's being out the way so important for our company sir?"

"Think Walker, with one less mouth that can talk about the Cold Fusion project, one less person to try to claim glory to it, one less person trying to recreate it we can have omnipotent power, and omniscience. No sharing, it would be the governments natural monopoly, not only to our own country, but the world. So let us make sure of it that the lawyer and Mr. Rogers do their job, so then we can take care of the lawyer ourselves soon after. Report any further information you find, we must be weary of how the case progresses Mr. Walker."

"Yes sir." Dominique begins to walk out the door.

"Mr. Walker."

"Sir."

"Leave the detective alone, let him follow, just make his path a bit more skewed, we can't make his journey an easy one."

"Yes sir." He walks out the room.

Chapter 56

At The Bob Casey Federal Court House

"Glad you're here early Sandra, and good to see you again Ryan. How was the flight over here?"

"Just fine, thank you Mr. Kennedy."

"And were you able to find the courthouse fine, no problems there?"

"No everything was perfect." Sandra replies.

"Okay good," Jack looks around, "and Michael?"

"Well…He just couldn't make it."

"I'm sorry to hear that."

"So am I Jack."

Jack takes a deep breath, "Well okay at least you two are here and I know Robert will be very happy to see you."

"Can we see him now?" Ryan asks.

"No not yet, you'll have to wait until the trial starts, you may have a few moments before the judge comes in, and a few moments after the trial, but other than that you'd have to visit him just like you have before."

"How did the first day go?"

"It was okay, there's a lot of…" He looks down at Ryan remembering not to cuss, "*garbage* that they are feeding the jury, but we just need to sort through the mess and make sure that the testimonies given are honest and something we can work with. Trials like these take a while, but so far as the witnesses that he has brought up, the prosecution looks pretty weak, as far as I can see I'll hopefully be able to find enough holes in the story to help Robert."

"Well we hope so too, is he holding up okay?" Sandra asks.

"Yeah, he's trying to keep as strong as he can, but I know he'll do a lot better now that you two are here."

"Good, is there anything we can do?"

"As of now, everything you have done so far is perfect, just being here is all Robert and I can ask for." Jack takes a look at his watch. "Hey I have to prepare a few things before the trial starts so if you two will excuse me?"

"Of course." Sandra says.

"I'll see you inside."

Phil stands on the other side of the hallway in the courthouse as he and Rogers prepare notes for the case and suddenly from the corner of his eye he sees a ghost from the past bringing his heart to nearly a complete halt. He looks up and as if it were an angel, she brushes her hair past her cheek and smiles as she talks to a young boy. "Sandra?" He thinks, "It couldn't be. She died, I saw her grave. It's not possible, is it?" His thoughts take charge of his being and everything goes blank up until he hears the strong voice of the bailiff.

"All rise!" Phil is suddenly brought back into the courtroom. He looks over in Robert's direction and there she is sitting behind him. Once again Phil is lost in his own world; he becomes trapped inside his own mind unable to escape. "What the hell is going on?" He asks himself as if to get a reasonable response. His head turned back towards the witness stand as he hears the first witness of the day.

"Officer Sherman Holder."

"Officer Holder, can you tell us your involvement in the case at hand?" Rogers asks.

"Yes, I was first on scene."

"Were you the only officer there at the time?"

"No sir, my partner officer Simone Towers was there as well."

"So it was just the two of you then?"

"Yes sir, when we first had gotten the call, we were the only officers sent and when officer Towers discovered the dead body we had called the paramedics and also for back up."

"So what happened when you first got to the scene of the crime?"

"Well we got to the hotel, the maid, Miss Perez met us at the front desk. She said that the disturbance was happening up in room five thirteen and just when we were heading up towards the room, another man came running to us and told us about the dead body outside. Officer Towers and I split up. I went upstairs to make sure everyone was safe, and Officer Towers went outside to find the body."

"That's when you called for backup?"

"Yes, I had called for backup on the way upstairs, and soon after the other officers had arrived with the paramedics at the scene."

"Once upstairs, what happened?"

"Well once upstairs, the manager, Mr. Joles approached me and explained the situation and that is when I put Mr. Heyward in cuffs, read him his rights, and then interviewed him. Afterwards I interviewed everyone else."

"I see, now…" Rogers was suddenly interrupted by the sound of the court's door closing. He looks back along with the rest of the courtroom.

There was Michael walking in trying to be as quiet as possible, already embarrassed by his late arrival and everyone staring at him. Sandra smiled as she sat there waiting for her child to come to the front of the courtroom. All Robert saw was his little boy, and was brought back in time to when Michael was a child like a lost boy looking for his father in the church between the pews. Michael finally locked eyes with Sandra and sat down next to her. She put her hand behind his head welcoming him. He looks at his father and nods his head in support. Robert returns the smile and looks at Jack, and Jack returns the same supportive look.

"Shall we continue Mr. Rogers?" The judge asks.

"Uh…uh yes your honor." He says with his concentration completely broken. He turns to the witness trying to salvage his flow.

Robert then through the corner of his eyes sees a blinking light. When he turns his head, he sees Phil looking at Sandra. He immediately had a theory of what the flashing light is. Anger and rage surge through his body as one of the closest people of his past sits across from him. Knowing that the only reason he sits in that seat is to ensure Robert's death. He remembers the evil smile upon Phil's face the night of the murder. Robert's eyes burn as he notices more and more that Phil's full attention is on Robert's family. He wants to jump over to him and squeeze the life out of the man who hurt him so much, the man who abandoned his family, and now is fighting with the law to have him killed. Robert remains seated and stares as to hope he can slowly kill Phil through his deadly thoughts.

Phil suddenly realizes the children are Michael and Ryan. "They have grown so much." He thinks to himself. His family, his old family. Sandra and the boys look over trying to see what Robert was looking at and see Phil. They exchange glances, Phil looks over at Robert, then turns his head and looks forward as if to ignore them and bypass the awkward situation. Phil's heart begins racing, trying to escape through his chest, and he starts breathing harder, pretending to focus on the case. But he doesn't even seem to be in the room anymore, as he steps back into the past.

"Isn't that Uncle Phil?" Ryan asks Sandra in a whisper.

"Shh…" She responds with an angered looked.

"Now officer where were we? Ah yes you had just cuffed Mr. Heyward and read him his rights correct?"

"Yes."

"Now why did you cuff Mr. Heyward and not Mr. Bryan Hodges?"

"Well when I got to the scene Mr. Bryan Hodges, Mr. Joles, and all the staff that were in the room and claimed Mr. Heyward to be the murderer, and therefore I didn't have much choice at the time."

"I see now when you interviewed Mr. Heyward did he say anything that would lead to some sort of a confession or anything that did not sit well with you."

"Objection, hearsay."

"Your honor this is an officer of the law and has made written reports of all the interviews he has conducted at the scene."

"Overruled."

"Well he said one thing that really stood out to me. He said, 'I didn't want to kill the guy, I'm not a murderer, I only wanted to talk to him.'" The confession was in bold red print on a projection screen for the entire court to see.

"Officer Holder how long have you been on the force?"

"Eighteen years."

"And in those eighteen years have you seen many murders?"

"Yes, plenty."

"I see, now when you spoke to Mr. Bryan Hodges, did he seem upset and delusional? Possibly even outraged?"

"Objection leading your honor!"

"Sustained."

"Okay, did or did the son of the murdered not seem upset?"

"He did."

"Did he seem angry?"

"Yes."

"Did he seem like a murderer?"

"No he did not."

"So are you saying that a man who seemed upset and angry, after a murder did not seem as if he were a murderer?"

"No, sir he did not."

"How can you prove that?"

"You can't, but from my experience, the way Mr. Bryan Hodges acted during the questioning and the way he seemed to be traumatized did not profile him as a possible suspect in such a case."

"I see, and when you fingerprinted the entire room did you find the fingerprints of Mr. Heyward 'most everywhere in the room, including the gun?"

"Yes, yes we did."

"Did you find Mr. Heyward's blood in various places of the room?"

"Yes."

"When you arrested Mr. Heyward did you find any weapons on his person?"

"Yes, we found a knife, which was about six inches long located in Mr. Heyward's back right pocket."

"Did you ask him about the knife?"

"Yes, he said he had it under his pants at first, but it fell out and then he put it in his back pocket."

"Were there any prints besides Mr. Heyward's on the knife?"

"No."

"Officer Holder what is the legal length of possession of a knife in the great state of Texas?"

"Five and a half inches."

"Well thank you Officer Holder. Your witness." When Rogers sits down on his chair he turns around and looks at Phil. "Wake up you fool, we need you in this case, not off somewhere daydreaming."

Phil snaps out of his disillusioned state and looks at Rogers. Rogers motions his eyes down to Phil's folder. Phil looks down as well and sees a red blinking light. "Oh sorry." He responds.

"Well let's stay on task." Rogers says then turns around. Phil then writes something into the folder and the light switches off.

"So eighteen years on the force huh Officer Holder?"

"Yes."

"Officer Holder, did Robert seem angry, and upset when you first saw him?"

"No, he pretty much seemed dazed and confused."

"How did he act when you questioned him?"

"Well, first I tried to give him some first aid for his head, and then I questioned him. When I did finally question him, he seemed to mumble a lot, but he was claiming that he didn't kill anyone. He said that Earl Hodges was already dead when he arrived."

"So in your eighteen years of service have you ever seen someone who was in the same state as Mr. Heyward dazed, confused, and denying the crime as a true prospect to a murder?"

"Well yes, yes I have."

"I see, and from all of these people in the same state what was the one thing they have had in common?"

"Well they were all drunk."

"When you checked Mr. Heyward's blood, was he drunk?"

The officer thinks for a moment, "No he was not, but he had lost a lot of blood that night, so it's hard to tell."

"So is it possible that Mr. Heyward was in the state he was by being beaten so badly and not by alcohol?"

"Yes."

"Officer Holder in your eighteen years have you ever heard the term immediate post homicidal depression?"

"Yes, but I have only seen it once."

"Can you explain what it is for the court's clarification?"

Roger gets up immediately, "Your honor, this phenomenon is found so few and far apart that many doctors don't even recognize it as an existing condition, rather most people find it is an excuse. Even the officer in question has seen it only once in eighteen years of duty."

"I believe any condition that would help exculpate my client is viable, furthermore, if the officer in question has heard about it and seen it then it should stand. If the prosecution would like I can have over a dozen expert testimonies from psychologists across the nation that would attest to such a condition." Jack explains.

"Mr. Rogers?" The judge asks.

He thinks for moment, "The prosecution will stipulate."

"You may answer the question Officer Holder." The judge tells the witness.

"Basically it is when someone commits a murder, usually a close loved one, and immediately after is so torn apart by the result so much so that they attempt to remove themselves from the crime and try to blame someone else for the murder, usually by killing them or severely beating them as to purge themselves from the situation. It's one of the rarer things I have heard of."

"But not impossible?"

"No, I guess not."

"Officer Holder, from your expert testimony is it possible that Mr. Bryan Hodges here suffered from immediate post homicidal depression, and Mr. Heyward did not murder Mr. Earl Hodges?"

"I guess so, if that were the case."

"When you fingerprinted the place did you discover the maid's finger prints all over the place?"

"Yes, but not any of the things that were entered into the room after Mr. Hodges checked in."

"Did you come across Bryan Hodges' prints everywhere?"

"Yes."

"Was Bryan Hodges' blood found in various places in the room?"

"Yes."

"Including on Mr. Heyward, and the gun?"

"Yes."

"Why do you suppose that is?"

"Well, from my investigation I found that Mr. Bryan Hodges fought with Mr. Heyward and gun whipped him several times on the top part of his head. Therefore both their blood types were found in various places."

"Was there any blood found on the knife Mr. Heyward was carrying, or any sign of use of the knife at the crime scene?"

"No."

"No further questions your honor. Thank you officer Holder." The officer walks off the stand, "The defense calls Dr. Ian Walters to the stand."

As the young doctor took the stand Phil started scribbling into the folder, and the trial became like a dream. He zoned into what he needed to do and completely took over. He first let Jack finish the first couple questions before he started his barrage of punches like a boxer fighting a child with nowhere to go. He looked over at Sandra quickly and back into his folder, he started writing as if he were proving something to her. Ever since the first day he met her in Dallas he's been trying to prove himself to her. He accidently introduced her to Robert trying to break an awkward silence they had and those two fell in love from then on. "She could have been mine." He thinks to himself. He then remembers his own family shakes it off and continues writing. If he hurts Robert, he hurts her, his first love, but they are no more his family. He must hurt them to protect himself. To protect his family, why else do anything?

"Doctor Ian Walters," The doctor begins, "I performed the autopsy on Mr. Earl Landon Hodges."

"Doctor Walters, were there any bruises on Mr. Hodges?"

"Just a few on his body and one on his face, and a few severe ones on his back, and of course the broken opened cranium from the back side."

"Was there sign of struggle?"

"Yes somewhat, it was obvious that there was a fight or beating of some sort."

"So on his body, were you able to find any sign that Mr. Hodges and Mr. Heyward here had a fight?"

"No."

"I see. So no, blood, skin, and fingerprint on the deceased that would point the finger to Mr. Heyward?"

"No."

"Did he have Bryan Hodges' prints on him?"

"Objection your honor the defense continuously is insinuating that the prosecution, the *son* of the deceased acted in this heinous act. And we request the court to strongly instruct Mr. Kennedy to keep away of such leading of the court's judgment and the jury of the trial. We further request the court to strike any testimony that is suggestive camp of Mr. Bryan Hodges committing the murder."

"I believe this testimony is just and admissible considering not one witness saw Mr. Bryan Hodges ever enter the hotel in the first place, or re-enter the room as it states in the police report nor did anyone see Mr. Robert Heyward enter the room or the hotel. As far as the defense is concerned they are both in the same boat and the defense asks that the court should not forget that and grant latitude to such questions and accusations." Jack says never turning around to address the existence of the prosecution.

"Hasn't this child been through enough your honor?"

The judge thinks for a moment. "The objection is overruled, but Mr. Kennedy though the testimony will be admissible, I want you to try to focus on defending your client as opposed to accusing the prosecution."

"Yes your honor."

Phil then smiles and scribbles into the folder. Every few moments Rogers would yell out objection leading, objection irrelevant, objection argumentative, objection, objection, objection! Bryan looks over at the digital note pad next to him blinking red and loses himself in it. It brings him back to when Phil, Rogers, and himself were sitting in Rogers' office discussing the case and how it should go.

"Okay we have a case now and we must be nothing, but perfect." Phil says looking at the other two, "When we go into court the defense already has a strike against them for the mere fact that the person is actually in court. The jury already has a slight preconceived notion of the defense being guilty. Our job is to play on the notion and make sure that the defense believes what they already think is true. Even though the law says innocent until proven guilty as far as the jury is concerned he needs to prove his innocence to them and that is all they're worried about. This trial is not about if he did it or not, it is about who can tell a better story, so if you need to, act like you're in kindergarten and the jurymen are your students then do so and tell the best damn story of your life. Now when Robert was questioned by the police he had no lawyer present so we need to find out what he told the police and use it against him. We must keep in mind the Miranda rights, 'Whatever you say can and will be held against you.'

Over eighty five percent of people whether innocent or guilty give incriminating evidence to the police unintentionally that can get them convicted. Rogers, when you are speaking to the jury you need to make sure that you are giving the jury a reason to convict Robert so no tricks just keep shoving in their face how he is a criminal and downplay the defense every chance you get. In old English times, they forced the person going to court to raise his right hand to see if he has any previous convictions against him. If you committed a crime the crime would be branded on to your right palm with a symbol depending on the crime, which would also make the sentencing harsher, depending on what crimes you've been already convicted for, if any. When they put Robert on stage we have to expose any incriminating evidence from the past and stamp it on to his palm."

"Ha, you know in ancient Rome they used to make you swear on your own balls as an oath." Rogers laughed

"Yeah, well if that were still true there'd be no crime, huh Rogers?"

"No I guess not."

"Anyway we will start off the case smooth letting the defense feel like they may have an edge but every so often we will object to throw him off balance. And once things start heating up we will object every few minutes even if there is nothing to object to. No story has ever been told beautifully being interrupted so many times, and we must make sure of it. We must stay composed, we must stay focused, we must stay perfect. When they call you on to the stand Bryan, you must say precisely what we will talk about. If you get stuck just try your best, but stick to what you know. There is no point in formulating stories because they will be cracked. If things go in a way we don't like we can always redirect. In this circus we must be the ringmasters. Even when they call me to the stand we must follow our script."

"Wait, why would they call you to the stand?" Bryan asks.

"I was your father's lawyer Bryan and closer to his affairs than most people. They're going ask me about my involvement with him, and I'm sure if they do bring me to the stand they'll dig into my past."

"What about your past?"

"Let's just worry about that if and when it happens."

"Okay…"

"Now, I have used digital pads like this since law school, and it has made my career. Even though I obviously won't be able to participate in anything during the trial, it doesn't mean I won't be able to talk, or tell you the next steps." He shows them the digital pad, "Now every time you want to tell me something you just write it onto here and press send, it will send it to my pad and alert me by flashing a red light. I will

respond in the same fashion, helping you every step of the way, so you won't have to worry about a single thing. Now Rogers let's start with your opening statement."

"Objection speculation!" Rogers yells out as Bryan is brought back into the courtroom, the red light still blinking.

"Your honor Mr. Rogers has objected countless times pointlessly to numerous questions, through three separate witnesses today already. He is only trying to disrupt my investigation and prolonging the interview, tiring the jury only hurting the case of my client. Would the court please instruct the prosecution to confine its objections so the defense can continue its investigation in a respectable manner?"

Rogers looks down at the note pad then back at the judge as he stands up, "Uh your honor, the prosecution believes that the defense is prolonging their interview to exhaust the jury with small facts, hearsay, and irrelevant testimony. The prosecution feels the need to continually object to expose the false extractions of various testimonies through precarious questioning."

"Are you fucking kidding me?" Jack addresses Rogers for the first time as he turns around. The people in the court take a gasp and begin to whisper to each other in disbelief.

"Order!" The judge slams his desk with his gavel, "Watch it Mr. Kennedy or I will have you in contempt."

"Your honor couldn't possibly take the previous statement by the prosecution seriously or into consideration. It is blatantly obvious what the prosecution is doing here and it is disrespectful and disgraceful, and once again we strongly point out that it is hurting the investigation of the defense!"

"Be that as it may be Mr. Kennedy, the prosecution is not breaking any particular rules or laws…"

"But…" Jack tries to interrupt.

"If," The judge regains control as he puts up his index finger as to quiet Jack, "if there are legitimate motions then neither you, I, nor anyone in this courtroom can put a halt to such objections."

"Yes your honor."

"Furthermore Mr. Rogers," He looks over to Rogers, "I will bequeath to you that the court will limit its tolerance on inessential objections."

"Noted your honor."

Jack looks at Rogers than at Phil sitting behind him trying his best to keep his composure. Phil gives him a dark half smile back. Jack looks down at the ground then at Robert; his focus gets diverted to his family behind him.

"Detective Frank Brown, when do you retire?" Jack asks almost half heartedly, feeling tired and defeated.

"Just over two months ago?"

"So why are you still on this case?"

"Because there are only a handful of cases in my whole career that have gone unsolved and those cases were in my earlier years."

"So why not let this case go? It's open and close isn't it? Robert Heyward committed the murder, you show it and then you retire and move on? Or you could have simply just let the next guy in line take it over."

"No. From all the crimes I've seen this one just doesn't seem to add up. This was my case, and I wanted to handle it, I have never passed on a case to someone else, and this situation should be no different."

"Doesn't seem to add up? What do you mean by that?"

"Like I said, I can't quite explain it, but I just think there's more to the case than what we see."

"Thank you detective Brown." Jack turns around and returns the half smile to Phil.

"That's enough for today, we shall meet in two days at nine in the morning." The judge slams the gavel.

"All rise!"

Robert turns around and hugs Sandra, and then Michael and Ryan.

"So you must be Michael." Jack says.

"Yeah, seems like you were having some trouble out there."

"Just a minor setback, it may actually help play the sympathy card for us."

"You okay dad?" Michael asks.

"Yeah...I am now." The officer in the court comes to take Robert away, "I'll see you guys soon." He says as he walks away.

"Look guys I need to take care of some things and put some notes together, why don't you guys take the day to yourselves and let's meet up tomorrow around lunch and we can talk some more."

"Okay sounds good." Sandra responds.

Jack puts his hand on Michael's shoulder, and then tries his best to smile, "I'm really glad all of you are here." Sandra nods her head at him and he walks away.

Outside of the courtroom in the hallway, Phil is signing some papers and looking in a folder while talking to Rogers and Bryan. He shakes their hands and they walk away. He starts walking back to the other side of the hallway. When he looks up he sees Sandra walking towards him. Stunned he stands there for a moment like a deer caught in headlights. When he finally comes to Sandra is only inches away from him.

"Sandra?"

Immediately, she slaps him, "Don't talk to me, you son of a bitch!" She says angrily.

"What?"

"We thought you were dead. Robert thought you were dead! All these years, he's been going crazy. And where were you? Huh? Our family trusted you to be there, but you disappeared. After all that Robert has done for you, how could you abandon him like that?!"

"He abandoned me!"

She puts her finger to his face, as tears start coming down her eyes, "Don't you dare feed me that crap. Every day he would call you, going more and more insane, trying to find you not knowing what happened to you, hoping you were okay. All the while his life and his family were falling apart, as his business burned to the ground and took down everything with it. And years later, after you left him to die in his own sorrows, here you are sitting, talking, contemplating with the prosecution to finish the job. You're nothing, but a piece of shit...I just want you to know you're going to burn in hell for this."

"You just don't understand Sandra."

She slaps him again, "Don't talk to me, I understand enough. If you went through half the things he did, you'd be dead by now. But you would have to be at least half the man he is, you could never measure up to such heights. He needed you...*I* needed you..."

"I thought you had died, I saw your grave."

She slaps him again, "That was my daughter you ignorant son of a bitch, you missed my daughter's funeral, you were going to be her godfather, but you were too busy running away like you always do." Her eyes are bright red from the tears, "Don't you dare ever utter her name again."

Phil holds his face as he looks up at Sandra and tears come down from his eyes as he realized what had just happened as he drops his head in shame. He looks up again only to see Sandra walking away, and her two sons just staring at him. She finally gets to them and they all walk away. His old family, walking away from him forever.

***

"Son of a bitch!" Jack says throwing his chair up against the wall.

"Calm down there Jack, you were going up against one of the best lawyers I have ever known in my life." Robert says as he sees his lawyer begin to fall apart pacing back and forth.

"What that douche bag, Rogers? He's a piece of crap, how the fuck does he keep trapping me? He doesn't even look that good, but for some God damn reason he's like two steps ahead of me." Jack thinks back to the trial trying to replay it looking for what mistakes he had made and he is thrown back into the fire and the splenetic feeling eats him alive. "Every two minutes objection, objection, objection! I mean what the fuck! Real lawyers go into to court to fight and argue a case, this son of a bitch goes into court to object."

"Calm down Jack I'm sure you'll do better when we get back in there."

"Ha, are you kidding me? I have to change my whole legal strategy, everything I've done all torn to shreds in one day, in one hearing."

"Calm down Jack." Robert says in a more stern voice.

"Don't tell me to calm down, my whole career, my whole case, everything I've worked for burned down in front of my own eyes today Robert! Do you even know how that feels Robert?" Jack looks him in the eyes.

"You're kidding right?"

Realizing what he just said he recoils a bit, "All my credibility for this case and any case I would ever take on in the future gone, videos of this hearing will be seen across the nation in about two and a half hours from now, so they can all laugh at me."

"You need to calm the hell down, right the hell now Jacky."

"Look I still have a future, ha, well had one. You've been so detached from the fucking world you wouldn't even know what that feels like anymore. So why the hell should I calm down Robert!" Jack gets in his face.

"Because it's my life you're defending!" Robert gets up from his chair, "Why the hell did you take this case? So you can get your fucking career boosted, so you can show your pretty little face on T.V.? Well fuck you I'm not bending over so you can climb on my back to get you to the top floor of some fancy law firm."

"Time's up boys, got to return you to your cell Heyward." The security guard says as he walks in.

"Read the sign out papers I still have him for another hour and a half." Jack keeps his strong gaze on Robert.

"No can do, warden is having outside top officials to do a cell evaluation check and needs all the inmates in at six fifteen."

"That still gives us twenty minutes."

"No, don't worry about it we're done here anyway." Robert says. "Like I said you're more than welcome to leave Jacky, I'll just find someone else to fight Phil." He starts walking towards the guard at the door.

"You mean *Anthony* Rogers."

Robert turns around, "No, I mean Phil Roderick. That pad that Rogers keeps writing in. That's the same pad that I've seen Phil use all his life, throughout his career. They're sending messages back and forth to each other. Everything happening in court is because of him. You stop him; you might have a better chance. But like I said I'll just find someone else. He just orchestrated that courtroom like a puppet master and you just fell into his trap like a rat drawn into a mousetrap with cheese." Robert walks out with the guard.

Jack picks up his phone and makes a call, "Hector, I need a favor. I need you to dig up some information on a Phillip Roderick." He hangs up. *"It's time to take care of this guy."* He thinks to himself.

Chapter 57

"Hate...one of the most vicious of vicious animals. Let it dwell within you and it will eat you alive starting with your heart, slowly killing you. Let it out and it will eventually kill everyone around you, it will become your face, it will wear your skin, it will drink your blood, and like a conductor at an orchestra it will compose its biddings through you. Do not befriend this animal, do not familiarize yourself with it, do not feed its hunger. Be wary, be cautious, and never turn your back on it. Be warned for the price of hate is hope."

Trying to shake off the dream Phil turns over in his bed as he puts his arm around Janis to hold her closer. He smells an unfamiliar odor in the atmosphere so he sniffs the air a couple times. Not knowing what it really was he ignores it, and falls back asleep all the while keeping his eyes closed too lazy to open them. Then all of a sudden he hears a scream. "Josh." He says as he immediately opens his eyes and tries to get out of bed, but he's thrown back by the flames trying to climb up into his bed.

"Phil?" Janis calls out behind him.

"Yeah, you okay?" He asks keeping his focus on the door trying to contemplate how to get out. His cell phone starts ringing and Phil's attention immediately goes to his bed stand. He sees Bryan's number, ignores it and gives Janis the phone to call the fire department.

"Where's Josh?!" She asks taking the phone.

"I'm going to go get him just make the phone call." He then runs into the bathroom and soaks a towel quickly in the bathtub. He then throws a few more in there to soak as he runs out the bathroom. As he approaches the door at the end of his room a blaze comes in as if to grab him and take him down to hell. He is knocked down to the ground by the heat.

"Phil!" He hears Janis' voice.

"Did you call the fire department?!" Phil asks trying to get back onto his feet.

"Yeah, they're on their way."

"Mom!" They hear their child's screeching voice.

"Get him Phil!"

He runs back into the bathroom and gets two more wet towels. He hands one to Janis and keeps the other. "Here, get out now!"

"But Josh!"

"Don't worry about him, I'll get him you just need to get out."

"I can't leave you here." The fire starts to heat up the room like a sauna as it creeps closer like water at the beach.

"Mom! Dad!...Ahhh!" The screams get louder and deadlier.

"Janis, get out now!" He looks her dead in the eyes, "Promise me you'll go straight down." She's quiet. "Promise me!" She finally unwillingly nods her head.

He puts the wet towel over her head and escorts her out the flaming door. They look at each other then part ways in the hallway. Coughing and keeping as low as possible Phil tries to make it to Josh's room. All of a sudden something falls in front of him and spits fire forward barely missing Phil's eyes catching the bottom of his jaw on his right side. He screams out and brushes it off. He looks up realizing that the stairs to the attic had fallen and there were two very narrow passages on either side of the stairway to get through. Both sides had fire raging and burning.

"Ow! Help! Dad! Mom!" The screams become flooded with tears.

"Josh I'm coming hold tight!" He begins to make his way to his son. He tries to lean against the hot wall on the right side to make his way through. Then without warning the stairs collapse on the same side he was trying to get through. "Shit!" He yells as he backs off. He then sees by collapsing onto the right side it left more room on the left side to get through. He backs up and then begins to run, and jumps over a pool of flames. As he makes his way over the fire; the flame's hands reach up trying to grab his legs and pull him in and all miss but one just grabbing the ends of his left heel. He lands clear as he is brought to his knees in pain. He slides forward scratching up his legs almost disabling him. He takes a couple short breaths to regain his strength.

"Dad!"

"Son!"

"I'm scared help! Please! Please! I promise to be good! Please help! Ahh…"

"I'm coming just stay away from the fire!" He pulls himself up with all his strength, but falls back down. He looks to his left and balances his weight up against the wall as he tries to pull himself up to a standing position. The hot wall creates blisters on his hands and Phil lets out a scream as he wills himself up at the thought of his son's grave danger. "I'm coming son!" He starts limping as fast as he can towards Joshua's room, he can hear the sound of fire trucks and police cars pulling up. "Thank God…God." He thinks to himself as he inches closer to Joshua's room. He finally started to believe ever since he met Janis, and here he was literally brought to his knees calling his name asking for help. In the most desperate of times even the devil believes in his creator. He finally makes it to his child's room. He sees that the doorknob is crimson colored so he doesn't attempt to touch it. He thinks for a moment then finally kicks the door open.

"Dad!" Joshua tries to run towards Phil, but frightened by the flames he retreats back into his corner.

"Stay there son, I'm going to come get you." Phil breathes harder as he wipes sweat from his brow, then remembering that the fumes were entering his lungs he gets lower to the ground again. He looks around to find the best way to get to Joshua. He finally sees an opening and starts making his way to his son through the devil's maze. When he finally reaches for his son, he wraps him up in the wet towel that he had brought, and picks him up. He starts to make his way back towards the hall as the ground begins to cave in behind him. He looks back almost falling backwards into the hole. He regains his balance and moves forward into the hallway. He walks up to the fallen stairway from the attic. It finally collapses almost wiping out both Joshua and Phil as it goes through the floor down to the first floor. Joshua lets out the most horrified scream grabbing Phil's neck half choking him as Phil drops down on the same knee that had hurt him earlier, and yells out as well. He tries to regain his strength, as he gets up. He looks behind him for some hope of an exit or escape but all he saw were cannibalistic flames forever consuming each other becoming stronger and greater. He lets out a grunt and pulls himself together as he moves forward.

The stairway that fell through the ground left a narrow passage along the wall. Phil puts his back up against the wall as he side steps his way ever so carefully holding Joshua to his chest. Josh looks down then hides his head in Phil's chest and lets out a scared moan. "Shh…Don't look down son." He tries to comfort Josh. The walls burn Phil's back; he just grimaces and continues as he fights off the pain. When they finally get to the end of the narrow passage, he lets out a sigh of relief as he makes his way to the stairwell that leads to the front door.

"Phil!" He suddenly hears Janis' voice.

He abruptly stops, "Janis?!"

"Phil!" He hears her again.

"Janis!" He thought she had gone and made it. The sudden fear chains his knees together, then he hears his son cough into his chest. As tears begin to form in eyes he makes his way back to his bedroom door and knocks it down by kicking it. He doesn't see her.

"Janis!" He calls out again.

"Phil!"

He goes inside the bathroom and sees nothing, just water overflowing onto the ground. He quickly realizes that the sounds were coming from outside their bedroom window and not from inside the house. When he turns around to run towards the door a wooden panel engulfed in flames falls in front of the door. With a feeling of defeat Phil starts breathing faster and faster then let's out the most choleric yell.

"Phil, get out of there!"

He looks around to find anything that would help him, he runs over to the dresser where there are a few water bottles to help put out the fire on the fallen wooden panel. He notices his arms getting tired as if the weight of the child would rip his limbs out of his shoulder. When he gets to the dresser he notices that Janis' secret box was opened and his eyes took him straight to a newspaper clipping in it. He couldn't help, but read it. And as soon as he had he was thrown back into the past.

"Phil!" A terrifying scream shatters his dream, and he is brought back into the carnage of his house. He grabs what he can from inside the box. He looks down at Josh and can't tell if he is still breathing anymore. He looks back at the door and there is nothing but fire and wood as he breathes deeper and deeper desperately praying for help, hoping someone or something would hear.

"Phil!" Janis yells out looking up at her window looking for some sign of hope. "Please help my husband, my child is still up in there! Oh my God! Josh, Phil." She begs tugging on the fireman's coat.

"We're trying our best ma'am we need you to stay back please while we do our job." The fireman talks into his radio, "Any news in there boys?"

"Nothing, this place is about to collapse we need to get out of here quick!" The man at the other end of the radio yelled.

The neighbors had come out and surrounded the building and flooded onto the street watching as Janis fell to her knees crying and praying for her husband and her son to come out. They hear an explosion from the bottom floor.

"No! Phil!" She cries, "Joshua, my baby, my baby. No…"

The firemen come out one after another in a line running, and not one, not a single one had either Phil or Josh as another explosion goes off. Janis runs up towards the house and the fireman near her grabs her. "Ma'am please, we can't do anything now. You can't do anything. They are in God's hands now."

"No I'm not going anywhere without my husband and my child. I will not live without them. Let me go! Please, God please!" She cried so much that her tears could put out the fire themselves. The firemen on the sides were doing their best to put out the flames as water mercilessly rushed out of the hoses, but nothing would help. Janis starts kicking and screaming louder. "Let me go! I want to be with my family!" She continues to cry. She then bites into the fireman's arm, he finally let go from the pain. She took off towards her house and other firemen started chasing after her. In the middle of the field she stopped and fell onto her knees and started to cry. "No! Why God why?" The firemen finally catch up to her and put their hands on her shoulders trying their best to comfort her as they slowly try to pull her back so any falling objects or debris would not hit her.

"Please save him, please. I'll do anything." She pleaded.

"We can't…" They start to pull her back.

She looks up and with all her might yells, "Phil! You promised!" Janis looks down in defeat and just as the firemen begin to pull her away something jumps out of the window and lands onto the ground. Everyone but Janis covered their heads to not got hit, they then slowly put down their arms as they lifted their heads to see what had fallen out of the window. A split second later Janis realized that it was Phil and immediately ran towards him. The firemen followed. Phil turned over and they found Josh clenched onto his chest.

"He still has a pulse, get the stretchers. The child has no pulse preparing to perform emergency CPR!" One of the firemen yells out.

"Thank you God." Janis looks up into the heavens and says. She lets out a small breath and collapses onto Phil and Josh's body.

Chapter 58

"Hey Hector what do you got for me?"

"Well don't ask me how I got this information, but I have some information on this guy Phil Roderick."

"Yeah?"

"Well did you know Mr. Roderick here was best friends with your boy Mr. Heyward. He practically helped shape the new face of Orion Industries after the death of Allen Heyward."

"Robert's father?"

"Yeah, after Robert had taken over the company, within just a year Phil had gained much interest within the company including stock and rank. Apparently Phil was upgraded immediately to the Orion's Stars club."

"That's the thing Orion had with the ring ceremonies right?"

"Exactly, after Orion burned down Roderick somehow ended up with Highland and here we are."

"Interesting."

"Well, it gets more interesting. Orion burnt down after the announcement of Cold Fusion."

"So?"

"So, after Earl Hodges announced the discovery of Cold Fusion look where he is now. And Roderick had high legal involvement in both scenarios."

"You think there's more to it?"

"Don't you?"

"You think Roderick is behind this?"

"I don't know that's your job."

"That son of a bitch, Brown was right."

"Did I hear my name?" Brown interrupts the phone call.

"Let me call you back Hector. Send me everything you know about him right away please." He hangs up the phone.

"You always find the need to sneak up around me?"

"Well you are in my work space."

Jack looks around, "The lab?"

Brown looks around as if to mock him, "Yeah."

"You know about this Roderick fellow?"

"Yeah, his whole family is in the hospital, and his house just burnt down."

***

Amber pours herself another half glass of wine as she looks over the videos and written reports of the case as soft music plays in the background. She takes a deep breath and thinks about her parents and all the struggles she's been through just to make it to where she is now. She thought about how her parents moved back to Pakistan after she graduated from high school and the decision she had to make, either go with them or stay in America. They said they came to the states so she could have a better future and with a full scholarship through college they had accomplished their goal and had to go back home, even though her choice in career wasn't what they really had in mind for her.

They gave her the option to follow them back to Pakistan, but she knew she had to stay. She would call them every day when they moved back. Then when her busy life started they still kept in touch, very few days would pass where they didn't talk. Days turned into weeks, and weeks to months. Now they would talk on occasions like birthdays, anniversaries and so on. Saddened by this she decides she should call them more often and reaches for her phone in her purse. As she reached down something caught her eye next to her purse. It was the digital recording from the night she last talked to Jack. Being so upset from that night, and being so busy actually working the case she had forgotten all about the recording. She picks it up and plays it as she takes another sip from her wine glass.

The recording plays like a silent film as the music in the background accompanies her. It starts off with Amber setting down her purse as she walks over to the evidence table. She leans over table to get a better look and Jack walks back. He turns around and takes a look at her butt and nods his head before he continues. Amber rolls her eyes and lets out a sigh in disgust as she watches the video. Jack then picks up his coffee moving the camera angle towards Robert's files completely blocking the view of everything else. All she sees is Robert's picture on the files. As the video moves forward she becomes more and more angry at his face. Too upset to move she takes another sip of her wine and sits there loathing. She closes her eyes for a moment then opens them and his face is still there with that cut under his left eye. She finally gets the energy to stand up and walk over to shut off the recording. As she gets closer she notices something under his picture. She immediately rushes back to her purse and searches through it emptying it out completely. "Damn it!" She yells out. Then she turns around and looks at Robert's face again. She slowly approaches it and then immediately takes out the recording and leaves. She picks up her phone.

"Jack."

"Hey hon, thought I'd never hear from you again."

"Are you at the lab?"

"Yeah."

"Is Brown there?"

"Yeah. Is everything okay?"

"I'll see you there." She hangs up the phone.

***

"I think Phil should be here if I'm going to do something like that."

"Don't worry, you have Mr. Rogers here to assist you, Mr. Hodges."

"Yes, but Mr. Rogers is the prosecuting lawyer, not my lawyer for legal affairs."

"Which may be true, but for signing a few simple papers you just need some legal representation and you should be fine."

"I think I'm going to call Phil."

"Go ahead Bryan," Rogers yells out, "I'm sure you'll find him quite busy." He and Max both laugh.

Bryan calls Phil a few times and gets nothing but voicemail, "Shit." He says under his breath.

"Did you get an answer? See he doesn't care about you, except when it comes to his assets. He cares about nothing but himself, and you can move on with your life away from all these selfish people."

"I still don't know."

"Bryan, what do you know about this company?"

"I know that it possesses the secrets to Cold Fusion and you want to get your filthy hands on it."

"Yeah, what else do you know?" Max pauses for an answer, "I didn't think you knew much more than that. Did you ever have any passion for this company before your father died? Did you have any passion for anything ever, or was riding horses on your father's ranch enough?" Bryan just looks at the ground embarrassed, "You know a man without passion is a man without a soul."

"Yeah you should know something about that?"

"Hmm," Max smiles, "So at least you have the same guts as your father. Bryan did you know that your father was going to sell me this company before his unfortunate accident?"

"Yes." Bryan thinks back to the night his father died and the talk they had about selling the company and doing something great with his life.

"This is what your father wanted son." Max approaches Bryan and puts his hands on Bryan's shoulders. "I know this is a difficult time for you, and there is nothing anyone can do to change what has happened. But we cannot forget our responsibilities, we cannot hold back the future, we cannot stop what we were meant to do. You were meant for great things, but other things. This is why your father was selling the company, to have a different life for you. You will do great things one day, but that will all be determined if you sign these papers or not."

"Sign the papers son, it is what your father wanted, it is your destiny." Rogers says as he puts his hand on Bryan's shoulder in support.

***

"Where the hell are my pictures Brown?!" Ambers says as she rushes into the lab. Jack and Brown look at her and then each other, and then back at her as if she were insane.

"What are you talking about?"

"Um…you're welcome for keeping the door open for you." Jack says as Amber rushes past him.

"Shut up Jack. Where the hell, are my pictures and if you ask me what pictures I'm talking about I'm going to dig my heels into your fucking ear."

"Ouch." Jack says with a disgusted look on his face.

"Now that is just mean Miss Khowja." Brown replies.

"Where are the pictures?"

"What pictures is she talking about?" Jack asks.

"My pictures I took from the bombing of Artemis Labs, which had a dud C4 bomb with a government logo on it. When I heard about this case I brought a few pictures with me just in case those markings came up again. Well they did, and now I can't find them. That night you caught me here, was the only night anyone but myself went through my purse. That means you found the pictures, and you took them." She says as she gets up on her toes and pokes Brown in his chest with her finger.

"Well you are a damn good investigator aren't you Miss Khowja?"

"What? What symbol? What the hell is going on?" Brown and Amber both look at Jack as if he were interrupting, and they weren't sure if they should tell him. He gives back a confused look. "What?"

Amber looks at Brown, Jack folds his arms and gives Brown a sarcastic yet interested look. Brown then hangs his head and lets out a defeated sigh. "Alright. When I read through the files for the first time I came across this symbol," He pulls out the pictures and sets them next to Robert's files to compare the two. "under the contracts written up by Max Johnson, and or passed on by his people. When I was going through your purse I saw that same exact symbol so I held on to it because I obviously felt there was much more to it. I've been on Max's trail ever since then, but for all my leads and every track I follow keep leading me back here to the beginning. They've obviously covered their tracks well, but I'll keep digging. I was going to look up Roderick, but with his house catching fire, and the whole family being hospitalized, just furthers my suspicion of Max and Apollo Industries."

"Why Apollo?" Asks Jack.

"Because of the Cold Fusion project." Amber answers.

"Exactly."

"Yeah, I just came across the coincidence of how Orion was destroyed, and how Hodges just died; both happening after announcing the discovery of Cold Fusion." He lets out a small laugh, "It's like the price of immortalization is death and ruins."

"And if Heyward was behind this then he wouldn't have bombed his own plant then killed Hodges, because he'd want all the power to himself." Amber says as if she were hit by an epiphany. Both Brown and Jack look over at Amber in shock that she would admit to such a thing. "What, I'm just thinking out loud."

"Well I thought the same thing at first, but then I thought what if Heyward bombed his own company for the money, and then out of jealousy of someone else possessing what he could of once had he killed Hodges. But like every track I've followed I keep coming back to this symbol and none of this has Heyward's fingerprints on it. So we have to look at the common denominators of both Orion and Highland and sort this out. Cold Fusion, Heyward, Apollo, Max, and…"

"Roderick." Jack adds.

"Exactly one of these three men are involved if not all and we need to figure out the true story."

"Heyward didn't fight Hodges." Amber says still in her hypnotic stage trying to put the pieces of the puzzle together in her head.

"What? How do you know that?" Jack asks.

"I remember from that first night I snuck in here. You said something about how tight Hodges' suit was on him."

"Yeah so?"

"So, if he were to get into a fight it would be difficult for him to fight, and throw a decent punch right?" She walks over to the evidence table.

"Yeah…"

"Yeah, so if his suit was so tight and Hodges was left handed, how did Heyward get such a horrible gash under his left eye when he was using his strong hand?" She picks up the suit and shows the rip on the left armpit. "At first I thought it could of probably have been from when Bryan Hodges beat him, but from the reports and the trial everyone said that he only beat him over the head. To have a scar like that he must have gotten it from somewhere else."

"Well it still could have been from the fight, or Bryan's beating, memory gets hazy at that point of where particular blows had landed." Jack says trying to make sense of the situation.

"No look at the scar, look how he got cut it's clearly from underneath. If Bryan was beating him from above the angle of the cut would be flipped around. This helps in your case as far as proving Robert not being there. I know it's farfetched because the doctor proved Hodges' time of death and Heyward's being in the room pretty close together, but you might be able to pull it off if he's innocent."

"I think she might have a point there Jack."

"So now you're on Heyward's side now?"

"I'm just saying let's find out what really happened." She flips the coat over hand and something falls out.

"What the hell is that?" Jack jumps.

"Relax Jacqueline." Brown finds a pair of tongues next to him and picks up the object. He examines it for a moment. "Cohiba. This is a cigar. Must have been Hodges'." He says turning the cigar in the air.

"Impossible," Jack interrupts, "I remember from the part of the file I actually bothered reading that he was in a non-smoking room. Why would he rent out a non-smoking room and then have a cigar? Brown can you have the lab do a saliva check on that?"

"It's pretty old, and there may be a few variables that might get in the way. I don't know it's a long shot, but we might as well try." He puts it in a plastic bag.

"Perfect, and good job Amber." She nods her head.

"You need to put both Roderick and Heyward on the stand, and depending on what this little sucker brings up, whoever's cigar this might be." Brown adds.

"How the hell am I going to put a man who just lost his home, with unknown conditions of him and his family on the stand?"

They all think in silence for a moment, "You can get a deposition." Brown suggests.

"Again, unknown conditions, and also he doesn't have to answer or say anything in a deposition if he actually did something…and if he did he probably won't, furthermore given recent circumstances chances are that the jury would sympathize with him especially if he lies."

"Would another lawyer actually lie on the stand?"Amber asks.

"Would you want to get the death penalty if someone else was probably going to get it instead?"

"I'll put Robert on the stand let's see how far that takes us for now and then we can see what we can do about Roderick after. It doesn't seem like he'll be going anywhere too soon."

Brown takes a sip of his coffee and sets it back down. Amber notices and immediately yells, "Hey don't put your coffee on the pictures it's not your coaster."

"Oh sorry."

"Look you made a ring stain now." She says as she picks up the picture and flashes it in his face.

"Wait a minute let me see that picture."

"What so you can ruin it some more? I don't think so I'm taking these back and putting them away." She puts it in her coat pocket.

"Come on let me see the pictures Miss Khowja."

"No go to hell."

Brown tries to brush off his frustration, "Alright whatever, anyway I think given some recent events I might have some new information on Max Johnson."

"Great! I'll cover the story with you." Amber says out of excitement.

"Yeah I'm coming too, this actually might help steer my case in the right direction."

"No you two kids need to stay put we don't know anything about him and so far in this case he's been the most discrete which also makes him the most dangerous. You need to focus on the case Jack. And Amber…stay out of trouble." He starts to walk out the door accidently giving her a small bump on the way.

"Wait that's it?" She says as he bumps into her.

"Yeah and," He looks her up and down, "nice coat?"

"Thanks." She replies sarcastically.

"Okay," He faces both of them again, "once I solve this, which I probably will soon if this new source checks out, the next time I'll see you two kids will probably be on the news. So before I leave Amber," She looks towards him, "just remember what Einstein said; we cannot despair of humanity, since we are ourselves human beings."

"And Jacqueline, remember that there is an ancient saying, famous among men, that thou shouldst not judge fully of a man's life before he dieth, whether it should be called blest or wretched."

"Sophocles?" Jack asks, Brown nods his yes, "And if we now shamefully fail, we shall become infamous to the whole world."

"Oh you want do presidents now Mr. Washington? It is better to be faithful than famous. Theodore Roosevelt."

"Touché."

"Do you two need a room or something?" Amber interrupts, They both look at her as if she didn't belong there. "Sorry just asking."

"Anyway Brown, I got to do what I got to do, and it's not just about the fame anymore honest, I just thought I'd join you in the banter before you leave."

"Okay take it ease Jacqueline, I'll have someone deliver the results of the cigar to you as soon as possible," He salutes him with two fingers, Jack nods his head back, "Miss Khowja." He tips his hat to her and walks off.

"What was that all about?"

"I don't know, but he turned out to be a pretty cool guy."

"So not about the fame anymore huh? I'm proud of you."

"Yeah, you know..." Jack says as he looks down at the ground like a shy child.

"Wow, for being so cocky I didn't think you'd be bad at taking compliments."

"Anyway," He tries to change the subject, "I have a long day tomorrow I have to change the whole way I was going to approach the trial, so I'm going to turn in early."

"Really?"

"Yeah unless you..."

"No, no I was going to get going as well. I think comparing these pictures to the contracts on Hodges' sale papers should help you." She reaches in her pocket.

"You know you're a lot cuter all the way here on my side of the case."

"What the fuck?!"

"What sorry, sorry, too soon?"

"No, that fucker Brown took the pictures. He must have grabbed them when he bumped into me!"

"Damn, that sucks. So no it wasn't too soon?"

Chapter 59

"Hang on, buddy we're going to take care of you." A man says as he grabs Phil's hand.

"We're losing her!" A voice shouts out from the side.

"We need another nurse here the bleeding won't stop!"

"Prepare the operating room!"

"Help!" Phil's mind shoots back in time and sees Janis' face.

"Janis…" He tries to yell, but a whisper trickles out of his mouth sending him back unconscious.

"Phil! Where are you going!" He hears Robert's voice.

"I'm sorry man I can't take this! I need to breathe for a little bit, I'll be right back just give me a minute!"

"Here lay Janis and Allen Heyward." Phil sees the priest standing in front of two coffins, everyone is in black and in their seats as Robert cries and Sandra holds his hand. Phil watches himself watching the funeral from the furthest corner of the cemetery where no one can see him.

"We're losing the kid again! He's coming close to flat line, get the defibulator!" Phil is shot back into reality for a moment and then is sent back to his dream state.

"Fuck you, no tornado can stop me!"

"Clear!"

"Now see I thought you had brown eyes all this time, but here you lay before me with those beautiful blue eyes."

"Can you hear me?" The doctor looks over Phil as she slightly opens his eyes. Phil nods his head. He tries to point to get information on Janis and Josh. "Try to be still, you need to conserve as much energy as possible." She says as she holds his hand down and injects him. Phil begins to feel numb.

"This is no miracle, this is a gift. Take this gift and the sun shall shine again. RAH."

"Shit he's going under again!"

"Doctor!"

"What?!"

"She's pregnant."

"I'm pregnant Phil we did it, we did it baby we did it!"

"I think we might have to either save her or the baby what should we do?" The nurse yells out.

"We have to contact a relative."

"There's no time doctor we got to pick one or we lose them both!"

"Janis." Phil faintly calls out.

"She'll be just fine." The nurse near him tries to calm him down.

"What are the chances of saving both?" The doctor starts to quickly walk towards Janis.

"Slim."

"Well let's get to work no one's dying tonight."

"We might have to do an emergency delivery here."

"Okay, go ahead and call in Doctor Bridges. John, I want you to stay with kid and don't leave his side; Doctor Smith will be there in a minute. I'm going to watch over the father make sure you come to me first with any updates."

"Yes, doctor."

"You have made my life complete. God sent you to me and you gave me strength to move forward. You lit the match in my darkest hour. You gave me breath under water. You held me tight when I feared the most. Now I shall hold onto you forever. Thank you, thank you for coming into my life. You are my north star, and with you by my side I shall never lose myself again. I promise to love you with all my heart not until the day I die, but until the end of time." Tears of joy flow down Janis' face as she awaits Phil to speak. Then there is an awkward moment of silence.

"Go, ahead son." The priest encourages Phil.

Nervous from the overwhelming sensation of his dreams coming true he was frozen lost in his new brides eyes. He shakes it off, "Yes…," He tensely looks down at a sheet of paper. The sweat on his hands make the ink run and he realizes if he doesn't read soon he will have nothing to read, "I love you. That is all. That is the beginning middle and end to our story. It started with I living lonesomely in this world. Our story became the one of love. And everything I will ever do from this moment will end with you. Therefore that is all, I love you. There will never be any more to how I can feel. No words can be forged, coined, or mastered to express in even a glimpse of how I feel about you." He pauses almost choking on his own tears. He regains his strength and continues,

"Never have I felt this way. Every day, I fall in love with you all over again. Every morning that I see your face I thank God I'm alive. Every night I fall asleep and like a child I painfully wait to see your face once more the next day. Like an angel you saved me and nursed me back to life. I am forever in your debt and I will live everyday proving my love to you for the rest of my life…Just like without water there would be no sea, without you there would be no me."

"You may place the ring."

Joshua looks up at his mother and new father in a little white tuxedo holding a white pillow. Phil and Janis both reach down and pick up the rings that rested on it. Phil begins to place the ring on Janis' finger, "With this ring I thee wed."

"With this ring forever I do."

Chapter 60

"Miss Sheppard, how long have you known Robert?" Rogers asks.

"Since I was about twenty."

"And in all this time has Robert ever acted violently, or acted in a way that would seem harmful to another human being?"

"No, never."

"Has he ever threatened anyone?"

"No, Robert was one of the sweetest guys I've ever met. He wouldn't ever hurt anyone."

"So, if someone were to describe Robert; murderer wouldn't show up on the list would it?"

"No."

"Miss Sheppard, why did you and Mr. Heyward separate?"

She looks over at Robert, he looks back awaiting the answer he has been waiting for, for many years. "We just didn't see eye to eye. We were on different paths, and had different priorities." Robert hangs his head not satisfied with the response.

"I see and what were your priorities."

"Objection irrelevant."

"Sustained."

"Miss Sheppard, did Mr. Heyward ever get angry with you?"

"Maybe a few times here and there. Every couple fights."

"When was your last fight before your divorce?"

"We had a fight just before I asked for the divorce. And that day we just yelled and screamed." Sandra looks down searching for answers, fighting to avoid going back to that awful day. She can't help, but to let her emotions take over. "We had never fought like that before, and then…"

"And then what Sandra?"

"Nothing."

"Miss Sheppard, you are under oath."

"And then he picked up a glass and threw it against the wall shattering it." She begins to cry.

"And did anyone witness this act?"

"Yes, my two sons."

"Where you afraid at that point?" Sandra looks up at Robert as she wipes her nose and holds her mouth. She tries to stop crying, but it only makes matters worse. "Miss Sheppard, I know this is tough, but we need you to answer."

"Yes, I was afraid. I'm sorry Robert."

"So, you admit that you lied Miss Sheppard?"

"Excuse me?"

"Just earlier you said Robert would never hurt anyone else, and now you said that he would?"

"No I didn't say that."

"Let me read it back to you." He reaches for the transcript. "And in all this time has Robert ever acted violent, or acted in a way that would seem harmful to another human being? You said, 'no, never' you later went on to say 'Robert was one of the sweetest guys I've ever met. He wouldn't ever hurt anyone.'"

"No I didn't mean it like that."

"So if he was never someone who you would consider dangerous, why would you fear him at such a moment? Why would he ever act in such a manner Miss Sheppard? You were so distraught from the divorce that you changed your name back within a month, isn't that right Miss Sheppard?"

"Objection badgering!"

"Sustained."

"No further questions."

"You may step down Miss Sheppard." The judge directs her off.

"Your honor the defense asks for a five minute recess before the next witness." Jack says standing up.

"Your honor the defense is fully aware that the next witness is the defendant, and asking for a recess is unfair and disruptive to the prosecution's stride."

"Your honor these are unordinary circumstances and the defense humbly asks for a five minute recess to assess unknown information to the defense in pretrial evaluation."

"And what is or are these unknown information that the defense had not known."

"...Your honor they are still unknown, the recess will help assess the information."

"I see..." The judge stares at Jack for a moment, "The court grants a *three* minute recess, you can assess the information on your own time Mr. Kennedy."

"Yes your honor thank you."

"The court will resume in three minutes from now." He slams his desk with the gavel and leaves the courtroom.

Jack finally reaches in his pocket and picks up his phone that had been vibrating and irritating him throughout the day's trial.

"Hello?"

"Jack Kennedy?"

"Yes this is Jack."

"Hi, this is Luke Watson, Frank Brown's brother-in-law."

"Yes, yes!"

"We were looking over the contents of the cigar you had recently found an unfortunately we were unable to find any conclusive evidence to help your case."

"What?!"

"I'm sorry, but the specimen was way too old and too damaged for us to find anything that would help."

"Nothing at all? No saliva, prints, nothing?" Jack shakes his head in frustration.

"No, nothing. I sent it over with some notes just in case you needed it today, but I'm not sure how much it'll help."

"Okay I'll take a look at it, well thank you for trying anyway." A young man hands him an envelope. "I think I just got your envelope."

"Oh perfect timing."

"Also, I haven't been able to get in contact with Brown, is it okay to contact you for any further questions with this kind of stuff?"

"Of course that's what we're here for."

"Thanks again for everything." He hangs up the phone. "God damn it!"

"What?" Robert asks.

"Nothing we found a cigar in Hodges' coat pocket, and were hoping to find traces leading to the owner of it, but it came up with nothing."

"Oh, didn't know Hodges smoked."

"Yeah, that's the thing he didn't, that's why we were so confused when we found the Cohiba in the pocket."

"Ha."

"What?"

"Nothing, just Phil used to smoke those all the time."

"What?"

"I mean it's no big deal just coincidence I guess."

"All rise!" The bailiff calls out.

"Your honor the prosecution would like to call Robert Allen Heyward."

Robert stands up slowly as he takes a deep breath. He turns around to look at his family. They stare back each with a different look on their faces. Sandra looks on apologetically and almost disgraced fearing the worst while her tears continue to flow. Ryan had a bit more of an encouraging look. He nods his head to show his support. And Michael stared at him as if he were just another on looker, as if what decision would be made, and what would happen did not matter. Robert tries to hold eye contact with Michael, and finally follows in Ryan's footsteps and nods his head as well. He then looks over to where Phil had been sitting all this time and saw an empty seat.

Robert is confused expecting Phil to be in the courtroom; on this day of all days he was missing. He shakes it off and walks over to the stand and takes his oath. Meanwhile Rogers looks at the notes Phil had given him and tried to commit them to memory one more time. Bryan looks at the notes as well and then his folder with the red light, knowing on one of the most important days in this trial the one man he could trust was in the hospital. He was almost brought to his knees when he found out what had happened to Phil. Bryan's whole world was crashing down and now he had no help. He thought about how selfish Phil was to not muster up the strength to still come to court on this day, after all his father had done for him. He had promised, he had lied.

"Please state your name for the court's record." Rogers begins.

"Robert Allen Heyward."

"Mr. Heyward, where were you on the night of April the eleventh?"

"Many places, where were you?"

"Will the court instruct the defendant to properly answer the questions?"

"Mr. Heyward would you please be mindful of the atmosphere and conduct yourself accordingly?"

Robert looks at the judge and nods his head in agreement.

"Now Mr. Heyward, where were you on the night of April the eleventh?"

"Like I said many places."

"And of all those places did you end up in Earl Hodges' room that night?"

"Yes."

"Where do you live Mr. Heyward?"

"Excuse me?"

"What city do you live in Mr. Heyward?"

"Dallas."

"Dallas? What were you doing approximately four hours away from your residence Mr. Heyward?"

"I went to go see Earl Hodges."

"And did you see Mr. Hodges?"

"No."

"Why not?"

"Because he was already dead when I got there."

"How did you know he had died?"

"Well when I got to his room I saw him outside on the ground."

"What did you do next?"

"Well, I was going to leave and that's when I encountered his son."

"I see, so why were your fingerprints all over the hotel room? Did you find the need to make sure everything was touched or is it that you had a meeting with Mr. Hodges' and then had a fight and threw him off the balcony?"

"No, I didn't kill him, I didn't kill anyone."

"So why were you there Mr. Heyward? What could have possibly been so important that in the middle of the night you decided to get up and travel four hours to see Earl Hodges? What was it Mr. Heyward?"

"I went to see him about the Cold Fusion project."

"The Cold Fusion project?"

"Yes."

"What is the Cold Fusion project Mr. Heyward?"

"Objection irrelevant."

"Sustained."

"Mr. Heyward why was it so urgent that you had to see Earl Hodges in a city four hours away from where you live in the middle of the night? Could this not wait? Is this you're your poor excuse for an alibi? Is this the story that you have played over and over in your head…"

"Objection your honor, the prosecution is acting in unnecessary badgering of the defendant, and downplaying the actions of that night in the eyes of the court and the jury. Motion to strike any specific questions regarding Cold Fusion, and the integrity of the defendant's story of what had happened on that night."

"Your honor, this whole case is about the integrity of the defendant's story. The other questions are for the acquirement of knowledge of the court and jury to see the context of the case. The prosecution asks for some leverage."

"The objection is sustained, and grants limited leverage to the prosecution, the motion is denied. Try to get to it quickly Mr. Rogers, and the court will not tolerate constant badgering."

"Yes, your honor. Mr. Heyward why was it so important that you meet with Earl Hodges in the middle of the night?"

"I had to see him before the announcement of the Cold Fusion project."

"Was it that urgent?"

"Yes, Cold Fusion was my baby. My company put it together and was ready for production. We were going to distribute it throughout the world."

"So out of jealousy you killed Hodges?"

"No! I wanted to make sure he knew exactly what he was doing. My father and I spent our entire careers trying to unlock the secrets of a power source that would benefit the world. Once discovered the world would have cheaper power, providing better life styles for everyone. Developing countries would become faster developed. And developed countries would reach heights never seen before. If this power source got into the wrong hands or even unassuming hands then they could corrupt the world's power, or even destroy it. We as humans many times do not understand the power we possess until it is too late. So quick we are to jump at the chance to become gods and yet we become enslaved because of it. I went to see Earl Hodges to make sure he didn't make the same mistakes as I did. I wanted to make sure that possibly with me on his side, we could take my knowledge and his power to turn Cold Fusion into what it was meant to do for the world. It was my chance to put my life back together."

"So you had noble reasons to see Earl Hodges and had no intent to kill, is that correct Mr. Heyward?"

"Yes."

"Then why the knife?" Robert sat there frozen reliving the conversations he had within his head on the way to Hodges' hotel that night. "Mr. Heyward," Rogers brings Robert back to reality, "why the knife?"

"I kept it with me for protection, I always have it by my side."

"I see and did you find the need for protection from the man you were just going to have a conversation with?"

"Yes, I mean no."

"Which one is it Mr. Heyward?"

"I...I don't know..."

"You don't know?"

Robert looks at his family for support, Ryan and Sandra look on for some sort of decent explanation, Michael has the same look on his face as Rogers, only more convicting, as if he were asking all the incriminating questions from all these years in this one question. He looks over to Jack. Jack looks on with no answer. Robert had to answer this question. This question was not about the knife, it was about his soul.

"Will the court please instruct the defendant to answer the question?" Rogers pleads with the judge.

"Mr. Heyward, please answer the question."

"I didn't kill him."

"So why did you have the knife? Was it for protection?"

"No, I don't know why okay. I just had it. I wasn't sure what would happen, and when I got there he was already dead. Didn't you read the autopsy papers, and police reports? There were no knives used."

"That is correct there were no knives used. Just like there was a gun on the scene and yet no shooting. Do you find that to be odd Mr. Heyward?"

"Well, that's not my job to figure out."

"Hmm..." Rogers smiles and thinks for a moment, "So walk me through this. What exactly happened?"

"Well like I said I was going to see Hodges..."

"With a knife tucked into the back of your pants." Rogers interrupts.

Robert looks at him with anger, but continues, "And when I got to the hotel I went up the stairs. I first went the wrong way and then when I figured out where the room was I went there. I walked into the room, and when I looked over the balcony I saw Hodges' body. I looked around the room to find clues to what happened. When I came to my senses and didn't want to be a part of what happened I began to leave, and that is when Hodges' son encountered me."

"So let me get this straight, you wanted to see Earl Hodges' to 'talk' to him in the middle of the night four hours away from your home, with a knife tucked into the back off your pants that had a blade longer than the legal limit. Once at the hotel, with the probable intent to kill Earl Hodges you get 'lost'. When you finally find your way to the room, you find that someone had already done the job that you had possibly intended to do. After the discovery of the dead body, you didn't decide to call the police you decided to play detective and search for clues on what had happened, as long as the finger didn't point to you it didn't matter you suddenly realize. After this sudden epiphany you decide to leave and that is when Bryan Hodges, Earl Hodges' son discovers you in their room and beats you with the back of his father's gun. Is that correct Mr. Heyward?"

"I was going to talk to him, and didn't want anyone to die, nor did I kill anyone." Robert angrily says trying to keep his cool.

"We'll get to that in a moment Mr. Heyward, now when you were being beaten by Bryan Hodges, did you fear for your life?"

"At one point yes."

"So why did you not protect yourself? After all, you did have a knife on you did you not…for protection?"

"I don't know I didn't think of it."

"You did not think that you had a knife on you? You did not think someone in front of me has a gun, I should probably protect myself?"

"No, I am not a murderer."

"I didn't say anything about *murdering* Mr. Heyward, I said protection."

Robert takes a deep breath feeling trapped, almost as if the water had come up to just under his nose, and he was going to begin to drown, "I know, I just didn't think of it. I thank God that I didn't think of it, because if I had done so then either I would have been dead, or this trial would be long over. I didn't kill Earl Hodges, and I did not pull out my knife."

"I see. Mr. Heyward, Earl Hodges is one of the most secretive businessmen in the world. How is it that you knew what hotel Earl Hodges would be in, let alone his room number?"

"I originally went to see him in his office. When I learned that I had been too late I begged the lady at the front desk to tell me where he was. When she didn't tell me I felt that all hope was lost for me. I had then overheard someone say that he was going to see Hodges at the Comfort Inn hotel off of Two Ninety East. A short moment later I went outside to go there. I bruised my leg only to find papers with the hotel information on it which had the room number on it as well. And that is how I got there."

"That sounds a bit farfetched wouldn't you agree Mr. Heyward?"

"It's the truth."

"I see…so, you had no intention of killing Earl Hodges?"

"No never."

"Never?"

"Never."

"You have never wanted to kill Earl Hodges or anyone else for that matter?"

"No, I'm not a violent person. I could never imagine doing such a thing."

Rogers walks back to his bench to pick up some papers, "Approach the witness?" He asks the judge.

"Go ahead."

"Mr. Heyward can you read this passage for me? This was an interview that you gave to Fallen Stars on one of their episodes. You only have to read the highlighted section."

Robert studies the document briefly and quickly remembers the interview. "I…I don't want to."

"Will your honor please instruct the witness?"

"Objection your honor. If the defendant refuses to read the document he should have the right to not read out loud."

"But your honor these are the words of the defendant himself. The court should have the right to hear it from his lips."

"Objection overruled. Mr. Heyward please read the document out loud."

Robert looks back at the document slowly trying to delay the inevitable as much as possible.

"Looking back what do you think of the life events that happened to you in the past few years?"

"Look I don't think or care about anything anymore. I hate everyone. If I ever see that bastard who took my company, or that low life lawyer who said he was my friend, or even that son of a bitch Earl Hodges, I will kill them. I will kill every last one of them!"

"Do you realize on national television you made death threats if I'm correct, against Maximus Edward Johnson president of Apollo industries and former military general, your former top lawyer Phillip Henry Roderick, and the president of Highland Corporations Earl Landon Hodges?"

"Yes and if you want to be added to the list you can be too."

"No…no sir. Not at all."

Robert shamefully puts down the document.

"Let me read that one more time for the court," Rogers says picking up the document, "even that son of a bitch Earl Hodges, I will kill them. I will kill every last one of them…if you want to be added to the list you can be too. Were these your words Mr. Heyward? Did you say these things on national television and expect it not to come back to you?"

"Yes I did say it, but I was in a bad place then. I was just venting I didn't mean a word of it. I swear it."

"We vent to our close friends, or our relatives. No one Mr. Heyward, no one vents on national television expecting you to not be literal in such threats."

"I swear I didn't mean a word of it."

"Just earlier you told us you never wanted to kill Hodges."

"I didn't, I didn't want to kill anyone."

A dark high-pitched voice begins to speak, "And they have rewarded me evil for good, and hatred for my love…Ha ha ha…Robert…" It says tauntingly.

"No…not now…" He puts his hands over his ears.

Rogers looks at him strangely, "Mr. Heyward must I read back the transcript to you?"

"Robert…I told you to kill him. Here you are now stuck because of your own stupidity! And now I am stuck with you! You are responsible once again! Set you a wicked man over him: and let Satan stand at his right hand. Ha, ha."

"No, no go away!"

Jack looks on confused, not sure what to do.

"I said, 'So, you had no intention of killing Earl Hodges?' and you said, 'No never.' I said 'Never?'"

"Go away!" Robert begins to shout.

"You said, 'Never.'" Rogers begins to talk louder, "Then I said, 'You have never wanted to kill Earl Hodges or anyone else for that matter?'"

"Stop…stop…stop…please stop…"

"They're going to get you Robert who will protect you now Robert?" Robert continues to hear his name randomly as if teasing him as the dark voice continues. "Where did that bitch go? Look at your so called wife." Robert moves his face in the opposite direction, "Look at her!" He is then forced to look, "Look at how she looks at you in fear like you were some animal. Look at your children how they hang their

346

heads in shame, while these men try to hang your head. Where is your Bible now? Here is your Bible verse, 'When he shall be judged, let him be condemned: and let his prayer become sin. Ha, ha, ha!' The voice lets out a dark evil laugh. The harsh laugh becomes darker, louder, and heavier. 'What good is this stupid book that you took your oath upon? Answer me!'

"You said, 'No, I'm not a violent person. I could never imagine doing such a thing.' You, killed Earl Hodges didn't you Heyward! You snuck into his room and shoved him off of his balcony!"

"Objection!"

"Cool it Mr. Rogers."

'Let his days be few; and let another take his office…Where is your God now? Only I am here.'

"Go away, not now please, not in front of my family." Robert begins to cry.

"Why the knife Robert?! Why the knife?! How did you really get the room number?! Tell us Mr. Heyward tell us the truth!"

"Your honor, stop this right now!"

"Mr. Rogers I am warning you better stop or I will have you in contempt!"

"Your honor, the defendant is putting on a show acting crazy so the court and jury will grant sympathy. This is a pathetic attempt and we strongly ask the court to look past this mockery. Permission to treat hostile!"

"Denied!" The judge angrily yells.

He looks back at Robert like a vicious monster, "Why did you go on national television and threaten Earl Hodges life! Why did you do it? You couldn't handle the fact that someone else had unlocked the secrets to your precious stone, to your fountain of youth! You could not let anyone else posses the power that could have made you a god! That's why you did it didn't you!"

"No!"

"Stop this right now!"

'Let his children be fatherless, and his wife a widow! This is what your Bible preaches! God is no longer here and therefore he is malevolent and I am not, I have stuck with you and I am therefore benevolent! Ha, ha, ha.'

"Stop!!!" Robert yells out as if the bats from hell had finally been released from deep within his chest. The court room becomes deathly silent, as tears flow from Robert's eyes. He sheepishly looks over at his family and then at Jack.

"Your honor, the defense asks for a five minute recess for the defendant to recuperate. And strongly requests a motion to strike due to the unruly hostility of the prosecution towards the defendant."

"Your honor I object to the motion."

"You cannot object to this motion."

"Your honor this is an act!"

"You, Mr. Rogers are completely out of line." He points his finger at him. "One more word, just one more inclination of misconduct in my courtroom from you, I will have you replaced and hold more weight to the defenses testimony and I will have you put in jail for contempt of court and on trial for immediate disbarment. I have never been so insulted in all my years of being a judge from such insubordinance. Do you understand what I am saying to you Mr. Rogers?"

Rogers cringes his teeth and reluctantly answers, "Yes your honor."

The judge looks back at the rest of the courtroom. "Now, we will take a short recess and in that time Mr. Kennedy I expect the defense to recuperate without further delay or other motions for recess. Is that understood?"

"Yes your honor."

The judge slams his gavel, "We shall return in five minutes."

"All rise!"

"You okay Robert?" Jack asks as he helps Robert walk back to his seat.

"Yeah."

"You sure, you want me to get you anything?"

"No…"

"Robby?"

"Dad you okay?" Ryan asks.

"Yeah son, I just need to breathe."

Time slowly passes as Robert listens to Jack speak of his plans of rebuttal to what had just happened. "Okay I think we can bring the jury on to our side more easily now. We can definitely play the sympathy card here and win them over. We can start off by talking about everything that has happened up until to Hodges' death in your life and trap the jury into falling in love with your story."

"What do you mean?"

"I mean think about it, with the outburst you just had, we have some brand new and very good avenues that just opened up for us to take. That son of a bitch Rogers is going to burn himself with his own flame. We can talk about other times you've had this outbreak and how you've reacted to them."

"You son of a bitch...you're going to try to convince them that I'm crazy aren't you?"

"Well it's one of the best options we have. Dozens of cases every month get acquitted on account of insanity. I'm sure we can get some leeway giving us limited in jail time followed by psychiatric treatment and you should be a free man in no time. With what just happened any jury would buy any psychology nut that comes in explaining that you probably weren't thinking right. And the jury witnessed your condition firsthand, so no one can say we're making this up."

"Fuck you, I'm not crazy and I didn't kill anyone. Even my own lawyer doesn't believe in me."

"It doesn't matter what I believe in, all that matters is what I can convince the jury to believe. Being a lawyer is the same as a sales man; I only win if I can sell them the product."

"Yeah and the product here is my life."

"Exactly so don't you think you should let a person who knows how to sell handle your product?"

"No I'm not lying so we can win this case. You either do it right Jack, or not at all. I'm sorry that's the way it has to be. I rather go down fighting than survive running."

"You can die for this."

"I didn't kill anyone."

"All rise!"

"I will not lose this case." Jack whispers to Robert as they stand waiting for the judge to take his seat.

"I hope not."

"Then you better be prepared to tell the whole truth. If I have a single suspicion of you lying, I'm going to do things my way, or you can rot in hell for all I care."

"So be it."

"Is the defense ready?"

"Yes your honor."

"You may proceed. You are still under oath Mr. Heyward."

Robert nods his head yes as he takes the stand once again. Jack starts soon after. "Mr. Heyward, did you kill Earl Hodges?"

"No."

"Was the interview you had with Fallen Stars an actual threat against Earl Hodges, or anyone else named in the interview?"

"No."

"Have you ever killed anyone?"

"No."

"Then why the knife? Did you have any intention to kill Earl Hodges?"

Robert stares Jack not sure how to answer the question. These series of questions were nothing like they had discussed earlier and now Robert was completely thrown off guard.

"Mr. Heyward?"

"Yes?"

"Did you intend to kill Earl Hodges when you drove over to his hotel on April the eleventh?"

Robert angrily shakes his head not answering the question looking Jack in his eyes as if he wished death and harm upon him.

Jack smiles and turns around and thinks for a moment. "Let's get back to that question later on. Mr. Heyward have you ever had an outburst like the one you had earlier in this courtroom ever before?"

Robert continues with his silence.

"Will the court please instruct the defendant to answer?"

"Mr. Heyward you must answer the questions that are being asked of you."

"And if I don't answer?"

"If you don't answer Mr. Heyward the jury may have the right to assume guilt when you don't answer the questions your own lawyer is asking you. It cannot be in your favor. Mr. Heyward, please answer your council's questions."

Robert looks back at Jack. "Yes, yes I have had other outbreaks like that before."

"When did you start having such outbreaks?"

"I don't remember, but after the divorce, after my family had left me."

"Have you ever acted violently due to these outbreaks?"

Robert looks on slowly becoming more and more upset, "Yes…"

"To whom did you act violently against?"

"No one else."

"No one else?"

"No, just myself."

"So from these violent outbursts you inflicted only yourself with violence, or pain?"

"Yes."

"So, self inflicted pain wasn't good enough anymore was it Mr. Heyward?"

"What?"

"You had to show someone else the same pain you felt, and who better than the one other person on this Earth who finally had the one thing you used to have? What better person to punish? What better target? Isn't that right Mr. Heyward? No one else would understand the same pain because no one else had what you had to lose what you had until Earl Hodges."

"What are you doing Jack?"

"You want to play nice Mr. Heyward?"

"You want me to answer that?"

"Permission to treat hostile."

"Excuse me Mr. Kennedy? You do realize you are on the defense?"

"Yes, your honor."

"Any objection Mr. Rogers?"

Rogers shrugs his shoulder confused, and shakes his head no.

"Okay, go ahead."

"Let's go back to our original question. Why the knife Heyward?"

Robert looks on without answering.

"You knew exactly what you were doing didn't you? You slipped the knife in the back of your pants not for protection, but for murder. Found out where Hodges was and followed him. Four hours is a long drive isn't Mr. Heyward? What were you thinking that whole time? Did you try to convince yourself out of it? Was it a long drive or short lived? Do you even remember the drive Robert? Only two kinds of people could have made that drive and not convinced themselves to kill that man; a crazy man, or a man set out for murder. Which one are you Mr. Heyward?"

"Neither, I didn't kill anyone."

"Then why the knife! Why was it on you?"

"I didn't kill anyone!"

"Why was it on you?! You *wanted* to kill him! You *had* to kill him! You had to take back what was yours!"

"I didn't do it!"

"I'm stopping this right now Mr. Kennedy."

"What else did you have to lose Robert?! Your wife? Your kids? You had nothing else but this didn't you?!"

"Stop it Mr. Kennedy!"

"That is why you drove over four hours. That is why you took the knife. And that is why you killed him isn't Robert!"

"Stop, you don't have to answer any of these questions Mr. Heyward!"

"You wanted to kill him didn't you Robert!"

"Yes, I thought about it and that's why I took the knife just in case. But that son of a bitch was already dead by the time I got there!" Robert starts to breathe deeply gasping for air.

Jack stands there quiet for a moment. "No further questions." Jack walks back to his desk and looks at his notes as Robert follows and sits down. They lock eyes and Jack shakes his head yes. Robert humbly reciprocates as he sits down. "Your honor, the defense had a witness on the list and due to medical reasons was not able to be here, nor was the defense able to get a deposition for the time being."

"What is the name of the witness?"

"Phillip Henry Roderick."

"I'm right here." Phil pushes a lever moving him forward into the courtroom in his electric wheelchair. Everyone in the courtroom looks back as they watch him make his way to the front. "If it'd please the court I would like to go ahead and testify." He looks Rogers in the eye as he pushes forward. Rogers looks back in shock.

"If the defense is prepared then I have no objection."

"The defense is prepared your honor."

"The prosecution objects to this."

"You cannot object to a witness being put on the stand that is not your own Mr. Rogers especially if you had pretrial knowledge of the witness list."

"Do you solemnly swear to tell the truth the whole truth and nothing but the truth under penalty of the law so help you God?" The bailiff asks.

"I do."

"You may take the stand."

Surprised and unprepared for Phil's arrival Jack shifts through his notes quickly.

"Go ahead Mr. Kennedy." The judge announces.

"Ahem, yes. Mr. Roderick." Jack says nervously, feeling uncomfortable and caught off guard for some reason.

"Yes…" Phil says impatiently.

"Do you know Robert Heyward?" Jack asks slowly trying to collect his thoughts.

"Yes."

"And how is it that you know him?"

"Is it relevant to the case?"

"Well it seems that you were at one time or another deeply involved with both Robert Heyward and Earl Hodges. I was just wondering how you knew Mr. Heyward."

"We were friends throughout college and we were roommates. When Robert took over Orion I agreed to work with him."

"So what happened?"

"Don't you read the papers son? Orion got bought out. The great Robert Heyward sold out and left all his friends behind in the dust."

"So then you moved to Highland Corporation?"

"Yes."

"Mr. Roderick what do you know about Cold Fusion?"

"I know enough."

"Why don't you tell us about it Mr. Roderick?"

"I don't see the relevance to this question nor am I at liberty to discuss the secrets of Cold Fusion in this case, or publically for that matter."

"Do you see the relevance of your being here?" Jack tries to irritate Phil into giving him a reaction.

"Do you want me to answer that?" Phil arrogantly replies.

"How well did you know Earl Hodges?"

"As well as any lawyer should know his boss."

"And what does that mean exactly?"

"It means I kept his legal affairs in order, and made sure he covered his butt whenever he did anything."

"Is that right?"

"Yes it is."

Jack tries to study Phil, but gets nothing back. There was no trap big enough to get the job done. Jack didn't even know why he wanted Phil on the stand. He was just hoping that he could find some connection that would help pull Robert away from the murder. But something had bothered him about Phil. The more he had learned about Phil the less the pieces of the puzzle would fit, especially everything leading up to the murder. He tries to hold back his arsenal waiting for the right moment to strike. Sometimes that right time never comes and a golden opportunity tarnishes. Jack continues to fight like an army man in war beyond the point of no return.

"Mr. Roderick, why were you in Houston April the eleventh?"

"Well my company had just announced the discovery of Cold Fusion and it was the eve of our annual gala. I had to be there."

"You mean the rediscovery."

"Sure."

"Can you explain why your prints were all over the files and all the things in Earl Hodges' room?"

"I was called in after the murder and I guess I had touched a lot of things while I was there, also I had handled many of the documents the night before and the morning of Earl Hodges departure for Houston."

"And did you decide to bleed all over those things also?"

"Excuse me?"

"Your blood was found in various places of the room, I was wondering as you decided to touch many things did you decide to bleed all over the room too?" Phil just sat there slowly becoming more and more quiet and angry. "Do you have an answer to that Mr. Roderick?"

"Yes, I had cut myself pretty badly when I was cooking that night I guess I didn't wrap it up properly, when I had heard what happened I left pretty quickly."

"I see, and where was that?"

"Where was what?"

"Where was it that you were cooking?"

"In the kitchen."

"The kitchen of your home over four and a half hours away from the murder scene or another kitchen Mr. Roderick? Because it wouldn't make sense for you to show up about fifteen minutes or so after you were called if you were that far away would it now?"

"It was from the kitchen of my hotel room."

"I see. Mr. Roderick. Have you ever seen Earl Hodges smoke?"

"No, but that's none of my business."

"Well it's just a simple question, did he ever smell like smoke?"

"No."

"That's odd because we found a Cohiba cigar in his jacket pocket. Isn't Cohiba the brand of smoke that you like? Isn't this your cigar? Approach the witness."

"Go ahead."

Jack hands over the used cigar that was found in Hodges' jacket.

"Yes this is my cigar."

"Why did Earl Hodges have your cigar?"

"Like I said we had a meeting the night before and he doesn't like people smoking around him. He held onto it and I guess he forgot it there. It's possible isn't it Mr. Kennedy?"

Jack stands there trying his best to get an edge on Phil, but can't get one. Jack becoming more frustrated tries to shoot questions at Phil to get him to say something that would help him.

"Did you see the interview where Robert threatened to kill you and Earl Hodges?"

"No, but I had recently heard about it."

"What did you think about?"

"What do you mean?"

"Are you having trouble understanding my questions Mr. Roderick?"

"Well if you ask the right questions, you'll get the right answer."

"Your honor." Jack addresses the judge.

"Please answer the questions Mr. Roderick."

"If you could please ask Mr. Kennedy here to clarify his questions I'd be more than happy to answer them."

"Mr. Kennedy…" The judge says somewhat irritated.

"Okay, I'll rephrase. When you heard Mr. Heyward's statements did it shock you or upset you at all?"

"Well it was weird, but Robert never hurt anyone. Didn't think he'd actually go through with it."

"How do you know Mr. Heyward did it?"

"Because you still haven't proven him innocent, this whole trial you've been dodging left and right trying to point the finger at someone else. Trying to allude and dilute facts. You're just trying to find enough information to show that he *might* have not done it hoping the jury will fall for your stupid little matchbook tricks and find reasonable doubt. You're no lawyer, you're just a used cars salesman."

"Fuck you Roderick!" His eyes lock in with Phil's eyes as he stares at him violently. Phil responds with half a smile.

"Order!" The judge slams his gavel, "You will calm down Mr. Kennedy." The judge calls out. Jack turns around to collect his thoughts.

"See there's the anger. So now are you going to grow up and become a real lawyer or what?" Phil asks Jack.

As if a flash bomb had blinded him Jack stood there staring into space in dead silence.

"Your honor it seems as if our young lawyer here is in shock and needs his mother. If you will allow I'd like to step down from the stand if there is nothing else."

"Mr. Kennedy, are there any further questions for the witness?" The judge waits a moment for a response. "Mr. Kennedy?" The silence continues.

"You may step down Mr. Roderick."

"Yes!" Jack suddenly catches himself. "Yes just one more question."

"Go ahead."

"What hotel?"

"I'm sorry?"

"What hotel? What hotel were you staying in, in Houston?" Phil gives Jack half a smile as if he finally asked the right question.

"I don't remember."

"You don't remember because there was no hotel room was there Mr. Roderick? Did you kill Earl Hodges?"

Phil takes a deep breath as if this was the moment he was waiting for. He then looks at Jack thanking him for finally asking the right question, "I have worked hard my whole life…"

"Answer the question please."

"On this fucking dream called Cold Fusion."

"Answer the question."

"And what have I gotten? Stabbed in the back by my best friend!" He looks at Robert.

"Will the court please instruct the witness…"

"I lost everything I ever had!"

"Mr. Roderick please answer the question." The judge tries to instruct Phil.

"I have nothing left except for one last task."

"Answer the question! Where was the hotel room? There was no hotel room was there? You killed Hodges, and escaped. When you heard Robert had been caught there it was the perfect scapegoat!"

"One last gift to return." He looks over to Robert.

"You killed him didn't you!" Jack stands right in front of Phil as he slams his hands down on the wooden bar that separated them.

Phil looks Jack in the eye. "Yeah, I hit that fat son of a bitch and he stumbled right off the ledge!" The courtroom fills with more silence than it could hold. Phil sits there staring at Jack in anger gasping for air. Realizing what had just happened he recollects himself and looks over at Robert. "You saved the life of the one I love and now we're even." He rolls his wheel chair off of the witness stand and tries to move forward towards Robert, but two officers intercept him and stand there. Jack stands there in shock as he watches Phil. Phil takes a look at his old family and they look back as if they were looking at each other through a glass wall. "I'm sorry." He says as tears begin to fall from his eyes.

"Motion for immediate sentencing and new trial. The defendant has rights." Jack says to the judge.

"Any objection Mr. Rogers?"

"No."

"Please apprehend Mr. Roderick." The judge says to the officers in the court. They begin to read him his rights as he continues to look at Robert and his family. He finally turns around as they escort him out.

Chapter 61

"As you have just witnessed Phillip Roderick has confessed to the murder of Earl Landon Hodges." Amber says looking into the camera, "What had been estimated to be a long drawn out trial has suddenly changed within a matter of weeks. The charges held against him will most likely lead him to the death penalty, but we will most definitely hear about that later. For now it seems as if Robert Heyward on the other hand will be let go with all charges against him being dropped." She turns around hearing rumbling behind her, "Here comes Mr. Roderick now, he is being accompanied by three police officers, one in front and one on either side of him."

The waves of reporters hit him with questions left and right. All he could hear is, "Mr. Roderick, Mr. Roderick!" The officers push the reporters back attempting to get Phil to the police car.

"Mr. Roderick!" Amber finally gets his attention. He stops and looks up at her, "Considering the recent events with your family, your house, and your condition why did you decide to still come and testify, which inevitably lead to your own incrimination?" Phil looks at her in silence as everyone also waits for an answer. Phil then takes a deep breath and without saying a word he moves forward towards the police car. "Mr. Roderick, Mr. Roderick!" The crowd follows. Amber looks back into the camera. "Well there you have it, silence. We'll be back with any updates America. This is Amber K. USN."

Phil gets into the car. After putting the wheelchair in the trunk two officers sit in the front and one gets into the back as they take off. Phil just looks down trying to clear his thoughts.

"Mr. Roderick." The officer next to him says in a dark voice. The voice sends chills down his spine.

"Yes?" He responds continuing to look down and trying not to break his concentration.

"That was very noble of you confessing even though you didn't have to."

"I don't want to talk about this."

"No matter, it still won't save your soul."

"What?"

"Just because I haven't killed you yet, doesn't mean I won't, it just means I haven't yet."

Phil suddenly realizes who's been talking to him. He turns to scream for help and possibly stop him, but it was too late.

"Max Johnson says, see you in hell you son of a bitch."

Phil looks up and then feels an immediate cold sensation in his stomach. He looks down and finds that the man has stabbed him. He looks up and sees Dominique in an officer's uniform.

"Hey what the hell is going on back there?" The officer in the passenger seat says as he looks back. "What the hell are you doing! Stop the car!" The car suddenly stops and the officers get out to stop Dominique.

"You? Why?" Phil asks in disbelief.

"We just needed you out the way. Don't worry your friend, Robert will be joining you soon." He then twists the knife within Phil.

Phil screams in pain as he holds his stomach. "No. Leave him alone." He says running out of breath.

One officer pulls Dominique out of the car and punches him in the face. He disarms him and then cuffs him.

"We need to get to the hospital now!" The other officer yells out as he examines Phil's wound.

***

"Thank you so much Jack."

"No need for thank you, I was only doing my job Sandra."

"Yes, but you saved Robert's life. We are forever indebted to you."

"Don't mention it."

"Will we get to see Robert soon?"

"Yeah, he should be out at any moment now. He just has to sign a few release papers and that should be about it."

"Okay, thank you. We'll go wait for him inside."

"Okay."

Sandra gives Jack a hug and walks away. Michael and Ryan both nod their heads at Jack one at a time then follow their mother. Jack starts to walk away from the courthouse with his hands in his pocket, somewhat disappointedly wondering where the media circus had gone. He then thinks to himself as he plays the last part of the trial scene through his head. "That slick son of a bitch." He says to himself as he shakes his head. The trial plays back in his head like a broken record. "If you ask the right questions, you'll get the right answers."…"You're no lawyer, you're just a used car salesman."…"Fuck you Roderick!" Jack is suddenly brought back to reality. Jack knew Phil was just toying with him. The whole thing was an act.

Phil wanted to see if he could have the upper hand. He controlled the courtroom from the seat of the witness stand. Just when there was no hope he gave a dying man some water. "Cooking in my kitchen…He set himself up," Jack thinks to himself, "I had nothing to do with it. Just when I thought I couldn't trap him he gave himself up to me…Why? I'm no great lawyer I just got a handout. He knew it, Robert knew it, and Robert's family knew it. It wasn't even a lucky break." Jack feels a thud in his back as someone grabs hold off him completely breaking his concentration.

"Hey there handsome."

"Hey, hey. Aren't we a little friendly today?"

"Well you fought one of the biggest cases of the century and won, you deserve a little friendliness."

"Ha, ha I see, but I don't think I did much at all. In fact…"

Amber grabs Jack's shirt and pulls him closer for a kiss. "Hey, hey I'm not that kind of guy."

"Not the kiss-the-girl-you've-been-trying-to-get-with kind of guy?"

"No, just not the just-won-the-biggest-case-of-the-century-then-kiss-the-first-beautiful-girl-that-I'm-crazy-about-and-falling-for kind of guy.

She smiles, "Come here…" She pulls him closer and kisses him on the lips.

Suddenly a beeping sound goes off, she ignores it. It goes off again.

"Hey I think you should get that."

"Yeah I should." She continues to kiss him. The beeping goes off again. "Oh God what is it?!" She looks at her phone. "Hey it's my boss give me a second. Hey Greg?"

"Amber where the hell are you?!"

"Still at the courthouse, why?"

"Because you need to get your ass back to work?"

"But the trial is over."

"The trial might be over, but you still have reporting to do!"

"What?"

"Phil Roderick just got stabbed on the way to the jail house!"

"Seriously?!"

"Yeah they're taking him to Memorial City Hospital. Get on it right away!"

"Okay." She hangs up.

"Jack!" A voice yells out. Jack turns around to look and sees Robert, Sandra, and the kids following.

"What's up?"

"Did you hear about Phil?"

"No what happened?"

"I just found out. Let's go, I don't know how much time we might have left!" Amber yells as she gets into the news van.

"Found out what?" Jack asks confused.

"I'll explain on the way." Amber yells out as she watches everyone get into the van. "Step on it Ed!"

They arrive shortly after at the hospital, soon realizing that the world had already beaten them there.

"Sorry, no media allowed inside." The officer says at the front gate.

"Okay, but I'm his friend I need to see him!" The officer looks at him strangely.

"You?"

"Yeah me."

"Sorry no can do. No one but patients can go inside at this moment for the safety of the patients inside. There are too many people here.

"Damn it!" Amber yells out.

Jack and Amber look around trying to find a way in. Suddenly Jack feels something in his pocket. It was his phone vibrating, "Brown."

"Hey kid, just heard about the case, and that Roderick character."

"Yeah, trying to get in to the hospital, but they won't let us."

"Really? There shouldn't be any security there."

"Yeah, but it's a media circus out here."

"So I'm assuming you're at Memorial City."

"Yeah."

"That is a cover these cops do to divert the attention away from what's really going on. Roderick should be held in Memorial Hermann Northwest Hospital. That's where we try to send the classified patients."

"Thanks buddy." He hangs up. "Let's go guys I know where he is!"

"What?" Robert replies.

"This is a cover up he's not being held here."

"How do you know?" Amber chimes in.

"Get in! I'll explain on the way. Ed, get us to Hermann Northwest."

"Where the hell is that?!"

"Here," Jack enters the location into his phone and hands it to Ed to guide him. "it says it's about ten minutes away."

"What the hell is going on?" Amber asks.

"Our boy Brown came through for us."

They arrive at Hermann Northwest soon after.

"We're here to see Phillip Roderick." Robert says as they all approach the lady at the front desk.

"Okay." She types the name into her computer. "He is in operating room four o three. Go down the hallway and take the elevator to the fourth floor and take a left."

"Thank you." Robert says and they all rush towards the elevator. When they finally make it to the room there is a nurse standing outside the door, with two officers next to her.

"Whoa, you can't go in there." The nurse says holding her hand up. Both officers had their hands near their guns, as they study the group.

"We're just here to see how he's doing and what happened." Robert says.
"We don't know yet, but he has severe damage in his abdominal area."
"What happened?" Sandra asks.
"He was stabbed in the car by someone posing as another officer."
"What the hell? By who?" Amber intervenes.
"I don't know I'm just a nurse here?"
"Who did this?" Robert looks at the officers.
"We can't say at this time sir. Aren't you the guy who was up on trial?"
One of the officers asks.
"Yes." He looks back at the nurse, "When can I go see him?"
"I'm not sure sir; they're operating on him right now. But for now you
and everyone else is going to have to wait out here."

*An hour had passed and still no word just random shouts from inside the room.
Everyone was in silence staring into space; they would periodically exchange short
glances with each other, each one wondering why they were even there. This man had no
debt to them, he had no true connection left with any of them, yet they were all there
waiting for the moment when the doctor will come out of the operating room. Robert
looked over at Sandra and she gave him the same worried look back, and they were
brought back to when they were younger and all was perfect, when they were all a family.*

*When Phil would come over for dinner and entertain the whole family, and tell
bedtime stories to the kids. Jack looks over at Amber and holds her hand as they stand
there in a worried state not quite sure why. Michal puts his arm around Ryan as Ryan
tries to hide the fact that he is crying. Suddenly the doctor comes out the doors and sighs
deeply as he takes off his elastic gloves.*

"Doctor how is he?" Robert asks immediately standing up.
"Who are you guys?"
"His friends." Sandra says.
"Um...Okay, well I'm sorry to say, we did all we could. He's not going
to make it. I can only let a couple of you in at a time, because there is a lot
of blood, and equipment lying around, and someone could get hurt. You
should go in quick he only has maybe ten minutes left."

"Thank you." Robert grabs Sandra's hand and they both go inside.
They walk in slowly seeing the blood splattered everywhere. The blood
makes Robert weak, but he continues moving forward. "Phil?" He calls
out to see if he was still conscious.

Phil looks to his side, "Robert?" Phil says in clear pain.

"You okay there buddy?" He asks as tears fall from his eyes from the look of his friend's face.

"You brought Sandra. I've missed you guys."

"Hey, you feeling okay?" Sandra asks fighting a losing battle against her tears.

"Yeah, but it's getting colder, they stopped working on me all together, so I guess I don't have much time left. Did they tell you how long?"

"About ten minutes." Robert responds.

Phil smiles, "Robert, that's not how you're supposed to answer that. Always straight forward huh?"

"I'm just kidding old friend you know you're going to live forever."

Phil lets out a small laugh, "There you go. Robert I'm sorry, but I wrecked the Porsche you gave me." He takes a deep breath and starts to cry. He coughs and some blood come out his mouth. He groans in pain.

"Shh, shh, quiet now, don't waste your energy."

"I'm so sorry, both of you. I missed your daughter's funeral. I left you guys I…" He looks away his voice becomes lighter, "I couldn't find you guys, you disappeared…I tried so hard to find you. I almost died in Florida. And here I am once again. But at least you two are here now, so I can go in peace." He looks back at them, "I'm so sorry." He says as he cries his voice almost a whisper now. The beeping in the background plays a familiar song for all of them.

"Don't, don't. I love you. I'm sorry I should have never left you in New York. I thought you walked out on us again." Robert tries to explain.

Phil tries to smile, "It would be typical of me."

"You…" He looks at Sandra, "You were my North Star, you always made me steer in the right direction. Thank you. I love you Sandra, I'm sorry…" He tries to reach for her hand. She grabs his hand, so he wouldn't have to move much more.

"Stop, Phil, I love you too."

"Please forgive me."

"Of course Phil, please forgive me too."

He closes his eyes and nods his head as he swallows his saliva and tries to breathe in fighting for his life. "Robert, it wasn't meant to be this way was it old pal?"

"No…It wasn't."

"Funny how life turns out. I didn't mean for you to take the blame, I had to do what was right...For my family...I'm sorry Rob..." He cringes in pain.

"Shh...don't worry about a thing. Whatever happened is behind us now. You're my friend Phil."

"And you're my brother." He pulls Sandra's hand and puts it on top of Robert's. They look at each other then back down. All three held each other's hand and at that moment felt as one. "It is the love that both of you had for each other that kept my faith in this world. I want to thank you for that. But, I want to say thank you especially to you Robert."

"For what?"

"You gave me my family." He reaches under his blanket and puts something in Robert's hands. Robert looks down, "Look at it later." Robert nods his head. "Tell the kids that Uncle Phil loves them both dearly. Tell them Uncle Phil said bye." He couldn't tell if he was talking in the past or the present anymore.

"I will." Robert sucks in both his lips trying his hardest not to cry, but his heart begins to hurt. He breathes in deeply, and lets go crying heavily.

Sandra covers her mouth as she cries as well. "Phil." She says.

"I love you both, I'll look after you. I have to go now."

"Phil no!" Robert yells out, "Please God no. I love you."

"Phil..." Sandra calls out.

"We couldn't save your son Mr. Roderick. His crushed ribs poked into his lungs puncturing them. We were too late." Phil touches his son's head as he sits there in his wheel chair completely quiet.

"And what about my wife and unborn child?"

"Your wife may not make it through the night. We had to pick between her and the child. During the operation, there were complications leading to too much blood loss, and the child had too much trauma to her brain and did not survive the operation."

"Can I go see her?"

"Of course."

"Janis?" Phil says as he rolls next to her.

"Phil?" She says very quietly.

"I'm here angel."

"Where's Joshua?"

"He's just fine, he'll be up and running in no time."

"And the baby?"

"They had to do an emergency operation, but the delivery was a success."

"Yeah? Is it a boy or girl?"

"Girl."

"What do you want to name her?"

"Let's name her after her mother."

She laughs, "Silly you'll always be calling out for both of us."

"Thought it would make things simpler, he smiles back."

"It's cold." Phil pulls the blanket over her upper body.

"You know I really thought I would lose you back there. You really scared me. Don't do that again please."

"I won't I will never leave you."

"Never?"

"Never."

"How about Sarah? It means princess." She says.

"That's perfect."

"I'm tired, I'm going to rest for a while."

Phil attempts to hold back his tears, "Okay baby."

"I love you."

"I love you too. I'll see you soon." He starts to move his wheelchair away. He pulls out what he had taken from Janis' box and reads it. It was the note she had read to him and a news paper clipping.

Thirty-five dead in an eleven-car pile when child throws his ball onto the Brooklyn Bridge. There was only one survivor, who was the motorcyclist in the accident, due to an anonymous organ donation. The death's included New York's finest humanitarian Allen Christopher Heyward and his wife Janis Livingston Heyward, parents of Robert Heyward. This tragedy…

"Robert." He thinks to himself not being able to read further. The whole night of Robert's parents' death replays in his head, when he walked away from Robert and Sandra because he could not take the pain of death and could not hold strong while others were falling apart. He remembers as he was walking away and all he could hear is Robert's voice calling out for him. His eyes filled with tears because of the pain, so he made up some excuse and said he'd be back in a bit. Then all of a sudden the doctors rush a woman in a biker's jacket across his path with blood on her face and she looks

up and screams for help. "Janis." He remembers her face perfectly now. He then reads the initials at the end of the letter she had shown him. RAH. "Robert Allen Heyward. My God what have I done?"

"You okay Mr. Roderick?" The doctor asks standing by the door behind him.

"Ever since I was a child I have been trying to fit in. Trying to find a family. Every time I have come close to someone I would lose them. This was my last chance; I thought I finally had a family, something to call my own. And now…I have lost my home, my wife, my kids, and I am crippled from the waist down. Tell me good doctor, what's the point of living when you have lost everything you have worked for your entire life? Where is our savior? Where is our so called God?"

"The point is to o move on Mr. Roderick, to prove that there is still good on this evil earth. The point of living isn't for your own salvation, but for the salvation for your fellow man. To have faith, when it is impossible to believe. To plant the seed of good in the soil of immorality."

"Hmm…Faith…" He pushes the lever on his wheelchair to move him forward.

"Where are you going Mr. Roderick?"

"I am going to finally go make things right." He presses the lever further and begins to leave the room.

He hears the beeping sound slowing down as he leaves, and it brings him back to reality. He looks over to Robert and Sandra, "I have to go be with my family now. I'll always be with your family." He looks up into the sky and sees his family surrounded in a white light. It was time for his judgment and his family would be there with him. The yelling and the tears in the background begin to fade away. He hears his name from both places. He looks back and sees Sandra and Robert on their knees crying. He was leaving his old family to be with his new family. He takes a deep breath and continues on forward.

The doctor rushes in, accompanied by his nurses, as the beeping becomes a solid sound. Jack, Amber, Michael, and Ryan follow them in to find Robert and Sandra in tears in each other's arms. They all run towards the two to try to comfort them. The nurses cover the body and prepare to move it out to the morgue. Michael and Ryan both run into their parent's arms as their eyes fill with tears.

***

368

Sitting there in his black suit with his family as he watched his friend and his friend's family being buried, reminded Robert of his daughter's funeral, and his parent's funeral. *"This was one funeral Phil showed up to."* He thinks to himself. All three funerals slowly began to mesh together; the misery didn't allow Robert to distinguish between the three. He looked down at a piece of paper. It was what Phil had given to him. The letter was what Robert had written to Janis years back when he donated his father's organs to her, behind it was a news paper clipping. The final item was a picture of Phil with Janis and Joshua. It was a close up of the three of them and Janis and Phil were hugging Joshua as they smiled to the ends of their cheeks. On the back of the picture, it had the names Phil, Janis, Joshua, and under it, it said, "Thank you Robert."

Tears fell from his eyes and slammed against the picture. He felt something brush up against his hand. He looked over and it was Sandra's hand covered in a black glove. He held onto her hand and they sat there as they said goodbye to their friend. After the funeral Robert and his family were walking away and came across Jack and Amber.

"What are you two a couple now?"

Jack and Amber look at each other. "Well, something like that." Jack says trying not to smile too much out of respect of the setting.

"Ugh, kids."

"Well, I guess this is goodbye Robert."

"I guess so kid."

"If you ever need a lawyer…"

"Well hopefully I'll be able to afford a good one if I do." They all laugh a little.

"Yeah, yeah."

"I'm just kidding, you'll be a big shot and you won't have time for people like me, but I hope you will have time for a friend." Robert puts out his hand.

"Definitely." Jack returns the gesture shaking Robert's hand.

"You kids be good now." He hugs Amber. Sandra gives Jack and Amber a hug. Michael and Ryan follow with a handshake with both.

Robert makes it to his car, "So you sure you can't stay any longer?"

Sandra tilts her head to the side, "Robert please…"

"Sorry I thought it was worth a shot."

"We'll stay in touch."

"Yeah."

"Dad, just in case you need company…" Michael says looking back at the car they came in.

Robert looks back and sees Ryan bringing a dog over. "Charlotte!" He yells. Charlotte barks and runs over to Robert. Robert bends down and hugs her. "Oh girl how have you been!" He says as he scratches her behind the ears, Charlotte barks in response.

"Thanks guys."

"Okay Robby our flight leaves soon."

"Okay." The two of them hug. The hug lasts longer than Robert expected so he does his best to take in every moment. Once he lets go he looks her in the eyes trying to tell her he loves her. He then looks at his kids. "Okay guys you better call me when you land. And I better hear from you more often, okay?!"

"Okay." Ryan says. Michael looks at Ryan and then back at Robert and finally shakes his head yes. They all hug and then Sandra and the boys begin to walk away.

Robert stood there with Charlotte as they watched their family walk away. Charlotte barks a couple times.

"If I thought that'd work I would've done it a long time ago." Robert says to her. "Don't worry we've got each other. Something will work out." Then he whispers to himself, "God I hope it does."

Chapter 62

Brown approaches an unbelievably tall building in a motorboat. Once inside he walks through a hallway nearly two miles long. "Whoa…" He thinks to himself as he begins his walk. At the end of his long hike he sees an elevator; he walks inside and sees numbers for every floor but the top, which was the symbol he had been following all this time. He pushes the button and then notices that the unbelievably large elevator box had a bench on the side so he decides to take a seat as he waits patiently. The elevator begins to move, "Is the elevator going down?" Brown thinks to himself in confusion. Once to the bottom floor he walks through another long hallway. The office building was almost desolate with the few exceptions of scattered people that paid no attention to him. None-the-less he didn't feel like he was alone in the journey he was taking. The eerie feeling of being watched haunted him in the back of his head. Every moment he felt as if he should look behind him, but he kept his stride. "I'm such a genius." He thinks to himself. "I can't believe I found this place." Even though he had found what he had been looking for, he found no comfort in it. The nervousness was overwhelming. He finally approaches a lady at a desk. She doesn't seem to pay much attention to him, as she shifts through some papers.

"Umm…Excuse me."

"Yes?" The lady responds while continuing to work.

"I'm looking for Max Johnson."

"Frank Brown?"

"Uhh…yes…" He says caught off guard by the fact that she knew his name.

"Go on in. He's been expecting you."

"Umm...okay. Just through those door?" He asks almost trying to get her attention.

"Yep." She says never losing sight of her work.

"Okay thank you."

"No problem."

Brown sees an old looking sign that read Maximus Edward Johnson. He then pulls the big door. It almost weighed a ton. He pulled it with all his might, but nothing happened.

"Umm...Miss?"

"You have to knock."

"I'm sorry?"

"You have to knock!" She says in an irritated voice.

"Okay..." Brown knocks in a sarcastic fashion. The door makes an odd sound as it releases air and the doors opened inward. Brown attempts to look inside, but only sees a long hallway with pillars leading to a desk. Brown takes a deep sigh, "More walking." He says to himself as he steps past the gigantic metal doors. The doors close behind him.

"You're a difficult man to distract Mr. Brown." A voice echoes through the room.

"Max Johnson."

"So how is it that you found me?"

"Oh that was the easy part; your secretary accidentally left a map of your location in your logo," He tries to look through the dim light to see where he was, but saw nothing. "and she's kind of rude too I would look into that."

"Well I don't pay her to be nice. So you say you found the map."

"It was clever, I had to look at it a couple times before I figured it out for certain. To have a base exactly forty-five miles west between both Florida and Cuba it's interesting."

"It is one of the most secret locations in the world Mr. Brown." Max finally turns around and locks eyes with Brown.

"Hey there." He smiles at Max. "For such a big secret you didn't hide it very well."

"Sometimes Mr. Brown you must be right in everyone's face to hide the best. This location has been here since the first World War."

"Well the sign outside with your name on it looks just as old."

Max lets out a deep dark laugh, "Incidentally Mr. Brown, that sign is just as old as this building."

"What?"

"Maximus Edward Johnson is an alias, every person who has taken this office has had to change their name to Max Johnson. This is our job. It is our sworn duty."

"Sounds sweet," Brown finally approaches the desk. "but the hours must suck."

"Have a seat Mr. Brown." He motions him to sit. "As you've noticed this base has minimal security. It is so minimal that even a dog like your self can get in without much trouble. All you would need is a boat of some sort. If the country is ever in danger, this is where the Vice-President comes. This is where all the buttons are to all the bombs. Everything…everything is at this base. This base reaches all the way to the bottom of the ocean, and then deeper than that. No one will ever know it, but this is the tallest building in the world. Now I'm sure you want something in particular Mr. Brown, or would you like to discuss the history of this office some more?"

Brown smiles, "Well I guess you told me more than I wanted to know about this building. So let's start by what I do know. I know that you were highly involved with both Orion Industries and Highland Corporation. I know that you are trying to combine those two companies with yours to make one super company possibly to take charge of the O.W.O.; obviously that includes the power of Cold Fusion. Therefore I suspect that you were involved with the bombing of Artemis labs, and possibly the murders of those who were involved with the project. This then leads me to think you were involved with Hodges' death and most likely with the burning down of Roderick's house and putting him in the hospital. Also, the fact that I know all this, and everything you have told me so far, and me finding the highest security building of the United States government, my life is obviously in danger. So, that about sums up most of it I believe. Now why don't you tell me what I don't know…Mr. Johnson?"

"Hmm…" Max leans back in his chair and studies Brown for a moment,

FARHAN NOORANI

"I have underestimated you Mr. Brown." Max stands up and turns around facing the wall, he looks through a window in which he could see out into the water, and thinks. "So you believe that there is more to the story?"

"Is there?"

"What is it that you want to know Mr. Brown?"

"Why is it that Cold Fusion is so important to the United States government?"

Max lets out a small laugh, "Good question. For years we have been trying to take control of the O.W.O. wanting to take a stronger economic power over the world, trying to make everything universal. And with Cold Fusion we could accomplish that and we would then become a natural monopoly."

"Why, would you want that?"

"Why? Tell me Mr. Brown, what is the point of different languages, they only beget cruel secrets? What is the point of different currency, they only cause confusion? What is the point of culture when it only creates hatred and ignorance? All religions Mr. Brown are bound together by and bow down to the great American dollar. They trust in us, and in God *we* trust. We the American government are the Messiah, we are the Prophet. Annuit coeptis, God has favored our undertaking. And we shall take this message and follow it through to its fullest extent. Novus ordo seclorum, a new order has begun. And the world shall come together under one flag, under one God, under one government, under their savior. E pluribus unum, one nation from many people. This is what is to come, this is what must be done. Everyone prays for peace on Earth, but we are the only ones who have the balls to do anything about it Mr. Brown. Now Mr. Brown we will need people like you and with intelligence like yours on our side. If you join our team your family will be taken care of for generations to come."

"Thank you, but I'm already retired, and you're fucking crazy. And everything you're doing here, all this…is wrong."

"You have your way. I have my way. As for the right way, the correct way, and the only way, it does not exist."

"Nietzsche? So all this talk about God and prophecy and you don't even believe in it?" Brown asks.

"God is just a means to an end Mr. Brown. Ha, ha, ha God…How many thousands of scriptures, books, and songs have been made about religion? It took God thousands of years to create religion. And we did it in a few hundred and in three sentences. Tell me Mr. Brown do you believe in God, and then tell me does God believe in you?"

"God isn't only a being, but a symbol of all that is good and all that can be good. He watches over us, but like children we must fall before we learn to walk so he allows bad things to happen. As long as God is there looking over my shoulder I know my path will be straight." Brown replies.

"So our dear detective is a philosopher. You spent your whole life digging through trash fighting burglars, thieves, and murders. So you read a couple books to keep you sane, to give some sort of meaning to your pitiful life, so when you talk to people they actually think you have half a brain instead of being a gun slinging buffoon. Clever Mr. Brown, but even a smart monkey at the end of the day is still…just…a monkey."

"I'm putting you under arrest for murder and conspiracy you overgrown pompous ass son of a bitch!" Brown stands up and walks closer to Max.

Max begins to laugh softly and it gradually becomes darker and louder. As soon as Brown gets close to him Max turns around and grabs him. "Do you think I dedicated my whole life to the military and the United States government just so a low life garbage sniffing rat like you could take me in?!" Max yells in his dark evil voice.

"It's funny isn't it; a monkey like me will be looking at you from the other side of the bars."

Max lets out a yell and punches Brown in the face and then in the stomach. Brown retaliates with a punch to the face and then the chest, but he is simply not strong enough. Seeing that Brown was completely out of breath Max picks him up by his shirt and presses a button and guns come out from every corner of the office, the ceiling, and the pillars and point at Brown.

Brown looks around, "That's a lot of guns for just me isn't it? So none of these bullets will hit you?"

"I'm wearing a pin Mr. Brown, and within that pin is a computer chip that flashes blue." Brown looks at the pin on Max's chest. "Whoever wears that pin is safe from these bullets."

Brown spits in Max's face and blood splatters over him. "Wow your pin didn't protect you from that? Interesting." Max yells and throws Brown across his long office; he then begins to walk back to his desk. Brown slides and stops midway.

"Mr. Brown." He says as he wipes the blood and spit from his face, "Did I mention that whoever enters my office on bad terms never lives to see the next day?"

"No," He says trying to get up while wiping the blood from his mouth, "but it is some good information I could have used earlier."

Max laughs, "I see that I haven't been able to beat your sense of humor out of you. No matter that'll be taken care of in a moment." Brown sits down on the floor and wipes his mouth as he laughs in defeat. "But before I press the button that will bring you to your ultimate demise Mr. Brown," Max says as he sits back into his chair, "that quote about God and all that fantasy you were talking about. Who said it?"

"That was all me mother fucker."

Max laughs, "I'm going to enjoy this."

"So am I."

Max presses the button and all of sudden all the guns point directly at Max. "What the hell?" He says with a worried look on his face. He tries to push some buttons to turn it off.

"When you've been in the business as long as I have you tend learn a thing or two." Brown says as he shows Max the pin with blue flashing light.

Max puts his hands up and yells. The bullets rip through him like paper. Brown also begins to yell as he covers his head closing himself into a ball trying to be as close to the floor as possible. Hot bullet shells fall to the ground chiming and echoing along with the sounds of the rampaging guns. Some burn Brown and many miss. A few moments later he hears the last shell bounce off the ground. He looks up and Max falls onto his desk as blood flows off of his desk and onto the ground. Brown picks himself up slowly and limps towards Max's desk. He presses a button to open the door, but the front door doesn't open a door behind the desk opens. With little choice Brown walks through the doors behind him. He quickly realizes it is an elevator and it takes him up to the ground floor. "I'm too old for this shit." He says to himself.

***

Thunder crashes as Robert makes his way into the kitchen in his pajamas. Charlotte barks as he pours a glass of milk for himself. "Quiet girl it's just a thunderstorm, we'll be just fine." He takes a sip from his glass and looks out the window and can only see the dark streets when lightning passes through. "Man I haven't seen rain like this in years." He says while petting Charlotte. "Let's catch the end of tonight's news shall we?" Charlotte barks in response as they make their way into the living room. Robert laughs, "Alright that's the spirit." He says as he sits in his couch turning on the television. Robert sees a woman speaking into the camera.

"With the merger of Apollo industries, to former Orion Industries, and Highland Corporation the Cold Fusion project is finally up and running. With me is the man who helped and was involved with all the mergers General Max Johnson. General Johnson, how were you able to merge all three companies and solve the Cold Fusion problem all at the same time?"

"Well both companies were in clear trouble when the government had acquired them. And being such big companies and everything they mean to the American public the government couldn't possibly let them fall without a fight. So we bought them out and used their resources and together we were able to stabilize the Cold Fusion project and here we are today." Says a tall burly man in an army suit.

"So what does this mean as far as the United States being involved with the O.W.O.?"

"Well we will be meeting with the One World Organization soon, and hopefully will be able to bring power to all countries at low costs. With that in hand, in the near future we hope to take third world countries from developing into developed countries, and bring other countries that are in debt out of debt, including ourselves."

"But then won't that mean that everyone will be indebted to you?"

"Well, I guess everything has its price. We just try to make sure that we have the cheapest price."

"One last question Mr. Johnson. What response do you have to the critics who talk about the 'curse' of the Cold Fusion project and how everyone who touches it eventually is ruined?"

"Well Nancy, I will be here for quite some time, I'm not going anywhere."

"Thank you General Johnson."

"Anytime."

"Back to you Amber."

"Well there you go. Cold Fusion is finally going to become a reality without another hiatus. In somewhat related news Dominique Walker is set to go to trial in two months after the murder of Phillip Henry Roderick, renowned lawyer of both Orion Industries and Highland Corporation. He was murdered shortly after confessing to Earl Landon Hodges murder. Well that's all the news for tonight. We'll be back tomorrow with more news same time same place. With USN I'm Amber K."

"And I'm Jim Rhines, goodnight America."

Charlotte barks at the television. "That's right girl let those sons of bitches deal with it." He laughs. She barks again, "Yeah I know I miss him too." Charlotte barks even louder at the door. "Oh come on leave it alone girl it's just the thunder, I promise it'll go away soon." She continues to bark. "What is it girl?" He then hears a noise at the door. Charlotte runs towards the door and scratches at it continuing to bark. "Get away from the door Charlotte." Robert reaches for something near him to protect him. His hand finally finds a baseball bat. He holds it up as he slowly gets closer to the door. The knocking becomes louder and faster. "Who the hell could be here at this time?" He says to himself. He finally gets to the door and opens it. "Sandra?"

The End